Praise for Thom Racina's riveting novels

Deadly Games

"The suspense never lets up in this fast-paced read."
—*Romantic Times*

"Thom Racina is one of the most exciting suspense authors of our time, always writing a book that's believable and unforgettable." —*Allreaders.com*

Never Forget

"Racina . . . has a deft ear for dialogue."
—*Publishers Weekly*

"[*Never Forget*] succeeds admirably . . . a novel that will not be forgotten by readers."
—*Midwest Book Review*

The Madman's Diary

"Fast-paced momentum . . . crisp dialogue and quirky characters." —*Publishers Weekly*

"Takes off at a rapid clip and never eases off the throttle. *The Madman's Diary* is an exciting thriller with an unexpected ending that begs for a sequel."
—*BookBrowser*

continued . . .

Secret Weekend

"Brimming with harrowing situations, romance, and mysterious characters . . . a suspense lover's dream. Racina has packed many surprises into this page-turner, with a special shocker saved for the end."
—*Romantic Times*

"A pulse-pounding suspense thriller. . . . Thom Racina has written an exciting winner."
—*Midwest Book Review*

Hidden Agenda

"A fast-paced thriller . . . a smart, up-to-date read."
—*San Francisco Examiner*

"Colorful . . . fiendish . . . good entertainment . . . could be a heck of a movie." —*Publishers Weekly*

"A timely story . . . filled with recognizable people."
—*Library Journal*

"A wild romp through my news terrain. . . . I had a great time with it!"
—Kelly Lange, NBC news anchor, Los Angeles, author of *Trophy Wife*

"A thrilling and savvy ride through the worlds of broadcasting, politics, and religion. . . . It's unique, and I was spellbound."
—Sally Sussman, head writer, *Days of Our Lives*, NBC-TV

"The power of television news taken to its logical extreme. Thom Racina's ingenious story gives the reader a peek into the media's well-hidden backstage."
—Bill O'Reilly, anchorman, Fox News

Snow Angel

"Chilling suspense." —Judith Gould

"Breathtaking . . . a devilish treat that will leave you crying for more. You may think you have this one figured out, but Racina pulls out all the stops and gives the reader one of the most exciting tales of the year. *Snow Angel* is topflight entertainment, a sure treat for any season." —*Romantic Times*

"Fast moving. . . . Racina spins a highly cinematic tale set against dramatic backdrops . . . a memorable villain who generates considerable suspense." —*Publishers Weekly*

"A chilling cliff-hanger chase." —*Booklist*

"A tale of obsessive love run nastily amok." —*Kirkus Reviews*

"Powerful, compelling. . . . A highly charged thriller with a surprise ending." —*Tulsa World*

Also by Thom Racina

Snow Angel
Hidden Agenda
Secret Weekend
The Madman's Diary
Never Forget
Deadly Games

DEEP FREEZE

Thom Racina

A SIGNET BOOK

SIGNET
Published by New American Library, a division of
Penguin Group (USA) Inc., 375 Hudson Street,
New York, New York 10014, USA
Penguin Group (Canada), 10 Alcorn Avenue, Toronto,
Ontario M4V 3B2, Canada (a division of Pearson Penguin Canada Inc.)
Penguin Books Ltd., 80 Strand, London WC2R 0RL, England
Penguin Ireland, 25 St. Stephen's Green, Dublin 2,
Ireland (a division of Penguin Books Ltd.)
Penguin Group (Australia), 250 Camberwell Road, Camberwell, Victoria 3124,
Australia (a division of Pearson Australia Group Pty. Ltd.)
Penguin Books India Pvt. Ltd., 11 Community Centre, Panchsheel Park,
New Delhi - 110 017, India
Penguin Group (NZ), cnr Airborne and Rosedale Roads, Albany,
Auckland 1310, New Zealand (a division of Pearson New Zealand Ltd.)
Penguin Books (South Africa) (Pty.) Ltd., 24 Sturdee Avenue,
Rosebank, Johannesburg 2196, South Africa

Penguin Books Ltd., Registered Offices:
80 Strand, London WC2R 0RL, England

First published by Signet, an imprint of New American Library,
a division of Penguin Group (USA) Inc.

First Printing, June 2005
10 9 8 7 6 5 4 3 2 1

For Les Rumsey
May all your Christmases be white.

Acknowledgments

As always, my thanks to Jane Dystel and Miriam Goderich for the direction, the support, and those great lunches.

And to Anne Bohner, my gorgeous new editor, who inherited this but made it her own.

Thanks also to Sheldon McArthur of The Mystery Bookstore in Westwood, California, for believing in this one for so many years. Hope it was worth the wait.

*It snowed and it snowed. . . . Our snow
was not only shaken from whitewash
buckets down the sky, it came shawling
out of the ground and swam and
drifted out of the arms and hands and
bodies of the trees; snow grew overnight on the roofs of the houses like a
pure and grandfather moss, minutely
white-ivied the walls and settled on the
postman, opening the gate, like a
dumb, numb thunderstorm of white, torn
Christmas cards.*

Dylan Thomas,
A Child's Christmas in Wales

The First Day
Thursday, January 15
High Temperature 40 Degrees, Low 24 Degrees

From his aisle seat, Robert Hanwell strained to see out the airplane's window. The woman sitting next to him, already staring out at the bleak landscape, shook her head. "Looks like we're landing in Anchorage, not L.A.," she remarked.

"I'd hoped it would change while I was gone."

They peered out at the depressing expanse of over-built land. Drizzle, fog and smog seemed crystallized in the air because of the temperature. It was just the same as the previous week, except that it was now colder. "You married?" the woman asked Bob.

"Yes. Wife and three kids."

"Bet she doesn't even want to go to the hairdresser in this."

Bob nodded. "Just before I left for Washington, Aileene said it was a chore even to go grocery shopping. She didn't want to have to bundle up, fight the wetness, drive on the slick roads."

"It's a horror movie," the woman said as they

touched down on the slippery runway. "All weathermen should be shot."

"One of my sons is a weatherman."

She smiled a little. "I'll bet he's popular right now, huh?"

"Hate mail by the sackful."

As they taxied to the American Airlines terminal, Bob conjured an image of Aileene sitting with him in front of the fire, reading, while Susan played the piano. Or her video games. Maybe they could do a Costco run and then hole up for the duration. But he worried about his daughter. It was just as likely that instead of listening to her entertain them at the piano (wishful thinking) or watching her obsess with video games (more realistic), they could be shooting her full of Demerol for pain every four hours. Susan suffered from a difficult illness called chronic pancreatitis, which was sometimes harder on her parents than on her. Even before the seat belt chime sounded and people were free to gather their things to deplane, Bob called home. His daughter answered with an enthusiastic, "Dad? Are you back?" Bob breathed easier. He could tell she was doing better.

"Is Mom picking me up?"

"No, Harry's coming," Susan said. He was her oldest brother.

"How are you feeling?"

"Good. Mom's right here, Dad. Want to talk to her?"

"Sure, honey. Put her on." The chime sounded on the plane. People jumped up from their seats and began the pointless mad dash to empty the overhead bins. Bob heard Aileene's voice and said, "We just arrived, still on board."

"Harry said he'd pick you up, had a meeting down that way."

"I'm glad you didn't chance driving in this. Looks like it's sleeting."

"NPR says it's going to get worse. They interviewed Cameron this morning on *All Things Considered*."

"What does Michael say about it?"

"Our youngest, being the optimist, doesn't sound too optimistic right now."

"I'll try to catch his newscast if I'm in the office by noon."

"Good luck. The freeways are a horror, they say."

"We're moving, have to grab my bag. I'll call you later, honey. Love you." He clicked off and slid his cell into his briefcase. When the perky flight attendant told him to enjoy his day as he was deplaning, Bob couldn't help but laugh. He was Platinum in the AAdvantage program, had been upgraded on his coach fare and thus had gotten a fairly decent hot breakfast. In fact American had done everything possible to take the edge off what had become a rigorous and unpleasant experience for frequent flyers like Bob, but exiting the aircraft destroyed all the goodwill the airline had created. A gloomy, cold edginess enveloped him, and he knew it was going to stick. L.A. was the city he loved, the place he'd gone after college to build a family and a life, but right now he could think of a lot of places he'd much rather be.

Standing outside the terminal on the departures level where he knew he could be whisked away faster, he scoured the traffic for Harry's big black SUV, but it seemed everyone in L.A. now drove big black SUVs, with the odd Mercedes or BMW sandwiched in between. He waited ten minutes, twelve, fifteen. Where the hell was his son? Had he forgotten their routine and gone to the arrivals level?

Just as he was about to call Harry's cell phone, a disturbance grabbed his attention. A crowd was growing around a policeman who seemed to be arguing with a woman wearing dark sunglasses on this dreary day. "You can't park there, lady!" the cop said loudly.

"I'm looking for someone," the woman countered. Bob knew that voice.

"Lady, move the car. This is departures, not arrivals."

"Can't you see it's *raining*?" She spoke to him as if he were a moron.

"Don't use that tone with me," the cop shot back at her.

"What tone? How dare you be so inconsiderate?"

"Goddamn it, lady, you're blocking traffic."

"Dolores!" Bob shouted from the back of the line of people checking bags outside. The woman standing up to the cop, the somewhat blowsy, somewhat elegant woman wearing dark glasses topped with a turban, was his son's wife.

She didn't hear him. She was focused on the cop. "Traffic? You call this mess *traffic*? You want to change places, be my guest. *You* spend three hours crawling along into this hellhole, and I'll stand there barking orders, okay?"

"Go for it!" someone yelled at the woman.

"Tell him, girlfriend," a young African American woman shouted.

"You go, Dee!" another voice chanted.

"Officer, it's okay. I'm her passenger," Bob said, pushing his way toward the curb.

"The white zone is for immediate unloading of passengers," Dolores now said in a nasal voice, mocking the well-known LAX recorded voice that blared from loudspeakers seemingly every ten seconds.

"I could arrest you for harassing an officer," the cop told her.

"Do you know who I am?" the woman said with her chin held high enough to spit in his face.

"Tell him, Dolores!" a fan called out. "Right on, baby." The crowd certainly knew who she was.

But Bob knew her in a way they did not, and he also knew that the cop could arrest her not only on harassment charges, but possibly, if he was correct in his intuition, for driving under the influence as well. He touched the cop's arm. "Officer, she's picking me up. It's okay. She's had a rough day."

"Me too. Get in that car and get her the hell out of this airport," the policeman hissed. "Now."

That car, Bob saw in the midst of the sea of stopped courtesy vans unloading passengers, like an apparition, was Dolores' prize possession, a huge white Cadillac convertible of ancient vintage that always got talked about, wherever she went. Which was the point. Whether she was on a summer beach jaunt, or a shopping excursion down to Mexico, or showing off in the Target parking lot, everyone noticed the relic from another era. But it was not the car you'd want to drive in bad weather. "Why'd you bring the Boat?" Bob asked Dolores as she pecked him on the cheek.

The cop was still watching them. "Save the loving reunion with the wife for later," he suggested.

"I am not *the wife*," Dolores snapped as she strutted around the front of the car in her silver fur and high-heeled Blahnik boots. Someone in the crowd whistled.

Bob had always called her "a classy dame," and even in this unappealing weather, when everyone was running around in their worst attire, Dolores looked like a million bucks. There she was, stopping them dead in a silver-white fox coat, dangling Bulgari earrings brushing her rich silk scarf, the turban covering her hair (colored a melange of reds, from deep bur-

gundy to bronze) and those signature sunglasses, despite the fact that it looked like midnight outside.
She'd learned to wear them as a child star, and though
the fame had faded, the appearance of celebrity had
not.

She popped the trunk lid and Bob quickly stowed
his roll-on bag. When he yanked open the passenger
door, he realized the heat was blasting and so he
started taking off his overcoat. "Get your ass in here,"
she squealed, "before Officer Krupke there threatens
to throw you in jail too." The reference to *West Side
Story* gave away her age. Bob got it, however, for he
was her contemporary, even though he was also her
father-in-law.

Bob threw his coat into the backseat and then slid
in with his briefcase. "Man, it's colder than—"

"A witch's tit?" Dolores howled as she checked the
rearview mirror. "God knows my tits are freezing."
She put the car in drive, then laid on the horn for the
Hummer that was blocking her path. "Look at that
thing. SUVs, the scourge of the modern world. Harry
wanted one. I said I'd divorce him if he bought it."

"The Escalade he drives isn't exactly small."

She focused on the short muscleman cleaning the
Hummer's back window now that he had dropped off
his passengers. "This one the cop doesn't mind. Go
figure. Look at him, the gym bunny. He can't even
reach the glass." She rolled down her window and
stuck her head out. "Hey, hire a cleaning lady to do
your windows, okay?" She rolled it back up without
listening to the man's reply, which, judging from the
way she accented it with his raised middle finger, wasn't
one she wanted to hear anyhow. "Little dick," she
said.

"What?" Bob wasn't sure he'd heard her correctly.

"That's why men drive them." She hit the horn

again, and this time the gym bunny gave up and got back inside. "Your oldest son excepted."

Bob laughed. "Information I don't need to know."

"Oh, come on," she added, with her signature bawdy giggle as she piloted the Boat back into the airport crawl. "Fathers must like hearing their boys are virile and strong, all that macho crap."

"I would rather be told they are good people."

"Michael is," she assured him.

He waited for her to say the same about Harry.

She did not.

As they inched toward the 405 on-ramp, Dolores explained that Harry—one of Hollywood's current crop of hotshot agents who had a schedule you could never count on—had a meeting that was likely to go on forever, so he'd asked her to pick up his dad. Living in Beverly Hills meant an LAX run was easier for Dolores than for Aileene, who would have had to come all the way from Los Feliz. "Susan's better today. She's over this one, I think."

"I know. I called when we landed." The windshield wipers were moving in slow motion, sounding as if they were in their death throes. "Hey, I understand why you keep this car. It's you. But why not get something safer for weather like this?"

She rolled her eyes, groaned and turned to him. She said his name as if to communicate that he was either the densest man on earth or was missing something that should have been obvious. "Bahhhhhhhhhb!"

He didn't understand. "What?"

She looked ahead again, gripping the wheel tightly to maneuver a lane change that would have shaken the toughest truck driver. The car behind her blasted her with its horn. "Screw you," she said nonchalantly.

"Dee, come on. I don't get it. You feel it's safer because it's so big? What?"

She turned to him again and with a haughty air tinged with self-deprecation, said, "What you forget is my public *expects* this."

And that said it all.

Dolores Delanova had grabbed fame early, as a child star, singing an unforgettable song in a forgettable holiday movie called *A Glitterfrost Christmas*. The movie was a mess, but the song had legs. And as with Rosemary Clooney and Bing Crosby, who'd introduced Christmas classics on celluloid in an earlier time, Dolores' fame was cemented forever with that piece of music. Trouble was, her career never again achieved that level of fame, and despite twelve albums, fifteen movies, and countless television appearances, she had been cast off to the sidelines of show biz as a has-been. Until Harry Hanwell, a young Hollywood agent and hustler whose own fame was mainly a result of dating young actresses rather than representing them, met her at a party and fell in love.

She would never admit her age, but it was a given that she had already passed fifty when she married Harry (after two previous marriages, both of them disasters that ended in divorce) when he was twenty-four. The tabloids loved it, fans ate it up, and Dolores Delanova, now Delanova-Hanwell, was back in the spotlight. Didn't hurt Harry's career any, either, because all of her contemporaries loved him, and slowly, one by one, he took over revamping their diminishing careers, making a fortune for his part in the transformations. He succeeded with most of them, bombing only with Dolores. The fact was that while she was still a gifted singer, she hadn't ever been a very good actress. And drinking to conceal the pain didn't help.

Bob and Aileene had initially worried that this woman was using their son to reignite a faded career. After all, she'd been a beautiful bombshell when they were young, a 1960s-era star, the "Latin Connie Stevens" she'd been called, the gal who won the hearts of Troy Donahue, Tab Hunter and Rock Hudson, moving on to Ryan O'Neal, Steve McQueen and Paul Newman in the 1970s, only to find herself playing 1980s B picture lunatics (the ones Bette Davis turned down) and, the ultimate humiliation in the 1990s, appearing as Brad Pitt's aging mother in a turkey that went straight to video.

The possible truth, embarrassing and difficult to admit, much less accept, was that the shoe might have been on the other foot. Harry, it was surmised by some, was the one using her. For she came with connections, a mansion in Beverly Hills, the instant entrée that her position gave him in Hollywood. Bob and Aileene had come to love Dolores as much as they loved their son, but somewhere in the back of their minds they questioned just how authentic his love for his wife really was. The emptiness and vulnerability that Dolores so desperately tried to hide—and that could have been brilliantly captured on camera had Harry had the foresight to put her together with the right director in the right film—broke her in-laws' hearts. They hoped there were no ulterior motives, prayed that mutual love and support was the basis of such a May-December marriage. But no one could be sure.

"I was hoping it would be warm and sunny when I got back," Bob said, changing the subject.

"January 2005 was only a dress rehearsal, I fear."

"Warm and sunny by comparison."

She turned the radio on. *You're listening to the*

music of sunshine on KIIS on this dreary Thursday in the City of Angels. "Why were you there? Harry doesn't tell me a goddamn thing."

"Government stuff."

"What's 'government stuff'? You're in PR."

"The weather. L.A. cares about its image. And one of my big clients is the City of L.A."

"Speaking of Washington, I'm doing a gig at the Kennedy Center in March."

Bob brightened. He knew she needed something like that. "What? A play? A concert?"

She laughed. "Trotting out the old hens, the one-hit wonders. Patti Page, Connie Francis, Polly Bergen, God knows who else. Hell, I told Harry if they really want to make money, rake up Dusty's ashes, reconstitute her and prop her up for "Wishin' and Hopin'."

"Let's not be ghoulish."

"It's a buck." She was riding the brake in painfully slow traffic. "But I'm tired. Maybe I can get Harry to pack it in and move to Maui."

Bob knew his son. "I doubt you'd get him to go anywhere there isn't a major art museum."

She shrugged. "Is it warm in Bilbao?"

"Raining there too," Bob advised her. "Weather all over the world is nuts."

The Santa Monica Freeway was barely moving. There was a string of red taillights as far as the eye could see. She suddenly cut off a driver, plowing across two lanes and over a patch of wet grass. "I'm gonna try streets."

Bob breathed again when they slid to a stop. She asked him if he thought it was going to get better soon. He shook his head. "I fear we're in for a long siege."

"You know what Michael said on TV last night?"

Bob turned to her, eager. "What?"

"He said he wouldn't be surprised if it snowed."

Bob laughed. "That's my boy. Should have been a comedian."

"He was serious, Bob," she said soberly. "Damn serious."

The people of Los Angeles—in that curious Southern California tradition—took it in stride, even enjoyed it. The general subject of discussion all over the city was the weather, from cell phone conversations to supermarket lines, at drive-ins and car washes, in the smallest apartments and the biggest hotels. The fact that it was the coldest January on record—or any month for that matter—fascinated most people; it was a phenomenon not unlike one of California's periodic devastating fires or an earthquake. Certainly not unique, but always captivating.

Others found it a chore. They patiently waited it out with dreams in their heads and suntan lotion in their hands, wondering where in the hell that beautiful California sun had gone and what was it doing there? It amused others, especially those who believed that life itself was crazily off-kilter in Southern California, so why not the weather as well? And then there were those who loved it, like the Beverly Hills matrons for whom it finally provided a reasonable excuse to parade around in heavy mink, even during the day, or the transplanted Easterners who longed for cold winter nights but without the snow that had driven them to the Left Coast in the first place. Still others loathed it. There wasn't a wet suit made that could keep surfers from feeling frostbite. Television crews were having a hard time shooting warm-weather scenes on location when actors felt like icicles were going to form on their lips. The tourist trade was drying up—and the city losing money—as hotel owners cursed the dark skies. But the one thing everyone agreed on was that it was *interesting*.

Perhaps more interesting to Michael Hanwell than to most people, for weather kept his blood flowing and his income steady—he was the weatherman on KTLA, whose studios on Sunset Boulevard this January morning were encased in an icy glaze. Wearing the wool turtleneck sweater his wife, Wendy, had recently given him for Christmas, Michael pressed a speed dial number on his phone while clutching a steaming mug of Peet's Mocha-Java in his other hand to keep warm as much as to drink. "Cameron, it's Mike," he said when the phone was answered. "Got your long johns on today?"

"I'm pulling out the ski clothes. How are you? The family?"

"Cold," Michael deadpanned, then added with gushing enthusiasm, as if on air, "but my spirit will never die."

"Your spirit will freeze long before you do. So, what's up?"

Michael rolled the turtleneck up over the lobes of his ears. "What's the dirt on this? I mean, is there hope or is it time to buy a ticket to Honolulu?"

Cameron Malcolm laughed, but it did not cover his deep concern. For nearly a year and a half, California had undergone the greatest change from previous weather patterns of any place in the world. A vast area of the Pacific Coast from San Diego in the south to Santa Barbara, two hundred miles north, was stunningly changed. In that time, the weather in this region had defied reason—storms, then warm breezes, followed suddenly by gale-force winds that forced panes of window glass into Malibu living rooms as if they were made of cellophane. Storms over the ocean itself were the reference point, and the effect of that weather on Los Angeles and the people living there was Cameron's biggest concern. He was the first African American man to run the Department of Science and Meteorology at the University of Southern California, and the mayor of L.A. had appointed him to oversee and advise on this growing problem.

He had the credentials. Several presidents had commended him publicly on past performance—forecasting the treacherous winter of 1977; being instrumental in preparing New York City for the previous December's weather, the hottest winter it had ever experienced, and thereby avoiding power blackouts and emotionally preparing residents for a Palm Springs kind of Christmas; predicting a flood in Wyoming a few years back, which, had he not warned authorities to get people out of the valley, would have killed hundreds more than the eighty-six lives it did take. His accuracy was on the money.

Thus he'd been urged to see what could be done here in Southern California after a month of sporadic rain, darkness and bone-chilling cold had taken a devastating toll: the loss of millions upon millions of dollars in crops and a spectacular upset to the nation's economy. The vital importance of Southern California beyond the entertainment industry was suddenly very visible to the world.

Michael Hanwell helped make it visible on a daily basis, with his thoughtful but cockeyed weather reports on the noon, six o'clock and late-evening newscasts. Staring at clouds for hours at a time as a little boy should have been a clue as to his future employment. But it wasn't until he watched the Weather Channel for days at a time while in high school that his family was sure where he was headed. He was doing what he loved, and in a humorous, offbeat, stand-up way. Which of course masked his seriousness.

"Cameron," he said to the man who was both his mentor and his godfather, revealing his fear, "I go in front of the cameras and keep saying *It's gonna get better!* or I sing *The sun will come up tomorrow!* but I sound like a blithering idiot when my report is just depressing."

"Giving hope isn't a bad thing."

"It is when there isn't any." He hesitated. "So, is there any?"

"Michael, my prediction is the same as yours."

"So I'd be lying to viewers if I told them this was going to get better?"

"Yes."

"Then I won't sugarcoat the truth."

"Be funny. You always are. But this is very serious."

Dolores dropped Bob off in front of a steely office building on Wilshire Boulevard. "See you at the house later," she said to him. "I'm off to get my hair done."

"Why bother? The turban looks great."

"I have to take it off sometime." She popped the trunk. "Meeting Harry at a goddamned gallery later. Better run."

Bob blew her a kiss and got out. When he'd pulled his suitcase from the vast trunk and closed it, he tapped on the metal to let her know she could pull away. Her wheels squealed on the slick pavement. It was really wet. And really cold. Bob feared her driving up the hill in Los Feliz that night, for if it got as cold as he figured it might, the wetness would turn to ice. But, hey, Dee wouldn't be driving the Great White Boat. Harry would be piloting the Great White Elephant, his Escalade, so why worry? As Bob was about to enter his building, there was the sound of crashing metal behind him, a fender bender involving at least four autos. He shook his head, thankful one of them wasn't Dolores. But it assured him there was reason to worry about everyone.

"Hey, Michele," Bob greeted his secretary when he arrived on the twelfth floor.

Michele DeVito, who'd been with him as long as his wife, hardly looked up from her computer screen. "Your son is making me scared."

"Harry?"

"Michael." She still didn't look up. Instead, she started reading to him. "*For a month, the turbulent air up in the polar region was held at bay by several giant high-pressure systems over Canada. The Canadian highs were in turn held in place by the natural east-west movement of air farther south,* blah blah."

Bob glanced at his watch. "He's not on the air yet. What are you reading?"

"Michael's page on the KTLA Web site. But wait," Michele said, "I'm just getting to the good part. *Same thing over Russia—turbulence buildup caused severe winter storms. But that energy broke up, a lot of it over Alaska, popping open like an aerosol can, like a broken dam, carrying the bitter cold into the atmosphere.*"

"That's what we expect for Alaska and Russia."

She finally looked up at him. "There's more," she said seriously. "*But the low-pressure area around San Francisco is diverting the great polar air mass south along the coast. Eventually, it's got to turn inland with the natural easterly air flow and deposit it somewhere. Unfortunately for us, L.A. is the most likely spot.*"

"Jesus," Bob said, shaking his head. "Is he predicting a snowstorm?"

"Get out the shovels."

"What shovels?"

Michele looked up to the clock near the door to his office. "He's on now."

"My watch is slow." Bob hurried into his private domain with a nice view of the Hollywood hills and the ocean on a clear day, and turned on the plasma screen that usually stayed hidden in a specially built bookcase. Michele leaned against the doorway as Michael Hanwell appeared in vivid color, the young weatherman as kooky kid, doing his usual dance in front of the map of the country that had all sorts of arrows and colors superimposed on it. ". . . but who really knows what any of that means?" Michael was saying, as a lead-in to the most popular feature of his forecasts, the "Whacked Weather" photo. He used a different shot for each newscast, weather photos sent in by viewers that he proceeded to twist to his needs. When he had predicted a battering storm for the coastal areas the previous summer, he used a picture of the deadliest typhoon in Burma, stating, "Here's Santa Monica during the storm." It brought laughs but also pointed up the seriousness of the situation and got people to board up their windows and sliding glass doors. For a particularly dry spell he once passed off the parched Sahara as "the San Fernando Valley getting a bit crispy." Today it was a shot of idyllic snow falling heavily on a Connecticut farmhouse. "Burbank tomorrow," he warned.

"Oh, man," Bob said.

"I live in Burbank," Michele reminded him. Then she brightened. "Maybe I could make a snowman for the first time in my life."

When the camera moved back to Michael live, he was dressed in a parka and huge ski gloves. Seriously, he told his audience that he was predicting snow, by tomorrow night at least. Perhaps several inches. And if the temperatures stayed where he thought they were going—below freezing—it was going to stick. "Get out your long underwear," he advised. "Put on the teakettle and see if you can't get a snow blower attachment for your lawn mower. We're in for something this part of the world has never seen before."

Bob clicked the screen off. "That's not true, really. Like I told the people in Washington, we have had snow here before."

"Back in 1977," Michele remembered. "I was a girl and it was the first time I ever saw it. But it didn't last."

"And there was a storm a year or so ago—the one that dumped the hail that looked like snow."

"I have friends on Bellhaven Street, in Englewood. Their car was covered."

"But nothing that lasted."

"Your kid says this is going to last. I only hope he's wrong."

As Michele left, Bob walked to his desk, lifted the phone, punched in a speed dial number and waited. When it was answered, he said, "Hey, you're scaring people."

"Dad, hi. You back?"

"Yes. I just saw you on-screen."

"Yeah, the storm over the Pacific is moving inland. By night we'll all be freezing, and the rain's going to turn to ice."

Bob looked out the wet window at the squiggles of color that were car headlights snaking along Wilshire Boulevard. "Ice will melt."

"It won't, Dad. The temperatures are going to stay below freezing for at least a week."

"Jesus, Michael, that's impossible. Not here."

"It is possible. Here. And the precipitation isn't going to stop. And that means snow."

"I think you should talk to Cameron and get his

expert opinion before you"—he wanted to make a point, but to jest as well—"before you incite viewers to riot."

Michael surprised him. "I talk to Cameron every day. He agrees."

"Oh boy."

"I'll see you up at the house later, Dad. Gotta run."

As Bob put the phone down and started to check his mail, his other son popped his head in the door. If Michael was the short, goofy kid with tousled hair and a winning grin, Harry Hanwell could play the straight man in their act. Tall, handsome, with piercing eyes and close-cropped dark hair and an earring that softened the tailored effect of his Thom Browne suits, he looked like a slick, hip lawyer, which is what he'd gotten a degree to be. But lawyers in Hollywood often became agents, and in a short time he'd risen to the top of the heap. At this moment, however, he looked like just another annoyed Los Angeles resident, wet, frazzled and impatient.

"This sucks big time," Harry said in greeting.

"Nice to see you too."

"I can't get to the client in Bel Air. It'll take a day in that traffic out there."

"Michael says it's going to snow."

"Right," he muttered, writing it off. "But in the meantime, I've got business to do. Can I use your desk?"

Bob stepped aside. "What, the mobile office in your SUV isn't working?"

"I've spent the day in it. Needed a break. Got any food here?"

"Michele can get sandwiches."

"Turkey breast, no dark meat, lettuce, soy mayo on low-carb bread."

Bob rolled his eyes. He called out, "Michele, get Harry a turkey on rye."

Harry was already dialing his cell phone. "This snow prediction. My little brother on the level?"

"He thinks so."

"Weathermen. Should never let them out of the asylum."

"You got him the job."

"I'll pay in hell one day." Harry swiveled toward the window in his father's chair to speak into the phone. "Hey, Arthur, Harry Hanwell. We're going to have to do this on the phone. Unless you have seven or eight hours to wait for me on this worst day of traffic in history." Harry turned back to his father. "What time's Susan's party tonight?"

"Eight."

"Right. Hey, Arthur, swell, I'll conference in Paramount and Warren, just give me a minute . . ." He looked out at the rain hitting the glass as he hung up. "Snow?" he said softly. "No way."

The same words were being spoken at the same moment at City Hall in downtown Los Angeles. The mayor and members of the city council were in a heated argument in one of the conference rooms. Cameron Malcolm had just addressed them, given them his expert opinion, which met with laughter, glares and distinct controversy. Snow? A siege? Impossible. Outrageous. Overreaction. Cameron said a fifty-fifty chance. No way. Listen, we've had flurries before. Pasadena got real snow a few years back. Palmdale gets it every year. Thousand Oaks had a major snowfall in 1908. We can handle it. We can't handle it. We don't even own snowplows. It would be beautiful. It's a fantasy. But what if? Do we have a "what if" plan?

Fact was that the City of Los Angeles had no plans for snow, and no clue how to even prepare for such an aberration. The best the city council could do was hope it wouldn't happen. Or, that if it did, it would be light and melt fast. From a mayor who greeted the news with total denial to a councilperson, Loretta Zane, who represented the outer fringe in Echo Park—the "Kook Konstituency," as the *Los Angeles Times* called them—who seemed eager for it to come about, the council was splintered in every direction, and thus no decision could be made as to how to prepare.

"Prepare, nothing," another noted council member said. "I'm worried about heat. We're using electricity and natural gas at a rate higher than the summer peak."

"And people are blaming Edison for their chilly bedrooms," another person said.

"Southern California Gas said their Web site crashed because of the irate traffic."

"We need to look like we're on top of this."

"We can't have panic."

"Bob Hanwell's firm is working on it," the mayor assured them.

One woman quipped, "He gonna keep them calm about snow too? Christ, it's his kid who has everyone riled by predicting it."

"Enough of this weather stuff," Mayor Larry Zarian shouted. "Anybody know anything about the Jeffrey King buzz?"

A councilman said, "They say he's going to run against you."

Mayor Zarian laughed. "On what ticket? Lunatic fringe?"

"He's got a lot of followers," Loretta Zane reminded him. She was a popular but austere woman in her mid-fifties, who seemed trapped in another time (hippie hair, little makeup, incongruous bell bottoms and fringed jackets) and thus might be called part of the lunatic fringe herself. "And they do a lot of good in the people's eyes."

Zarian blew up. Jeffrey King, a former Lakers star whose getting into trouble with the law had led him to found his own wacky religion (only in California) with the millions he'd made by doing endorsements, was a particular sore spot with him. "The 'good' he does, Loretta, is only to pull the wool over people's eyes. He's nothing but a cult leader like Jim Jones, David Koresh and our own Charles Manson. Nobody that evil could be elected here."

Loretta stared at him a moment and then gave him a slight grin. "If you say so."

He adjourned the meeting with a rap of his fist.

Everyone left the room but Loretta. The windows had become steamed up from all the hot air that had blown off. She got up and walked to them, looking at the beauty of the beveled glass in the old metal frames. She ran her finger over a pane in a vertical line. Then another, close to it. Then a horizontal line through the center, joining them to create the letter *H*. Then a capital *E*. And an *L*. And so on until she made a word: HELTER.

She suddenly looked fearful, turning to see if anyone else was still in the room. She was alone. So she continued, compelled to complete the thought. Zarian had unwittingly given her the inspiration. Under HEL-TER she drew a capital *S*, then a *K*, then an *E* and an *L* and another *T* and another *ER*. SKELTER. HELTER SKELTER.

A smile that looked unworldly creased her face.

She brought her left hand to the window to wipe out her artistic creation, but then thought better of it.

No. She'd leave it there. If it evaporated before anyone saw it, fine. But if by chance someone came along,
it might startle them. They were words that could still
incite deep feelings in Los Angeles.

And what Loretta now knew, after hearing Cameron predict snow, was that the words were once again
a warning. A warning that Charlie and Squeaky and
Tex were right. And that Zarian was right as well in
his unspoken fear over the enigmatic Jeffrey King. He
was to be feared, for many reasons. She shivered with
anticipation at what might come to pass if snow really
fell. Snow could change everything.

Helter Skelter.

There is a kind of building typical to Los Angeles—
the stucco apartment house built around a swimming
pool and a few palm trees. Its thin walls force the
neighbors, like it or not, to become one big family.
Places like that were usually comfortable and af-
fordable, and it was for those reasons that Michael
Hanwell and his wife and daughter lived in one.

It was called Kings Carriage House for the fact that
it was on lovely Kings Road in West Hollywood. They
all had names like that. Laurel Towers (on Laurel
Canyon, but only two stories high), Bali Hai, the
Palms, Westerly Plaza—all with colored floodlights
adding a vaguely garish year-round Christmas quality
by night. But for Southern California and the type of
weather that is the norm there, they were perfect—
large windows for the ocean breezes, air-conditioning
for the summer heat, gas space heaters for the winters
when the nights dipped into the forties.

But what was happening this January was different
from what had ever happened in any previous winter.
The space heaters were working overtime and hard,
and the result was just enough heat to keep reasonably

warm. The city's gas supply was being drained in the face of an already mounting natural gas shortage, which was a prime concern Bob Hanwell had taken with him to Washington, and something the city council had pondered this very afternoon. Bob's job as a public relations man was to help the city convey the news to the people in a way that they could not only understand but accept.

Residents were understanding it already; accepting it was quite another thing. The mayor's office was overwhelmed with calls, the Department of Water and Power felt like it was under attack, and the media only seemed to invite panic. The cable networks were a step beyond Michael Hanwell's prediction of snow; they were already lining up the "experts" for sound bites on what was going to happen if Los Angeles was besieged by a blizzard. Retired weathermen were being yanked out of retirement—in some cases, literally out of bed—to wax poetic on envisioning Griffith Park as a ski slope, Lake Hollywood as an ice-skating rink, Ventura Boulevard as the tundra. In an exclusive interview on Fox, the reclusive but bigger-than-life former sports hero Jeffrey King said, "I've told my followers that Armageddon is coming. The Bible did not specify, but it could be another word for snow."

Parijata MacKay watched the TV with a sense of amusement and a deep sense of fear—fear of the Lord seeking revenge. Was King right? Was this the coming end of the world? Was this the Lord's retribution for the sins of Los Angeles? She would accept her fate, come what may, but she would not let on that she was scared. No. She needed to be the nurturer, the leader. As manager of the Kings Carriage House, she chose not to reveal her deep religious fears, choosing instead to be strong and in control, as she always had done, from her days raising four kids as a young wife in

Mexico City to today, when she was a grandmother who had the love of a family of friends.

She turned off the television, trying to tell herself it was all nonsense. These shows were just that, show business, make-believe, fantasy. But she trusted Michael, the most decent and honest tenant she had, and his prediction gave her pause. As she wrapped a sweater she'd knitted for his and Wendy's little girl, who was turning six months today, she worried most about the children. Yesterday a gas heater in an apartment in East L.A. had exploded, killing three innocent bambinos. Dying in a fire, she thought. There could be no more horrifying ending. A few days before, another baby had perished from the toxic gases of a charcoal fire his desperate but uneducated father had set up in a bedroom to keep the family warm. Parijata made the sign of the cross.

Upstairs, Wendy Hanwell popped into the apartment laden with groceries, chilled to the bone. "Ugh!" she shouted to let off steam. She shook her short hair like a dog who'd just emerged from the ocean.

Michael, who was sitting on the sofa attempting to teach patty-cake to little Rachel, looked up. "Mrs. Hanwell, you're a mess."

She walked to the heater and rubbed her hands over her face in front of the warmth. "We're moving. To a real house. We can afford one now. It's time."

"With a real furnace?" he guessed. The Kings Carriage House was an upscale building on a desirable street where they'd moved when they decided to live together three years before. They'd been married more than a year, but because money had been tight, they'd stayed in the apartment. But now, since Michael had a real job at KTLA and a real salary to go with it, there was no economic reason to stay there.

"I guess we should buy a house. I'll miss everyone here, though."

"I think that's what's kept us here this long," Wendy replied. "But it's time. Life goes on."

She thought about what she'd just said. "It doesn't for some, really. I visited a family this afternoon, Michael, and their roof leaks, there's no food, they—"

"Honey, you promised. Don't bring work home with you."

"It isn't work. I care about people."

"That's why you're a social worker. And I value that. But we have our own problems. Like the coming snowstorm."

"It's better that Hank stood in for you tonight on the six and ten both. Let people lynch him instead of you."

"Come on," Michael groaned. "This is no dire prediction that should upset people. It's really going to snow. And we need to be prepared."

"The baby okay?" Wendy sat down with them, changing the subject.

"Of course. She likes any excuse to wear that little hooded Gap sweatshirt Mom got her." Michael had picked up Rachel from Parijata when he came home from the studio before Wendy. "We took a dip in the pool together," he kidded. "Then we got to her dance lesson on time and—"

"Don't kid yourself. They grow up fast. That stuff will be happening soon enough." Her baby reached out and squeezed one of her fingers, letting out a shrill cry of delight as she bounced on Daddy's knees. "You really want to move?"

He thought about it and nodded. "But don't tell Parijata. Not until we find a place. And hopefully nearby. I won't want to lose the best babysitter in the world."

"Matthew can help us."

"But he just started in real estate." Michael was cautious about working with their friend who lived in the same building. "My mom has better connections."

"Yeah," Wendy reacted with a scornful laugh. "For million-plus places in Los Feliz. Come on, Michael, get real. You're not Al Roker yet."

"Someday."

"Even then we'll live in WeHo."

He smiled. And bounced the baby some more.

Rachel Hanwell was a beautiful child, which wasn't surprising since both her parents were attractive, but in opposite ways. Wendy was dark, with thick brown hair and green saucer eyes. She had a stunning body, and although she was small, she was strong and athletic. In fact, she could outrun Michael any day, and she beat him at tennis every game they played on his parents' court.

Michael resembled his mother more than Bob (tall, wiry Harry was more the image of their father), meaning it wasn't physical beauty as much as character that made him so attractive. That off-kilter smile, his animated gestures, punctuated with large hands and a grin as wide as his face—his whole aura was one that charmed people. Though he was only five nine, his spirit made him appear taller, and there wasn't a place on his body where the muscle had not been toned by working out.

Had he not developed his fascination with weather, he might have become an actor, or certainly a stand-up comedian of some sort. He was comfortable in front of people, loved the applause, the knowledge that he was reaching millions of viewers with each broadcast. He had always been a natural ham, the practical joker, the guy whose next move you couldn't guess. His geeky interest in high- and low-pressure systems gave him a unique position when it came to run-of-the-mill television meteorologists. He stood out. He was different. He was controversial. He would go places.

But tonight he was only going to the house in which he had grown up, several miles away in the hills adjacent to Griffith Park, to a birthday celebration for his little sister and a half-birthday party for his own daughter. Before Rachel was born, Susan was all he had to dote on. He'd spoiled her rotten, was her best friend, and worried about her constantly. Pancreatitis was a tough disease for anyone to be saddled with, but he cringed that his little sis had been dealt this hand. From the time at age three when she suddenly doubled over and started screaming in pain, Michael had been there to hold her, comfort her, get her to the emergency room, pray for her. She had been sick this past week—Bob had almost canceled his Washington trip because of it—and Michael knew she was not out of danger yet.

Wendy abruptly put her arm around his shoulder. She knew what he was thinking. "She's going to be all right," she said gently. "Don't worry. There will always be reliable doctors and hospitals if she needs them."

"I hope," he said without enthusiasm.

"And if even if not, your mother will handle things."

"What's that supposed to mean?" Aileene Hanwell was the one sore spot in their relationship. And Michael hated it.

"That means she's a control freak, and we both know it."

"If Rachel had pancreatitis, you'd be out to protect her and do anything for her too."

"Yes, but . . ." Wendy let it drift off. No point

getting into it again. The subtle friction between her and her mother-in-law was a given, seeing that they were cut from totally different cloths. Wendy was fiercely independent, whereas Aileene had always depended on a man. Wendy was out to save the world, while Aileene lived her fairly isolated life in a rich neighborhood in the hills. Wendy worked in a free clinic helping the poor. Aileene sold big houses to wealthy buyers. Wendy was warm and ingratiating. Aileene had a veneer you had to work at sanding down. Once you did, you had a loyal friend for life, but Wendy was unwilling to go that far. She decided to steer the conversation down a different road. "So who's coming tonight?"

"The family. Harry, Dee, us, maybe Cameron."

"Dolores is going out in this weather?" Wendy exclaimed. "She's not afraid her hair might melt?"

"She picked Dad up at LAX this afternoon."

"You know, Michael, I like her so much. I mean she can be a real girl, down and dirty and fun and sassy. But when she gets into that fearful mode, it's so pathetic."

"It's so vulnerable."

"Afraid of her own shadow."

"It's the booze. And the unhappiness. It's the one thing I resent about my brother."

"Don't blame Harry. Dolores has to take responsibility for herself."

"Hey, Dr. Phil, enough. You analyze too much."

"Your family brings it out in me."

Michael lifted Rachel into the air and nuzzled her as he brought her down toward his chin. "Happy half a birthday, my precious darling!"

"Oh, please, you sound like a Josh Groban song."

"What's wrong with Josh Groban?" Michael asked.

"For me he's the male Celine Dion."

"That's a bad thing? Listen, Wendy, I think we should all just have fun tonight. Man, we could all freeze to death in the next week, so let's go for it, huh?"

"Michael, stop being so morbid."

He said nothing more. But an hour later, when they were bundled up and leaving for Los Feliz, as they exited the building they looked down in a mixture of wonder and concern: the steps were coated with ice.

The moisture was in a turbulent air mass that had been created above Siberia only three days before. But now it was being pushed toward the California coast by the first punch of the developing polar outbreak. As the air mass reached southern California, it particularly threatened Los Angeles because it ran into an even colder mass of air already in the area. Because of its weakness, the warmer mass rose above the other systems and in doing so, began to cool as it moved higher and higher. The moisture grew heavy in the colder air. It had to release. When it did, it would fall through the cold air at ground level. That air was already below freezing.

It was the ideal situation for sleet, snow, and—as Wendy and Michael had just discovered on their steps—ice.

Harry Hanwell entered the auction room to find Dolores already seated in the middle of the crowd. He slid in next to her. "Fuck this weather."

"Good afternoon to you too. I've been sitting here over two hours."

"How did you get here on time? It's hell out there."

"It's hell in *here*."

"What? You're surrounded by great art and you're bitching?"

"The only art I like is Garfunkel."

Harry didn't answer. His focus was fixed on the sculpture that was up next. He raised his paddle and bid. "Where would we put it?" Dolores asked.

"In the hall."

"Maybe you could cement it to the hood of your SUV."

"Very funny." He raised his arm, indicating a four-thousand-dollar bid.

"It's awful."

"I thought you weren't interested in art."

"I'm interested enough to know that's ugly. And that Gloria won't like dusting it."

"Shhh. Shit, no, it's not worth two grand. Forget it." He looked in the catalog for the next item. "I dropped the car at home so we could go to Dad's together. Be crazy to take two vehicles. Took a cab here. What an experience. Driver was a lunatic smoking dope and going on about Tahiti."

"I wish I were."

"What? In Tahiti?"

"Stoned."

Harry didn't respond. He bid on another painting he liked. But he dropped out the moment it went over the price he wanted to pay. He was a shrewd collector, and he knew art. It was his one true passion, his only hobby. Because he had developed his interest in art at about the time that he married Dolores, people speculated that he did it to impress her or to cement his new social position. Or to fill the walls of the mansion that came along with Dolores. But as time passed even his own brother, who was the most skeptical, had to admit that he'd found an interest that he cared about—now that he had the money to pursue it. But Harry never seemed to have enough; every week he was in another gallery, often buying.

"My ass hurts," Dolores told him, fidgeting. She was bored and restless. Sitting there politically correct in uncomfortable straight-back chairs, she felt a little like they were at a wake. Hushed, somber, serious as hell, staring at a Cotman watercolor instead of the corpse surrounded with flowers. Even the attendants looked like undertakers and ushers. She needed a drink. "We're due at your parents' house."

"Shhh." He lifted his hand. Then pulled it down. "Shit, wrong one."

"Huh?"

"You always do that to me."

"What?"

"Distract me. I want the one with the grapes, not the peaches."

She let out a laugh loud enough to make everyone turn to them. "Oh, I'm sorry, baby, but if you could only hear yourself. I mean, in all seriousness, *I want the one with the grapes, not the peaches.* Peaches!"

"Dolores; shut up."

"Hey, bid on that one."

"What?"

She pointed at the enormous painting that was being displayed. "We could hang it out in front of the house to scare people and save money to boot by getting rid of the security patrol."

"It's a masterpiece."

"Butt ugly. And anyway, why *do* we pay some fat retired cop to drive around every four hours? They don't know if I'm being raped or murdered inside there."

"Baby, trust me. No one wants to murder you, much less rape you."

"Go to hell," she hissed.

Harry bid on the painting.

She knew it wasn't because he even remotely wanted it. He did it to get back at her.

Screw him. She raised her hand and raised his bid by two thousand dollars.

"What are you doing?"

She'd show him. "I fancy it suddenly." She raised her own bid by another thousand.

"This isn't funny, Dolores." The startled auctioneer was staring at Harry, asking if there was another bid— going once, going twice. Thankfully another man raised her. And Harry shuffled Dolores out of there, yanking her to the foyer. "What were you doing?"

"Enjoying myself."

"Are you crazy, bidding against me? Raising the goddamned price?"

"It's my money in either case, so what the hell are you worried about?"

He glared at her. That was a low blow. He wasn't going to take it. "It was your money, a long time ago. But the situation has reversed itself, or haven't you noticed?"

"Oh, sorry, I forgot you're the reincarnation of Michael Ovitz."

"He's not dead."

"He should be."

"We're getting the hell out of here," Harry growled, heading for the front door.

"That's what I wanted to do in the first place."

Outside, waiting for a perky attendant to bring the car, Dolores said, "I'm not going to the Degas thing."

"What Degas thing?" he snapped.

"This weekend."

"It's Van Gogh. At the Getty. It's the biggest show of the year. You're coming."

"I'll barf if I have to look at another old master."

"Van Gogh is an Impressionist."

"Worse yet." The car arrived. Harry glared at her, letting her open her own door as he walked around to the driver's side. As he slipped the young attendant a folded bill, Dolores called to the boy from inside, "Slam the door on his foot. He deserves it."

"Pay no attention to her," Harry told the teenager, with a smile. "Too much wine." But the minute he shut his door, the smile died. "What a clever thing to say. You happy when you make me look ridiculous?"

"I haven't been happy in so long I've forgotten what it's like."

The words had just spilled from her lips when brake lights lit up in front of him. He reacted, too harshly, stopping on a dime, their seat belts gripping in a tight hold. The car behind them blasted its horn.

"Jesus!" Dolores cried. "You trying to see if the air bags work?"

"God*damn* this fucking weather!" Harry cursed. "What did we do to deserve this?"

Dolores laughed. "We married each other, that's what we did."

Aileene Hanwell sat in her den, reading a book on California history. One particular passage gave her pause:

> On a cold day in January, in 1542, a Spanish explorer named Juan Cabrillo was leading an expedition along the coast of California. His ship's log revealed the plight of his sailors, who were caught in an unusually severe winter storm.
>
> Without warning, Cabrillo's small group of ships were forced to take refuge at an island thirty miles offshore, near Santa Catalina. There they waited

as ice-cold winds and driving rain and sleet at-
tacked them for over a month. The bitter cold was
the worst part of the ordeal, and it was noted that
ice—several inches thick—formed at times on the
surface of their water barrels. The ship's rigging
was coated with ice and was unusable. The men
had to build extra fires belowdecks, thus endanger-
ing their boats. There was little wood to be found
on the brush-covered island, and the wild winds
thwarted any attempt they made to sail away from
the island until March of that year.

To emphasize the magnitude of this severe polar
weather, it should be noted that Cabrillo and his
men were offshore, where the sea usually warms
the air. One can only imagine what it was like on
the land, then, the land around Santa Monica Bay
where the Indian village that eventually would be-
come Los Angeles lay . . .

She closed the book and shook her head. She remembered the big snowfall in Newhall back in the
mid-1980s. Highway 5 had been closed because of the
drifts, and that was just thirty-five miles from the center of L.A. It had snowed in Silverlake in the 1950s,
she'd just read in the paper. And a few years back
there had been flurries right there in their yard. So
this cold weather and the rain they were having
weren't unheard of. She looked out the window. At
least it wasn't snowing.

Fires roared in all three fireplaces—in the living
room, in the den just off it, and down in the family
room on a lower level. Burning the trees they'd cut
down during the summer helped save gas. Aileene
sipped her coffee and pulled her feet under her on the
comfy chair. She could smell the roast and potatoes. It
would be just like Christmas again, she thought hap-

pily, with the whole family here. It would ease some of the gloom.

Bob and Aileene Hanwell had long lived on Waverly Drive, in one of the most beautiful homes in the Los Feliz district, an older section of town between Hollywood and Glendale, where famous stars of the 1920s had built houses—Cecil B. DeMille, W. C. Fields—that attracted modern-day stars—Lily Tomlin, Bette Midler, Tom Hanks—decades later. The house was a three-story Spanish Colonial, built on a hillside in 1929, with a pool, spa, outdoor fireplace and tennis court added in later years.

On the lower level was a large family room off the driveway, with a heating room where old gravity furnaces still provided toasty heat in weather like the kind Los Angeles had been having. The main level was dominated by a huge living room off the foyer, the focal point of which was a Steinway grand sitting in the far corner. The piano had been Aileene's mother's until she passed away, and now it belonged to the granddaughter, Susan, who played it with love and vigor (but who most often would rather play *The Sims*).

Bookshelves lined all four walls of the adjacent den, with two corner windows looking out onto the red-brick pool deck. There was a formal dining room looking over the big fir tree in the front yard and a kitchen that, despite state-of-the-art stainless-steel Viking everything, still retained the red Spanish pavers, dark distressed-cherry cabinets and old rusted light fixtures that kept it warm and comfortable.

What had originally been a maid's quarters—and Michael's room when he was a teenager because it had its own French doors opening to the outside—was now Susan's, who was proud to step up to (actually down to, from upstairs) her adored brother's digs.

Being on the main floor, it also made it easier for Bob or Aileene to tend to her when she was sick. One entire wall was a sea of video games and the flat-screen computer on which to play them. She had her own spiffy tile bathroom, an enormous armoire that held her growing wardrobe—what teenage girl wasn't all about clothes?—and, next to it, the basket that Herschel, her beloved, slightly dim, a little over-wrought, but always lovable Sheltie, slept in each night.

The top floor was spacious, filled with light from windows that framed the trees and mountains and lights of the city like so many paintings. The master bedroom had a lovely balcony porch of its own, with two doors opening onto it, where Bob and Aileene spent many a morning reading the paper and drinking coffee, at the same level as birds in the trees. Harry and Michael had grown up in each of the two smaller bedrooms at the back of the house, until Susan came along—a surprise, ten years after Michael was born—and needed a room of her own. Harry's old room was now a guest suite, and the other one was used by Bob as an office. Aileene, who had sold a lot of houses in the area, always felt she had kept the best for herself.

Outside, the grounds were expansive. Geraniums, roses and jasmine covered every inch of the acre of land. The pool was a large oval—built for the athletic boys—surrounded by an expansive terrace. A high red-brick wall surrounded three sides of the property, which masked the charm with a slight fortress look when they added the electric gate at the foot of the drive. But it was secure. Many years ago, Charles Manson had sent his followers to this street to kill Leno and Rosemary LaBianca in one of the most famous and riveting murder sprees in American history.

Because it happened just two doors from the Hanwells, Aileene felt safety was of utmost importance.

She went into the kitchen and pulled the roasting
pan from the oven. Holding the cutting board piled
with vegetables, she slid them around the meat, then
put the pan back into the oven. She could see through
the window that the drizzle had finally stopped, but a
cold wind seemed to be rattling the panes of glass.
She pulled her sweater tighter. Looking at the scene
outside gave her the chills. The computer on the
kitchen desk made a dinging sound. Aileene pushed
a speaker button on the wall. "Let the walls come
tumbling down!" the voice sang.

"That could only be my kid," she said, and then
pressed the button to open the front gates.

She watched out the dining room window as their
car made it up the steep driveway, then took a bottle
of Yellowtail out of the refrigerator and set it into the
bucket she had already filled with ice. She pressed the
START button on the coffeemaker so the thermos
would be filled and hot when they had the birthday
cake. Then she went to Susan's door, knocked lightly
and entered.

Her daughter didn't look good. Aileene could see
the pain in her eyes; no matter how well Susan masked
it, a mother knew. But she also knew better than to
comment on it. It had drawn them closer, this constant
struggle to be without pain, to stay healthy, to get
well. Aileene used to panic when she saw the telltale
signs that an attack was coming on—she felt so powerless knowing that within two days her only girl was
going to be lying on a table in an emergency room
screaming in pain. But she had turned this gift of prediction into something constructive; they were better
able to prepare for the attacks, to warn the doctor

ahead of time, not in the middle of the night when the first pain struck. And, at times, they could even ward off the attacks.

Whether or not to put her in the hospital again was always a hard decision, one that Bob and Aileene had faced countless times in the thirteen years she'd been their unexpected and bittersweet joy. Aileene found Susan's difficult premature birth, ten years after Michael, to be the great blessing of her life. Their only girl was pretty and smart and talented and so very much alive, with eyes filled with wonder and a zest for living. But to have been born with a chronic illness seemed like an awful trick. They'd wallowed in it at first, but over the years they had come to think of Susan's affliction—and so much pain—as the very reason she lived her days so fully, almost desperately. When they got tired of asking themselves "Why her?" or "Why us?" they began to understand it. Not why she had been saddled with the illness—no one would ever understand God's plan for them—but the illness itself. They knew it inside and out, how to deal with it, how to handle it, how to comfort Susan when she was really hurting, how to make the healthy days better for her, and how to prevent or at least how to minimize the next attack.

Susan was an unusual case. Pancreatitis was usually associated with alcoholism, but in her case it was the result of her premature birth, the cells in the organ not quite having formed to do what they were supposed to do—supply insulin and secrete the enzymes to properly digest food. She was not diabetic—her insulin levels were fine—and the normal output of enzymes let her eat normally. What was wrong was that when the pancreas malfunctioned, the enzymes it produced did not exit the organ, so they started to digest the organ itself, causing intense and acute pain. The inflammation soon spread to the surrounding organs and tissue, enveloping her stomach and back in agony that could be relieved only by narcotic painkillers. Sometimes she could manage it at home, but other times she needed to be hospitalized. This time Aileene and Bob didn't know which way it was going to go.

"Michael's here," Aileene told her little girl, who was sitting—where else?—in front of the computer screen. Herschel was curled at her feet. "Hey, turn that thing off." At that moment, the dog heard them entering downstairs, barked, then hightailed it out of the room and down the stairs to the first level. Susan pulled away from the screen. She turned to Aileene.

"Hurt much?" her mother asked.

"Just a little."

"It's different this time."

Susan nodded. "It isn't getting worse. Same thing for days."

"Up to eating?"

"I'm not sure," Susan said, not wanting to risk inflaming the pancreas more. "But I want to play 'Happy Birthday' for Rachel."

"And for yourself."

Michael burst into the room. "Hey, sis, hate to talk shop, but how do you like this weather?"

Susan said, "I think you should create a computer game about it."

Michael smiled. "Hmmm. Call it *Ice Storm L.A.*"

Susan took him seriously. "You would have to drive a car from one end of Sunset Boulevard to the other. It could be so cool."

"There were accidents everywhere," Wendy said, carrying the well-wrapped baby into the room. She put Rachel on Susan's bed.

"Wow," Susan said.

"What?" Michael asked, shedding his coat quickly, turning to start unbuttoning the baby.

"She's getting bigger."

"Babies grow," Aileene said. "Look at my own brood."

Michael rose to his tiptoes and gave her a sour look. "Arrested development, Mom. Gimme a few more inches, if you don't mind."

"Give up on it, bro," Susan warned him. "Harry swiped those extra inches for himself."

"Just be glad television makes you look taller," Wendy joked.

"Wonderful," Michael grumbled. "So, what do we have to drink around here?"

"Considering the weather," his mother said, "I think we should all be having hot chocolate."

"Alcohol will warm me much quicker," Michael said, heading toward the kitchen.

As they sat in the living room with their wine and appetizers, Aileene began to worry about Harry and Dolores. "He called from his cell a long time ago, saying they'd left the gallery and were on their way."

"Traffic," Wendy reminded her. "You're lucky, Aileene. You haven't had to go out there."

Aileene took it more harshly than Wendy had meant it. "That doesn't mean I can't appreciate the difficulties."

"Be glad you can stay home," Wendy said, not wanting to pick a fight. "We envy you."

"Susan is precarious. We're waiting for the results of the test from last week. I can't take her out and I can't leave her."

Michael reached over and put his arm around his mother's shoulder. "She's going to be all right, Mom. You know that."

Aileene nodded, but she didn't look convinced. She changed the subject. "Your father is late because he was meeting with Cameron. I told him to drag him along if he could persuade him."

"Great," Michael said. He enjoyed his godfather more than anyone else she could invite.

Wendy cringed. "That means we'll talk weather all night."

Herschel started barking, running to one of the big living room windows. Aileene got up to go to the kitchen to press the gate control, but Michael beat her to it. "I'll get it, Mom."

As he left, Aileene stared at the beautiful little girl. "I just can't believe I'm a grandmother. I always thought, Oh no, it'll make me feel so old. You know what it really does?"

"What?" Wendy asked, getting on her knees to stoke the wood in the fireplace.

"It makes me feel young again."

"Goddamn drivers, they don't know what the hell they're doing out there!" Dolores shouted as she made her entrance, shaking the wet off her fur.

"Man," Harry added, "it's awful. Intersections blocked, cars smashed, trucks sideways. Let's all go to Hawaii, tomorrow."

"I need a drink first," Dolores said, hurrying to the dining room where the wine sat on the antique hutch. But she reached inside the hutch for the one bottle that wasn't red or white, the caramel-colored Dewar's, pouring herself a glassful with two cubes. "One plus in this weather is that if we run out of ice, we can always go chip some off the pool."

"That could happen, Dee," Michael quipped. "But it wouldn't be fun."

She giggled as the Scotch warmed her throat. "I

think it would be a gas. Ice skating on swimming pools, what fun."

"The ice would crack the plaster. It could be very dangerous."

"Oh, Mike," Harry said. "What a spoilsport."

"No talking shop," Aileene ordered. "Not tonight. This is a birthday party and we are not going to be morbid."

Dolores rolled her eyes. "It's your son who's morbid. I'm thinking about tobogganing down Western Avenue. It's wild."

Bob and Cameron Malcolm arrived a few minutes later, joining the others for drinks in front of the warm fire while Aileene put the finishing touches on the meal. The subject didn't change; in fact, with Cameron present the talk was exclusively about the weather. How the city was ill prepared for it and its cost. "I think we're facing something devastating," Cameron admitted.

"Come on," Harry interjected. "You think this is something new? Weather always wreaks havoc here. Man, every year the place burns, then rains flood what has burned, sending houses into the ocean, and we rebuild them immediately. It's a cycle. No sweat."

Wendy said, "I think Cameron's right about the cost. And I think it will only mean another reduction in funds for government programs and places like the free clinic."

"Yeah," Michael said. "A lot more depends on the weather here than our mood. We produce most of the fruits and vegetables for the country, and nuts and fish and cotton. It's staggering how the country depends on us. The economic fallout could be disastrous."

"It could affect the business too," Harry said.

Dolores immediately explained. "By business he

means the *movie* business. In his book, it's the only business worth caring about."

"It pays our bills," Harry snapped.

Aileene put her head in. "Soup's on." She disappeared just as quickly as she'd come.

Dolores moaned. "I hope not literally. I've never been a soup kind of girl."

"Yeah, all you like is sauce," Harry added under his breath.

Dolores gave him a look as icy as the weather.

Aileene hadn't made soup, just salad, roast and veggies, and they were a hit, warm comfort food on a cold winter's night. The baby was fast asleep and Wendy was finally relaxing, curled up in Michael's arms on the sofa, while Harry and Dolores kept a safe distance from one another. Cameron came in from the den, where he'd been talking on the phone. "National Weather Bureau won't admit snow."

Michael blinked. "It's a given."

"Denial. They're 'hoping' it'll blow itself out over the water."

Michael shook his head. "I feel an intuition about this one, Cameron."

Cameron, an exacting scientist who had little room for intuition, had to agree. "It would surprise me if it didn't happen."

"It's going to be chaos, right?"

Cameron said emphatically, "Unless I can convince the city to prepare for it."

"Fat chance," Michael said. "What do they know from snow?"

Dolores set her fourth glass of Scotch on the grand piano and said, "Enough already! Sounds like we're in Siberia." She parked her hefty butt on the bench,

opened the fall board and tinkled the keys. She loved
the sound of this old Steinway, made back when they
were consistently perfect and bright. The song she
played was one she'd played for them less than a
month ago, on Christmas Eve. Michael started laughing. "Talk about a good choice."

"Oh, the weather outside is frightful," she sang
softly, *"but the fire is so delightful . . ."*

Michael joined in on the title line. *"Let it snow, let
it snow, let it snow."*

When Susan walked in, Dolores stopped playing.
"Hi, honey. Happy birthday. How are you?"

"Hi, Auntie Dee. Better." Susan had always chosen
to call her "auntie" even though she was her sister-
in-law. And Dolores liked the term of endearment,
since she was no one's aunt in reality. The girl went
over to the piano, where Dolores hugged her and
made room. Susan slid in and took over the song,
fully, richly, and everyone, despite their feelings about
whether or not it was going to come true, sang about
the snow. When Susan finished, she was about to start
another song, but Dolores put her hands on hers to
stop her. She knew the girl was going to play "A
Glitterfrost Christmas." "Not tonight," Dolores
begged. "After singing it about forty thousand times,
I don't think I could get through it again without vom-
iting."

Aileene appeared holding the birthday cake that
she'd expertly decorated with HAPPY BIRTHDAY
SUSAN & RACHEL on top of the icing. Susan played
"Happy Birthday" while everyone sang it to her and
the baby, who slept through the entire experience.
"We'll wake her for her first," Michael promised.
"For sure."

As they had ice cream and cake and coffee, Michael
turned on the eleven o'clock news on Channel 2. He

didn't dare tell anyone at his own station, but Ann Martin was his current favorite anchor. He'd grown up watching KNBC, where the anchor, Kelly Lange, had inspired him to join the business one day. He had pictures of her plastered all over his room (this being a teenage boy, it helped that she was stunningly beautiful), plus one of Paul Moyer, and another idol, Fritz Coleman, the Channel 4 weatherman. When Kelly left KNBC to become a novelist, Michael discovered Ann Martin, who he thought was just terrific. But tonight he was surprised to see Ann doing an on-location interview with the mayor of Los Angeles, out in front of the Disney Concert Hall as patrons exited after a concert. "Why there?" Wendy asked him.

"Effect." Harry was sure. "Life goes on. A little rain and cold won't stop us."

"Like hell," Cameron muttered.

A moment later, Cameron was startled to hear Ann Martin mention his name. "We all know that Cameron Malcolm, one of the most respected voices when it comes to weather, today backed up Michael Hanwell's startling prediction for Los Angeles: snow. What's your take on this, Mayor Zarian?"

Larry Zarian looked surprisingly amused. "I think it's a little fanciful. More likely we're in for heavy rain and freezing temperatures. But we are putting snow crews on alert because we do value Mr. Malcolm's expertise."

Cameron laughed out loud. "What snow crews?"

"This city doesn't even own a plow," Bob added. "We might bolt a few to the front ends of trucks when mud cuts off Pacific Coast Highway, but snowplows?"

"Los Angelenos," the Mayor Zarian insisted, "will weather the storm, as they always have in the past. It's a great city with great people, and a little bad weather will not get us down."

"Thank you, Mayor," Ann Martin said. Turning to the camera, she added, "There, you've heard it. The Los Angeles battle cry."

Dolores trumpeted a battle cry of her own. "Not get us down? Half the population is in a goddamned depression."

"And the other half thinks it's fun," Bob said. "Which worries the hell out of me."

Half an hour later, Michael walked into Susan's room. She was not, as he had expected, in front of the computer. She was lying on her bed. "Sis?" Michael said as he sat down next to her. "Is it hurting after you had the cake?"

She knew she couldn't hide it. She nodded.

"Not doing too well, huh?" He brought a strong hand to her shoulder. "Where does it hurt more this time? Front or back?"

"More in the middle tonight. Did you have the TV on?"

"Yes, to hear the weather report."

"Are they agreeing with you?"

"Hardly. But already everything's encased in ice. You could see it behind the location crew. Everything was shimmering."

Her eyes brightened. "Really?"

"Really."

Herschel stood by the French doors that led from her bedroom to the backyard. He whined a bit, then pawed one of the doors.

"He wants to go out," Susan said.

"Come here," Michael offered, giving her a hand to help her up. "I'll show you." He unlocked the door and clicked on the outside overhead light. When he opened it, the dog scampered out as usual, but this time was not usual at all. It was as if, realizing he was skating on a thin layer of ice over the bricks, he put on brakes. On all frozen fours, he slid—stopping just before the pool.

Michael and Susan stepped outside as the freaked animal ran back in. "I've never seen this," Susan exclaimed. Everything was glistening because of the ice, like a movie set that had been sprayed with water and then fast-frozen. It sparkled. It was beautiful. "How cold is it, Michael?"

Michael guessed. "High twenties. Probably twenty-six or twenty-seven right now."

"Cool."

"Literally." Michael walked toward the pool, holding Susan's hand so she wouldn't fall. He wanted to see something, curious if it was happening, something he'd never thought he'd see in his life in Los Angeles. And sure enough. When he bent down and poked his finger into the dark water of the swimming pool in which he'd spent most of his youth, he found a thin layer of ice floating on top.

And even though he had predicted it, it startled him.

Was it just the beginning?

The Second Day
Friday, January 16
High Temperature 35 Degrees, Low 22 Degrees

The respite from the wet weather didn't last long. By morning a steady drizzle was falling, and people cursed it as they left their homes and apartments to go to work. Los Angeles boasted of the world's best drivers; the assumption was that one *had* to be a good driver to survive the freeway culture. But a curious thing happened when it rained. Those "best" drivers didn't know what to do. They didn't have a clue. The arteries to and from the city became tangled with bumper-to-bumper traffic, small accidents tied up roads for hours and the people living in the Hollywood hills thought they'd suddenly relocated to San Francisco because the sound of squealing tires and grinding brakes filled the normally quiet air.

The city was not quiet this morning, not by any means. Car horns resonated like in the streets of Manhattan. Children on their way to school slid and squealed across puddles that were still icy. The subway was packed; every available car had been put on the trains. And every bus the city owned was hauled into operation because so many people had wisely decided not to drive, so the roar of big engines and the smell of exhaust fumes lay heavy in the dank urban air. All along the ocean, winds battered the houses and the waves threatened moorings.

At ten a.m., when most people were at their jobs, it seemed to be business as usual, and some of the tension was being forgotten. Some people felt they deserved a little hell—the weather for most of the year had been as good as it gets—especially when the rest of the country was being torn apart by tornadoes, hurricanes, flooded riverbanks and, in the Great Plains, drought. California was still the promised land.

"It was down to eighteen degrees in the high desert last night," Cameron told Michael over the phone in his dressing room at the studio.

"I guess the storm over Baja kept it from getting that cold here."

"Yeah, didn't dip past twenty-six."

Michael didn't sound relieved. "But that storm's gone now. The desert air is moving in."

"Jeffrey King had one of his spokesmen on *The Today Show*. Said it's the end of modern civilization."

"Atonement for our sins, huh?" Michael asked.

"He mentioned you."

Michael let out a laugh. "Me? Just 'cause I was first to say it? Hell, Cameron, you're the one who got the credit on NBC last night." Michael was distracted by someone at his dressing room door. "Come in."

With a sour face, his assistant handed him a computer printout.

"What?" he asked.

"Read it," she said.

Letting Cameron wait because it was from the National Center for Atmospheric Research, Michael glanced at the report. "Wow. Cameron, we're vindicated."

"How?"

"Let me read: *Snow Possible—Santa Barbara South to and including San Diego County—Within Forty-eight Hours*."

"I'll be damned." Cameron told Michael to hold on. A few moments later he said, "I got the report from the long-range prediction group in Camp Springs, Maryland. It says just how long the arctic winds are going to continue is anybody's guess, but they're sure the trend of polar air will bring snow along with forceful winds, creating—get this, Mike—blizzard-like conditions."

Even Michael was startled. "A blizzard? In L.A.?"

"Yesterday you were derided, now you're a prophet."

"Look, what we do is an inexact science at best and this sounds lunatic."

"But we now have backup. I've got to tell the city."

"Good luck." Michael knew that L.A. had had no experience in dealing with this in the past, so how could the city prepare for the unthinkable? Rain, yes—and they were ready for it this year. The previous January, the national weather team in Camp Springs, Maryland, had issued a "severe" weather warning for Southern California, but it had been met with applause, for after two dry years, water was going to be welcomed. But no one had ever dreamed of snow.

"Mike, I talked to my friend Steve over at NCAR yesterday, and there is the chance this could be headed off."

"That likely?"

"Nope. I think we're in for it."

"I'm on the air in a while. Gotta prepare."

"Carry a shovel. I'm off to see the mayor."

"Cameron, thanks, and good luck."

* * *

The temperature was so cold that the rain was coming down as sleet by the time Cameron arrived at City Hall. The sound of the heavy, wet precipitation hitting his umbrella as he made his way to the door was astounding. Once inside, he realized his shoes were covered with white ice. It didn't give him hope.

When Cameron was ushered into the big conference room, the city council was watching Michael Hanwell giving the weather report. Cameron chuckled to himself to see Michael standing naked except for swimming trunks under the glare of lights. "So," Michael was saying, "if we just think sun and beach and iced tea, we can re-create a nice hot winter day inside our apartments and homes while looking out the windows to see a winter wonderland."

The council members muttered; some laughed, some seemed pained by the performance. One woman said, "He's so cute. Great body."

Another said, "He's nuts."

An African American man grumbled, "If it happens, you know what part of the city'll suffer the most?"

"Your district, my district," Loretta Zane said. "No one cares. We had three apartment fires last night in Echo Park because of gas explosions. The ice has downed power lines. We get snow, our streets will be plowed last."

"Listen up," the mayor said. They hushed and looked back at the screen. Michael Hanwell was saying, "All kidding aside, the National Weather Bureau has now admitted we're facing a storm you'd more likely find on an open Midwest prairie."

"He's overwrought," the mayor muttered, hitting the remote in his hand.

Cameron stepped up. "I was just about to tell you the same, Larry."

"Even if you agree with him, we'll handle it," the mayor assured him.

Loretta said, "Think of the chaos we'll have at the airports, the train stations, the subway. We are not prepared for this, Mayor. We are not equipped."

"She's right," the African American councilman warned. "We need to get equipment in here from mountain areas, where they know how to deal with snow. We need to make firm plans."

"Right. The one thing we can't do is live in denial," said the woman who thought Michael Hanwell was a hunk. "We owe it to the people to be forthright."

The mayor said emphatically, "Nobody wants to believe this."

"Maybe they'll believe that," Cameron said, gesturing toward the windows. They were covered with sleet.

Bob and Aileene didn't see Michael's prediction in beachwear because they were on the phone with Susan's doctor. Natalie Shemonsky explained the results of the tests they'd done the previous week. "She has a cyst on the pancreas, and there's an obstruction we're not sure about that's stopping up the duct, enlarging the organ, and there's considerable pressure on the portal vein."

"From what?" Bob asked. It hit him suddenly that this was not a run-of-the-mill attack that was lingering in Susan. It was something worse. And far more dangerous. "Is this pressure coming from the pancreas?"

"No. It's the scar tissue from the cholecystectomy— the gall bladder removal—we did a few years back. It's created a kind of webbing in her upper body that's pressing on the vein."

"What does this mean? Could it be cancer?"

"There are sometimes worse things than cancer," the doctor said. "This can be difficult."

Aileene bit her lip. "Hasn't she been through enough?"

"Honey," Bob cautioned, "we can't beat ourselves up." Then he addressed the doctor again. "Doctor, tell us what to do."

"Is she eating?" Natalie asked.

"Only a little. Too much pain."

"I think you'd better take her down to Hollywood Presbyterian for an IV today or tomorrow."

"In this weather?" Aileene said with a shiver.

"I'd ask you to come here to Cedars, but considering the streets, it's out of the question. We need to build her up, perhaps give her blood."

"For surgery?" Bob asked.

"Yes. We need to schedule this before it gets worse. I want Mitch Karlan to do it—he's the best man there is. He's due back in town in a couple of days."

"Is that okay?" Bob was clearly worried. "To wait?"

"Mitch can't operate until the inflammation is gone, in any case. The acute pain is gone. It'll be okay."

"Thanks, Natalie. We appreciate it."

"We're almost out of syringes," Aileene reminded them.

"Have the pharmacy call me," the doctor said. "Gotta run. I'm at the hospital and most of the nurses are sitting in their cars on the Pomona Freeway."

"What are they expecting, the blitz, for Christ's sake?" Dolores exclaimed as she stood staring at the other desperate shoppers in Ralph's Supermarket.

"Jesus, there's nothing left on the shelves," Harry added, incredulous.

It was nearly true. Some shelves were almost empty, most of the stock depleted. People were buying everything, stocking up. Husbands pushed one cart while wives piloted another and kids followed them with yet another, all filled to the brim. The lines at the check-out lanes extended to the back of the store. "Ten minutes to shop," Dolores commented, "then an hour to check out."

She and Harry found what they could. Most canned items were long gone, except for the expensive gour-met brands, which they actually preferred. There wasn't a box of Kleenex or a roll of toilet tissue left in the store. People hovered around a poor stock boy on his knees in a white apron, attacking cans of dog food as he pried the cases open; others simply took whole cases. "We should have tried Trader Joe's," Dolores said.

"I drove past one this morning coming from Fox," Harry told her. "Cars were queued up for the parking lot like a gas station line during a fuel crisis."

Liquor didn't seem to be moving so fast, or perhaps the store just had a big supply, Dolores thought. She put two bottles of Dewar's into the cart and told Harry to get in line. "By the time I'm done, you might have a head start on a cashier."

After he'd stood there twenty minutes, she showed up with a box of cereal under one arm, a bag of onions hanging from a finger, and two more bottles of Scotch for good measure.

"You're getting four of them?" Harry asked in astonishment.

"If we're in for the blitz," she announced, "I plan to *be* blitzed."

He glared at her. "You know, sometimes I think you drink partly just to irritate me."

She smiled. "You're partly right."

When they finally reached the Great White Boat, sleet was blinding them. "Of all days I booked to ser-vice the SUV," Harry muttered.

"Yeah," Dolores groaned, "and I've got to drive this thing back home once I drop you off at the dealer."

They put the groceries and bottles in the backseat of the Boat and hurried inside. Harry started the car as Dolores uncapped one of the Dewar's bottles and helped herself to a sip. He held in his comment. The windshield was so encrusted with ice that he had to get back out and scrape it with his key. Still the wipers would not move. Harry yanked the door open. "Give me that bottle."

"What?" she said.

"The Scotch. Give me."

"What for? You drink vodka."

"If we had vodka, I'd use it. I need to deice the windshield."

She looked apoplectic. "You're going to pour Dewar's on the goddamned car?"

He reached out and snatched it from her fist. "Jesus," he growled, "it's only booze." He uncapped it and splashed it over the entire windshield, using a good fourth of the bottle. He turned the wipers on again when he got back inside. They groaned, but then started to move, finally swiping the ice right off the glass.

"It worked," Harry said with delight.

"Works for me too," Dolores added, taking another little sip.

"I've noticed."

As the Boat snaked down the street, Dolores turned on NPR. Someone was talking, of course, about the weather. "I think that's Cameron," she said.

"Turn it up."

She did. Cameron Malcolm was saying, "It's not confirmed, but a major snowstorm could hit Los Angeles within the next two days. A massive polar outbreak of proportions rarely seen anywhere on this continent is heading down from the north."

"No wonder the shelves were empty," Dolores said. "And I thought it was all my brother's fault."

Cameron continued. "I've just seen evidence of a second storm out of the Alaskan gulf, taking the same path as the first storm. At best we'll get a few inches of snow; at worst, who knows? The temperature of the ocean is very low for this area, and the westerlies are feeding cold air into the Southland. The clouds are heavy with precipitation. One thing for sure, even if we don't get snow, we're going to get some ice."

"Harry," Dolores pleaded, "let's get out of here." She meant it. "Let's get on a plane, go somewhere, anywhere."

"The only place we're going is the Cadillac dealer so we'll have my vehicle to get us to the Getty tonight."

"*Tonight*? In this? Are you crazy?"

"If you think a little ice storm is going to keep me from partying with Vincent van Gogh, *you're* crazy."

Loretta Zane sipped herbal tea in the living room of her funky clapboard house in Eagle Rock. There was an enormous skylight over the living room that leaked at the very prediction of rain. Today, with the sleet striking it like moist gravel falling from the sky, water poured down from all four corners, into pans, a garbage can and a plastic pail. The wind that propelled the sleet howled through the cracks in the insulation—this was one of those canyon places often found in the L.A. Basin that were little more than upgraded shacks—and the space heater bravely tried to take the chill off, to no avail. But Loretta didn't care.

She was deeply immersed in a book. One she had

read many times before, but was reading again for inspiration: *The Future of Kings,* by Jeffrey King, who was, for her, the wisest man on earth, the most charismatic, and the closest person to God she'd ever known. His story had the makings of a movie:

Poor white boy grows up tough in L.A.'s black ghetto. Aimless, arrested many times for petty crimes, addicted to drugs by the time he is ten. He never meets his father. His mother dies of a drive-by when he is in high school, and he himself almost dies shortly thereafter as a result of snorting cocaine that was cut with rat poison. Then the miracle—finding redemption in sports, the sudden realization of this six-six skinny giant that he has a gift, the gift to play basketball. Drying out, practicing night and day, he's discovered on a fluke by a scout for the NBA. A couple of years of real polishing, hard work, swearing off drugs and drink and women follow, then the moment—being signed by his heroes, the Lakers, and making history.

Though history can take terrible turns, Loretta thought. This same guy who leads the Lakers to victory after victory is fighting the demons that still live inside him, and once the money they throw at him (the Lakers as well as Reebok and other companies eager for his endorsement) is spent on all he desires (houses, cars, vacation villas, sports scholarship endowments to inner-city schools), drugs are still tempting him. Heroin and sex prove a lethal combination one night in Salt Lake City, and he is arrested for rape and possession. In the trial of the year, he beats the sex charge (some say only because of his high-powered attorneys) but does a year in prison on the drug conviction. When he emerges, he's grown up, changed, but still very rich.

This is where Loretta pictured the movie's sound track getting lush and full. Jeffrey King, who found

Jesus in jail, sometimes confuses Jesus and himself.
His shadow grows larger as he sets up a foundation
that offers services that government agencies should
provide—day care centers, drug help for teens, food
for the homeless. People liken it to the social services
the clerics provided in Iraq when there was no functioning government for the .people to turn to after
the American occupation. They are mesmerized by his
fame, by his kindness and the results of his foundation's actions. He turns his infamous notoriety into
something bigger than life: a group anyone can join,
the Kings, followers who believe that he alone can
change the world.

"And he will," Loretta said aloud even though no
one was there to hear her. "He'll pick up where Charlie was stopped." The agenda, the manifesto, the prediction, whatever you wanted to call it, it was going
to come true. It was going to snow. Snow. The catalyst
for the dream. Charlie's and Jeffrey's both.

The phone rang. Loretta checked the caller ID,
planning not to answer if it was anyone from the city
council. She grabbed the phone because it was Andy,
one of the followers, one of the Kings. "Yes."

"I don't understand," a twentysomething male voice
said. "They told me. I mean, I'm coming to the meeting, but I don't get it."

"You will, Andrew," she assured him.

"But the dude never said nothing about snow."

"It's what will happen *because* of that snow. You'll
see. Trust me. Trust the Father."

The boy hesitated. "I'm in Topanga and only have
my Harley. Getting to Eagle Rock on these roads
could be dicey."

"The streets are clear. We got some salt into the
city this morning. I mean, we're not that unprepared."

"It's fucked out there," he said. "I can't risk taking

a spill. You're gonna need me, The Kings are gonna need me."

"Get a ride with Jack. He's out your way."

"Yeah. I forgot. Yeah."

"I'll see you in a few hours."

The boy took a deep breath. "I can't believe it's gonna happen." The idea seemed to mesmerize him.

"Good-bye." Loretta hung up and brought her feet under her on the ratty chair. *Oh, Andy. So young, so impressionable, so hot. Kids,* she thought. *Children.* But who wasn't still a child? Hell, they'd all been kids when it happened the first time, when a messiah had lived among them. She was old enough to remember, not like these young people who had never heard of Squeaky or Tex, or even Charlie. She remembered that Sharon Tate was a kid herself, a kid carrying a kid. Children were always the future, weren't they? Andy was dumb as a stump, gangly, directionless and immature. But he believed, and that was what they needed. Believers who would see to the new order. Jeffrey would be proud.

She set the book back on the shelf, only to notice the one next to it. *Helter Skelter.* By Vincent Bugliosi. A scathing indictment of everything she believed in. But also her secret bible. Jeffrey King was the new Charlie. And he would lead them to glory.

After the midday news, Michael had time to run home before the six o'clock broadcast. A producer getting into his Audi A8 Quattro said, "Hey, Mike, you like your car?"

"I do," Michael admitted as he opened the door of his new Prius. "And I feel good about it."

"Hey, environmentally sound is great, but does green work in this weather?" the producer asked.

"So far." Michael grinned. "I sure wish I had Quattro, though. When the snow comes, you're probably going to get a lot farther than I do."

The producer tossed his bag and some scripts into the car. "I'm heading for Palm Desert tonight, getting out of this."

"Don't blame you. Good luck. Drive safely." Michael slid into his vehicle.

"You too," the producer called, doing the same.

Michael dialed the clinic. "Free Clinic, Wendy speaking."

"Hey."

"Hey."

"I'm going home for a few hours. Can you leave?"

"Huh?"

"Let's make love."

"You're kidding."

"Not in the least. It's the best way to keep warm."

"Listen, horny husband, you tell that to my waiting room filled with frightened people, sick people, people chilled to the bone."

He shrugged. She sometimes took her work much too seriously. "I was only kidding," he said, even though he wasn't.

"I really can't talk," she said, making a kiss sound into the phone, and hanging up.

That stung a little. He put the car in gear and left the studio lot. Three blocks away he got stuck in a bottleneck. Nothing moved either way. He thought of his wife's voice, how sexy it was, and what they could be doing at home this afternoon while Parijata watched Rachel, and how—

He felt a stirring in his pants and tried to turn off the impulse. A city bus was creeping up next to him. *Yeah, just my luck, I'll be beating off to the audience of forty women peering through the bus windows.* The car in front of him moved a little. Then a little more. He finally made it through the intersection, then everything again stopped dead. Looking in the rear-view mirror, he thought he saw someone he knew. He turned, glanced at the people struggling to cross the street in the wind, then was sure. It was his friend and neighbor Matt Bamberg, the actor/real estate agent. Opening the door, he called, "Matthew! Hey, Matthew!" He hit the horn at the same time. The guy noticed him.

"Michael!" Matthew called, hurrying to the car.

"Get in."

Matthew did, thankfully. "Man, this sucks."

"I'll say. Where were you going?"

"Home."

"Me too. Good timing."

"I'll say."

"Where were you? Showing a house?"

Matthew shook his head. "I had an audition. Tim says he'll be at the hospital until late—too many sick doggies, so he couldn't pick me up."

"You get the part?"

Matthew, a handsome guy in his mid-twenties who had talent and drive but not great luck getting acting parts, shrugged. "Who knows? Listen, tell your brother to sign me. I'd have a much better chance."

"Your agent not working for you?"

"Sending me to a cattle call like the one I just did? Forty wet queers hoping to get seven lines in the new Sofia Coppola picture?"

Michael blinked. "They were all gay?"

"Well," Matthew confessed, "they were all cute, so naturally I assumed."

"I'm cute," Michael joked, "but I'm not."

"You're ugly and you know it. Hey, I heard two hunks talking about you in the holding pen. About your broadcast today."

"Oh boy."

"About your pecs, about your swim trunks, wondering how big—"

"God, you guys are fixated on one thing. You should take a clue from us straight boys. We are not so obsessed. I mean, all we think about is tits. Big tits, bigger tits, the biggest tits."

"Yeah, we'll try to emulate you from now on." Matthew laughed. "I'm surprised they don't invent a Viagra pill for women's breasts. I mean, pump them up for a date."

"You could make money off that."

"More than I'm making as an actor, I'm sure," Matthew said, somewhat depressed.

"It's a tough business, pal. You gotta hang in there. You've got the talent."

"I also have the talent to sell houses, and that's what's paying the bills. That and Tim's salary." Matthew looked out the window as the traffic started to move. "This is pretty incredible. You guys going anywhere on your vacation? Anywhere warm?"

Michael shrugged. "We planned just to take a few day trips. Now I think we'll stay in bed and snuggle."

"Sounds good to me."

Michael slammed on the brakes and felt the car slide. "Where'd you grow up?"

"Wisconsin. I feel like I'm back home."

"Unlike back there, where roads are ready for this and people know how to drive in it, we're really going to be in trouble when the snow hits."

"Total gridlock?"

Michael nodded. "Nothing is going to move. Nothing."

It was already happening on the San Diego Freeway, where Dolores Delanova-Hanwell was cursing.

"I told you we should have gone straight home. No, you've got to go down to the car dealer on Wilshire."

Harry groaned. "We could have shopped in Santa Monica. They have markets there too, you know. But no, you have to go to your *favorite* Ralph's."

"Sure. Blame me."

"Look out that side for me."

She turned to the window. "It's covered with sleet."

"Open it!"

"Not on your life."

"Goddamn it, Dee, I need to get over to get on the Santa Monica freeway. I can't see a thing."

Grumbling, she rolled down the window. As it lowered, the ice stayed in place, as if there was another window outside the one that sank into the doorframe. "Will you look at that!" A second later, it simply collapsed inward. In her lap. "Shit!"

Harry, amused but more intent on changing lanes, shouted at her to stick her head out and tell him when it was safe to do so. Dolores felt freezing rain and wind hit her face. She flagged the car next to them to hold back so Harry could get over. "Okay, now, go."

Harry changed lanes, and she rolled the window back up. He made out the sign to Santa Monica and turned toward the ramp, cutting off another car, which caused a barrage of horns and fingers sticking up in windows. "Oh, go fuck yourselves," Dolores muttered, at no one car in particular.

Harry said, "It's bumper cars at the carnival."

Then they were hit in the driver's side by a pickup truck. Dolores freaked out, for this was her car, her pride and joy, her reminder of the day she was a star, the last vestige of another time in which she was much happier. "Harry, stop! Don't let them get away."

"I can see there's no damage. It's just a bump."

"Stop!"

"Dolores, nobody's stopping out here to exchange insurance company cards, you understand? This thing is built of steel, it doesn't dent. If anything, the truck's bumper is history."

"No wonder I drink."

"Oh man, now what?" Harry saw the cars in front of him stop dead. Whereas the 405 had been moving a bit, the 10 was a parking lot. He thought fast. Maybe, just maybe— He turned the wheel right, said, "Hold on" and gunned the engine.

"What are you doing?"

"Going through the ivy." Indeed, he piloted the car over the bump of the curb at the side of the ramp and plowed through the icy greenery—where, incongruously, automatic sprinklers were roaring in the freezing rain. "I think I can get up the hill."

"You're not in your goddamned SUV, Harry!"

The Great White Boat lunged and bounced. Dolores reached into the backseat when she heard the bottles clinking, trying to protect them. But it was for naught. A moment later, as Harry turned the wheel again to avoid what looked like an easy chair that had been discarded on the side of the road, the car began to slide—it was on a steep incline—and Dolores came slamming up against him, the groceries and bottles tumbled all over the rear seat, and the car finally came to rest against a light pole. "Jesus, Harry, what were you doing? Trying to kill us?"

"Yes," he snapped, glaring at her.

For a moment she thought he meant it.

He had to climb over her to get out to check on the damage, for it was doubtful whether the driver's door, wrapped around the firm steel pole now, was ever going to open again. He had trouble standing on the steep hillside, holding on to the car for dear life.

He saw the wheels sunk into the mud under the ivy and realized this was the end of their journey. "Come on," he told her.

She was startled. "Come on? Where?"

"I don't know. Out. We can't stay here."

"Call the auto club."

"Get serious."

She looked around and realized it was a silly notion. Nothing was moving, the freeway was stopped, their car was dead and the weather was getting worse. Harry's dark brown hair was already white with sleet. He reached inside, offering his hand. She grabbed it with one hand, firmly gripping the half-empty Dewar's bottle with the other. She wasn't about to leave it behind.

Just then a voice called from behind Harry. He looked up to see a guy in a parka and big boots coming down the slope. "Hey, I got a truck above. Saw what happened. Thought I could help."

"Thanks, man," Harry said gratefully. He looked inside at Dolores. "Come on. This guy's gonna help us get out of here."

"Aren't there cops around? We can't just abandon the car! What about the food?"

"Dolores, come on, grab my hand." He reached out again as the fellow who had offered help grabbed his shoulders to steady him.

"I can't go up that hill in these shoes," Dolores protested.

"You'll go up barefoot if you have to. We don't have a choice."

"Come on, lady," the other man said encouragingly. "Don't be afraid. They say this is nothing compared to what's coming."

Harry bent down and grabbed her arm, attempting to pull her out of the vehicle. She protested. "Wait a frigging minute!"

The good Samaritan said to Harry, rather curiously, "This your mother?"

"Wife," Harry corrected him.

The guy just raised his eyebrows.

Dolores got to her knees on the seat, reaching over the back of it to grab one of the bags on the floor. The car reeked of booze, so she knew at least one of the bottles had broken. But one had survived. Yanking it over the seat, clutching it to her, she turned to Harry and said, "Help me, for Christ's sake."

He wanted to kill her. "What do you think we've been doing?" The two men eased her out, stood her against the car, giving her a moment to catch her breath.

"Hey, I know you," said the truck driver, who appeared to be in his fifties as well, as he reached to take the bag from her. "Aren't you what's-her-name?"

"That's me, all right," Dolores deadpanned. "Sandra Dee."

"Really?" the guy asked, looking confused.

"Close. Dolores Delanova. But they do call me Dee."

His eyes brightened. "Oh, yeah. You were in *Summer Love*."

"I'll never live it down."

"You were one of my favorites."

"Well, honey," she said, turning on the charm, "you think you could carry me up there?"

Harry said, "Get walking." And they did.

But Harry fell backward into the muddy soil when he stepped on something hiding in the ivy that was too slick. It stunned Dolores, suddenly finding him in the sludge looking surprised and vulnerable. Tears welled in her eyes. "Harry, are you all right?" He reached up, she grasped his hand, the truck driver helped him to his feet, but through it all Dolores didn't take her eyes off him. She pulled him to her, tears rolling down her face. "I'm so sorry, honey. Forgive me, please."

"It's all right, Dee. I'm fine."

"I hate this. I hate this so much," she said, coming apart.

"Come on, be strong for me, baby," he ordered. "Let's get up to the top. Just a little more to go—"

"Dolores Delanova. I'll be damned," the trucker said, bringing up the rear. "My wife won't believe this one."

Bob Hanwell walked into the ER waiting area and saw his wife holding a novel. He went over to her and sat down. "What are you reading?"

"A thriller. *Deadly Games*. Sheldon at the Mystery Bookstore in Westwood recommended it. It's thought-provoking."

"So's the weather."

She looked up to see that he was covered with ice. "Oh, it isn't!"

"It is." They had gotten to the hospital right after talking to Dr. Shemonsky, when the sleet was still rain. While Susan got her IV, Bob had left Aileene there and gone to the pharmacy to pick up syringes and vials of Demerol and atropine. "We've got to get home before the roads get too slick."

"Fifteen minutes more," Aileene said, glancing up at the clock. "Is it hell out there?"

"Yes. Cars are skidding, people falling, the wind is getting ferocious, and it's coming down sideways. Sheets of ice."

"You know, Bob, I drove on ice as a girl in Minnesota, but it's been years."

"Not true. You did it at Tahoe a few winters ago."

"Yes, with snow tires."

"Maybe you won't have to. I'm here."

"I hope it won't frighten Susan."

He smiled. "She'd love it, but I think she'll sleep all the way home."

Love it? Could anyone really love it? Her resentment of the pain her daughter had to go through made her look at the world through a different lens. Would they get their daughter home safely on the streets? Would the house stay warm enough to keep Susan comfortable? Could they get an ambulance quickly if Susan needed one? Love it? She hated it.

Aileene put her head on Bob's shoulder and closed her eyes.

The accident Wendy was in was much more serious than the minor mishap that sidelined Dolores and Harry. When a car slammed into the side of the bus on which she was riding, the bus driver lost control, and the bus came to rest on its side on the front lawn of a house. Wendy's car had not started when they closed the clinic early because of the weather. It would not turn over no matter how much she tried, and she couldn't even get the hood open because there was such a layer of ice on it. She gave up. She'd probably feel safer on a bus anyhow. They were bigger. So the impact was even more startling to her because she was feeling so safe. When she felt the impact, everything spun, as though she were suddenly dizzy, faint. Clothing, bags, umbrellas and briefcases and raincoats were instantly airborne. There was an eerie momentary silence that seemed longer than it actually was, then the cry of a child's voice, then shouts of pain, confusion and shock.

Wendy was unhurt except for a little cut above her eye. She felt the blood run down her face as she knelt on one of the broken windows. She grabbed a kerchief she saw lying near her and pressed it to her head. She curled up against what had been the ceiling of the bus and caught her breath as people stepped on one another in an effort to get to their feet, clamoring to get out. Wendy felt a stabbing pain as a man braced his foot on her shoulder, trying desperately to push himself up through one of the windows. A female passenger fell against her as she lost her footing trying to move toward the door, where people were already reaching inside to pull the passengers out.

Finally, Wendy got up. She felt dazed, but she knew she was all right. Three men—one, the bus driver himself—helped her up and out. She sat on top of the side of the bus that was facing toward the sky, for a moment in the sleet, and caught her breath. "You okay?" a man asked.

"Yes. My head hurts, though."

"Let me see. I'm a nurse." He pulled her hand away and saw the cut was minor. "It isn't bleeding anymore. Keep it cold, put pressure on it." He rubbed the bloody kerchief in the ice that was building up on the bus and pressed it back against Wendy's forehead. "It'll be fine."

"Can I help? I work at the Free Clinic."

Before he could answer, she had jumped down to the ground, where people were lying about, in pain, hurt, in shock. A man was bleeding profusely from his hand, which had evidently gone through a window. She turned to another man. "Give me your necktie!" He didn't question why. He pulled it off and handed it to her, and she quickly tied the tourniquet on the injured man's arm. When the nurse took over, she spied a bystander standing in suit and tie and quickly approached him. "Can I have your tie too, please?"

"Sure," he said, sounding terribly unsure. As he began to unfasten it, she heard why. "It cost me two hundred dollars."

"It's going to prove well worth it." She grabbed it and tied it around her own head to hold the kerchief in place.

Then she helped care for others. After about fifteen minutes, she could hear sirens in the distance, but she knew they would be a long time coming. What was happening was happening everywhere on the streets of L.A. this afternoon. Gridlock. She fixed a temporary splint for a little boy whose leg looked like it was broken, calmed a woman who was worried about her purse, assuring her it was safe inside the bus, and hugged a little girl who would not stop crying over her injured mother. When the first ambulance arrived, she led the paramedics to the most severely injured and then helped direct things as police cars and a rescue squad showed up. The wet soaked through her coat, through her clothes to her skin, and the sleet formed a kind of ice helmet over her hair. She helped distribute the articles that were recovered from the bus, including her own shoulder bag. By the time it was over, she felt she'd been there for days.

Refusing any medical attention for herself and assuring the police officers that she lived within walking distance, she sat down under the tree in the yard in which the overturned bus lay, and found her cell phone to call Michael. But she couldn't even push the button to dial him. She simply started to cry.

Matthew drifted to the window. "This is the freakiest thing I've ever seen."

Michael looked out as well. "I wonder about getting back to the studio for the six o'clock. I shouldn't have left."

"Have some soup, boys," Parijata said, coming from the kitchen. They were in her first-floor apartment, staying warm together.

"I will," Matthew said happily, " 'cause I don't think Tim is going to be cooking me dinner tonight." He let her fill his mug. "Looks good. I never learned how."

"I'll teach you," Parijata said, "but we start Mexican, *sí*?"

Matthew winked. "Terrific." He glanced out the window. "In fact, I think we should start the cooking classes *in* Mexico, where it's warm."

"We'll all go," Michael added, letting Parijata ladle soup for him as well.

Sitting on the sofa, Michael clicked on the television. It was tuned to MSNBC, where he saw Contessa Brewer sounding like him: talking about the weather. The rest of the country was simply mesmerized by the situation on the West Coast and by the beautiful, striking anchor reporter. "There's an almost gleeful *It's your turn!* attitude from people who have suffered through snowy winters for most of their lives." Contessa smiled. "Of course, that might have more to do with the East Coast–West Coast rivalry than anything else. But the thing we are all sure of, no matter where in the country you are—and I'm here in L.A. today, in the thick of it—it's hell."

"She's so damned refreshing," Michael gushed. "You believe her."

"Sexy too," Matthew added.

Michael raised his eyebrows.

"For a girl," Matthew clarified.

"When it snows," Parijata said, "the bambinos are going to be loving it. Most have never seen snow. It will be magic."

Michael groaned. "It'll be like a ride at Disneyland

at first, astonishing and wild. But how much will we get? That's the problem. I mean, what will we do with it all?"

"Shovel," Matthew muttered. "Like my dad made me do all winter long as a kid."

Michael got up and went to the window. The sleet was still coming down. He didn't look happy as he glanced at his watch. "I'd better head back."

"Good luck," Matthew told him.

Michael went to the bedroom to kiss his sleeping child and get his coat. But just as he was putting it on, his cell phone rang. "Hey, honey," he said as he realized it was his wife. "No, I'm home—at Parijata's as a matter of fact, about to head back to the studio. How's the situation there?" A look of panic glazed Michael's face. Matthew and Parijata stared at him as he stood there with his coat in one hand, the phone in the other. "Oh God, honey, you weren't hurt, were you?"

"What happened?" Matthew asked, concerned.

Parijata made the sign of the cross.

Michael listened as Wendy explained about the bus accident. "Where are you? Should I come get you? You're sure you're okay?"

They could all hear her through the phone yelling that she was fine, she was only a few blocks away on foot, she would be there soon. Her nerves were obviously shattered. She softened and said, "I just needed to hear your voice, Michael."

"Honey, I love you," he responded.

"Go to the studio. I'll see you later. I'm almost there."

Michael shut his phone and put his jacket down. "She was in an accident, her car wouldn't start so she took a bus. It tipped over. But she's okay, she says."

"My God!" Matthew exclaimed.

Michael looked ambivalent, glancing at the window again, not knowing what to do.

"You've got to do the weather," Matthew urged him. "People need your reassurance. Trust Wendy that she's fine."

Without a word, a worried Michael slipped his heavy coat on and left the building.

Loretta Zane sat on the arm of her sofa, facing the people who had gathered in her living room. "The King has predicted the end would come. He has told us we would be saved if we believed. Well, we have believed, and we are going to be saved. Look outside. Just look outside." Everyone turned to the dark windows, where sleet was clinging to the glass. "It's the start of the end. The end of the world as we know it. The Kings will be the only ones to make it through this. We will survive the snow."

There was a lot of chatter about whether or not it was really going to snow. One guy said that he was sure it was too preposterous to believe. Loretta countered with, "You want to tell that to the Father to his face?" The man shrugged. Another said she believed her, but how would they survive it? Would something miraculous happen that protected them? "We will be given instructions from the Father. We need to trust he will tell us how to outlast the weather."

Andy Rakos jumped to his feet. "Man," the wild-looking young man ranted, "I don't know. I mean, hell, we hear Armageddon is coming soon, but don't that mean the whole earth? Like, dudes, this is just L.A. So hey, we survive this storm, and then what? How do we start the New Order that the Father preaches?"

"Trust him," Loretta said firmly.

"Yeah, trust him, man," an old black fellow said. A chorus of voices added their agreement. Someone spit, "Death to pigs."

When the group left after Loretta's promise that the King would instruct them at a candlelight vigil out near King's compound in Chatsworth the next night, Andy Rakos stayed behind. It wasn't unusual, for she and Andy had been having sex since they first met at a retreat that Jeffrey King had conducted in the mountains two years before, when the kid was only seventeen. But Andy didn't want sex tonight. He wanted enlightenment. And history. He was the youngest of the followers who was fascinated about someone that Loretta had personally known, the Jeffrey King of his time, Charles Manson.

After a million questions, and a million answers, Loretta told Andy she was tired. He reminded her he'd come with another disciple and had no way of getting home. This was his night off, but he had to work tomorrow evening, so she offered to drive him. But they took a detour on the way to his place out in Topanga. They drove up Waverly Drive in Los Feliz— where she stopped in front of a house.

"What's this?" he asked.

"Where Leno and Rosemary LaBianca bit the dust."

He looked like he'd been zapped by electricity. "Wow. Cool."

"It's been remodeled over the years, but it's still the same place."

He looked up and next to it. "What's that big wall to one side?"

"Was a convent," she said. "Now it's some kind of prayer house for priests, a retreat I guess. Catholic church owns it."

"I never knew that."

"Surprisingly, not much was ever made of it," she admitted. "Not even in the TV movie they made."

"I watched your tape of it. It was crap."

"Charlie liked it."

Andy brightened, surprised. "He saw it?"

"They have TV sets in prison, you know." She turned the wipers faster. The sleet was caking on the windshield.

"Was he everything Jeffrey is today?"

She swooned. "Everything and more."

"They portray him as a scuzzy, insignificant junkie."

"His name defines the last century. When he's paroled, people will see."

He rubbed his hands together in anticipation. "Man, I'd give anything to meet him."

"That's why we have to survive this. That's why we have to trust Jeffrey." She put her warm hand on his leg, pressing down on his crotch. The windows were steaming up. "Andy, I feel the fever burning because what Jeffrey's saying matches Charlie perfectly. The Father says Armageddon, Charlie said a race war. Both mean the end of the world as we know it."

His heart was pumping blood faster now. He felt her zeal. He pressed her hands against the hardness under his zipper. "The world will end because of the snow? It won't stop?"

"It will be the catalyst for a new order. When this happens—when the snow comes—it's going to delineate once and for all the two classes, the rich and the poor, white and black. The race war will come because of the snow."

"And we'll start it."

She grinned. "Yes, we'll start it." Then she kissed him, wet and passionate, sucking his chin and licking his cheeks as well. "Oh, yes, it'll be like nothing the world has ever seen. You. Me. The survivors, starting over again."

"I want to make love to you," the boy panted.

She sat up straight and put her hands back on the steering wheel. "No. It's time to go." She put the car in gear and turned around, heading down Waverly toward Rowena Avenue. "We'll have all the time in the world for love once this has happened."

They passed the long convent wall. At the end of it was another house, a big Spanish structure hugging the hillside behind gates. All the windows were warmly lit. "That's a nice one," Andy murmured, looking up at the edifice.

"They'll die too," Loretta said flatly. "They all will. The whole street, all these rich, smug, entitled bastards who keep the rest down under."

The car slid sideways going down the slope. Loretta righted the wheel, turning into the skid, while Andy held on for dear life. "Man, this really is getting bad," he said, shaken.

"I love it," she said.

Aileene Hanwell gasped as she looked out their living room window at the street, where the lights of a car seemed to be moving sideways. "Oh God, that car's going to hit the—" But it didn't. She breathed a sigh of relief. "They are so lucky." She sipped from the cup of tea she held in her hand, then walked back toward the fireplace. Susan had fallen asleep there on the sofa when they'd returned from the hospital, and she still slept soundly. Bob had stoked the fire several times, gone outside for more wood, but all the time with a remote phone glued to his ear. When he walked in now the call had finally ended. "Who was that for so long?" Aileene asked.

"Conference call with the mayor and Cameron. Everyone is at wits' end on how to handle this thing. They're setting up a command post at Griffith Observatory."

Aileene blinked. "Because it's so high up?"

"And helicopters can get in and out. They're turning over the reins to an Army general, Parker Van Hecke. They drag him out for all major disasters, apparently."

"What are you doing for them?"

"The old PR trick. Keep everyone calm. Keep them from panicking. I called Mike to get his support—he's the one who first warned of snow. I want him to impress upon people that it is a grave situation, but one we can make it through."

"What did he say?"

"He was caught in traffic on the way back to the studio, not sure he'd make it in time."

She checked the big clock on the mantel. "He's got just a few more minutes."

"Wendy was in some kind of bus accident."

Aileene looked concerned. "Is she okay?"

"Michael said she's fine. I guess it shook them both up, though."

Herschel, who was sound asleep next to Susan on the sofa, raised his head, as if instinctively knowing she was about to awaken. Sure enough, her eyes opened. They did not speak of much pain, Aileene thought. "Honey, how are you?"

"Okay. I slept."

"You sure did."

"It looks like midnight."

Bob laughed. "It's looked like midnight all day. It's almost six. Want to watch your brother on TV?"

"Sure," Susan said, rubbing her eyes and petting the dog at the same time.

Bob helped her up. "Let's go down to the family room, the big screen. I can light us another fire there."

On the other side of town, in Beverly Hills, Dolores walked into her kitchen dressed in a chenille robe. Her hair was wrapped in a towel. She'd taken a hot bath the minute they got home—which hadn't been easy. By the time they reached the man's truck, she'd broken a heel, and water had soaked through her shoes. Harry was covered with mud from the spill he'd taken in the ivy, so when they slid into the cab of the truck, the mud went with them. On top of that, Dolores had rubbed up against something greasy in the dirty truck and black goo stuck to her fox coat like paint. She was grateful she'd rescued the Scotch. She had nearly finished the open bottle in the two hours it took them to get to the Cadillac dealer.

Grateful for the ride through hell, they had the driver leave them on Wilshire Boulevard in Santa Monica, where they picked up Harry's SUV. From there on, it was fairly smooth sailing, and the Escalade had gotten them home faster than the truck had taken them to West L.A., but perhaps that was more a result of Harry's expert navigation of side streets than of the vehicle itself. When they pulled into the garage on Roxbury Drive, into the magnificent house that Dolores had owned for most of her adult life, they were both thoroughly on edge. While she bathed, he showered in his own bathroom, and was sitting drinking vodka on the rocks when she finally drifted into the warm and cozy den. "What about my car?" she asked.

"What about it?"

"I want my car." She used the whiny voice he hated.

"I'll go back and get your car in the morning." He hoped she would just say fine.

She didn't. "Leaving it there all night? Someone could steal it. Or they might tow it away someplace."

"There's nothing we can do."

"I think we should call the auto club."

He shouted, "So go call the goddamned auto club. You've got a voice. You've got a phone."

She did. And they told her precisely what Harry had said. There was nothing they could do tonight—hers was one of more than seven hundred calls in their area of Los Angeles alone—but they would put it on the list for tomorrow, depending on what the weather did.

When she came back to the den, Harry was watching Michael. No clowning around tonight. Michael Hanwell was instead giving a pep talk about snow. "It will be met with wonder and fascination, and it's going to be fun if we see it that way. So don't think, 'Oh no, what a burden,' or about how awful it will be to drive in. Stay home. Schools will undoubtedly be closed. No one has to go out. Eat what's in the freezer, play games and read books and just enjoy this wonderful freak of nature. This won't be a tsunami that will destroy our paradise. It won't happen again for a long, long time, if ever. Remember it to tell your grandkids. Build snowmen. Enjoy it."

"But," the anchorperson said to Michael from the studio desk, "how much are we going to get? Do you know yet?"

Michael shrugged. He held up a Whacked Weather photo. It showed a cabin with a light dusting of snow on the roof. "Could be this much." Then he held up another, the typical Christmas card picture of a forest covered with snow that was fairly deep. "Or this much." Then he showed another, in which a swirling blizzard had blown drifts up over the roofs of cars. "Or this. But we hope not."

The anchor, knowing that Michael's mission was to keep people calm, said, "You know, Mike, we're Californians. We take earthquakes, fires and floods in stride. We just have to do the same with this."

"Right." Michael grabbed a grease pen, which, as in the old days of weather reporting, he liked to use as a prop. On top of the photo of the drifts he wrote "20 degrees." "The low for tonight. And I'm not kidding."

"Jesus," Dolores muttered. "Every plant out there's going to die. You know what it'll cost to replant this place?"

"The trees might make it," Harry said hopefully.

"I should give them a little Dewar's."

"Listen, I'll go see about your car in the morning."

"Take the Great White Behemoth to find the Great White Boat," she sang, "in the great white snowstorm."

"I was supposed to go to a screening at ICM tonight."

"No movie ever made is worth driving in this." Then she grinned. "With the exception of a few of mine."

"And *Casablanca*." Harry was getting hungry. "What's for dinner?"

"Hell if I know. You're the cook."

"We still have that veal?"

She swirled the ice around in her glass. "Oh yeah, you bought it the day we thought Kate and Steven and the kids were coming to dinner. But there's too much."

"So I'll cook it up and we can have it for sandwiches. Or freeze what we don't eat."

"Hey," she said with a grin, "just set it out in the yard. No need to even put it back in the Sub-Zero."

The wind slammed wet sleet against the dark window. It was so loud they both looked up. "Michael's right," Harry said. "This is just whacked."

Matthew and Parijata helped Wendy into Parijata's apartment. "You'll catch your death," Parijata told her, urging her out of her wet clothes. She brought a blanket to wrap around her, while Matthew ran upstairs to the Hanwells' apartment to get her some warm clothes. "Were people injured?"

Wendy nodded, accepting the cup of hot tea gratefully. "It was pretty bad. But no one died. Thank God for that."

"You walked here?"

Wendy nodded yes. "I think I got here faster than if I'd been in a car."

She warmed herself with the tea, then changed into dry clothes. Rachel woke up and Wendy fed her. Tim showed up after Michael's newscast, hugged his partner and collapsed on Parijata's sofa. "Animals who have never felt temperatures lower than fifty degrees are being brought in with frostbite, paws that are raw and infected. It's something I never thought I'd see here." He turned to Matthew. "How'd the audition go?"

Matthew shrugged. "Like all the others."

"I heard most movie and TV production has shut down."

"I don't think anyone can get to work. And location stuff, for sure," Wendy replied. "I think the whole city is coming to a standstill."

"What's it like in the Valley?" Matthew asked.

The animal hospital where Tim worked was in North Hollywood. "Ghastly," he said.

"Maybe Michael will tell us more." Parijata turned the television back on. The ten o'clock newscast was one horror story after another—accidents, fires, people evacuating, rioting in a grocery store, a general being called in from the Pentagon to oversee things, a state of emergency being declared by the governor. Michael's weather report was his usual clown act, a welcome respite from the grim news. He sang, "Baby, It's Cold Outside," doing harmony with a recording of the song that Dee had done on an album back in 1971. The prediction for tomorrow's high and low startled everyone. It would barely rise above freezing, and the temperature could dip to eighteen degrees. Millions of viewers felt shivers as he said it.

Michael seriously warned people to stay off the ice. Now that the temperature was dropping for the night, the ice would be slick, dangerous, even deadly. Fifty-three people had already died in ice-related accidents today. When the news picked up after Michael was done, it showed thousands of people stranded in their cars on ice-encrusted freeways at rush hour. People trying to stand on patches of slick black ice. People huddled under the canopies of gas stations and hotel lobbies, under the eaves of buildings, waiting—praying—for the sleet to stop. The minicams showed enormous trucks spilling salt onto the streets of the city.

In bed later, Michael held Wendy close to him. He was exhausted from his drive home after the news. It had taken him almost two and a half hours. At one point, he had thought about abandoning the car. Every four blocks, he had to get out and chip ice off the windshield, for the defrosters were doing no good; it was coming down too fast and too hard and it was just too cold. After his shower, he crawled into the warm bed and curled up against her soft, smooth skin. A moment later Wendy was surprised to feel his penis erect against her thigh. She turned to him, but he was sound asleep. It was not a sexual reaction, it was just what happened when a man fell asleep. She kissed him on the cheek and closed her eyes, feeling the afterglow that she'd felt so many times after lovemaking, that place where the body goes numb but the mind seems to keep climaxing. They were one together now, their minds making love, and yet resting, slowly relaxing.

Wendy suddenly opened her eyes. She had no idea how long they'd been asleep, but she realized she'd not turned off the light. Reaching up, trying not to disturb Michael, she felt for the little knob to turn the bedside lamp off. When she did, the room turned black, but then, after her eyes had adjusted for a few moments, she saw the dim light from the building next door. But the light was refracted through ice, a thick coating of ice that covered the window from end to end.

In Los Feliz, Bob Hanwell stepped outside to get more firewood for the night, since Susan had fallen asleep again in front of the fireplace in the family room and he wanted to make sure she was going to be warm and toasty. She hadn't needed pain medication, and for that he was grateful. He prayed she would sleep soundly all night long.

He couldn't believe how cold it was. This was a bone-warping, mind-numbing arctic embrace that he had never felt in Southern California. He crouched over the wood piled under the protection of the eaves of the house and lifted four logs into his arms. Could he manage a fifth? Sure he could. But he was wrong. As he stood up, the top one fell off, rolled toward the pool and fell in. "Shit," Bob muttered.

But then something startled him. The log hadn't splashed into the water. It had rolled across the surface. Huh? Bob walked to the water's edge. Sure

enough, the log was lying there, not floating, not bob-
bing in the cold water, just lying on top of it. He bent
his knees and, setting the logs down, he tapped the
surface with his right hand. It was solid ice.

It took three hard hits with his fist to crack it. When
he did, and lifted up a chunk, he saw that it was almost
two inches thick.

And for the first time he was scared.

Harry Hanwell stood next to the Great White Boat, seething. Not only was the car's driver's door wrapped around the light pole, the back window had been knocked out, the trunk was open and the spare missing, and what was left of the groceries had been taken. Only a stalk of celery remained, frozen, on the Scotch-stained backseat. The freeway traffic was moving, slowly but surely, so it was almost as if nothing had happened. It pissed him off.

When he got into the car to attempt to start it, he was startled. The steering wheel was gone. The whole damned steering wheel! And the radio had been pried out, leaving a gaping hole in the dashboard. He shook his head. Parts for antique cars could fetch a lot of money on eBay. This weather brought out the worst in people. He cursed himself for allowing Dolores to keep the thing this long. Well, no more. He would have it towed to a body shop, then they could send it to a scrap yard. No, wait, he told himself. He'd talk to someone who specialized in classic cars. Hell, he could sell it on eBay himself. He might make good money off what was left of it.

A highway patrol car pulled up and two officers got out. They were pleasant enough, but warned Harry that he'd better make arrangements to have the car moved or they'd do it for him with a ticket to boot. It wasn't impeding traffic, but it wasn't exactly a legal parking place either. Harry grumbled that he'd already called AAA, and as he was assuring the officers of that, the tow truck arrived.

He climbed back into his Escalade and drove away, confident that he'd never have to look at the Cadillac convertible again. It would be towed, stored, then sold. Just what he should have done long ago. His cell phone rang. "Harry Hanwell." It was an actor he represented who had been sitting in Hugo's in West Hollywood waiting for their power breakfast for more than two hours now. "I'm coming, I'm coming," Harry assured him. "Maybe you didn't notice, but it's a bit of a fucking mess outside." He hung up. Actors. Was he crazy? He actually was going to eat with one? There had to be better things to do with his life than to put up with their selfishness. However, he knew of no easier way to make money.

Michael hung up the phone as Wendy came from the bedroom, dressed for work. "It was Mom. She wants us to come up there."

"When?"

"Now."

Wendy looked surprised. "Today? What for? I have a job and you're on the air at noon. Your vacation doesn't start till tomorrow."

"Damn. I wish I'd never put in for it."

"You only did it because I thought I could get off

too," she reminded him. "A week in Puerto Vallarta sounded great."

"Mom thinks we'll be safer there."

Wendy shook her head as she donned her coat. "Jesus, Michael, she's the kind of person you were trying to reach last night. Telling to stay calm."

"I know."

"How's your sister doing?" Wendy was concerned.

"Holding on."

She nodded. Michael grabbed his leather jacket while Wendy lifted the baby. "You start the car while I take her down to Parijata. Then maybe you can jump my car and juice it up enough so I can drive it home tonight."

"No," he corrected her. "Best thing is when it starts, I take it. I'll leave you mine. That way your battery will get a good charge."

"I just don't want you to be late," she said. "Your job's more important than mine."

He laughed out loud. "Prancing around as the weather clown? You save lives."

She opened the door. "Hey, Michael," she said immediately, "it feels warmer."

He stepped out behind her. "As expected."

"Don't you think it will last?"

"That would be nice," he admitted, locking the door. "But it's more like the calm before the storm."

"No blue plastic bag in the driveway today," Bob told his wife when she came down to join him for coffee. "First time I can ever remember the *New York Times* not arriving."

"Maybe someone stole it."

"He always tosses it past the gates." He shook his head. "I don't think he made it. I was the only idiot out there," he admitted with a grin. "Almost broke my neck, slid all the way down. But it's melting; it's warming up."

Aileene took milk from the refrigerator, poured some into her coffee, and sat at the table in the breakfast area with him. "I called Michael. I told him they should come here for a few days."

"And?"

"No dice."

"They have their own lives, honey. They have their family of friends where they live. And they have jobs to do."

"But Michael's vacation starts tomorrow. And they aren't going anywhere."

"Let them be." Bob changed the subject. "Susan had a good night. She got up and had some juice, a little yogurt. She's showering now."

"It wasn't as easy as you think."

Bob looked alarmed. "What?"

"I heard her moaning around three. When I came down, she was in a lot of pain."

"Did you give her Demerol?"

She shook her head. "She refused. She said she'd get through it. She's terribly afraid of becoming addicted."

Bob rejected that notion. "It would take hundreds of shots over a short period of time. It's an irrational fear."

"She fell back asleep in my arms after about an hour."

"But she's better now."

Aileene nodded. "I didn't sleep much of the night myself."

He took her hand across the table. "Honey, I'm sorry. You hungry?"

She nodded her head. "I'm in the mood for an omelet. But I think we're out of eggs."

"Should we go to the food store?"

"I had the set on while I was dressing," she warned him. "They showed an Albertson's that looked like Baghdad after the bombs fell. I don't think we want to go there."

He got up and opened the refrigerator. "We are low on things. I suppose we should have stopped at the Mayfair yesterday when we went to the hospital."

"With Susan? Impossible."

"How about frozen waffles?" He grinned. "Sorry to use that word. But I know we have some."

"Fine." Aileene poured herself a bit more coffee. "I'm worried that crummy apartment house they live in won't withstand the cold."

"Michael and Wendy? It's a lovely place and you know it."

"You think I want my only grandchild to freeze to death in West Hollywood?"

He had to laugh. "Anchorage, perhaps, or Antarctica, but the notion of that happening in West Hollywood—"

"I know, it's absurd." She opened the wooden blinds that covered the kitchen windows. "I wonder if it is warming?" She couldn't see much from there because the wall of the convent came to within four feet of their property, but she could tell that the ice was melting. "I hope the worst is over. I wonder how the sisters are doing?"

Next door, which was a very big next door indeed, almost twenty acres, sat the estate that was once the home of a Beverly Hills car dealer and real estate baron, which he'd willed to the archdiocese upon his death. Thus, the thirty-five-room mansion and guest houses and swimming pool and gardens and fountains and towering oak trees had become the home of the Sisters of the Immaculate Heart of Mary, who would become known as the "Rebel Nuns" in the activist days of the 1970s. Today it was called the Cardinal Timothy Manning House of Prayer for Priests. It was used for that purpose, but also as a retreat house by Catholics from the Archdiocese of Los Angeles. Bob and Aileene, fallen Irish Catholics, had never gone there for that reason, but they did love the place. In fact, Bob thought, one would be hard-pressed to find a more spiritual setting than this beautiful estate on the edge of Griffith Park.

In these days of not only fallen Catholics but also fallen clergy, Aileene felt it was a shame that the Spanish castle next to them was going unappreciated and virtually unused. The Hanwells and other neighbors like Sally and Tony Morina, and Robin Rosenberg and Rosie Fiorentino, the two women who lived on the other side of Bob and Aileene, had often taken walks through the grounds and enjoyed it immensely. Back when Waverly Drive was in the news, after Charles Manson and his followers had murdered the LaBianca family on the other side of the convent walls, the nuns living there had virtually held the neighborhood together with their kindness and prayers. It had been, and was again, a quiet, residential street lined with lovely homes that were occupied by good people. The Manson thing had been an aberration.

"I'll bet the sisters and the good fathers are praying for the whole city," Bob allowed today. "Have you talked to Harry or Dee?"

Aileene nodded and shrugged. "Terrible story. They ended up abandoning her car on the Santa Monica Freeway, and today it was towed away, probably for good, Dee said. She's beside herself. She doesn't have a vehicle."

"They have Harry's."

"His traveling office? And when is he ever home?"

Bob thought about it. "Why don't we tell them to come here too? Until this is over. It would be good to have the family together."

"I already asked. Dee said Harry was determined to go to some art opening tonight."

"Van Gogh at the Getty," Bob clarified.

"Oh, sure. Dee didn't say, but of course that's it. I want to see it too."

"Not in this weather you don't," Bob cautioned. "It's here six weeks, so no sweat." He went to the laundry room and grabbed his jacket from a hook on the wall.

"Where are you going?"

"Garage. That big heavy mackinaw I wore up at Mammoth last year. It's out there in a box, isn't it?"

She smiled. "Yes, where we put the camping gear, the backpacks and bedrolls. Didn't think we'd need that again for a while." She glanced out the window. "But aren't you overdoing it? Isn't it too warm for that?"

"You heard your son last night. It's supposed to get down to eighteen this evening."

"I guess I just don't want to believe it."

Bob looked in on Susan as he passed her door. Herschel put his head up next to her, staring at Bob with his big sad eyes. She had her face to the wall, but he was sure she wasn't sleeping. Her legs were drawn up to her chin, a pillow between them and her stomach. He didn't say anything, and closed the door, knowing she was in pain again.

Ten minutes later, Bob came back inside with their mountain clothes. None of the Hanwells had skied until Harry discovered the sport in his teens; he'd dragged them to all the good slopes over the years—from Big Bear to Vail to Aspen to Park City—and treated them all to a long weekend in Deer Valley in

February, where everyone took to the slopes but Dolores, who preferred to spend the afternoon in the bar at the Stein Eriksen, "keeping warm." Bob handed Aileene their matching North Face jackets and tossed Susan's heavy coat onto a chair. "I wonder if it'll even fit her."

While they were downstairs, he checked the furnace pilot lights. They were fine. The water heater too. Aileene pulled some food from the freezer down there to defrost in the kitchen fridge. Bob told her he was going up to shower, but when he did, he walked into the office at the rear of the second floor to look down over the backyard. The day was brighter than yesterday had been, and there was no sleet or rain coming down now. Everything was wet, but not icy the way it was last night. But one thing hadn't changed. There was still a layer of ice covering the swimming pool.

In a small, cold house on a winding street in rustic Topanga Canyon, Andy Rakos had just returned home from his job as a night watchman at a Washington Mutual branch in Van Nuys. He aimed to take a long hot shower and sleep all day, his usual routine. But today would be like no other.

He had to leave his Harley at the bottom of the hill, for although the temperature had warmed considerably after dropping into the teens during the night, the canyons were colder than other places, and a thick sheet of ice made climbing the asphalt driveway impossible. Because he walked to the house, his roommate didn't hear him arrive. When he stepped into the living area—the house was little more than a shack consisting of a living room, two tiny bedrooms, one bath and a galley kitchen—he found his roommate sitting in front of the one thing of value in the place, his laptop computer. That in itself would not have been startling, but it was the guy's reaction to Andy's sudden appearance that said something was wrong here.

"Hey, Andy, man, didn't hear you drive up."

"I didn't drive up."

"So, like, hey, how's it going?"

"What are you doing on my computer?"

"Doing? Oh, man, just playing a little solitaire."

"That isn't solitaire on the screen."

The young man turned red. "Yeah, shit, I hit something wrong when I heard the door open. I don't know what came up." He turned to close the lid.

"Don't touch it," Andy ordered, walking up to him.

Keith, sitting there in his undershorts, tried to look nonchalant, but the sweat that had appeared on his forehead gave him away. "Man, some weather, huh? How were the roads? How can you drive a bike on them? I'll bet you froze your nuts off last night out in that bank parking lot, huh? Want me to make you some coffee?"

"Shut up," Andy said sharply. "Move."

Keith nervously got up and stepped aside. Andy sat down. He looked at the screen, scrolled down it, then clicked on the other pages that Keith had open and had obviously been reading. Sure that he was not overreacting, Andy spun around in the dilapidated desk chair and glared at him. "So you know."

"Hey, dude, I was just playing around."

"Enjoy yourself?"

Keith seemed to sweat more. He paced under Andy's stare. He searched for words but wasn't sure where to start. "Listen, I have to say . . . I mean, is this . . . shit, I don't know if . . ."

"Cut the crap," Andy snapped. "Yes, it's true. Inevitable. A prophecy whose time has come."

"Man, come on, that's insane. Like, okay, King was

the greatest basketball player of his time. And he's done a lot to help people. But what he preaches lately is . . ." Keith searched for words. "You can't agree with him on everything."

"We've waited a very long time." Andy folded his arms and stretched his legs out. "Sit down. You're making me nervous." Keith fell into a ratty chair. "You're also making me cold."

Keith realized he was sitting there in nothing but his undershorts. Knowing Andy wouldn't be back to the house before eight, he'd sat down at the computer the minute he'd awakened, at seven. To continue reading the manifesto, which he'd been doing for days now. Rather than go back into his room for his jeans, he grabbed the ripped blanket that covered the hole in the chair and pulled it around his middle. "So," he said. "What? You've waited a very long time for what?"

"For people to see that Jeffrey is the only person who will lead us to a better place."

Keith shook his head. "Yes, I just read it. I know the agenda." Keith mustered his guts. He grinned. "Come on, Andy, you don't really believe this crap."

"Crap?"

It seemed to hit Keith. "You're one of them?"

"A King."

"It's a cult. *60 Minutes* exposed it last year. They're anarchists, terrorists. They use bombs and kill people."

"To bring about awareness, to make change."

"Andy, the government has been trying to bring an indictment against him for a long, long time."

Andy grinned. "They don't understand. We do."

"You and how many others?"

"There are more than you think." Andy's voice was confident.

"How? Why? I mean, why you?"

"When I was growing up in Athens, I needed a hero. Never found one. When we moved to America, Jeffrey King became that because I was nuts about L.A. and sports. But even then I felt he was something more than just a sports star, he was mesmerizing, special, a god."

"*Is* God, your computer says."

"Maybe so. Certainly a prophet."

Keith began to sweat again. "Tell me what I read isn't going to happen."

"The end of the world as we know it? What does snow in Los Angeles sound like to you?"

"But you're not going to . . ." Keith couldn't bring himself to say it. This was his roommate, an acquaintance for more than a year, someone he'd shared this place with for almost eight months, a guy he thought he knew. "Tell me you're not going to."

"To what? Kill people?" Andy said with an almost prideful tone. "We won't have to. The snow will do that."

"Then what?"

Andy grinned with a smugness that reeked of superiority. "Then the new order. The Kings will have their own world."

"Loretta Zane," Keith said, bringing up a well-known Los Angeles name. "She the same one on the city council?"

Andy suddenly realized how much Keith knew. "Yes. She became King's publicity agent back when he left the Lakers. Getting her into local government gave him political power that he might not have been able to gain on his own. But nothing means anything anymore. The only thing we care about now is survival."

"It's crazy. You're crazy."

Andy smirked. "So, you aren't going to join us, huh?"

Keith squirmed. "Join you? For what? For what happens after Armageddon? Man, you're deluded. You can't be serious."

"Wait and see."

"I think I'm gonna pray it doesn't snow."

Andy suddenly realized something. He tensed up. "You're going to tell someone."

Keith's demeanor changed suddenly as well. He sat erect, scared. "No. Hell no. Who'd believe me anyhow?"

"Indeed." Andy turned to look at the laptop. "So we're cool?"

"Sure, man."

Andy didn't believe him, but gave him the benefit of the doubt. In another day or two, if the prediction was correct, it wouldn't matter anyhow; the snow would change everything. People like Keith, who didn't have a pot to piss in, would join the blacks and the Hispanics and the Vietnamese refugees who were kept under the thumb of the white establishment would rise up against them, just the way Loretta said Charles Manson had predicted decades ago. Revolution, as the Beatles sang. "Helter Skelter." Then on the other side of the snowstorm, when most everyone lay dead, the Kings would rise to rule the world. Andy knew he sounded mad, and he decided not to try any harder to convince his roommate. He would simply see for himself. Soon.

Hours later, Andy woke up from a deep sleep with a sense of mission, a sneaky feeling that something was happening—at this moment—that he should know about. He sat up. He heard nothing at first. But then, when he stood up, he heard a muffled voice coming from behind the closed door. Assuming Keith was talking to someone else in the house, and alarmed because he had no friends and no one else was supposed to be there, Andy did two things. He slipped on a pair of board shorts. Then he pulled a revolver from under his mattress.

He opened the door and tiptoed slowly into the living room. He could hear Andy more clearly now. He was not speaking to someone in person, he was on the telephone. "Give me a detective, then, man, who will listen." Pause. "It's not as crazy as you think." Pause. "No, I'm not giving you any names until I talk to someone who sounds receptive." Pause. "Thank you. Sure, I'll hold."

But when the senior detective with the LAPD finally picked up, the line was dead.

That was because forty seconds before, Keith had set the phone back into the cradle when Andy Rakos had appeared with the gun. He had pleaded for his life in a gasp, just as Andy shot him through the head, and he now lay motionless on the cold linoleum floor.

Dolores could hear the sound of Harry's shower running as she sat at the vanity in her dressing room. She rubbed some expensive Neiman Marcus cream into her cheeks and then rinsed her hands in the water from the gold-plated fixtures and dried them with a soft, fluffy towel. The bedroom was her sanctuary, her retreat; the dressing room, her own little theater. She turned the sunlamp on and propped her chin on her hands.

The sound of running water stopped, and Harry opened the sliding glass doors and continued where he'd left off. "Are you coming with me or not?"

"Oh, stop already. I told you yesterday I wasn't going."

He stepped into her dressing room, bare naked, drying his hair. "Come on, Dee. It'll be depressing sitting home alone."

"It'll be more depressing standing there making idle chitchat with those stuffed shirts." She glanced at him in the mirror, lithe, muscular, his buttocks as firm as the day they'd met. She was drawn to the image for a second, but immediately turned away. "Put some clothes on."

He stopped messing with his hair, letting the towel drop to his shoulders. "Why?"

"Because you're so sexy."

He looked startled. "I am?"

She swiveled on her stool and looked up into his eyes. "And it's very frustrating to see you naked because we so seldom make love anymore." There. She'd said it. And was proud of herself for being so honest. Without the help of Mr. Dewar.

"Oh." He brought the towel down to his waist, wrapped it around himself, fastened it as he sucked in his washboard stomach for a moment. He stood there, on the spot. She hadn't asked a question, but he felt it deserved an answer. "It's the work, baby. I'm so damned exhausted when I get home, you know? And the mental pressure. Shrinks' offices are filled with guys like me, guys who can't perform because they're so driven."

She reached out and pressed the bump in the front of his towel. "I could relax you."

He touched her hair, then bent forward and kissed her lovingly. But as she lifted her other hand around his ass, just as she was about to unfasten the towel, he stepped away. "I'm going to be late for the cocktail hour."

"So what?"

He smiled and ducked back into his bathroom.

Dolores went to the kitchen and poured herself a

drink. She hit the RADIO button on the media panel above the desk, and NPR filled the rooms as she made her way back to her private lair. The news report said patches of sunlight had appeared in various spots over Los Angeles, and all the ice—even in the highest elevations in the city, the Santa Monica Mountains, the nearby San Gabriel Mountains—had melted. Freezing temperatures could again be expected for the night; however, there was no sign of any precipitation. The sleet storm that had wreaked havoc yesterday would not repeat itself. Government offices would be open as usual on Monday, mail would be delivered, life would go on; there was no emergency, no reason to be alarmed.

However, Colorado and Utah were experiencing the biggest snowstorms of the last fifty years.

Harry, who heard the report from the speakers Dolores had turned on throughout the entire house, couldn't care less about Colorado or Utah, other than looking forward to the slopes in Deer Valley. He hit the speaker button to shut it off in his room, then pulled one of his tuxedos out of the closet.

Dolores sat down at her dressing table again, aiming the sunlamp at her face. Taking a healthy swig of Scotch, she put the chair in the lounge position, closed her eyes, pressed plastic eye protectors over them and leaned back to soak up the sun. Screw the weather. She was going to pretend she was on the beach in Barbados. Where, she wished, her naked husband would come out of the water and make love to her.

Aileene found Susan twisted into a grotesque position on the mattress, clenching her pillow with tight fists. Even Herschel looked frightened at the foot of the bed, for she was moaning in pain. Seeing her daughter in such misery, Aileene understood why most doctors had told them that pancreatitis can be one of the most painful diseases known to medical science.

Aileene acted fast; she was nearly expert at it already. She prepared the hypo, drawing the liquid Demerol and atropine from the vials with the syringe, then held it up in front of her eyes, pushing the plunger until all the air was out of it—until the liquid squirted from the needle—and then she said, "Okay, Susan, honey, on your side."

Aileene pulled Susan's sweat pants down slightly to reveal the muscle at the top of her buttocks, the tender area where so many needles had penetrated. She didn't hesitate. She rubbed the area with alcohol and then jabbed the needle full length into the skin and pushed the medication into her body. She pulled it out as quickly as it had gone in and pressed her fingers on the little wad of cotton where the needle had been, rubbing gently to help disperse the medication into her bloodstream. "I'd make a good nurse," Aileene said.

"You're the best," Susan said softly.

"It'll be gone in a little while, try to help it along, breathe deeply, try to relax a little, darling." Aileene sat there for twenty minutes, rubbing Susan's shoulders, keeping her company, waiting to see the results of what she'd just done. Relaxation was important; even though the pain was severe, fighting the medicine was counterproductive.

Aileene finally saw the drug was working. Susan's eyes grew heavy, her speech grew languid and lethargic. But she became talkative. Demerol acted a little like truth serum. Susan reminisced about days when she was little and Michael and Harry were fighting about something and they both needed her to keep a secret. Aileene didn't understand it all, but she played along. Soon Susan was asleep. Herschel took Aileene's place on the bed with Susan when she got up. She saw the computer was still on. She shut it down, sure that Susan would not be using it for a while. Then she left the room.

Aileene wandered to the den, sat herself down in her favorite chair and looked out the window at the weather. Despite the fact that there was no one there to hear her, she said out loud, "She should be in the hospital."

To take her mind off her daughter's precarious situation, she turned to the books. She'd read most of them, but now she scoured the shelves for something she had always promised herself she'd read on a rainy day. There was Ingrid Bergman's biography, which she couldn't recall if she had ever read or not. Madeleine Albright's book, which she indeed had. *Cashelmara*, a novel she recalled loving some years ago. *House of Sand and Fog. The Da Vinci Code. Helter Skelter. The Essential Guide to Prescription Drugs* . . .

Helter Skelter? It made her wince. And made her think about chaos. And to a woman whose life was all about order, it truly gave pause.

At five p.m., Mayor Larry Zarian went on television again to speak to the people. "I'm proud to say that at this hour, some semblance of normalcy has returned to our great city. The ice storm is over. The roads have been cleared of stalled automobiles, the freeways are running smoothly, there are extra trains on all Metro lines, the airports right on schedule. Overanxious buyers have caused unnecessary reductions of certain food supplies, but all the major food chains have assured me personally that sufficient quantities are on the way.

"We need to get back to normal, and we all have

to pitch in to do that. We must conserve energy, for the cold spell might still be with us for a time. I ask that you heat your homes only enough to remain moderately comfortable. The Department of Water and Power suggests sixty-five degrees, so pull out that down comforter or wear a sweater to bed tonight. Shut off warm-air vents to rooms that are not being used. Though the forecast still calls for snow, we are optimistic that, judging from the warming today, this will not come to pass.

"This is a time for continued optimism. There is no need for panic or even great worry. Together here in Los Angeles, we have survived a lot worse. I promise you, good people of Los Angeles, I won't let you down. We will not let each other down. The City of Angels will prevail."

Cameron Malcolm turned off the TV set in the makeshift communications center that had been set up only hours earlier on one of the highest peaks in the Los Angeles Basin, at the Griffith Observatory. "Sounds like the guy's running for president," he said to soldiers who were installing a phone that would connect him directly to Washington.

"He might," one of the men said.

Cameron knew he shouldn't be criticizing; he was here to advise. The real responsibility in getting the city through this would not rest in the mayor's hands in any case. It was to be given to General Parker Van Hecke, who was due to arrive from Andrews Air Force Base any minute. It was going to be his show and he was going to run it. The governor and mayor had given him full authority, and Cameron hoped that the city, with disaster relief money in hand, thanks to the president, would, to use a familar phrase, weather the storm. A storm that seemed like a notion out of a science fiction novel.

Cameron for once in his life hoped to hell he was wrong. He wanted nothing more than to have the elements prove him incorrect, and then he could just go home. But he was convinced that the huge snowstorm that was burying the Rocky Mountains at this moment was going to swoop down on the city. Michael Hanwell and Cameron Malcolm were no longer the only two weathermen convinced it was going to happen. The National Weather Bureau now was on their side. Even the mayor, despite the denial in his televised pep talk, believed it might come about. Cameron was glad the Army was taking charge. He could certainly warn people about driving their Mazdas in a freezing rain, but heavy guns were needed if something white dumped on the city. The Army was necessary to keep this city alive.

Cameron heard two soldiers preparing for the task. One asked about oil reserve supplies. They turned out to be too low. How about snow removal equipment? They had nothing. Did the airports have heating elements built into the runways? Of course not. Did anyone even own a real snow shovel? Stores had never even stocked them. The soldier got on the phone and barked orders to the National Guard, putting them on alert so they would be ready when the general took over. Cameron pointed at the latest update coming across the computer screen: LIGHT SNOW FALLING IN MERCED, FRESNO, MOST OF THE SAN JOAQUIN VALLEY . . .

Not entirely familiar with the layout of California, the soldier turned to a big map already placed on the wall. "That's pretty far away."

Cameron shook his head. "Not far at all, in terms of weather." In fact, too close to feel confident that it might avoid them.

Another soldier ran in from outside. "The chopper

is here with General Van Hecke." He showed Cameron a small handheld device. "Sir," he said with alarm, "look. The temperature is dropping. *Fast.*"

It finally began to happen. Even though the sleet had stopped coming down, the moisture was still up there, in the heavy clouds. Water molecules floating in the air over the L.A. Basin had risen into a cold region of the atmosphere, cold enough to cause them to condense and freeze. The collected weight of the crystals could not be supported by the air under them. The result was they began to plunge toward earth. If, as they descended, they hit warm air, there was the possibility that the flakes would melt before they hit the ground. But the temperature of the air never rose above freezing, and the crystals made the journey of several miles completely whole.

The drizzle had started again as Harry gave up the Escalade to a valet and boarded the small tram that would take him up to the glittering Getty Museum, where he was surprised to find such a small number of people. This was the biggest art event of the year, and the cowards hadn't shown. He hated them, the selfish bastards, afraid to go out on a slippery street, afraid to get cold, get rain on their hairdos. What he did like was that the people, like himself, who did show up were the antithesis of those who were in the supermarkets at that hour.

There was no panic here. Here they wore diamonds and tuxedos, here they smelled of Tiffany cologne, here they talked of art and culture. They balanced glasses of champagne while nibbling on caviar canapes and cold shrimp. Everyone was smiling. No one spoke much about the weather, as if it were nothing more than an annoyance. They talked about the new acquisitions to their own collections, shared art world gossip, discussed the new biography of de Kooning that the reviewers had found so controversial. The curator of the Norton Simon, one of the world's most renowned Van Gogh experts, gave an introduction to the collection they were about to see, adding, with a touch of humor, "And if we're all snowed in by the time it's over, well, we have some nice things to look at until they come dig us out."

Muted laughter.

There was a sense, a feeling, an air about the people standing there in their gowns and jewels that their money and position guaranteed them immunity, sanctuary, protection from any crisis. Much less the elements. No one bothered to think that a Mercedes would require tire chains if snow were to fall on the streets; chains were for pedestrian vehicles like Chevrolets and Kias.

And who could blame them? Los Angeles was a comfortable place where they lived comfortable lives. Threats came and went, and tremors and mud slides were part of the price they paid to live in paradise. You paid more taxes in these ZIP codes, but those taxes bought you an insurance policy of the kind you couldn't purchase from Allstate: insulation insurance, from the rest of the world.

Harry took a piece of seared tuna steak from a tray and popped it into his mouth, then thanked the pretty blonde who was holding it. His eyes went wide. Her smile was infectious. A once-over told him she had a gorgeous body. And she didn't move away, focusing her attention on him for way too long. Then she told him, in a sexy soft voice, to have another. He said, "Well, hell, why not? I'm a growing boy."

"I'll bet you are," she added, clearly flirting, then moving away.

A big-breasted woman, at that moment, grasped him by the arm. "Darling, how wonderful to see you."

Harry gave her a blank look.

"Jinger," she said. "Jinger with a *J*. Remember?"

"Sure!" He had no clue.

"Remember my husband, Jay, also with a *J*?"

"Absolutely!" Christ, who was she? Who was *he*? A client? A fellow art patron? Did he know her because she was Jay's wife? Hell, maybe she was someone he had screwed. She wasn't bad-looking. He took the safe route, pretending they were long-lost friends. "You know, Jinger with a J, you look wonderful, as always." He winked with his most sexy look.

"Harry, you just have a way about you, don't you?"

"So, where *is* Jay?" He could be standing right next to them and Harry wouldn't have known.

"London."

"Pity. I love your dress." He said it staring at her breasts.

His flattery worked. She swooned. "Have you seen the paintings yet?"

His eyes were locked with those of the waitress, over Jinger's shoulder. "No, not yet. Listen, Jinger, I was just going to—"

She grasped his arm and pulled him toward the gallery. "Let's have a look together." He gave the server girl another smile as they drifted through the doorway. "Harry," Jinger asked, "where's Dee tonight? I was sure she'd be here with you."

Harry didn't say it, but he was glad she wasn't.

Bob told Aileene that the supermarket, where he'd gone hours ago, had been hell. People were like animals, with carts lined up for miles, shelves completely empty, everyone snarling at one another, the police trying to control them. She told him about Susan's growing discomfort, which made them both feel disheartened. There wasn't much for them to say as they ate supper. The temperature was now down to twenty-three degrees. That in itself was incredible, and depressing. Bob considered turning on the pool heater to keep the ice from getting thicker and cracking the sides, but the waste of gas would have been sinful. Aileene suggested they drain the pool. He said he would open the valve in the morning, when, he hoped, the escaping water wouldn't form an ice-skating rink in Robin and Rosie's backyard. The house that belonged to the two wonderful women who lived next door was down the hill from them, where the water would go.

As they drank coffee and finished leftover Christmas cookies, Aileene continued to worry about her new grandchild. "I think we should encourage them to come here."

"Aileene." Bob tried to be clear. "They are adults. They'll make their own decision. I want them here too, but Michael's a man now, with his own life."

"Harry I don't worry about. Michael I do."

"Michael has an inner strength that people don't recognize. The clownish exterior isn't what he's about and you know it."

"Family should be together at a time like this."

Bob was about to say something more when Herschel entered the room, followed by Susan. She'd been given her second shot of Demerol only an hour earlier, so they were both shocked that she was standing there. "What is it, darling?" Aileene asked.

Bob jumped to his feet. "Susan, hey, are you okay?"

Susan steadied herself by holding on to the granite counter. She looked drugged and in pain, but there was something on her face that both her parents read as determination. She moved toward the dining room.

"Honey, where are you going?" Bob asked, glancing at Aileene.

They followed her into the dining room. Bob moved to her side and helped her, let her lean on him. She led him to the big front window. "Turn the outside light on," she whispered. Herschel already was at the glass, his paws on the low windowsill, almost licking one of the panes. "See."

Bob gave Aileene a glance. It wouldn't be the first time the powerful narcotic had caused Susan to hallucinate. Aileene reached into the foyer and clicked on the switch for the front outdoor lights. And then they saw it. Something they had never seen before in all the years they had lived in this house, this city. Ice was one thing, but this was quite another. What Susan had seen from the window of her room was so startling that she had to get proof from her parents that it was true.

It was. It was snowing.

Dolores felt lonely. And bored. A hundred-plus channels and she could find nothing she wanted to watch on TV. She curled up with a book for about ten minutes. She ate leftover pizza from a week before, doctoring it with a healthy shake of oregano and cheese, and dunked each bite into olive oil. But she wanted to *do* something. She should have gone to the goddamned art thing after all. At least she could be dishing people there, which always proved to be fairly amusing.

She went through a pile of CDs, but there was nothing she particularly wanted to listen to. She had some old vinyl albums under her bed, she remembered, so she dragged them out. The sound track from *Ben Hur*. *Melanie's Greatest Hits*. Melanie? She'd forgotten about her. She knew Lulu, but had never met Melanie.

Back when you only needed a first name. What was she saving these for? There were several of her own records, but she hesitated to listen to them. Sitting there all alone in a seven-thousand-square-foot house listening to her glory days that were long past would only depress her more. Norma Desmond lives!

She went back downstairs and called next door. "Karen," she said when her neighbor picked up, "whatcha doing?"

Karen Hughes said, "Chris is in Chicago on business, so Jacob and I are having a quiet evening just sitting by the fire."

"Why don't you come over?"

Karen seemed surprised. "Now? What for?"

"Dessert," Dolores said. "I'm a hunting-season widow tonight."

Karen didn't understand. "You're a what?"

Dolores laughed. "Harry's off hunting."

"Hunting?" The woman gasped. "I would never have guessed."

"Not deer. Art."

"I see. Dolores, we're in our pajamas, in for the night."

"I'll come over," Dolores suggested as an alternative. Her voice quavered as she finished yet another glass of Scotch. "I just can't stand being alone, honey."

"Dee, you don't want to go out in this."

"Hey, a fur coat will get me through anything."

"No, I mean it's slippery."

"Slippery? All that ice melted today."

"Dolores, haven't you looked outside?"

"Not since Harry left."

"I think you should."

Dolores walked to the window and turned on the yard lights. With the phone still to her ear, she opened one of the bank of French doors that spilled onto the enormous rear patio and stepped outside. The first thing she saw was the steam rising from the pool. They had kept the heat on because Harry liked to burn money by swimming laps early each morning. But now it looked like some boiling cauldron. What was odd was that the patio was all white.

Dolores looked up. "Oh my," she gasped as she saw the flakes drifting toward earth in front of her. "I don't believe it." She walked out from under the overhang. *Glitterfrost*. She felt the flakes land on her. On her hair, on her shoulders and arms, on her face. She was back on a movie set—back in that terrible *Holiday Inn* rip-off she did years ago. Singing about glitterfrost while men poured bags of Ivory Flakes in front of fans, making it look a lot like Christmas. But this was real. She just gaped in wonder.

"Dolores, are you there?"

"Shit," Dolores Delanova-Hanwell finally said, "it just doesn't get any crazier than this."

Parijata was the first to run to the window when she heard Tim Jensen in the courtyard shouting, "It's snowing! Everybody, it's snowing!" She saw, in the spotlights that were aimed up at the building's name—THE KINGS CARRIAGE HOUSE—that it was really coming down. Wet and thick and white. Everyone who was there ran outside, Michael and Wendy, Matthew and Tim, old Mr. Rosenberg in his nightshirt, the Asian couple who had just moved in at Thanksgiving. Michael leaned over the railing from the second floor and shouted, "I'm vindicated!"

"Yeah," Matthew yelled up to him. "We're going to blame you."

"I love it," Parijata said excitedly, reaching down to touch the light layer that had fallen.

Michael lifted his hands to the sky, cupping them

in toward him, doing his best impression of Madonna doing Eva Perón. "*Don't cry for me, West Covina,*" he sang.

"Hey, Evita," Tim shouted. "But will it stick?"

Michael looked down and saw his breath. "It's cold enough. Yes."

"Cool," Tim said.

Wendy grasped Michael's hand. "It's so pretty," she said softly.

"From the looks of it," Michael said, "it's been coming down for at least an hour. The first flakes all melted, but it got so cold suddenly that I think we're going to have a good accumulation."

"Too bad it's the weekend," she said. "You'd have a field day on the air with this."

"Hey, everybody," Michael shouted down, "snowball fight in thirty minutes!"

"You got it, buddy," Matthew yelled, and everyone ducked inside to don their jackets and gloves.

"I'm going to build a snowman," Wendy vowed. "It's something I've wanted to do all my life."

At the Getty, Harry ducked into an emergency exit staircase after giving the waitress a look that said "follow me." A minute later she did. He was waiting, drink in hand, eyes poised for seduction. "Hi."

She smiled the same smile that had melted him. "Hi."

"I've been watching you all night."

"I know." She walked right up to him. "This your private office?"

"My private office is only a few miles away. And it has a comfy sofa in it."

She purred. "That sounds nice."

Harry took her hand. "This isn't very warm, but it'll do."

She looked quizzical. And sexy. With a heavy sensual undertone, she said, "Do for what?"

"For this." He pulled her to him and kissed her passionately on the lips.

"Ah," she said when she moved her head away. "But I don't even know your name."

"I'm Harry. But I know yours. Calla."

"Mind reading one of your talents?"

"Another server told me."

"Ali. I saw you chatting with him. I thought you were trying to pick *him* up."

Harry blinked. "I think you'll keep me satisfied tonight."

"You're flirtatious. With everyone."

Harry grinned. "I'm an agent. I have to be."

"So, is this true love?"

He shrugged. "Want the truth?"

"I appreciate honesty."

He laughed. "Like I said, I'm an agent, so that doesn't come easily. Except in situations like this."

"So," she said, running her fingers down the starched front of his tuxedo shirt to rest on the band of his pants, "tell me the truth." Her little finger dug into his shirt and touched the hair just below his navel.

"I just want to get laid."

She offered her lips again, and he kissed her as her hand moved farther inside his shirt. "Me too," she said.

"So we have a deal memo?"

She pressed her body to his. "Now kiss me like you really mean it . . ."

He started to, but suddenly they heard shouting. Something had happened, something was going on in the reception area. They looked at one another, knowing they had to part, they had to see what it was about.

"Don't leave here without me," Harry warned her, one hand on her right breast.

"Promise," she said, brushing her hand over the lump in his pants for good measure. They kissed quickly again and returned to the warmth of the exhibition hall to see what the commotion was about.

No one saw them enter, because everyone had their backs to them. All the guests were lined up at the windows. "What is it?" Harry asked people he knew. "What's going on?"

"Snow," a woman said.

"Oh, Harry, look!" Jinger with a J called to him. "Have you ever seen anything like this in L.A. before?"

The side of the mountain was white, glistening. He couldn't see the courtyard proper because everyone was pressed up against the glass, but he heard the reactions. The sound of the voices went from awe and fascination to fear and upset. Harry didn't understand. He tried to get closer to the glass. "Well, look at that," a man's voice rose above the rest of them as Harry pushed his way in front of him.

"Who the hell would do a thing like that?" a woman muttered loudly.

Harry moved to an opening in the crush of people to get a clear look out at the courtyard. Indeed, everything was covered with about an inch of white. That may have been what captivated people initially, but it wasn't what had prompted the man's outrage, what was causing the stir. What was shocking everyone was what was written in the freshly fallen snow. In huge letters, someone with heavy boots had walked out the words DEATH TO PIGS like a message a skywriting plane might leave floating under the clouds. The art patrons, in their gowns and tuxedos, looked out, completely befuddled.

"Holy shit," Harry whispered.

*   *   *

The beautiful white flakes were being viewed in quite a different way across town at the communications center in Griffith Park, however. "Why'd it have to happen so damned fast after I got here?" General Parker Van Hecke muttered. He and Cameron and a representative from the Red Cross and several aides from the mayor's office looked over maps. "Get plows ordered," he bellowed. "Anywhere we can get them." In the background, Mayor Zarian, on television again, was promising that the streets would be cleared shortly, warning people not to drive if they didn't absolutely have to, assuring them the snow would melt in the morning when the temperature again rose above freezing. He was spouting everything Bob Hanwell had told him to say. But no one was listening this time. People were greeting the phenomenon with absolute delight. Except at the communications center on top of Mount Hollywood. No one there liked this at all.

Already there was a crisis in the highlands. The resort towns of Big Bear Lake and Lake Arrowhead were buried. It had been snowing in the San Bernardino Mountains since late September, the earliest snowfall in that area on record, and although early on it was controlled, for the ski resorts were prepared for snow—it brought in most of their revenue—it soon became too difficult to handle. Residents abandoned their houses and attempted to get down the mountainside to San Bernardino, Riverside and Redlands, but the snow seemed to follow them. Indeed, for the past month, it had been snowing at elevations lower than anyone could ever remember. Roads had to be closed. Tire chains did no good; even SUVs twisted and turned and dropped off cliffs like toys falling off store shelves. Massive accidents and stalled vehicles—including several highway patrol cars and rescue trucks—blocked the routes to and from the resort towns. The windchill factor had brought the temperature down to well under zero. It had never occurred to anyone that such weather could come down the mountains.

Several people died of asphyxiation as they sat in their cars hoping to be rescued, running their engines so the heaters would keep them warm. Hordes of people gathered at ski lodges, churches, hotels and other large insulated buildings, where there were supplies of food and enough gas and firewood to keep warm. But how long those resources would last was anyone's guess, because how long the treacherous mountain blizzard would last was just as much a guessing game. And now that it was snowing down in what they called the Inland Empire, the bleakness was overwhelming.

Things were much worse in the Palmdale/Lancaster area, in the higher desert elevation just to the north and east of Los Angeles proper. Residents there were used to cold winters and some snow, but nothing like what was happening outside their doors these days. It seemed to come all at once, great chunks of white, layers almost, dropping to the ground to create another foot of snow where just days earlier, desert plants had been visible. And the wind. It wouldn't have been so bad had it not been for the wind. The force blew icy flakes into people's eyes, through their clothing, knocking them to the ground, against walls, and hands froze to the bone as they clutched trees and signposts in desperation. The ice had been around longer than it had been in the city of L.A. For three weeks, Palmdale's nights had been in the twenties. Cars with the improper amount of antifreeze in their cooling systems were dead for the winter, making travel to safer areas—if there were any—unrealistic, impossible.

Indeed, all routes into Los Angeles were cut off or had come to a standstill within an hour of the first flakes that fell in the city. Popular routes like the Grapevine and Pacific Coast Highway, being too treacherous, were closed. Trucks jackknifed and over-turned, blocking entire freeways. City streets were lined with cars going nowhere, an overload of desert-ers who simply could not move. People would have to stay put and deal with it.

But no one really knew how.

Most everyone had left the Getty Museum. Van Gogh had been upstaged by snow. All those rich col-ors, Harry thought, overshadowed by pure white. But the snow had taken a backseat to the unsettling mes-sage that some crackpot had drawn with boots in the blanket in the courtyard. Not that it really upset any-one; ten minutes later they were getting into their Jag-uars, BMWs and a Bentley or two. Ten minutes later they had forgotten it had even happened, more intent on being able to drive in something most had never had to drive in. Harry lingered, having yet another martini. It wasn't so much that he didn't want to go, it was that he would have to go home to Dolores. And that he hadn't gotten even a taste of Calla.

Where was she? She'd disappeared, it seemed, once he'd gone to the window to see the message in the snow. He found Ali, the handsome young waiter who'd told him her name, and inquired about her. Ali shrugged. "Lots of staff split already," he said, car-rying a tray of halved acorn squash that were now filled with used toothpicks.

"You know her phone number?" Harry boldly asked.

"Man," Ali said with a disappointed air, "and here I was hoping you'd ask for mine."

"You must be an actor."

Ali grinned. "And you're one of the hottest agents at CAA. Oh well, can't blame me for trying. But no, I don't have her number. I only see her on jobs now and then. Sorry."

Harry nodded and drifted away. Some force propelled him back into the exhibit hall, where he stood in front of his favorite painting of the collection, Van Gogh's *Congregation Leaving the Reformed Church in Nuenen.* He raised his glass to Vincent. Harry loved creative genius. Vincent was the epitome in his book.

"It was painted in 1884," a voice said from Harry's side.

He looked to his right. The curator was standing there. "You know it was stolen once."

Harry nodded. "This and one other, which was it?"

"View of the Sea at Scheveningen." He pointed to it across the room.

Harry nodded again. "1882."

"You know your stuff," the curator said with admiration. "He's the best, isn't he?"

"Without a doubt. Man, I wish I could represent him."

The curator let out a laugh. "They were both lifted from the Van Gogh Museum in Amsterdam in 2002. Found them just before Christmas in 2003."

"In Spain, I recall," Harry said. "Hey, the name is coming back to me—Octavia?"

"Octave was his name—Octave Durham. A thirty-one-year-old art nut with balls."

"Who'd name a son Octave?"

"His mother."

Harry looked up at the painting again, wondering what it would feel like to have it all for oneself. He couldn't imagine the thrill. "Moron."

"Pardon me?"

"The moron got caught. If I'd had them, no one would ever have known."

The curator saw the look on Harry's face. "Is it one of your favorites?"

"Little-known paintings always have the most appeal for me." Harry took his gaze off the ancient colors. "Well, quite a night. I think we're the last people here."

"The snow sent everyone running."

"And the words out on the terrace."

The curator was puzzled. "What to make of that? Crazy. I just wonder who did it? And why?"

Harry shrugged. "This is a town full of crazies."

"Hey, Harry, before you go—in my office is a copy of the manuscript. I'm finally done."

"Terrific, Ben. Can I read it?"

"Your name's on the envelope. I sure hope CAA can place it."

"You're one of the great voices in the art world. It's about time you wrote a book."

The man looked impressed. "You really think you can sell it?"

"Slam dunk."

"Instead of money, make the deal this way: just introduce me to Julia Roberts."

Harry smiled. "I'll do both."

The curator walked Harry to the doors of the exhibit hall. "I'm ducking out the back way, going home before this gets worse. Just close the door to the office when you get the manuscript. One of the guards will see you down the hill."

"Good night, Ben. And thanks." Harry made his way past the few catering staff who were folding tables and putting away bottles, ascended the stairs, which took him to a comfortable office lined with every book on art ever published. His cell phone started to ring, but stopped. He checked the bars on the screen: in and out of service. He checked the caller ID. It was Dolores. Christ, he thought, she's only going to say it's snowing, where are you? He decided not to even try calling her back.

As he put the phone away, he saw the envelope with his name on it. He unfastened the clip, opened it, and slid the manuscript out. *Great Museum Thefts and Forgeries*. Ben had told him only that he was finally writing an art book; he'd never told Harry the subject of it. Curious, intrigued, Harry sat down on the comfortable sofa and read a few paragraphs. Under the pages were photographs, numbered for insertion into the book. They fascinated him. Yes, there were the two Van Goghs, the two they were just talking about, one of which hung downstairs at this very moment. Harry turned to the chapter on Van Gogh and started reading about *Congregation Leaving the Reformed Church in Nuenen,* from its creation by a brilliant young man named Vincent to the cold night, when it was worth tens of millions of dollars, that it was stolen in Holland. He became engrossed.

And soon forgot that the mounting snow even existed.

Dolores tried Harry's cell phone three times, and finally left a message. "Honey, I'm starting to get worried. It doesn't look like this fucking snow is going to stop. Are you still at the museum? Or are you on your way home? I don't know what to do." She poured herself another drink and sat in the breakfast nook. It was coming down hard and fast now, covering everything in sight—lawn chairs, diving board, built-in bar and grill, statues—with a fluffy white blanket. She clicked on the television. Fritz Coleman was looking frazzled, predicting feet of the stuff, warning people not to drive, not to go out, to make sure their roofs were capable of supporting heavy wet snow. She turned him off. What the hell was she supposed to do, climb into the attic and see what kind of posts held up the roof beams? Call a roofer? "Can you hurry over and tell me if the snow will make my roof fall in?" She thought he was being silly. But it scared her.

She got up and walked into the dark living room, made her way behind the big Baldwin grand that had been a gift to her after a recording session, to peer out the window overlooking the sloping lawn and the street. She could see nothing but a winter wonderland. She had no idea where the lawn stopped and the driveway began, no idea where the curb was or where the street was. Everything was simply shrouded in white. The evergreen trees were magnificent, beautiful. The lights surrounding the modern place across the street, a house she hated, cast glimmering pools on the sparkling flakes, giving everything a fairy-tale appearance. Then a car made its way up the street, very slowly, sliding slightly from one side to the other, looking like the shots of Buffalo they played on the news each winter to make Californians feel superior.

It suddenly occurred to her that she was trapped. As she went to the phone in the foyer, she felt sweat beading on her forehead. "Harry, Harry, answer," she begged, as the cell rang and rang and then went to voice mail once again. "Harry," she said when she heard the beep, "please call me. I'm scared, honey." She pressed the red button to hang up, then pushed #4 and held it. It dialed Bob and Aileene.

Aileene answered. "Dee, hi. How are you two?"

"I'm alone." Dolores explained that she could not reach Harry and didn't know what to do.

"He might be just a block away at this very moment," Aileene said, hearing the alarm in her voice.

"Or maybe not." Dolores finished the drink. "What if he's deep in the bowels of the Getty and doesn't even know what's happening out there?"

"That's unlikely," Aileene assured her. "Everyone knows by now."

"What if his car's stuck in the parking lot? What if he got into an accident?"

"Dee, he'll be home soon, you just have to trust that. And you're fine there. It's a big, warm house with plenty of food."

"I can't stay in this mausoleum," Dolores said. "Not alone. I believed Michael all along, that this would happen. Everyone laughed at him, and now he's a seer. Even Fritz What's-his-name has joined the bandwagon."

Bob, who had been listening on an extension, suddenly said, "Dee, why don't you come here? We should be together. Leave Harry a message to come here too."

Aileene sounded enthusiastic. "Oh yes. We'll convince Michael and Wendy and the baby to come too. Family belongs together at a time like this."

Dolores looked out one of the glass panes in the front door. "Can I drive in this?"

"If you're going to do it," Bob warned, "do it now. The streets are slippery but passable. They won't be in a matter of hours."

"Yes. Yes, I can do it." Then something occurred to Dolores. "What am I saying? I don't have a car!"

"What?" Aileene asked.

Bob remembered. "Sure, the Great White Boat is no more. And Harry took the SUV."

"Can you come get me?"

Bob told her his fears. "I hate to leave Aileene and Susan alone, Dee. Susan is in the midst of one of her attacks. If we need to get her to the hospital, I'll have to do it. And by the time I get to you, who knows if we'll make it back."

"Can you call a taxi?" Aileene asked.

Dee laughed. "I should risk my life with someone who doesn't speak English who's probably never driven in snow before? Are you crazy?" But then she thought of something. "Jake."

"What?" Bob asked.

"Jacob Hughes, next door. The teenager. He's got a car and he's always doing chores for us for money. I'll pay him to drive me."

"You think his mom will let him?"

"She got kicked in the teeth in that divorce. She needs money too."

"Dee," Bob said, "let's not talk anymore. Pack some things and get on the road. I want to call Michael now."

"Okay," Dolores said, with enthusiasm. "I'll see you as soon as I can get there."

" 'Bye," Aileene said. "Godspeed."

"Dee," Bob added, "good luck."

"I'm sure as hell going to need it." Dolores hung up, went to the kitchen to dig out Jake's cell phone number from the junk drawer. He answered on the first ring, and when he heard her voice he immediately said, "Hey, Mrs. H. You want me to shovel your driveway?"

"I want you to do more than that, honey," she purred.

"Yeah? Cool. I never shoveled snow before."

"You want to make some money?"

"Of course."

"Lots of money?"

"Huh?"

"Turn down that awful music behind you and listen to me," she told him. "I have a proposition for you."

He obeyed. "Okay, let's talk deal."

She laid it out. He seemed reluctant for two reasons. One, he loved his car, the first automobile of his young life, and two, he doubted his mom would go for it. "You can talk her into anything," Dolores assured him.

"She won't let me drive in this."

"Then let me rent your car," Dee suggested.

"My *car*?" He sounded like she had just asked him to donate his liver.

"Yes, your goddamned car."

He got over the shock quickly. "How much?"

"Five hundred bucks." She thought she heard him gasp. Silence. "You there?"

"Yeah, hey, man, wow."

"That a yes?"

"When will you bring it back?"

"Hell, I dunno. After the snow, I guess."

"TV says it's dangerous driving out there. I don't want it in an accident, 'cause at my age insurance costs—"

She cut him off. "I'll pay for it if there's any damage. In fact, if I crack it up, I'll buy the damned thing. Get you a new one."

"Awesome."

She giggled. "Now he *wants* me to crash it."

"My ma's not going to like this. And her boyfriend, Chris, he'll—"

"Convince her."

Softly, he said, "Maybe a few bucks more and . . ."

"You little pisher! All right, here's the deal—five

hundred for you and five hundred for her, okay? You wouldn't make that kind of money shoveling snow if you did it for the rest of your natural life."

"Done. When do you want it?"

"I'll be over in a few minutes."

"Um, it's kind of a mess. I mean, it's full of stuff."

"For a thousand dollars, get your ass in the garage and clean it out." She disconnected and started dialing Harry again, but stopped as she came up with a better idea. She looked up the number for the Getty Museum. She hoped that the switchboard could find Harry if he was still there. They could put her through. But a night guard said everyone had left.

Slamming the phone back onto the charger, she thought about what she might need. Cosmetics, clothes and medication topped the list. Food, she should take some food. Who knew how long a siege they would be in for? Scotch—that was a no-brainer. When she got upstairs and opened a drawer looking for Valium, she saw some jewelry. Well, why not? She tossed it into the Vuitton bag she'd placed on the bed. She unlocked the wall safe behind a painting and stuffed a wad of papers into the bag. She withdrew a few pieces of really expensive jewelry that were not in the vault in the bank and put them in there as well. Perhaps it was an overreaction, a silly thing to do, but she did it nonetheless; she could always put it back. Homes were going to be empty, and burglars knew this, she was certain. She doubted the old fart on their security patrol was going to be driving by in a snowmobile to protect the upscale houses.

Aileene shook her head. "I want them here."

Bob took her hand. "Honey, come on. You're sounding like a broken record. They're our family, yes, but Michael has his own family now. And he wants to be with them." Michael had just declined their offer to join them in Los Feliz. "We have to respect it."

"But that apartment. I don't think it's safe."

"Honey, it's a palace compared to where we lived when we were first married." Bob really did agree with her about having them there, but he knew there was nothing they could do about their younger son's decision. "They want to stick it out there with the people they live with."

"It's her."

He blinked. "What? Who?"

"Wendy. She's never felt comfortable with us. She's the one who won't come here."

Bob shrugged. "Even if that's true, we still have to respect Michael's decision."

"I got along well with your mother."

"You did, yes. But Wendy isn't you." He tried to make her understand something he'd told her many times before. "She comes from a broken home, a father who abandoned her when she was what—three? A mother who was seldom there for her. The big happy family on the hill isn't her reality."

"But that's what she said she wanted!" Aileene reminded him. "Michael told us when he met her that we were the family she never had."

"Yes, she's attracted to it but also repelled by it because it scares her—she doesn't yet know how to handle it, or maybe she feels she doesn't deserve it."

"My grandchild is going to be raised with love and nurturing and warmth."

Bob smiled. "Yes. And Michael and Wendy will create that for her. It's not our responsibility to see that that happens."

Aileene closed her eyes and looked sad. "I just want my family together here."

Bob put his arms around her and kissed her. And

changed the subject. "I'm going to close the vents to the rooms that don't need to be used. Both furnaces are working at capacity. Overtaxing them is courting disaster." The house, though solid and well built, and equipped with two gravity heat furnaces, one for the lower two floors and one for the upper level, nevertheless did not have the proper insulation for sub-zero weather. It was eighteen degrees already, and if the trend continued, it might well dip below zero before it started to rise again.

Bob built a roaring fire in the living room fireplace and closed the heating duct slightly; that would keep Susan's room toasty warm. They planned to put Dolores and Harry in the guest room, so Bob shut the vent in his office and pulled the door tight; Harry and Dee could also snuggle under a down comforter. If Michael did come, he and Wendy and Rachel could have the master bedroom. Aileene would sleep with Susan, and Bob could sack out on the sofa in the living room or in a chair in the den.

Aileene was upstairs putting out fresh towels for Harry and Dee when the lights suddenly flickered. "Bob?" she called.

"Yeah, honey, don't worry," he shouted up the stairs. "Electricity only goes out in rainstorms, not this." He walked to the door that led to the pool area and looked out over the backyard. It was an astonishingly beautiful and serene sight. Everything from the palm trees to the yard lanterns to the top of the fence hiding the pool heater and pump was covered with a shimmering layer of frosty white. He went to the lighting panel near the back door and flipped a switch. The pool lights turned on, revealing thick ice floating on top of the water. Then he pulled a small lever and illuminated the tennis court. What he saw worried him. The electrical lines leading to the light poles—installed years before wires like that were sunk in the ground—were sagging under the weight of the thick, wet snow. What if all the wires that connected all of the great grid that was Los Angeles were doing the same? What if that snow got too heavy?

Bob dug out all the candles and flashlights they owned. Just in case.

Andy Rakos stood with three other believers on a cul-de-sac named El Cielo Drive in Coldwater Canyon, looking up to where the original house at 10050 had stood before it was razed and rebuilt. "It's where it happened, where it started," he said to the others. "Sharon Tate called it her 'love house.' I can't believe you've never seen it before."

"Yeah," a girl said. "But who were these people? Why are you so obsessed with them, Andy?"

"Loretta says Jeffrey is going to make Manson's prediction come true." Andy looked proud that he could teach them something. His zeal was as strong as Loretta's. "In June of 1969, Manson took Watkins aside, down near the old trailer at the Spahn Ranch, and confided, 'The only thing blackie knows is what whitey has told him. *I'm* going to show them how to do it.' Watkins defected, Loretta said. She was his girlfriend then. But we won't defect. We're gonna show the world Charlie wasn't crazy. That Jeffrey the King isn't either."

The girl wondered, "If it, like, really snows, is the rest of the planet going to hear us?"

"What is going to happen here in Los Angeles," Andy said convincingly, "will outshine any movement, any revolution, any coup that the world has ever seen. The snow will be only a catalyst for the slaughter to come. It'll make the news. It'll be headlines the world over. And we—the Kings—will be the survivors."

"Hey," one boy said cautiously, seeing headlights turning onto the street. "Pigs."

But it wasn't a police car; it was a security patrol car. The white Taurus pulled up next to them. The driver was alone in it and rolled down his window. "You folks lost?"

"Yes, as a matter of fact," Andy said, secretly thanking the man for the alibi. "We are looking for a friend's house, but the snow . . ."

"I'd recommend that once you get there, stay there. Nobody should be driving in this."

Andy said, "I'll call our friends on my cell phone and check the address." He pulled out his telephone to continue the charade.

"Was this the place Charles Manson killed Sharon Tate and all those people?" one of the guys smugly asked the security guard.

"It was. But aren't you too young to know about that?"

"I'm a movie nut," the boy said.

"Oh, yeah, they remade that movie about them." He shook off the unpleasant memory. "I'm a sports nut," the man offered. "Never go to the movies now that I got ESPN."

"You like Jeffrey King?"

The man looked ambivalent. "He was the greatest in his day. Sad to see what's become of him."

"Hey, dude," Andy said, "he may not be pushing tennies and tank tops anymore, but he sure is helping people see the light."

"Blinded by him, that's what those people are." The security guard shook his head. "He brainwashes people. That's not good. You all stay warm now, hear?" He rolled up his window and continued his slow drive.

"We'll see who's brainwashed," Andy said to the other three. "We'll see soon."

*   *   *

Something had caught hold of Harry Hanwell by the time he finished reading the manuscript. He leaned back in the chair, a faraway look in his eyes, removed from reality. Had anyone walked in, they might have asked if he was ill, for something surely was wrong. His skin, always tanned and healthy, looked pale and clammy. He felt a longing in his bones, a desire greater than any he'd ever known for something beyond his reach. He bit his lip and pressed his hands to his crotch, almost as if to curtail the feeling if it were to become sensual. It was a sense of overwhelming desire, but it was not sensual; it was not for a woman. It was for art.

Suddenly the faraway sound of a closing door echoing in the empty space of the museum brought him back to the real world. What time was it? His Rolex told him he'd been sitting there almost two hours. He pulled his phone out again. The caller ID had registered, even though a ring had not come through. Dolores had tried again. He picked up the phone on the desk and pressed one of the buttons on the base. He got a dial tone, dialed 9, and then his number. She did not answer, so he did it again, calling her cell phone. She picked up on the third ring. "Where are you?" she screamed at him.

"Hello to you too. I'm still at the museum."

"They told me everyone left."

"I'm the last one."

"You're trapped there?"

He shrugged, getting up to look out the window. "I don't know. I don't think so. Is it that bad?"

"Baby," she said with irony, "it's cold outside."

"Why didn't you answer the house phone?"

"I'm next door. I've just commandeered Jake Hughes' junker."

It startled Harry. "You what? What for?"

"To drive to your father's house."

He saw the snow was falling harder than before. He thought he could make out drifts on the expanse of land looking out toward the hills behind the building. "You can't drive in this. Not that shitty car!"

"Had you been here and not living it up at some stinking party with all your goddamn artsy-fartsy pals I wouldn't have to. We could have gone together. In *your* vehicle."

"Dee, listen to me. Go home and wait for me. You can't drive in this. And you're drunk."

"I am not. I'm just scared."

"Of what?"

Her voice sounded pathetic. "Of being alone."

"I didn't desert you tonight on purpose. You wouldn't come. I didn't know it was going to snow."

"Everybody knew it was going to snow."

He knew he couldn't reason with her. But he couldn't understand why she wanted to go to his family's place on the other side of town. It had to be the booze. The lonely fear. "Dee, all right, it's probably not that bad out yet. But don't drive the kid next door's deathtrap. Take a taxi or something."

She laughed out loud. "Taxi? Try finding one. Turn on a television. Cars are sliding all over the streets. People can't get up hills."

"Please, baby, I'm on my way. I'm leaving now. I'll be there soon. Wait for me."

"I promised Bob and Aileene I'm coming. They need me."

"They need you? What for?"

"Susan is sick."

"Jesus. Dolores, all right, if you have to do it, do it. But we have tire chains. Use them."

"What the hell do I know about tire chains?"

He snickered. The thought of her in heels and a turban and mink down on her knees attempting to put chains on the wheels was priceless. She would do it too, if she had no one to help her. He was sure of that. "Ask Jake to put them on."

"*Pay* Jake to do it, you mean. Where are they?"

"Hell if I know. In the garage somewhere. Been two years since we used them at Mammoth. Stay on big streets. Take Sunset all the way to Vermont."

"I'm taking some things for you."

"Things? What things?"

"Clothes. What are you going to do, wear your father's underwear? Food too. We can't expect them to provide everything."

He shook his head. "Dee, promise me, not another drink until you get to Los Feliz."

"Screw you."

"Promise me, baby."

She took a deep breath. "Promise."

He heard someone talking to her. "Who's that?"

"Jacob." She told the boy to go look in her garage for tire chains. "Harry, are you leaving now?"

He looked out the curator's window again. Incredible. Everything was white, still coming down. "I may stay the night right here."

"At the museum?"

"Or maybe at the office." CAA was right down on Wilshire, easier to get to than the house. It might make sense to go there where it was warm and safe and wait until morning when the snow melted. "I'll come to Dad's in the morning."

"I have to get going."

"Dolores, lock the house, and set the alarm."

She said, "Wish me luck."

"Good luck."

She waited for more, something more, anything

more. Did he miss her a bit? Was he fearful for her journey? Worried about her? Did he love her? Couldn't he say it now, for old times' sake if for nothing else? "Thanks," she said coldly and hung up.

Harry placed the receiver in the cradle and almost immediately thoughts of his wife and snow went out of his head and the glassy stare returned. He felt strange, almost giddy, in a sinister kind of way. He glanced over at the curator's manuscript and ran his fingers over the pages he'd just leafed through. It was almost midnight. He suddenly had a big grin on his face, and then he shook his head. No, it was too crazy. It was utterly preposterous. And yet the manuscript said it was the simplest thing in the world. Given the right circumstances, all it took was guts. Did he have real guts?

He pressed his nose to the window and watched the view of the white hills disappear in the fog of his warm breath. Given the right circumstances. Were these the right circumstances? Was it possible that snow, of all things, was going to change his life? Could he count on it to last, at least long enough? It would mean leaving everything behind, changing his life as he knew it, making a break, becoming a new person. Because they'd know he did it. The last guy left in the place. His passion for art. His love for Van Gogh.

A new person. Himself, finally. Not what others wanted him to do, not what he could grasp because of his famous and well-connected wife. His. His villa on an island somewhere. And he could do it. He already had the money, the network that might help him. What would he end up with if he worked in the same mold all his life? More of what he had now, which was empty and ultimately meaningless. He'd never be famous; he only represented famous people.

This one act would put him on the map forever. He could work his ass off for the rest of time and never be able to afford what was hanging down these very stairs leading from the office. He would never own such perfection, such beauty, such fortune, such satisfaction. Tonight it could be his for the taking.

He paced the office, charged like a panther with an excitement and zeal that went beyond sexual. Calla had been a rush, and the thought of getting a blow job from her had been enticing, but nothing got him as hard as this did. This *power*. That's what it had always been about with women—power. He'd have to give up the power he'd attained in Hollywood, but the scandal would give him a potency he would never be able to duplicate. He would have to forgo everything. The house, the cars, his marriage. What marriage? Dolores had ceased being his wife long ago, and there were young, hot Callas all over the world. He'd fallen madly in love with Dolores at first, then stayed with her because her life was vital and exciting and glamorous, but then it was because he felt sorry for her. No more. She would survive. She had her fuel. He'd made her feel young again for a very long time, which he knew was more than most gals her age could say. He'd done his good deed. He wasn't obligated to care for the elderly forever.

He pulled his head away from the window. He had to piss. He tried a door behind the desk, and sure enough, it opened to the curator's private bathroom. The wall behind the toilet was covered in mirrors, and as he peed he looked at himself and said, out loud, "What the hell is the matter with you? You nuts?" He finished, flushed and zipped up. But he stood still. His eyes seemed to fall back into that other world again, pulled back into the dream that was sizzling with ambition and the promise of riches he could barely fathom. *Try,* he told himself. *Try, just for the hell of it.*

It became, thus, a challenge. Just to see if he could pull it off, even halfway. Right now: empty building, priceless paintings, a manuscript that said it was easy, and the desire to do something bold and dangerous for the first time in his life. It was powerful motivation.

Harry descended the stairs from the office. Slowly. Looking around. There was no one there. Perhaps he was right, perhaps the place was already deserted. He walked across the still brightly lit floor where just two hours ago martini glasses had clinked and the hems of thousand-dollar dresses had dusted the marble. To the window that looked over the courtyard. The strange letters that someone had walked off out there had disappeared now, under the newly fallen snow. Suddenly the lights in the ceiling shut down, which caught Harry by surprise. Then others clicked off, and an eerie glow filled the space from little work lights spaced every ten feet or so along the walls. Outside, the gleaming spotlights suddenly turned to black as well. But Harry could still see the wind blowing the snow against the window.

Then he heard a distant voice. "So, you okay here?"

And another one. "Have to set the alarms in Exhibit Three by hand."

"Still malfunctioning, huh?"

"Shit, don't have nothing to worry about tonight, Frank. Who the hell is gonna be out in this?"

"You got a point."

"Naw, go home. It's really nasty out there. I may sack out here 'cause the night shift ain't coming in."

"Figured. What you eating?"

"Stuff left over from the party. Damn good. Got me a bottle of wine too."

"Nice label. Wish I could stay and share with you, Frankie, but I gotta go all the way to Torrance."

" 'Night, Dave."

Harry heard a door close. Then he walked slowly through the darkened reception hall and peeked around the corner toward the front desk and the panel of monitors and security apparatus. The fat guard was drinking wine and stuffing his face from a platter left behind. He wasn't even looking at the screens. Harry counted on him to be asleep within half an hour. Before he bothered to set the alarms in the room holding the Van Goghs by hand. Or would he remember and do that first? Harry knew he could not risk it. So he sat down on the floor, just around the corner from the man, waiting. Anticipating. His mind strayed from the quest to Calla. Man, he wished they'd had another ten minutes. She had the lips to give great head. Or maybe he could have bent her over the stairs and thrown a fast one into her right there. Like he and Dolores had done when they first met. Sexy, wild, older, experienced Dolores. But the booze, the weight, the neediness, it all turned him off now. He looked at the black wall of glass being pelted with wet snow and wondered if she was on the road. She had to be insane to want to drive in this.

As if what he was planning wasn't.

Dolores, being used to big cars, felt like she was driving in a pod of some kind, or a baked potato. That's what the color of the bashed-up VW Golf looked like to her, the hue of a potato skin when it's been left in the oven too long, a shell of brown, gray and black, slightly crinkled and crushed. But the damn thing worked, knock on wood—even though there was none to knock on. What she wouldn't give for that Lexus SUV with the shining wood trim that Karen

Hughes herself drove. How a woman with such taste could let her son buy this piece of crap, Dolores couldn't imagine. Maybe she was teaching him something about saving money. You want a car at your age, she had told the boy, pay for it yourself. That edict began the endless pleas for odd jobs around the Hanwell mansion. Hell, what a payoff. Dolores probably gave Jake more money to drive this tin can tonight than he originally paid at the seedy used-car lot out in Van Nuys.

She turned onto Sunset and slid sideways into a lane she wasn't aiming for, even with the chains fastened. She had never in her life driven in snow this thick, this heavy, this deep. But as she made her way carefully down the wide boulevard of dreams, she saw that traffic had made it wet, not as slippery as the side streets she'd taken from her house. She felt confidence returning as the chains dug into the mushy snow. She sat far forward on the seat, her bosom actually touching the steering wheel. She felt safer that way. She couldn't imagine how Jacob drove from the position the seat was in when she got inside. It was as if he drove from the backseat.

She craned her neck forward to see out the windshield. The air was so cold that the snow seemed to freeze on the glass in little bumps, little patches, everywhere but the two spots where the blowers hit the glass. She had the heat up all the way and was nearly dying, sweating. The back glass on the hatch was all steamed up. She rolled her window down a bit. It helped.

It was slow going, about twenty miles per hour at the most, stop and go, stop and go. Snow covered palm trees, parked cars, the buildings of UCLA. On the Sunset Strip she saw people coming out of bars and restaurants, madly trying to get their automobiles out of snowed-in parking lots, most of them not bothering. It looked like young men were robbing the Hustler Store. A young black guy, who on a sunny day might have had the forbidding look of a rap artist, now looked cold and helpless. Dolores wanted to pick him up, but there was no room. The car was filled with things she had deemed too important to leave behind.

It was two in the morning when she reached the corner of Sunset and Crescent Heights. Young kids were hanging out outside the Virgin Record store. And the Starbucks there was still open—she figured the staff probably couldn't get home anyway so they stayed to sell out every bean in the store. She pulled over toward what she thought was the curb and called to a boy who looked as drunk as she was. "Hey, get me a coffee?" She whipped a twenty from her purse. "You can have the change."

"Hell, yes," he said and walked into the store.

She pulled out the cell. It was still showing a signal. She dialed Bob. "I know it's late, but I wanted to tell you I'm on Sunset."

"Go up to Hollywood Boulevard," Bob suggested. "I talked to Cameron a little while ago and he said it was one of the first streets plowed."

"I'm plowed," she said.

"Dee, you sure you should be driving?"

"I see my coffee coming now," she told him. "I'll see you soon, I hope."

The boy handed it to her. "Yukon Blend, they said."

"Jesus," she muttered. "For twenty bucks you couldn't have gotten a vente? Cheapskate."

"Hey, lady, you didn't say."

"You got a cigarette?" she suddenly asked. She hadn't had a cigarette in months. It was time.

"I guess." He reluctantly handed her one. "This is pretty cool, huh?"

She rolled her eyes. "Yeah. Cool." She rolled the window back up, took a sip of the hot liquid and pushed the lighter in. She was amazed that it was even there. And more amazed that it worked. She lit the Winston with delight and took a deep drag. *Shit, that'll sober me up.* She put the car in gear and continued the treacherous drive.

By the time she reached the street Bob had told her to drive on, she'd smoked four stale cigarettes she'd found in the glove compartment. And had guzzled some of the Cragganmore that sat in a place of honor on the front passenger seat. She'd opened the window all the way to get rid of the smoke and to stay awake.

Suddenly, incongruously, on plowed Hollywood Boulevard, the car stopped moving. She could barely see through the windshield because the wipers were sagging under the weight of the snow. She stepped on the gas, but nothing happened; the car seemed only to rock back and forth. She felt it was sliding slightly sideways. She pressed the accelerator again, but the rocking motion continued. Finally she gunned it, and this time it really did spin out sideways, slamming against the side of a Mercedes. She screamed at the crushing sound of the impact and then tried to pull away a bit, but after the noise of the engine died down as she finally took her foot off the gas, she heard a voice yell, "Give up on it, lady, for Christ's sake. We're stuck."

Indeed they were. She got out of the car, stepping into a snowbank. She'd put on a chic pair of designer boots that were made for cold weather but never for snow; in any case, the stuff went up to her knees. She cursed and made her way around the front of the car and assessed the situation. The other driver, who had

had to crawl out his passenger door because Jake's little Golf was now mated to the left side of his C320, stood nearby. "You all right?" he asked.

"I've had better nightmares." She looked at the mounds of snow. "Where did all this come from?"

"Plows," the man said. He turned to look at the side of his automobile that would never be quite right again.

"I'm so sorry," Dolores gushed. "I've never driven in this before."

"I have," he said with a shrug. "I'm a ski instructor, but obviously that doesn't help. I've been stuck for ten minutes."

"I have chains," Dolores said as if to give a reason this shouldn't be happening to her.

"I got all-weather tires. Lotsa luck."

She looked at the rear wheels. One of the chains was missing; she guessed Jake hadn't fastened it correctly. The other tire seemed to have tried to dig a hole in the street. "What can I do?" she cried.

"Get in, put it in low gear, hit the gas real slow. I'll try to rock you out."

"Oh, how kind of you," she said as she got back into the car. She did as she was told, but the wheels spun, and the tire with the chain intact dug even deeper with a horrible sound and the smell of melting rubber coming from deep below.

The man put his head in the window. "You gotta go it on foot. We both do."

"No!" she cried. She couldn't abandon the car. She couldn't walk in this. She couldn't carry all the stuff she'd brought.

"There are patrols moving up and down the major streets—weren't you listening to the radio? Trucks are picking up stranded people."

"And taking them where?" She was beside herself.

"Dunno. Shelters, probably. Schools, hotels, wherever."

"Will you go with me?" He had a kind face and seemed to be just this side of brawny, though it was hard to tell because some of the bulk could have been his parka. "I can't make it on my own."

He nodded. "I'm gonna get some things and lock up my car."

"Yes, sure, of course," she said, knowing she had to do the same. But what things? She turned in the seat and tried to figure out what she could carry. Jewelry, yes, absolutely. She stuffed a handful of necklaces into the coat pockets, then dumped the rings into her purse. The papers could stay—they were bound to get wet anyhow. She picked up the Ziploc bag that held the wad of rainy day cash she had grabbed from the back of the freezer and pushed it down her bra, shivering because it felt so cold. Then she turned off the engine and killed the lights.

And looked at the booze. How would she carry it? She'd have to leave it. But what if Bob didn't have any? She grabbed one bottle and tried to put it into the pocket of her coat, which luckily had been constructed with fairly large patch pockets—thank you, Blackglama—so she could manage to wedge it in with the necklaces. She took two others with her as she stepped out of the car again, went around to the hatch, opened it, unzipped the roll-on overnight case she'd brought the clothes in, pulled out some panties and a sweater to make room and stuffed the bottles inside. She lifted the bag out, stood it in the snow, closed and locked the hatch, then went back for her purse, rolled up the driver's window and locked the door.

"Leave the flashers on," the other driver warned her. She saw his were blinking through the white. "Yes, of course." She opened the car again and felt around like a blind woman, having no idea where the emergency flashers were located. Finally she found them, pressed the triangular button and locked the car again. She was scared. Not for the vehicle—she couldn't care less about the piece of crap. She was leaving behind a fortune in St. John outfits, Blahnik shoes, DKNY jeans, a Kate Spade bag and four beautiful bottles of Cragganmore Scotch. It killed her.

But she told herself not to panic—there was absolutely nothing she could do. Harry would have to make arrangements for someone to get the car in the morning. If they towed it, well, hell, it would just be a replay of the Great White Boat. Or Jake could come and retrieve it. Or, hell, maybe someone should break in and take it. The thought of some boulevard bum prancing around in a new St. John ensemble was kind of delicious. And the food might really help someone who needed it.

She turned and headed toward the sidewalk, where the guy was waiting. Dragging the wheeled bag was almost impossible—it felt more like she was pulling a show shovel—and when he advised her to leave it behind, her refusal was so sharp that he agreed to pull it for her, thinking it must contain every treasure she'd saved her whole life long. She pulled the mink tight in front of her, and when she saw a glimpse of one of the stars along the Hollywood Walk of Fame, she wondered if it was her own. She looked at the building they were in front of. No, hers was back two blocks, probably covered with snow. As they walked, they made enormous footprints in the snow, just as so many stars had done in wet cement across the street.

"I feel like I'm hallucinating," she told the man. "I mean, I know you're real, but we're in the same nightmare."

"My name is Jeff Troyer, by the way."

"I'm Dolores Hanwell."

He stopped walking and put his palm up in the air. "It's changing."

"What is?"

"The snow. It's getting drier. Feel."

She did. He was right. It was softer, not as heavy. "Is that good or bad?"

"If it keeps coming down, and the wind continues, I think it's bad."

"Why?" she asked.

"Because then it will be a real blizzard." He wrapped his scarf around his mouth. "Come on," he urged, "take my arm. The wind is the worst of it."

At the Los Angeles International Airport air traffic controllers got the final and expected word: closed. Some were amazed that they'd taken this long to finally shut things down. Controllers were used to closing runways at the slightest notice when thick fog lolled along the coastline, making arrivals and takeoffs impossible. While the facility had held on bravely despite the snow—the city had attached plows to garbage trucks—the mounting white was no match for unheated runways.

One older controller was shocked into awareness of the situation outside when he stood up from his computer screen and experienced a feeling of déjà vu. He'd worked in the tower first at the Minneapolis-St. Paul airport and then at Chicago's massive O'Hare. What he was looking at now was equal to the worst storms he'd seen in those other cities. But this was L.A. Unthinkable.

The bustling airport had quickly become, in the waning hours of the day, a ghost town of the Old West. A pack of seagulls, desperate for warmth, huddled inside the mouth of a huge hangar that serviced 747s. Cars, attempting to get into or out of the sprawling facility, had been abandoned like toys in the drifts. A Wally Park shuttle van lay abandoned, on its side. Several airport employees, mainly the last of the airline maintenance people, desk clerks and cleaning people, braved wind and ice-encrusted faces to walk out, not knowing how in the world they would eventually get to their homes and families.

On the lower level of Terminal 3, an elderly African American man who had worked most of his life as a TWA porter sat on the edge of one of the baggage belts, eating an apple along with a bag of Fritos. Not knowing what to do with his life when American Airlines, who bought that once-great carrier, had retired him, he continued to come to the airport each day, as a kind of good will ambassador and fixture of another time. Tonight he was speaking to a younger black man, a porter for Alaska Airlines, who reminded him of himself years before. "You talkin' nonsense, boy," Willy told the kid.

"Bull. There's this book, see. Science fiction, was out a long time ago, before I's born. And in this book is this blizzard just like we got goin' now."

"So what?" Willy asked, crunching on the corn chips.

"In that book, man, the black people rise up."

"What you sayin', boy? Rise up?"

"Against the white man."

"What for?"

" 'Cause the white man he got the big houses, he got the furnaces, he got the fireplaces. The black man he got nothing. The King, he say we gonna be saved if we believe. Jeffrey King, he the man."

"He a white man," the guy reminded him.

"He got a black soul, dig? So like the dudes from

Watts and here in Inglewood, they're freezing, their roofs fall in, they got nowhere to go to keep warm, so they go to the white man's house."

Willy smiled. "Beverly Hills."

"Yeah, man, and Newport Beach and all those jazzy rich places. And the race war starts."

Willy shook his head. "You sayin' that gonna happen here?"

"That's what I's sayin'. They gonna murder each other. And Jeffrey King's people, they gonna be left."

"Alma and I, we got a comfortable house. We got a good furnace, we got two fireplaces. We're in the Baldwin Hills. This race war gonna get us too 'cause we live like the white man?" Willy finished the bag of Fritos and crunched it in his fist. "Snow. You think snow is gonna make the black man rise finally?"

"That book I said, it's comin' true. And that means death to pigs. That be what Jeffrey says. He da King."

The old man had heard the same words long ago, but coming from this youth, a boy only in his early twenties, a boy raised on hip-hop who wore pants three sizes too big and kept his hair in tight cornrows, it simply confused and befuddled him. "What somebody made up in a fiction book ain't gonna happen. It's nonsense, boy."

The youth pulled on his jacket.

"You leaving?"

He nodded. "Gotta be there, Gramps, gotta do my part."

"What in hell are you talking about?"

"I said helter-skelter. It was in the song. The Beatles song. *The White Album*, dude. I aks you, you remember that? People say Jeffrey be the new Charlie. It gonna come down." He grinned from ear to ear. "From the sky."

And with that he fled out the automatic doors, into

the darkness, into the snow, as the old man put the last bite of apple into his mouth.

On the roof of the building at that very moment, a lone figure made its way out to a small platform where numerous odd-shaped instruments sat. The man quickly rounded the platform, looking at the dials and scales, taking notes despite the ice that was starting to crust over him. He paused a second, looking incredulous, and then made a swift retreat back to shelter and kicked his feet free of snow. His mind felt stunned into reality as he looked at the numbers he'd just written down. It couldn't be, but it was. The instruments didn't lie. Already ten inches of icy wet snow had fallen, and the storm was only six hours old and holding strong.

Michael Hanwell was sweating. He, Tim and Matthew were up on the roof of the King's Carriage House, shoveling off the accumulated snow. Because it was wet and heavy, they feared the flat roof would collapse under the weight. Accomplishing little with the garden shovels they managed to find—and one dustpan they were using as a scoop—they worried about the section they'd not yet gotten to. Wendy had gone to all the people who were still in the upstairs apartments at midnight, warning them of the danger, urging them to come down to Parijata's apartment. The guys had worked for hours on the roof, taking turns to go inside to dry off and warm up, but it was a losing battle. Their muscles were aching and they were dead tired. They knew they weren't going to be able to do it all. And whenever they finished a section and turned back, it was covered with white again.

A flat roof posed real problems. The early snow had melted, and because it so seldom even rained, the drains were not often cleaned, meaning the water from the melting snow accumulated on the rooftop, and then froze. Indeed, Michael fell twice just trying to walk up there, for there was what appeared to be an ice-skating rink under the fresh powder. Wendy brought up a thermos of coffee around two in the morning, but as she appeared on the ladder she heard a creaking sound. So did the guys. They all froze, feeling the roof moving, just like one of the periodic earth tremors that they were accustomed to. But this was no quake. This was simply the giving out of a framework not designed to support such weight.

Wendy screamed as a whole section of the roof just in front of Michael disappeared. It simply fell in, collapsing like a sinkhole. The sound of shattering glass— windows blowing out—and collapsing stucco rocked them. Wendy gripped the ladder tightly, letting the thermos fall to the ground, as Michael fell reaching out for her to hold the ladder safely against the side of the roof. Matthew and Tim grabbed each other and hung on for dear life, Matthew pulling Tim away from the hole that appeared in the snow just inches from his feet. They found themselves looking down into the vacant apartment that had been freshly painted only days before.

When they walked into the recreation room, which adjoined Parijata's unit, the others breathed a sigh of relief. No one had been killed, no one injured. But several people were now homeless, and everyone was afraid of what would happen next. Would the snow and ice that had fallen into the upstairs apartments melt? What would happen if all that frozen water suddenly warmed?

They decided they would all stay in the recreation room, which had a soaring, pitched cathedral ceiling, with no dangerous second story above it. They dragged mattresses in from other apartments, clearing space, everyone pitching in with blankets and pillows and food rescued from other kitchens. Michael braved going back upstairs for Penelope Marlin, a beauty of an actress who needed insulin from her refrigerator. The snow prevented him from getting a good grip on the fallen beams and tar paper and plywood, the rubble of what had been a lovely apartment. He managed, but just barely. What really frightened him was a sparking electrical wire.

After Michael called to him, Matthew found the master breaker and tripped it, stopping the flow of electricity to half of the building. No fires had started, thank God. They felt they were safe. Wendy and Penelope and three others broke up chairs and some wooden drawers the guys dragged in to burn as firewood. The guys changed from their wet, soggy clothes to warm woolies, or pajamas, in Michael's case, with little snowflakes on them that Wendy had bought him for Christmas and he'd sworn (liking to sleep naked) he'd never wear. Tonight he was grateful for them.

Parijata insisted that Michael and Wendy sleep with Rachel in her bed, saying she would stay on the cot she often used when her nieces and nephew came from Mexico City. Once in bed, Michael and Wendy said nothing for a few minutes. The baby was sleeping soundly, having no idea of the danger and chaos around her. Finally, Wendy voiced it. "You want to go to your parents' house?"

"I don't know," Michael replied. He'd turned his mother down all three times she'd called earlier that night. Even though Dee and Harry had agreed to go there, even though he was now on vacation for a week, even though he knew it would be the wisest decision, he didn't want to desert his family of friends. This was where they belonged.

But the danger of the situation wouldn't let him

close his eyes. Sheer exhaustion should have put him into a coma, he knew. But he just couldn't sleep. He kept staring at it, at the wet, icy white striking the window. And feeling impotent, completely powerless, that he could no longer really forecast anything.

Harry Hanwell waited until the guard had fallen into a stupor of alcohol and sleep, then he made his move. Taking a razor blade from the curator's bathroom, he carefully slit the inside edge of the first painting. Then the other side, then the other two, and the canvas dropped into his hands. He carefully, almost reverently, his heart racing and his pulse pounding, set it on the floor. Then he did the same to the other one. He got two of the posters of the paintings that the museum had left at the door of the exhibit hall for everyone to take and taped them inside the frames, so at first glance the naked eye might not notice what had happened. When he stepped back to examine his handiwork, as an artist might after signing one of his works, he realized he was sexually excited. Well, imagine that.

He didn't know what time it was—hell, he didn't even know what day it was; years could have passed. Time meant nothing. He'd completed the first stage of the most ingenious, outrageous, and courageous art heist in history. One for the books—one, he was sure, that would go into the curator's own book that he'd just read. He rolled the canvases gently, lovingly, and then picked them up and cradled them in his arms— his babies, his little loves—and carried them up the stairs to the curator's office.

He suddenly realized how heavy old oil paintings were. He set them down on the desk and ran his fingers through his hair. *God, I've done it! I don't believe it.* He looked giddy suddenly, then that expression disappeared behind a mask of despair. *Jesus, what the hell am I thinking?* But when he looked out the window at the monster storm that showed no sign of abating, the sense of beauty that existed on top of the danger won him over. The snow was as beautiful as the paintings, as his act had been; the danger was a part of it, a piece of it, something that made it even more compelling.

But the snow shocked him into another reality: how was he going to get out of there? How was he going to get them outside? How would he get them home? Just carry them? Just walk through the snowstorm with them in his arms? How about wrapping them in the brown paper tube that the posters had come in? Lot of protection that would offer. He looked around the room, eyes frantic, racing, trying to find something plastic, rubber, something resistant to water. His crazed expression melted again, and he dropped into a chair.

He seriously contemplated giving up the whole scheme, walking out, pretending ignorance when questioned, as he surely would be. But then there was that dream of a villa on some beautiful island inlet, the money he'd socked away in a Cayman account, and the airport was not far away. He was faced with a choice. Stay in his rotten stinking life that was going nowhere—despite his famous clients and the best tables in all the power restaurants—or make a break with the biggest booty of all time. Was there really a choice to be made?

Hell, even if they caught him, he'd go to the electric chair—he wasn't even sure, did they still do that in California?—knowing that he had had the greatest thrill of his life by walking out the doors with those works of art under his arms; anything and everything was worth the risk. He was living tonight for the first time ever, not just going through the motions, not just pretending. Suddenly he envisioned himself in an old Hollywood Western (for which he'd probably represented at least two of the stars), where the townsfolk gathered at the oak tree on the hill to watch him swing. And he laughed at them, spit at them, because he had the last laugh, he was the one with the guts, the nerve, the balls! None of them could even come close in their tired, fearful little lives. No thrill on earth, not even sex, could match the explosion of sheer electricity that had surged through him as he held those paintings in his arms. His. They were his now.

He got up and searched again. His eyes focused on a square garbage can in the bathroom, but that would mean folding the canvases, which was risky; they were probably even too old to be rolled, but it was necessary. He found a raincoat in the curator's closet, and wrapped it around them. But just as he was pulling the arms tightly around the paintings, he glimpsed something outside the open door. Hanging on the wall, encased in glass, was a fire hose.

A fire hose. Waterproof. Pliable. Thick enough to slide rolled canvases into. Easy enough to carry over one's shoulder. A goddamn old-fashioned fire hose! Harry felt his blood surge with excitement again. There was no lock on the device. He opened the glass door, unfastened the hose from the water connection, and lifted it. It was heavier than he'd imagined it would be. He dragged it into the office, where he cut roughly a quarter of it off with the razor blade. He carefully laid it out, slid the rolled paintings into it, and then stuffed the ends with hacked-off bits of the raincoat. He rolled up the unused part and replaced it in the case at the top of the stairs. Then he returned to the office, slung the nine-foot section over his shoulder and looked in the bathroom mirror. All he needed was a fireman's helmet.

In the office again, he couldn't resist something. Setting the hose down for a moment, he flipped through the pages of the manuscript until he came to a passage that described what he'd just done, quickly slitting paintings from their frames and replacing them with forgeries. He grabbed a black marking pen and after the line which read, *But how ever to get them out under the guard's nose, no one could figure that out,* he wrote in block letters, not unlike the letters out in the snow earlier, SOMEONE DID.

He walked down the stairs in his stocking feet, with his shoes in his other hand, just to be sure not to disturb the snoozing guard. His was the only coat in the checkroom, and once he had donned it and buttoned up, he slid his shoes back on again and then lifted the fire hose to his sturdy shoulder. He walked past the guard as if the man was not there.

When he stepped outside, the shock of the weather hit him. It was worse than the ice storm had been, absolutely astonishing. Just as Michael had predicted. Snow everywhere, wet and clammy, heavy and seeming to come sideways, not from the heavens at all. No one would be here for days, he was sure, not even the cleaning people. He'd be long gone before they even discovered it.

Now, however, a new challenge faced him, one far more difficult than stealing two of the most priceless paintings known to mankind. How the hell would he get down to his car at the bottom of the hill? And, after that, out of Los Angeles?

Never mind the details. He had the will. The zeal. The drive. Tonight, he felt bigger than life, like that lunatic Jeffrey King seemed to always feel. He now understood the fervor of madmen. Nuzzling the fire hose on his shoulder with his cheek as if it were a puppy he was saving from the flood, he pulled his collar up and headed down into the storm.

Michael glanced at the screen on his Nokia when it woke him. "Mom? You okay?"

"Yes. You?"

"All right." Wendy was still sleeping next to him. The baby wasn't where they'd left her, so he knew Parijata had come to feed her. "Are Harry and Dee there?"

"No," Aileene said, her voice laden with worry. "We last heard from Dee as she was driving, heading toward Hollywood Boulevard, maybe one o'clock or so. Harry's cell isn't working or he's not answering. Susan had a rough night. Dad just gave her another shot. TV says that buildings are burning because of gas fires, buildings like yours, Michael."

"Our roof pretty much caved in."

She gasped. "You're all okay?"

"Yes. But several are homeless. What time is it?"

"Five in the morning."

He sat up and wiped the sleep from his eyes. "It's still snowing," he said after a quick glance to the window.

"Please, Michael," his mother begged. "It's gotten much worse than even you predicted. Everything is covered with snow. Please join us, if you still can."

He considered it this time. "I think you're right. I'll talk to Wendy about it and call you back, Mom. Love you. 'Bye." He hung up just as Wendy sat up. "I think maybe we should go to Los Feliz."

"Something happen?"

He shook his head. "It's the safest place, that's all."

"We're going to abandon our home and friends?"

He jumped out of bed. "Wendy, for God's sake,

stop being the social worker. Forget about your degree for a minute. In regular weather this is a beautiful building and a great, safe place to live. Now it's an orange crate full of snow and plaster and mush. We're all going to have to leave if this keeps up. And it looks like it's going to."

She had never seen him so adamant. But so was she. "I love these people, and they need us. I'm staying. I'm not going until I'm forced out."

Michael dressed as fast as he could, without a word to her, and walked out.

He forgot about the argument in seconds as he smelled the distinctive odor of natural gas. It overwhelmed him. They'd shut down the electricity but not the gas. He ran to the door of the recreation room, warning everyone. "Get out, now, until we can turn it off!" He went to two of the occupied apartments over on the other side of the building, where the second floor had not yet caved in, and banged on the doors, rousing the tenants. "Evacuate the building till we can shut the gas off!" Within ten minutes everyone was dressed for the weather and gathered across the street, which was now nothing but a winter wonderland. With the help of the Asian man from the far apartment, who knew more about gas lines than Michael did, they managed to find the master valve for the entire building.

Everyone stood patiently in the snow. Wendy held her baby close to her body, covered with three blankets. Parijata rubbed her hands together. Tim leaned against his boyfriend, his head on his shoulder, worrying, praying, weary. Penelope and the other tenants stood by, shivering. A woman from the building they were standing in front of brought out coffee and offered a place to warm up. No one accepted; they were all too concerned about their home, their building.

They wanted to watch it, as if their vigil would protect it from destruction.

Michael finally came sliding across the street. "He found the valve . . . couldn't turn it . . . got some tools . . ." He was out of breath, his lips purple, his nose red. When it seemed to be taking time, a few of them decided to have a snowball fight, while others did take the neighbor up on her offer of warmth. The heat in the apartment was coming from an open electric oven.

Twenty minutes more and they were all back home. They trudged across the street, cold again, afraid, hoping that was the end of it, but the snow was still coming down. Inside each of them lay the suspicion that there was more yet to come; a few of them—Michael especially—felt that what had already happened was nothing compared to what was in store for them in the future.

"I have faith," Parijata said, fingering rosary beads.

"Yes," Lorna said. "And I have this incredible desire to build Frosty!" She ran to the middle of the front yard, right outside the sign that said THE KINGS CARRIAGE HOUSE. "Come on, everybody," she shouted, the perennial cheerleader. "This isn't going to get us down!"

"You guys roll the body," Tim shouted back. "I'll do the head."

They dug into the wet snow, forming snowballs, and rolled them until they got bigger and bigger, until they'd made three of them, a large one, a medium-sized middle and the head. They set them on top of one another and stuck the two brooms Penelope had found into the center snowball for arms. Matthew pulled his scarf off and wrapped it around the neck. "Don't worry," he told Tim in anticipation. "I've got another."

"Eyes, nose, mouth," Parijata said. Then she lifted her index finger, telling them to hold on, to wait, as she hurried back inside the apartment. She returned seconds later with three plastic glasses—blue ones for the eyes and red for a nose—and one of those wax lips and teeth things that they sell in costume stores.

"Where the hell did you get that?" Michael asked her.

She shrugged. "I think somebody dropped it at Halloween. I had it in a drawer."

"Perfect," Lorna pronounced. Matthew told them to stay put and returned in a moment with his digital camera. He snapped four or five shots of them horsing around with Frosty, and then handed the Nikon to Penelope, who included him in a few pictures. It would be the perfect way to remember what had turned out to be an unforgettable night with friends.

As they all went back inside, leaving Frosty on guard out front, Michael secretly wondered if in the morning all the fun would be over.

The U.S. Army Hummer stopped in front of the gates of a house on a winding street in the beautiful Los Feliz area of Los Angeles. The woman who'd been riding in it with the National Guardsmen picked up her suitcase and purse and pushed the turban farther down on her head. She thanked them, but the words were stilted. She was in shock and they knew it, but she had survived. One of the soldiers, a wide-eyed boy Dolores thought reminded her of Jake Hughes next door, pushed the button on the gate panel after he chipped the ice off it. When a voice asked who was there, he told them who he was and that he was sorry for waking them at this hour, but he had a Mrs. Hanwell with him. Could someone come down the driveway and help her in? The man's voice sounded delighted, and he assured them he'd be right there. Then the gates opened just a few feet, straining against the weight of the drift in the driveway. But it was enough for her to slip through.

Dolores, without shoes, her feet nearly frostbitten, her legs cut, her face reddened by the ice that had pelted her all night, began trekking up the steep driveway. In a moment Bob was there, hugging her, then grabbing hold of the suitcase she was pulling. "I had to abandon the car," she gasped, trying at once to explain everything, "and Jeff Troyer—this wonderful guy—helped me for over a mile, but I had to go up Western and he was going down, so we parted—a heel broke off, I couldn't walk, lost my boots—" She started to sob.

Bob let the suitcase fall into the snow and took her in his arms. "It's okay. You're here now—you made it," he said in encouragement. "We've got to get you inside and put you in a warm tub and pour hot tea into you."

She grinned through her tears. "A little Cragganmore wouldn't hurt, either." She straightened up and sucked in her breath. "I feel like I'm in some goddamned Russell Crowe epic."

"We all do." Bob picked up the suitcase and helped her toward the house, where he could see Aileene waiting in the window.

"Harry?" she said. "Did Harry get here?"

"No," Bob admitted. "He said he was spending the night at CAA. He thought it might be easier to get here tomorrow."

"Bullshit," Dolores said. "It's gonna be worse."

They reached the lower door off the driveway, where Aileene met them with a warm towel. Dolores let her wipe her face with it, thankful for the gesture. "My God," Aileene said, seeing the state her daughter-in-law was in, "you look like you've been to hell and back."

"I have," Dee said. "And it's covered with ice. No fire at all."

About the time Dolores slid into a hot bubble bath at Bob and Aileene's house, Harry entered his warm, plush office. He thought it was a miracle he was there at all. He'd trudged all the way down the hill from the Getty—sliding like a kid on the snow—to find the Escalade nearly buried in the snow. Stowing the fire hose in the back, he used a folder that was sitting on the rear seat as a kind of scraper and got most of the snow off the windshield. The powerful defroster did the rest, and soon he was on the 405, along with only seven other vehicles. It was awesome and uncanny and positively unnerving. The trip down Wilshire Boulevard into Beverly Hills was excruciatingly slow and dangerous. His vehicle came into contact with three others on the trip, fender benders that normally would have prompted shouting in the street along with several cops to assess the damage—but not this time. Harry never stopped once.

Dented, frazzled, but ultimately feeling that he'd survived the first test of his new journey, Harry found the CAA building completely empty. He'd never seen it without guards, custodians, some other agent working late into the night, but tonight everyone had fled. He scanned his key card to open the garage door, parked in his usual spot and assessed the damage. The Escalade looked like it had done duty in Iraq. But who cared? It was something he was going to be leaving behind.

Once in the office, he kicked off his soaked shoes, stripped his wet, clammy tuxedo from his body and hid in his private shower for a full ten minutes, finally feeling warm again. When he got out, he slipped on sweatpants that he kept in the office to wear at the gym and a sweatshirt Demi Moore had given him from one of her kids' schools in Montana. Tired and bleary-eyed, he sat at his desk and went online, almost more from force of habit than wanting to check his e-mail. In fact he didn't even open his in-box. He clicked on the weather.

What he read wasn't good. It sounded preposterous, like one of his younger brother's on-air jokes. "Snow has also pounded Palm Springs and the surrounding desert resort areas, with the accumulation in La Quinta reaching three inches, the first significant snow-fall to be recorded there in modern times." The out-look for the next few days sounded worse. The storm would significantly change as the winds blew dry air into the area from the desert—but the precipitation was not about to stop, meaning the snowstorm would become a blizzard. The temperatures could dip down to zero in the next few days. Blah blah blah.

He clicked on the news. It was startling. Fires were raging all over the city as a result of explosions in gas heaters that were being overtaxed. Everywhere, roofs were collapsing from the weight of the snow. Hospitals were filled to capacity; there were not enough doctors to treat emergency trauma patients. Road accidents were lethal, for few rescue crews could get to them. The mayor was begging people not to panic, the gov-ernor assuring everyone that the area would be de-clared a disaster area by morning (as if, Harry thought, that was going to be some kind of consola-tion), and shelters were opening up all over the South-land. And, perhaps wackiest of all, a drive-by shooting had been reported in Watts, not from a car—from a snowmobile. Nothing, Harry noted with a grin, about Van Gogh paintings missing from the Getty.

But something did grab his attention. In an MSNBC online news clip, the energetic Contessa Brewer, the babe of an anchor that Harry had always adored and secretly wanted to make love to, was in Los Angeles for a few days—a few longer than expected, Harry thought, with the planes all grounded—and got a tip on something happening in the San Fernando Valley. She was reporting from an odd candlelight vigil in Chatsworth at sundown, when the snow was coming down hard. It looked to Harry like some kind of Christmas celebration, a procession to the church before Midnight Mass, but this was nothing of the sort.

As Contessa informed the viewers, the participants in the vigil wouldn't allow her cameras to come close, but what it represented was chilling. Yes, she was standing only a mile from the heavily guarded compound where Jeffrey King lived like, well, a king, but this spot was exactly where the Spahn Ranch had stood, the old movie ranch that was, in the late sixties, home to the Family, the ragtag group of druggies and hippies that included Susan Atkins, Linda Kasabian, Bruce Davis, Squeaky Fromme, Leslie Van Houten, Charles "Tex" Watson, and the leader who convinced most of his followers that he was Jesus Christ and that the Beatles spoke to him through their songs, Charles Milles Manson. "But the center of attention here tonight, the man who instigated this rally, is Jeffrey King, as famous today as Charles Manson ever was in his."

Contessa managed to nab a moment with the man. Suave and towering above her, King appeared to be wearing a dark hooded robe of some kind, and his face was ghostly white, making him look like a living version of the usual depiction of the Grim Reaper. "What's this all about, Mr. King?" she asked.

"It's about prayer. It's about what's coming."

"The end of the world?"

He smiled an enigmatic smile. "Armageddon by any name you wish."

"Why here?"

"It has significance."

"A connection with Charles Manson?"

King smiled some more. "It is rare to find a man who believes in his convictions the way Manson did in his."

"Unafraid, then, of public opinion?"

King laughed. "He was frightened of everything. Like a coyote, he used to say. That meant he missed nothing."

"But what is the purpose of this tonight?"

"Commemoration. Concern. Continuity."

She grinned. "And that means?"

"You should attend one of our retreats."

"If it's the end of the world," Contessa quipped, "I think it's too late to sign up."

He wasn't amused. "My followers have a certain affinity toward other prophets who have come before me."

"This is the first time you have publicly connected yourself to Manson. People say you have planned to run for office. This can't help."

"I'm a convicted felon. I can't run for office. Anyhow, baby, it's moot now." He put his palm out to catch some snow. "This is the end."

"What makes your followers come here in a snowstorm that even people in Alaska wouldn't venture out in?"

A woman pushed her way to the mike. "I'm Loretta Zane," she said. "I'm on the Los Angeles City Council. I am here to show my support for this man, the King, who will lead us to the sunlight again." Contessa looked at the woman as if she were loony, but she let her continue. "I knew Manson myself. I do not condone what steps he took. But he was right in his prediction."

Contessa pressed her. "Many of us weren't even born when the Family went on their murder spree that shattered Los Angeles. So enlighten us. What does helter-skelter have to do with snow?"

Loretta looked at Jeffrey. He nodded to her. She said, "Charlie said, 'When the shit comes down, the black man will be on one side and the white man on the other.' Well," she added, looking to the sky, "it's coming down. It sure is."

"This snowfall somehow portends a race war?" Contessa asked incredulously.

King took over. "There will be a revolution because of this, and only my followers will be left standing."

Loretta grabbed the mike in the freezing wind. "Susan Atkins said it best. She said, *A couple of black people—some of the spades from Watts—would come up into the Bel Air and Beverly Hills district—up in the rich piggy district—and just wipe some people out, just cutting bodies up and smearing blood and writing things on the wall in blood.*"

"And you believe such anarchy will take place because of the snow?"

Jeffrey King grinned devilishly. "Black people are gonna want to get warm, they're gonna want roofs over their heads, they're gonna say they've finally had enough. So where are they gonna go? Bel Air. That's where."

"This is a celebration, then, of helter-skelter? Of Manson's vision coming true?"

"Hey, baby," he said with a wink, "your own newscast said tonight that poor people are being burned outta their buildings, that their flimsy roofs are collapsing. Helter-skelter, baby, helter-skelter."

Contessa said, "Mr. King, you live in one of the biggest mansions in the San Fernando Valley. Do you think you're safe?"

"I'll open my doors to all my followers."

In the background, Contessa and her viewers heard the group singing the Beatles' "Sexy Sadie." "I frankly don't know what to make of this," she admitted to Keith Olbermann, who was anchoring his *Countdown with Keith Olbermann* newscast from the studio in New Jersey. The Manson followers playing in the snow was today's number one story.

"And a city council member is supporting him?" Keith said. Keith turned to his right and immediately added, "Contessa, an interesting item just in— apparently earlier this evening, at the Getty Museum, someone wrote DEATH TO PIGS in the snow. It's a phrase that Jeffrey King used in his book and that has often been quoted by his followers. And it was exactly what was written in blood on the wall at the LaBianca house the night after the Tate murders."

Contessa turned to King and asked him about it. He just started to sing, *"You say you want a revolution . . ."*

Contessa turned it back to Keith, not quite knowing if she should laugh or feel scared.

Harry turned off the computer and dialed his desk phone. The lines were still up; it still worked. He called his father. Bob answered on the first ring, sounding awake, but Harry knew he'd been sleeping. "Dad, sorry. I thought I'd better let you know—"

"Yes, son, we've been worried. Dee is here."

"Thank God she made it."

"Are you in the office? I didn't look at the ID to see where the call came from."

"Yeah. Listen, can I talk to her? She's probably pretty ticked at me."

"I think she's worried about you," Bob corrected him and then told him to hang on.

After what seemed like ages, Dolores picked up an extension. "I was asleep. After what I've been through, I should be dead. Where the hell are you?"

"CAA. Dee, I'm proud of you."

It startled her. "Why?"

"Because you did it, you made it. I know what it's like. I was out in it."

"In a fucking tank. I *walked*."

"Walked?"

"Never mind." She was weary and didn't want to have this conversation now when her nerves were coming apart and she so badly needed rest. "Let me sleep, Harry. I'll talk to you mañana."

"Yeah. I just called to say good-bye."

"What? Good-bye? Where do you think you're going?" She added a note of humor. "Or is this your way of telling me you're divorcing me?"

"I mean good-bye now, from this call, that's all."

"Harry, you been drinking?"

"No."

"Maybe you should. I'll talk to you in the morning." And she hung up.

Harry took her advice, poured himself some of the Grey Goose he kept in the bar over by the sofa and two leather chairs, drank it neat, and drifted into a slumber that would better be described as a coma.

Dolores tried to get back to sleep after Harry's call, but couldn't. She got up, looked out the window at what seemed not to have changed at all, then went downstairs to the kitchen to get herself a drink. She

figured she'd use Bob's Scotch first, and so she finished
his bottle of Dewar's. She peeked in on Susan, whose
sleep had been induced by yet another shot of Demerol for pain. "Got any for me?" Dee whispered,
and then kissed the girl on the cheek, patted the dog,
and closed the door. Wandering the dark living room,
Dolores looked out toward the street as she saw lights
reflecting off the walls. Vehicles were moving up Waverly Drive. Were they Jeeps? Four-wheel-drive vehicles like the one that had delivered her to the gates?
No, it seemed to her they looked like cars. Well, didn't
they have the damned luck? Cars making it up an icy
street without sliding back down?

She stood there wondering if Jeff Troyer had made
it safely home. She had his card and had promised to
call him. He deserved a gift, her angel of the night;
she would send him something wonderful. A ticket to
Tahiti, she thought, with a snicker. Maybe she'd go
with him. Another car went by, this one looking to
her like an SUV almost like Harry's. Her heart raced
for a moment, but it didn't turn into the driveway at
3449, it continued up the hill. What the hell was going
on up there? Were the priests next door having a
party? Or maybe they'd turned the place into a
shelter.

Whatever. She slugged down the Scotch, which
warmed her, and walked back up the grand staircase
to bed.

What she didn't know was those vehicles were not
going next door, to the House of Prayer, but rather
to the house just beyond it, the house at 3301 Waverly
Drive, where another vigil was being held this night,
a commemoration rather than a celebration of the
prophecy. At the moment Dolores Hanwell turned out
the bed lamp just two doors away, a group of true
believers had seized the former LaBianca house, eager

to show the world that it wasn't over yet, that lightning could strike twice in the same place, that Jeffrey King would prevail, proving that Charlie was right after all.

And about then the snow finally stopped.

And as the first light of early morning crept over the area, the City of Angels looked different than anyone had ever seen it look since the day explorers had discovered the basin. It was blanketed with white. What was astonishing about that vision was the purity of it all, the incredible soft beauty that could have been painted by Van Gogh.

And yet, under that pastoral, heavenly facade, as exemplified by what was happening inside the La-Bianca house at that very moment, lay nothing but pure hell.

The Fourth Day
Sunday, January 18
High Temperature 23 Degrees, Low 14 Degrees

From NBC Studios in New York City, Katie Couric, leading off with the big news on the *Today* show, seemed a bit stunned by what she was reading. "The president has conferred with General Parker Van Hecke, director of operations in the Los Angeles area, and has promised federal assistance immediately; it is expected that the city will be formally designated a disaster area in a few hours. The mayor of Los Angeles stated that the city is 'completely helpless' in the situation and has asked the military to begin the evacuation of hard-stricken areas—especially poverty areas—and to air-drop badly needed supplies to stranded residents. The governor of California has concurred.

"Whenever you have large air masses fighting one another, as Al Roker will explain in more depth in a minute, you get the most potent storm. L.A. has been hit by the most potent storm in its history. Power is out in many parts of the sprawling city, and hospitals and other rescue and shelter institutions are functioning on auxiliary generators. LAX and all area airports closed yesterday afternoon and cannot reopen their runways. Cold, exasperated residents spent hours unearthing their cars from snowdrifts that have blown higher than most people, while others walked in the wet, slushy streets or trekked through semi-shoveled sidewalks on their way to coffee shops, bars, and convenience stores to escape cabin fever. Groups of neighbors have had shoveling parties, where everyone pitches in to dig out.

"It is indeed impossible to get out, difficult even to get word out. Long-distance carriers say lines are down throughout Southern California, and cell phone service is iffy because of overloads. There is as yet no report on deaths because of the freak snowstorm, but sources estimate that over five hundred people may have died in the area from Santa Barbara down through San Diego."

Couric looked up from the monitor. "I spoke to a friend out on the coast a little while ago, and he said that despite the dangerous situation, spirits were high, and everyone was planning to build snowmen and toboggan down the hilly streets in the Hollywood hills, and then gather to pray that it will all melt."

Matt Lauer interjected, "But it isn't going to. It's still well below freezing."

"And," Couric added, "there is more snow headed for the area. Isn't this all just too incredible?"

"I saw that movie," Lauer said, "the one about the coming ice age . . ."

"The Day After Tomorrow."

"Yes, and I thought the shot of L.A. buried in snow was kind of put there for the people on the East Coast who want to trash L.A. But now it's come true."

Katie nodded. "All the harder to believe when we

realize the temperature here in New York this January morning is seventy-five degrees. We'll have some tape of the snowstorm that hit Los Angeles yesterday in the next half hour. Breaking news at any moment. And, of course, Al Roker to let us know just what's in store for L.A. today, on *Today* . . ."

"My God! Michael, look!" Wendy was peering out Parijata's window as Michael walked out of the shower, toweling his hair. He stood next to her, gaping at the sight before them. Across the courtyard, which was inundated with snow, Matthew was crawling through a window into his apartment. "I don't believe it," Wendy said.

"More than I even thought," Michael agreed. It had built up; it was staying. Their Frosty had a hat of new snow on his head many inches high. No longer was it mushy and damp as it had been in the night; no longer was it the kind of snow that had caused the roof of the building to fall in. This was no longer wet. The snow that was falling now was thick and dry and piling up.

Outside, a little while earlier, Tim and Matthew had tried to open their apartment door so they could go inside to get some heavier clothes, but the door moved two inches at most. They couldn't even dig it out because the snow was encrusted with ice—the temperature had dipped so low in the night. All the water on the patio had frozen solid, with eight inches of snow piled on top of that, frosted with ice you could crack. So the window seemed the next best bet, and it worked.

Michael dressed and got outside in time to help Matthew and Tim carry some things to Parijata's apartment. Tim, who loved to cook, brought his biggest stockpot so he could make soup with everyone's veggies and chicken and meat. He would miss his gas range, but he was glad Parijata had an electric one—with the gas off he wouldn't have been cooking anything otherwise. Out in the courtyard, Penelope and Kenny Rupp, who left 4A this morning after he couldn't stand the cold any longer, had the same expression on their faces: bewilderment and enchantment. It was beautiful, but they'd thought for sure it would be gone in the morning. This morning wasn't getting warmer, as the others had. It looked like it wasn't going to melt, and new stuff was starting to accumulate on top of it.

"Will you look at this?" Penelope said to the rest of them. "I always wanted to walk on water." Sure enough, she was standing on the surface of the pool. The ice was thick enough to hold her.

"It's frozen solid," Tim gasped. "Two weeks ago I was swimming in this," he said, making a run for the ice, "and now I'm skating on it!" He slid halfway across it, grabbing Penelope's hands as though they were two figure skaters starting their routine. Then he fell flat on his ass.

Everyone laughed, but it was strained laughter at best. Parijata came out with a blanket over her shoulders, and they all talked of what was going to happen, speculating on the sun, on the snow, on their chances to stay warm. Tim went inside to start the soup. The rest of them looked up when the flurries that had been falling turned to real snow.

"I'd give anything to be doing the weather today," Michael admitted to Wendy.

"Nothing's broadcasting from L.A.," she told him, "not even the major networks. I think CNN and MSNBC had some live reports yesterday, but that was about it."

Michael nodded. "I doubt anybody can get to the studios."

"Electricity is going to go everywhere," Matthew predicted. "Nothing in this city was planned to withstand anything like this. It's worse than an earthquake in many ways."

They went back into Parijata's apartment. Wendy and Tim made breakfast, eggs and tortillas and orange juice that was a blend from cartons in five or six apartment refrigerators. The Asian couple who'd stayed in their own apartment on the first floor, as Kenny had done the night before, came to the door to tell everyone they were leaving. They were going to attempt to get to the desert, where they had relatives and it wasn't nearly as bad. They gave them everything they had in their refrigerator and cupboards and wished everyone well. And asked for everyone's prayers. Parijata lit a candle in front of a statue of the Blessed Virgin.

When Tim discovered three frozen chickens in one of the Trader Joe's bags the couple had left behind, he said he'd add them to the soup that was already cooking, for which Wendy and Penelope were chopping vegetables while Michael fed Rachel. But Parijata objected. "No, I make you good arroz con pollo for dinner tonight."

Kenny liked the sound of that. "If they're anything like your tamales, Mrs. McKay, I'm ready."

Parijata blinked, not used to being called by her married name. "Trouble is, when you call me that, I am reminded of the man I divorced."

"And that's a good thing?" Michael asked.

"Yes, because he was a bad thing."

Wendy joked, "You should have married a Mexican."

Parijata laughed. "You sound like my mother."

Kenny raised a fist. "This is survival central, dudes!

We're the Carriage House Gorillas. Nothing's gonna stop us."

After breakfast, Michael and Matthew went outside to shovel a path from the door to the street. As they dug up the hard snow, they found a crack in the concrete coping around the pool. "When it warms up, the pool's going to have to be drained," Michael said.

"Right now, who cares?" Matthew tossed a shovelful of snow onto the pile they were building. But it seemed pointless, for it was coming down again as fast as they could remove it.

Dolores woke with a start, and a headache. At first she didn't know where she was or what was happening. She pulled off her sleep mask, expecting bright sunshine to be coming in her wall of French doors. But she wasn't even in her own house. In a moment, as she rubbed the sleep out of her eyes, it all came back to her. She felt the swelling in her feet, the aching of her bones, and the warmth of the heat blowing through the vents on the floor. She ran her fingers through her hair. *God, what a mess!* It felt thick and dirty and knotted. Her face was puffy from the icy wind of the night, and too much booze. She didn't dare look into a mirror, not for at least an hour. What she didn't know for sure wouldn't hurt her.

She got out of bed and peered out the window. Everything was white, and nothing had hard edges, thanks to the blanket of snow. And it was still falling from the skies. For as far as she could see, down the hill, over neighbors' roofs, snow filled the air, sat on tree branches, on rooftops, crusted onto power lines. And it all seemed to be covered with ice.

Then it came back to her. The nightmare from last night replayed itself in full color—really, mostly the black of night and pure white—and seemed to haunt her. She leaned against the cold windowpane and saw it steam up under her breath. "Harry," she whispered, "where are you? Come soon. Maybe it will be all right." Her voice revealed a good amount of fear.

Just up the street, fear was the last thing anyone was feeling inside the house where Rosemary and Leno LaBianca had been so brutally slaughtered on the night of August 10, 1969. There was a kind of giddy joy, a sense of winning, almost as if the squatters were witnessing the Second Coming. Loretta Zane sat on the sofa in the living room and looked at the words scrawled on the wall in the dark of night: DEATH TO PIGS 2. HELTER SKELTER 2. THE KINGS LIVE! written in the blood of the current residents, who perhaps this morning no longer qualified as "current" because they were dead, their bodies thrown outside in the snow. *Former* residents they were, Loretta thought as she drank coffee and helped herself to the box of Krispy Kreme doughnuts that someone had brought.

"Hey, Loretta," Andy said, popping in from one of the bedrooms in workout pants and a sweatshirt. "Morning." He'd gone with her from the candlelight vigil in Chatsworth to this house, to their destiny. "Awesome, the vigil last night."

"Made national news," she said with pride. "They'll see."

"Hey, there's something I never thought of."

"What's that?"

He scratched his nose nervously, reluctant to voice it. "Well, saying national news . . . made me think . . . kinda wondering . . ."

"What?" she snapped.

"If we're gonna be, like, the only people left after

Armageddon, what's gonna wipe out the people in other places?"

"Huh?"

"The snow ain't everywhere, baby. It's here. Everyone here might die and we'll be saved, but how about the people in Florida and Maine and France and places?"

She looked intently into his eyes. "Trust the King. It isn't for us to know. We must believe what he says."

"You think maybe something else is gonna wipe everybody else out?" He blinked. "Like, hopefully?"

"It's bigger than we can know."

He shrugged, taking her word for it. He stretched, yawned and drifted to the window. "Man, the snow was real red with blood. Now it's just kinda pink."

"Gives a whole new meaning to the phrase 'cold-blooded killer,' doesn't it?"

He laughed. "Sure does. But it's almost gone."

"What?"

"The evidence."

"How so?"

"Look. It's snowing again. Harder than before."

"Good. It'll put even more pressure on the blacks down in South Central."

"They'll be here soon," the young man said, his eyes wild again. "In droves."

"That's okay," she purred. "Let them come. There are plenty of big warm houses like this one to welcome them."

Harry Hanwell woke up to find the afghan on the floor, one leg up over the top of the sofa and an erection pressing between his legs. He'd been dreaming about Calla. She'd just started going down on him when he opened his eyes. He felt like he was sweating.

His office was dark—what time was it? He'd gone to bed with the lights on. What happened to them?

He got up and tried the switch. Nothing. The power was gone. But the heat was on, blowing from the vent high on the wall. How in hell could a blower be working if the lights were out? He figured it was some kind of different generator or electrical system. He pulled the drapes open and looked out at the next building. Sure enough, there were lights on. That gave him hope. The walls were encrusted with ice, and snow was blowing through the air the way it had when he'd accompanied Dolores on a singing gig in Minneapolis in winter. He was looking out at absolute unreality. This was Beverly Hills.

Plans of escaping on a plane today died. He'd surmised that with security so tight, he'd have to find something other than a fire hose to put the paintings into—a large suitcase, perhaps a mailing tube. But now, knowing the airport wasn't going to be open, the logistics of disguising the paintings weren't important. The important thing was only how he was going to get away. Train? Bus? He shuddered at the thought; he hadn't taken a bus since he was in his early twenties.

But no damn blizzard was going to keep him down. An article on the young agents at CAA two years earlier had called him, "Irrepressible, the kind of guy who finds no challenge daunting." Except perhaps one, at this moment: the desire for food. He was starving, and it wasn't like he could pick up the phone to have his secretary order in. The last thing he'd eaten was some caviar on a water biscuit. The clock on the desk glowed 8:20, but it had to be later than that. Sure enough, his watch told him it was afternoon. Long sleep.

Inside the refrigerator under his coffeemaker were

melted ice cubes, a warm Diet Coke, some vodka and a rotten half sandwich he'd forgotten to toss. His stomach growled. He went into his bathroom, brushed his teeth, splashed some cold water on his face, and then headed for the hall to see what was in other refrigerators. Out there, he heard a voice. He stopped walking, turning toward the front doors. "Somebody here?"

"Yes, sir, Mr. Harry," a familiar and jovial man's voice said. "I been here all day. How the hell'd you get in?"

Harry found the guard, John Dorroh, sitting at the reception desk, feet up on top of it. "John, good to see you. I spent the night. It's nasty out there."

"You got that right, Mr. Harry. My wife, she's yelling at me not to go in today, nobody is working anywhere, stay home, don't desert me, you're gonna get killed out there on those streets. But hell, Mr. Harry, I gotta say, if I stayed home with her all day, I'm the one that would kill *her*. Can't spend all that much time with that woman, you know? Here nobody yells at me."

Harry laughed. "The way it looks out there, Johnny, this may be home for quite a while."

"Praise Jesus."

"We got any food around?"

John smirked, reached under the part of the desk Harry couldn't see, and lifted out a white Igloo cooler. "One thing that woman is, she's a good cook. She loaded me up." He handed it to Harry.

"Great." Harry opened it. Fried chicken, biscuits, two beers and some salad in a plastic Glad container. "Man, this is just what I was praying for."

"No restaurants open today, Mr. Harry. Even the TV stations shut down 'cause nobody can get to them, it's all New York news on, and the cable guys, they're saying it's the end of the world for California, like we just had the big one and dropped in the ocean. They keep quoting that asshole Jeffrey King that it's Armageddon."

"We're not gone yet."

"But we're in trouble. Oh yes. People dying everywhere 'cause nobody can get to hospitals, roads leading out of the place are all jammed with accidents, big fires and buildings being abandoned 'cause they got no heat, rich people worried the poor people are gonna come take over their places. It's bad. Real bad."

"Where do you live, John?"

"Culver City. Took me four hours to get here."

Harry bit into a chicken leg. "This is damn good."

"Where's the Mrs., Mr. Harry?"

"At my parents' place in Los Feliz. I wanted to join her there last night, but I gave up."

"I hear they're running a rescue thing at the Griffith Observatory up there. No matter, we'll be okay here."

"I can't stay," Harry told him. "I gotta go to Dee."

John studied Harry's gym outfit. "You got warm clothes?"

Harry shook his head. "Tuxedo, that's all."

"You're gonna freeze 'em off out there."

Harry nodded, enjoying the food. He popped open a beer. "I'm gonna call Dee, see what the options are."

"Trust me, you need some long johns. There's that ski shop around the corner, up on Wilshire."

Harry blinked. "They gonna be open?"

John laughed. "You can open it. All the way here, I seen people breaking into places, smashing the windows. There's no police no more, Mr. Harry. It's chaos out there."

Harry was startled. "People are breaking into buildings? Banks? Stealing?"

"Grocery stores, drugstores, clothing stores. What good is money in this? People want to survive."

Harry hadn't thought it through. It seemed that suddenly everything was upside down. Priorities had changed. The idea of breaking into a store to get a warm jacket and boots had never occurred to him in his life. But then too, the heist of two of the world's most precious paintings hadn't really been in his plans either. Until last night. Until the snow.

He picked up a second piece of chicken and bit into it. "Christ, I'm famished."

Bob Hanwell's cell phone rang. "Bob, Cameron here. Glad to see you still have service."

Bob said, "We have electricity, so I charged up all our phone batteries. Signal is getting wonky, though. How's it going?"

"Operation White, they're calling it. More and more buildings—apartments especially—are without the capability to withstand this. Much of the city is on fire."

"Fire and ice."

"Private plane tried to take off from the Van Nuys Airport. Guy was selling seats for a lot of dough."

"What?" Bob was stunned. "How'd they clear the runway?"

"Makeshift plow in front of the guy's Hummer."

"They make it?"

"Smashed into the terminal building," Cameron told him. "At least fifty dead. People were gathering there, homeless now, hoping to get out."

"You need more shelters," Bob told him. "Tell the general to open up an auditorium or warehouse nearby and get medical supply trucks in there."

"Larry Zarian's done a good job of that. He's opened every major building with available space to shelter people. And we have Guardsmen coming in from all neighboring states."

"And get word out that people shouldn't try to leave, they should stay put. They're safer that way."

"Tell that to those in South Central." Cameron changed the subject. "How's Susan?"

Bob told him that her pain was considerable. "If things were normal, she'd be in surgery already."

"Hospitals are without staff, overcrowded. No one can do a delicate surgery like she needs in this situation."

"I doubt that the surgeon Dr. Shemonsky wanted for her ever made it back to town. We have no choice but to wait."

"Can she?"

Bob swallowed hard. "She has to."

"No one can get in. Getting out is just as bad. I know the mayor spouted some nonsense about getting everyone evacuated, but it isn't going to happen."

Dolores and Aileene crouched over Bob's shoulders, listening. "How long do you think it's going to last?"

"Michael was right on the money. Another few days for sure. Maybe a week total."

"Susan can't last a week!"

Aileene gasped and shivered. Dolores put a hand on her arm.

Bob was sorry he was upsetting Aileene, but it was a gut reaction. "We've got to get her to a hospital, Cameron."

"Bob, there are people standing in lines in the snow waiting to get into the hospitals. Strokes, frostbite, broken bones, on top of regular illnesses."

Bob looked stricken. Dolores said, "Ask him how much snow we're in for."

"I heard her," Cameron said. "Six feet, I'd say."

"That's preposterous." Aileene gasped.

"Tell me you're kidding," Bob said.

"We got nine feet in the Sierras already."

"Sierras, yes, that's normal," Bob said. "This is Los Angeles, Cameron."

"Van Nuys got two feet. Pasadena has three plus. More in Eagle Rock and down in Chino."

"Jesus."

"Bob," Cameron cautioned, "keep your family and friends together, stay inside, stay warm. Conserve food and fuel, keep water dripping so the pipes won't freeze. I'll see what I can do about helping Susan."

Bob had to ask it. "Can you get her out?"

"I don't know, my friend. Nothing's flying in this. So much snow is coming down that it's almost impossible for choppers to maneuver. If we get more wind, it's going to become a full-scale blizzard, and then we're really sunk." Cameron took a deep breath. "But I'll do whatever I can for my godchild."

"Cameron, thanks."

"I gotta go, Bob. I'm right above you, up on the hill. Doubt I'll be leaving here."

"Hey," Bob said, trying to joke, "if you get bored, ski down the hill for coffee."

"Dallas Raines told me he was cross-country skiing in Beverly Hills this morning. It's just surreal, isn't it?"

"So, the Channel Seven weatherman is just as nuts as my son, huh?"

Cameron laughed. "Looks that way."

"Stay warm. I'll be in touch later."

Dolores looked perplexed as Bob turned his phone off. "He said it'll become a blizzard. What the hell was I walking in last night?"

"Technically, we had an ice storm, then massive

snow. A blizzard needs extremely high winds to blow the already fallen and falling snow around. It's far worse."

"I need a drink," Dee said, going to the bottle of Scotch in the dining room hutch. It was her third glass since she'd awakened.

Aileene gave Bob a cautionary look, but he ignored it. If that was what Dee needed to relieve the stress, fine with him. He put an arm around Aileene. "I'd do anything to get Susan to a doctor. Anything."

She nodded silently.

Bob fed the dog and put on his jacket. "I've got to try to drain the pool."

"What?" Dolores gasped. "Why?"

"The ice is going to crack the sides and forty thousand gallons of pool water will wipe out the family room, and then the entire house will slide down the hill."

Bob made his way through the snow to the far end of the yard and brushed the white from the pool equipment, the heater and pump and filter. He tripped the switch that turned off all power to the system, so it wouldn't accidentally be activated later, trying to pump solid ice through the filters. Then he opened a valve down near the garage, a siphon that usually drained the water slowly into a little ravine, a gully, which took it down the side of the property to the gutter in the street, and eventually down the hill to the sewers. He had to whack the frozen valve handle with a hammer to get it to turn, but once he did, water gushed out. Steam rose as the slightly warmer water hit the ice and snow.

He went into the garage and grabbed an ax. Back at the pool level, he was curious about something. Could he walk on it? Would it support his full weight? He had to try it. Stepping gingerly onto the top of his pool, he guessed it was several inches thick. And it supported him. He saw Aileene in the window, taking a photograph, and he posed like Paul Bunyan about to fell a tree. Stepping back onto the security of the brick patio, he sunk the ax head into the ice. He chopped at it until a large crack appeared across the surface. Water splashed up through the split. He remembered growing up in the Midwest, going ice fishing with his dad and grandfather in the winter. He felt he was doing the same thing here, only the point was to crack the ice so the pressure would be relieved and the pieces, once the water was gone, would rest on the bottom.

He put the ax to one side and grabbed a garden shovel to clear the steps leading to the patio from the garage, just in case they had to use them, to take Susan to the car, for Michael and Wendy and Rachel to get in, should they come. He looked up at the wall up the hill at the east side of the house, wondering if the retreat house had been turned into a shelter. Dolores had said many cars went up that way last night. Well, the priests there didn't have to worry because they had an automatic blessing at that shelter: they had God on their side.

His hands suddenly felt frozen solid. He looked at his watch. Almost two o'clock. He suddenly wondered about Harry, about Michael. Had either of them called? How were they? He stomped snow from his boots at the back door and entered the house. In time to hear part of the confrontation.

"How can you just let her *lie* there? At least let me hold her!" Dolores was shouting at Aileene. Bob knew what was happening. Dolores wanted to do something to aid Susan, and she objected to Aileene's attitude. He walked into the hall just outside the kitchen to find the two women standing in the laundry room, just outside Susan's closed door.

"I know my daughter," Aileene said firmly, "and I know what's best for her."

"But some *comfort*, that's all I'm saying, for Christ's sake." Dolores sipped her drink. "I just want to *do* something for the poor thing."

A sense of pride and resentment colored Aileene's words. "She is not *the poor thing*. I know what is best for her. Dee, we've been through this since she was three. Painful as it is for us, leaving her alone is the only option."

"I just wanted to *do* something for her."

"And what would that be?" Aileene snapped without thinking. "Give her a drink?"

Dolores looked as though she'd been slapped in the face.

Before she could respond, Bob stepped in. "Hey, girls, come on. Susan can hear through the wall." He saw an empty syringe in Aileene's hand. "Did you give her another shot?"

Aileene nodded. "And Florence Nightingale here doesn't approve of that."

"I didn't say that," Dee pleaded. "I just wanted to go in and sit with her."

Bob said to Dee, "We've been through this her whole life, Dee. I know it's hard to watch it."

"You give her one of these," Aileene said, indicating the syringe, which she now tossed into the plastic container for empty ones, "and leave her be. And you think that doesn't hurt a mother?" She sounded suddenly on the verge of tears. "You think I like having to be this cool and collected, this regimented? Oh, honey, you just don't know."

"I only wanted to help," Dolores said pathetically, softly, walking into the living room.

Bob looked at Aileene. "I'm sorry," she said, "but we both know Susan doesn't want someone hugging and gushing over her." They both heard her cry out in pain. "And she especially doesn't want people watching her writhe in pain."

He nodded. "Darling, I understand, but Dee's never had a child. She doesn't know. She's worried about Harry. Be a little less harsh on her. She's only trying to show that she cares."

"She's tried Harry several times. Nothing."

"Michael?"

Aileene shrugged. "Yes. They're still determined to stay put."

Bob shook his head. "I'm heading for a warm bath. While we still have hot water." On his way up the stairs, he saw Dolores sitting alone on the piano bench. He watched her for a moment. She put her fingers to the keys and played a few bars of "Moon River," which had been Harry's favorite song since the day, as a boy, when he discovered Bob's vinyl album of the sound track to the movie *Breakfast at Tiffany's*. Dolores stopped, wiping tears from her eyes. Suddenly, Bob cursed his son for what he'd done to her. If they couldn't have a child of their own, they could have adopted. She needed someone to love, someone to give to. It might have turned out differently. They might have had a good marriage instead of a bitter, unhappy cold war.

He started taking off his wet shirt as he continued up the stairs.

The Kings Carriage House was beginning to look like a refugee camp. The recreation room adjoining Parijata's apartment was filled with broken furniture piled up to burn in the fireplace that Michael and Matthew were building. They'd dragged in one of the outdoor gas barbecue grills and ripped out the range hood from one of the abandoned apartments, hooking it up over the grill in the living room. Surrounding it, they set up a metal trash can from which they'd cut out a big hole, creating a kind of primitive fireplace. They fashioned an exhaust chimney from some duct-work they had ripped out of the rubble at the other end of the building, fastening it with duct tape. They knocked out one of the tall windows and replaced it with plywood, into which they cut a round hole the size of the ductwork, to lead the poisonous fumes out-side, and they taped around that too, to keep out the cold air. They figured they had enough propane—five tanks total—to last a while. And if they used it mainly as a fire starter to burn wood, they could make the bottled gas last a week or more.

Matthew and Tim had brought in their mattress and set it in the corner of Parijata's living room, next to the sofa bed that Penelope had used the night before, near the heater. Parijata slept in her Barcalounger. Kenny slept in a sleeping bag, while another resident who gave up trying to make it in his own apartment, Jim Farrick, curled up on a cot they had found. The kitchen was filled with food, cans and boxes and bottles, everything they could get from the apartments. Tim had climbed to the second-story balcony and raided the kitchens of the apartments where the roof had fallen in. They had enough food to last the rest of the year.

They called the rec room Snow City, and when they were all gathered they tossed the first wood on the fire, the leg of a living room cocktail table that flared up when Michael squirted some charcoal lighter fluid on it. They added the pieces of the rest of the table and soon had a roaring fire in front of them, filling and warming the room. It was going to work.

Parijata entertained them with a story about a snow-storm she was caught in as a little girl in the mountains of Mexico. Bandits had come to their village and forced everyone out. "We had to march over hills in two feet of snow with all our possessions on our backs, an old mule, walk for days until we find shelter." They lived in an abandoned mine for five days while a blizzard raged. "We make fire too, just like here."

"Everyone survive it?" Penelope asked.

Parijata shook her head. "My mother's friend, her child die. But perhaps it was a blessing. I saw bambinos so cold you wanted to kill them just to stop their suffering."

Wendy winced. And pulled Rachel closer to her warm body.

"This is the way we learn about life. This is how we learn faith. But the children, they should not suffer." Parijata crossed herself.

"Were you rescued?" Matthew asked.

Parijata said, "We make our way back to the village. The bandits, they are gone, one is dead, frozen. We stay in the church there until other people return. The Blessed Mother, she protect us all."

Jim Farrick, who, ironically, had just retired to California because of its weather, said, "I was in Chicago for the big blizzard back in—what year was that?— 1967. We went to bed at night and woke up to so much snow we couldn't open the door. I remember going with my mother to an A&P store on Clark Street, but there wasn't a thing left on the shelves. A bread truck pulled up—how it got there, I don't know—and people attacked the driver and robbed it of everything."

"People do anything to feed the bambinos," Parijata said with a nod.

"Twenty-three inches fell in five hours," Jim told them, "and then more storms added another foot to that. But the worst thing was the wind."

"Chicago," Michael said with a shrug. "The Windy City." He glanced at the window. The weather stripping wasn't holding back the sound of increasing winds. "Sounds like we're there now."

"Fifty miles an hour," Jim assured them. "It blew the snow into twelve-foot drifts. People took refuge in tollway plazas, gas stations, any place they could find. I think there were three thousand buses stranded on the streets. I remember seven hundred of them couldn't even be located."

Wendy asked, "How do you remember the numbers? The details?"

"I worked for the *Chicago Sun-Times*," Jim explained. "I was a copy editor, so I read every word again and again."

Michael said, "Listen to that." They all heard the howling. "The winds today could get up to gale force just like there. You can feel it coming through the walls."

They did. They all shivered. And the sound of the high-pitched, whistling gusts frightened them.

"This is depressing," Penelope said.

"Yeah," Kenny added. "Let's have some music." He found a CD and put it on. Michael Bublé filled the room. His wonderful voice was a relief.

"Hey, Michael," Jim said, "I recall a weatherman back in Chicago—Harry Volkman was his name—who predicted four inches. Well, there was already four inches on the ground when he left for the station that morning. He never got there to do his noon show. It was the snowstorm of the century."

Wendy laughed. "It's a new century."

"And this is ours," Michael added.

Loretta Zane sat in the crowded living room of the former LaBianca house and listened with delight to

what one of her cohorts was telling her on the phone.
". . . and so we broke in and got the pigs and then
we tossed them out, just like you did, and this band
of blacks, they came up the hill about three in the
morning and we invited them in, we told them they
were following the prophecy of the King—one kid
wore a Lakers jersey—and that they were going to
come out of this winning the war that they'd been
fighting for ages."

"No police?" Loretta asked.

"Yeah. Some kind of patrol found one of the bodies
out front. I don't know how, snow had covered him
by then, but three uniformed guys came to the door."

Loretta stiffened. "And?"

"We shot them."

She smiled. "I hear they are rising up in South Central, bands of people moving toward higher ground,
toward the rich white houses."

"How are things there?"

"It's like an airport when flights are delayed. Too
many people. We just took over the house next door.
There's another one, though, that intrigues me. Big
old Spanish place, gated, just under the church property. Andy noticed it one night from the car. It looks
warm and cozy, you know what I mean?"

"Cool."

Loretta took a cup of soup some black girl she'd
never seen before handed her. "I need two hands to
eat, gotta go."

"Hey, one more thing," the voice said. "Does the
King know? Have you spoken with him? I mean does
he realize?"

Loretta looked dreamy. "Of course he does. It's all
over the news. How could he not."

"Even more cool. 'Bye."

*   *   *

Just down the hill, the Hanwell house still had electricity. And cable. MSNBC kept them riveted. They watched Contessa Brewer holding tightly to a palm tree as she attempted to report on the snowstorm, but the howling wind and swirling snow nearly blew her down the street. Palms bent under the force of the blizzard winds, and in front of the snow-covered houses behind her, you could not tell where lawns ended or streets began. Everything was covered with white. When Contessa found a spot where she could steady herself—holding on to a street sign that was buried half its height in a drift—the cameraman, in a valiant attempt to get close to her, took a nosedive and that ended the segment.

"Transmission from Los Angeles has been lost," Keith Olbermann said, "owing to the fact that Contessa has just blown away. Is this bizarre or what? In some places, we understand, drifts reach as high as thirty-two inches. Fires are beginning to plague the city—you might have noticed the black smoke beyond Contessa in the final shot—and many deaths have been attributed to the fires, and to the cold. The winds are dry, making it worse, and the temperature is, at this hour, a very bone-rattling sixteen degrees, with a windchill factor that puts it below zero. People attempting to shovel, some for the first time in their lives, have suffered heart attacks. We are told that in some parts of the San Fernando Valley, the National Guard is working hard to get the injured to places where doctors can help, such as schools and meeting halls that have been designated makeshift shelters.

"Power is out in most areas from Santa Maria in the north to the far southern boundary of Orange County, and east to and including San Bernardino and Riverside counties. Reports have come in from all over the area. San Diego, which remains warmer so that the snow falling there continues to melt, has never had so many car accidents in all the years of recording such happenings. Boats anchored in Newport Beach have been blown into one another by the winds, which are more severe near the water. Yachts have sunk. The Balboa Beach Club was gutted by fire, and homes along the ocean have collapsed under the strain of ever-mounting snow as the freezing sea spray adds to the weight. Food and clothing are at a premium, with little left on grocery shelves because there is no way for trucks to get in to replenish the staples. Food, medicine and warm clothes are being air-dropped near designated shelters, although helicopters will be grounded if the blizzard-like conditions of the storm continue. In Glendale, where the local Kiwanis Club was meeting in the Elks Club hall on Colorado Boulevard as the snow began to fall, people are welcome to take refuge there. The Kiwanis spokeswoman, Susan Dell, says they're 'having a big party until this is over.'

"This just in: polar bears have escaped from the Los Angeles Zoo." Keith smiled. "They must think they're in heaven."

Harry Hanwell thought he was in hell. It was getting dark already and here he was standing in a ski shop he'd just broken the window of, changing his clothes right there in one of the aisles. He slid into the warmest thermal pants he could find, chose the most expensive pair of boots and sat down to lace them up. As he stripped off his sweatshirt so he could put on a thermal shirt under a fleece garment, he heard voices. Crouching down, he got the fleece over his head just as four boys, two blacks and two Hispanics, burst into the shop. All the way there, he'd seen looters scurrying out of stores, loaded down with everything they could carry. He loved it. Half the city had to be looted by now. It would make the heist at the museum look all the more natural.

But these boys eyed him with distrust. "Hey, dude, what's going down?"

"Just helping myself to some warm clothes," Harry answered.

"Shit, man, this is my dad's digs, so you gotta pay me," said the ringleader, a husky black kid with earrings in both his ears, his right eyebrow and the corner of his upper lip. The three others snickered.

Harry called his bluff. "Yeah, and I own the building, so your dad owes me."

"Dude," the other black boy said, looking through things. "Gonna warm my ass fine with this stuff."

The two Hispanic boys looked Harry over, getting close to him. Harry thought it was time to go. He put on a thick insulated ski jacket, then a tight-fitting cap that he could pull down over his face in the blizzard, and picked up the fire hose. But one of the two stood in front of him, hands buried in the pockets of his jeans, which looked like the crotch had been dragging in the snow. "Where you goin', man? A fire?"

"What's with the fuckin' hose?" the ringleader asked.

"Nothing," Harry said. He wasn't very convincing. One of the Hispanics grabbed it, pulling it from his shoulder, yanking the rolled-up plastic raincoat out of the end.

"Hey," Harry shouted, "get your goddamned hands off that."

"Owieeeeee," the other black boy squealed, "dude don't like us messin' with his hose."

The other kid relished the innuendo. "Never hearda no white dude wit a big hose."

"You know what they say about those white guys,"

one of the Hispanics said, which Harry thought was mildly clever.

But Harry wasn't about to give up millions of dollars' worth of paintings to four scumbags who didn't know Van Gogh from Van Nuys. "There's nothing in there you'd want."

"You got money in there?" one asked.

"Money?" Harry laughed. "No money. No."

The ringleader pulled out part of one of the canvases. He unrolled it a bit. He looked perplexed. "What this shit be?"

"I . . . I'm an artist." Harry tried to look a little nuts. Like Vincent might have had he been caught in the same situation.

"Shit," the boy spat. "Some mutherfuckin' painting."

"Shit's right," another said. "Coulda been fifty grand in that thing."

The kid holding the canvas dropped it. Harry started stuffing it back into the hose. "It's my life's work," he said, thinking for a moment he wasn't kidding, playing the nutty artist. "I'm gonna be in museums all over the world one day. I have to save my masterpieces from the snow."

The boys looked at one another and broke up into laughter. "You do that, Picasso," the husky one said.

Harry thought, *At least he knows Picasso was an artist.*

"Hey, man, cool phone," the ringleader said. He was holding Harry's hotshot, state-of-the-art Nokia. "Man, a camera too. Too cool."

"I need that," Harry said.

"Me too, man, me too," the leader said, pocketing it. Then he grabbed a scarf from a shelf, made a big deal of wrapping it around his neck and started out the broken display window. "Come on, guys. We got better places to go."

"Wait, I want some stuff," one of the others called out.

Harry couldn't give a damn whether they were staying or leaving. He was leaving. Somehow he was going to make it to his parents' house. Not because Dolores was there, but because it was the only way he could think of that he might get away, out of this city, out of this madness. He grabbed the hose, put it back on his shoulder, stepped over his discarded tuxedo pants, pulled his ski cap down and headed once more into what was now a raging blizzard.

Bob Hanwell went out again, just before it got dark, and took pictures of the incredible scene. It was harder than he'd figured—snow constantly covered the lens, but he managed to snap some shots from the windows of the house. As the sun—what sun?—set somewhere behind the snow clouds, the house took on a warmth and a beauty he thought he'd never seen there before. The fireplace lit the living room windows with its orange glow. The yard lights were on, illuminating the snow piling up around the pool. The ice level was going down, and a huge formation of solid ice was being created where the pool water flowed into the gully, like a frozen waterfall. When he went inside, Bob smelled something baking, cookies or a cake. Dolores sat in front of the crackling oak logs in the living room fireplace, listening to what sounded like a Broadway musical.

"What is this?" Bob asked.

"It's *The Boy from Oz*. Peter Allen was my good friend, you remember, and Harry and I saw Hugh Jackman do the show."

"Heard he was great."

She nodded. "Listening to it gives me comfort."

Bob understood. "Takes your mind off the rest."

As Bob left her, he saw her fingers holding tightly to the glass of Scotch, which hadn't left her hand since her confrontation with Aileene.

Though concentrating on the original-cast album, Dolores soon heard other things as well. Susan screaming in pain, until Bob gave her another shot of Demerol, which reduced her agony to a low moan, and then sound sleep. She then heard what she thought was a gunshot, which startled her. Running to the living room window, she looked out to see if she could tell where it had come from. She could not. But then she heard another one. Bob walked in to find her sitting shaking on the piano bench, looking out. "Dee?"

"I swear I heard gunshots," Dolores said.

"I did too. But it could have been a car backfiring."

"There are no cars moving out there." She looked alarmed. "Bob, there's a lot of people across the street. Look. I swear, there's a struggle of some kind."

Bob hurried to the window. They couldn't see well with the blowing snow, but between gusts it looked like a large group of people were at the doors and windows of the house directly across from them. "My God, it looks like they're trying to break into Flo Brennan's place!"

"It's one of the few houses on this street I didn't sell," Aileene said, joining them. "I think that's where the shots came from."

Bob stood on his toes, trying to see, but it was impossible. It was like looking at something through water. The lights in Flo's windows grew brighter as the sky got darker, and then it looked like people were crawling in through them. "Bob, maybe you should call the police."

Bob did just that. They only sighed. It was happening everywhere, they told him—the less fortunate breaking into homes of the more fortunate. "Don't tell anybody I said this," the cop offered, "but if you have a gun, I'd get it ready."

Twenty minutes later there was a loud pounding at the front door. When Bob pulled it open, Flo, a big, sturdy, pretty but completely frazzled woman wearing nothing but a housedress, fell into his arms. "Bob, Bob," she cried, "they shot Lady, they killed Lady . . ."

Bob helped her in. Aileene brought her a shawl, made her tea in an attempt to warm her. But Flo wasn't cold at all. She was in shock. "They were at the windows, just staring in at me. Lady heard them and started barking. One of them shot her, right through the glass, shot her dead on the floor of the parlor."

"My God," Dolores said. "That was the sound I heard."

Flo was crying. "And then more, into the air, and they just burst in, through the windows, strangers, invaders. Who are they? Why did they do this? How could they kill my dog?"

Aileene, whose heart was breaking over the poor woman's loss, went to her, took her in her arms and just held her, silently trying to comfort her. At that moment, Herschel walked into the room and Flo completely fell apart. Sobbing, she reached to pet him, then hugged him, then held him for dear life. The loving animal licked her cheek. She dissolved in grief.

Bob walked over. "Flo," he said, touching her shoulder, "I know this is no consolation, but just be grateful they didn't kill you too."

*   *   *

Most disasters last only a few brief moments. An earthquake can level a city in one minute, a hurricane can do its damage in just as short a time, sweeping from city to city. A tornado can carry off a house faster than you can see it coming. But a blizzard can go on for three, four, even five days, continuously battering the land with snow and cold.

In Los Angeles, the second massive storm had nothing immediately behind it to push it out of the way. The storm it nudged was caught over the Rockies between the L.A. Basin and higher mountains to the east. Out off the coast another storm front prevented movement of air to the west. So the storm stayed put, dumping foot after foot of snow on the city. The fate of Los Angeles now hinged on the air mass that lay hundreds of miles away, on the other side of the mountains, and there was nothing that could be done about it.

The snow fell through the night, with Sunday quietly turning to Monday, but under that surface were scenes of death and devastation unheard of in the history of Los Angeles. It had been—for all its uniqueness—one of the dullest days Los Angeles had ever known. There was nothing to do, nothing anyone could do. People had little choice other than to sit inside and wait, hope, pray. Unless of course that peaceful marking of time was interrupted by explosions or fires or cold. Or by desperate people at the door, people who were willing to kill dogs, or worse, other people, to get warm, to eat, to survive. The quiet pastoral white scene of the surface was a lie. It covered something ugly and desperate.

At the Kings Carriage House, everyone had gone to sleep in good spirits. The makeshift fireplace was keeping the chill out, candles and kerosene lamps lit the rooms, it felt cozy and warm. The electricity lasted until dinner was ready, so they ate by candlelight. Matthew, who never slept soundly, promised to get up every few hours to make sure the fire was still burning. By eleven p.m., everyone was sound asleep.

Until four-fifteen a.m., when suddenly there was a great shudder. It felt like an earthquake at first. The front wall facing the street shook, the whole building rattled. Everyone sat up in bed.

Michael ran in from the bedroom. "What happened?"

Matthew shrugged. Tim shook his head, half asleep. Parijata got up from her chair and crossed herself. Kenny crawled out of his sleeping bag. Jim put his glasses on. They saw that plaster had fallen from the front wall. The plaster was cracked where it looked like something had nearly come through the stucco. Penelope looked out the window. "Something on the street, flashing lights."

The guys put shoes and coats on and went outside. Pressing against the front wall of their apartment was a huge city truck with its yellow lights flashing. It had nearly gone through the building. The driver was dazed, almost incoherent, as they helped him out of the vehicle. "I was putting sand on the street . . . a car . . . lost control . . . hit hard . . ." He sat down in the snow, shaken.

"You're okay, man," Michael assured him. "It's just an accident." He looked around for another car but didn't see one. It looked like the driver had lost control and had gone into a spin, with their building acting like a guardrail.

Wendy joined them now. "Bring him inside," she called out. "Get him out of the snow."

"Yeah," Matthew offered. "Come inside Snow City and warm up. Nobody should be driving in this, even city trucks trying to help."

They started to help the man to his feet, but the next second they were all knocked down. Behind them, the dark of night flashed hot and white and dazzling, almost as if the sun had suddenly returned. But it wasn't the sun. The brightness was a wall of fire. An explosion.

As they picked themselves up from their hands and knees in the snow, they saw that their building was now on fire. Michael knew immediately what had happened. The impact of the truck hitting the wall had either knocked one of the propane tanks into the flames or had jolted the burning fire in the grill so harshly that the gas line had been severed, igniting the propane. The fuel supply had become a firebomb. The rec room was aflame.

"Rachel!" Wendy screamed.

Michael gasped. Parijata was still in there. Penelope too, and Jim and Kenny. And—Michael's heart stopped—his baby. He ran back to the door. Tim and Matthew were right behind him. So was Wendy, but Matthew turned and stopped her, holding her back. "No. It's too dangerous," he said.

Wendy screamed for her daughter as Matthew refused to let her go. "Trust him," he told her.

Wendy shouted past them, "Michael, be careful! But get her, please, get Rachel!"

Michael rubbed snow on his face and hands and disappeared into the building.

"I'm going in too," Matthew said, letting Wendy go.

The truck driver moved up to them and took Wendy's arm, trying to pull her away.

"Get her to the other side of the street," Tim said, letting go of her. He turned and followed his partner to the flames.

Matthew looked at him. "Ready?"

Tim just nodded. And they disappeared inside.

Outside, with the truck driver attempting to drag her a safe distance from the flames, Wendy held her breath, praying.

The flames rose higher, turning the whole section of the structure into an inferno.

But no one came out of the building.

The Fifth Day
Monday, January 19
High Temperature 19 Degrees, Low 10 Degrees

The exploding propane cylinders caused the fire to roar and burst through the front wall of the apartment building with such force and heat that Frosty, the mascot of a snowman they'd built the night before, was immediately scorched black and started to melt.

Wendy's mouth gaped open. It seemed like an eternity that Michael had been in there. Where was he? Had he found their daughter? What had happened to him? And to Matthew and to Tim? Where were Penelope and Kenny and Jim? The truck driver pulled her into the street. "It isn't safe," he explained. He was trying to protect her, but she yanked away, hurrying back toward the building, directly to the frame where the front door had stood. The man tackled her. "You can't go in there!"

"My baby's in there! My husband!"

Suddenly Wendy saw figures emerging from the burning building. Her heart leaped in hope. Matthew and Tim had Penelope, who was coughing violently from the smoke. Jim literally dragged Kenny Rupp to safety, and the truck driver let Wendy go so he could help them get Penelope across the street, away from the danger. Wendy didn't know if she should aid Penelope and the others or rush in in an attempt to find Michael and her daughter. "Michael," she shouted, "What happened to Michael?"

No one had an answer but Kenny. He gasped, "I saw him go into the bedroom."

Wendy turned back to the building, praying. The front section, where the fireplace had been, was the inferno. The area where Parijata's bedroom had been seemed not to be burning yet. My God—Parijata! It dawned on Wendy. "Where's Parijata?"

No one had seen her.

Inside, after wetting a towel to press to his face, Michael felt his way into the bedroom. His daughter was not on the bed. But he did see Parijata, on her knees on the floor, bending over under the window. He called her name, reaching for her, but he quickly discovered she could not react. She did not move. He turned her head to discover that her face was covered with blood coming from a gash in her head. She had been hit by one of the wooden beams that fell from the bedroom ceiling. He grasped her wrist and did not feel a pulse. He was in shock, terrified, aghast. Parijata was dead. Where was his daughter?

"Rachel? Rachel!" he cried. Then he heard the whimper. It seemed to be coming from right in front of him. Yes! She was under Parijata. Parijata had had the baby in her arms and was heading for the window when the beam struck her. There on the floor, protected by Parijata's body, which Michael now lifted off her, was his little girl, looking up at him with bright, terrified eyes.

He reached for her, feeling the wet blood of the

woman who had saved her, lifted her into his arms, which scared her so much that she started screaming. Michael put the damp cloth over her face, held it tight and quickly assessed whether he could get out through the rec room door. No way. It looked like a blast furnace out there. He turned his back to the window, lifted his foot and kicked through it with his shoe, protecting his baby as the glass shattered. Then he stepped through it, into a drift, which caused him to lose his balance—but Matthew was there to catch Rachel as Michael sprawled in the snow. Matthew took the baby, and Tim leaned over Michael as he started to vomit.

"Mike, come on, come on," Tim said, trying to pull him to his feet. "Cough, puke, do whatever, but we can't stay here. It's gonna blow!"

They crossed the street just as Matthew was putting the baby into Wendy's arms. When Penelope saw Michael and Tim coming without Parijata, she cried out in anguish, knowing what had happened. Kenny threw up from the smoke and the horror. Jim couldn't look. Behind them, their world ceased to exist as an explosion blew snow and ice and fire into the sky.

Michael threw himself over Wendy and Rachel, while the others dove for cover or ran farther down the street. Matthew pounded his fists into the snow. Tim crouched next to him, pulling him close, his arms around him, trying to comfort him. The truck driver reached out to Penelope, whom he didn't even know, touching her arm to comfort her in some small way. Wendy moaned in agony, clutching her baby to her.

And Michael started to cry.

Harry Hanwell had made it only two miles after he'd set out into the howling blizzard late the previous afternoon. Despite his ski outfit, he was freezing, and the ever-increasing, battering wind kept setting him back. At one point he thought he would join the people who had filled the lower floors of the big Hustler building at the corner of Wilshire and La Cienega. Maybe Larry Flynt had invited them all in to stay warm. God knows, Harry thought, the reading matter in the waiting room had to be pretty hot. It made him think of beautiful Calla, and he cursed his luck and kept going.

Just after midnight he found himself taking refuge in an ironic place: his father's office building, just across the street from the Los Angeles County Museum of Art, where a shelter had been set up in the lobby. He tried to get up to his father's office, but of course the elevators were not working and the stairs had been closed off. He didn't have a key anyhow. What would he do there?

In the lobby he drank hot soup and found himself a spot on the floor, where he laid his head on the fire hose and slept a good six hours. He woke to the sound of a ringing cell phone and thought for a deluded moment that he was at his desk doing business as usual. Some cell phones were working at the shelter this morning, some were not. He borrowed one to call his father. But the call would not complete. So he thought of something else. Cameron Malcolm, Michael's mentor, the family's dear friend. He called information for his cell provider. "Come on, Verizon!" Indeed, someone answered; the 800 information number was working, probably because the call center was in Nevada. Miraculously, he got through to the man. "Cameron, thank the guy that found you for me!"

"Harry?"

"Yup."

"How are you? Where are you?"

"Mars, I think. But I'm fine."

Cameron told him that he was in touch with Bob by shortwave radio. And that Dolores had made it there and everyone was okay, but that his little sister was in bad shape. Cameron assured him that he was trying to find a way to airlift them out.

That convinced Harry that he was right in heading toward Los Feliz. He would get out with them, and then he would take off forever. He knew that with the complete breakdown in communications, lawlessness would prevail for a long time and that the theft at the Getty would not be discovered for days or even weeks. And would anyone even care when the human tragedy was so overwhelming? He felt safe.

But getting to his dad's place before Cameron got them out was the important thing. Once back on the street, however, Harry could see nothing but blowing snow. It was going to be a long, hard trek to the house he'd grown up in, a lot of it straight uphill. But he would do it. He had no alternative.

Dolores was worried sick about her husband. She'd had a nearly sleepless night after the neighbor showed up in such terror. Florence Brennan was a gentle, kindhearted woman, it was clear, who would never tend toward exaggeration. Never an animal lover, but still she wondered how anyone could be desperate enough to shoot a person's beloved dog. How could they just invade her house, take it over as if they felt it was now theirs? And what if the same thing happened here? Bob had made sure the front gates were tightly closed after they got Flo settled on the sofa in the den. But gates and walls could never keep out those determined to get in, Dolores surmised. Hunger and the desire for shelter drove people to do desperate things.

She wished she had her sleeping pills, but she'd left

them in Jake's car. She smirked, wondering what had
happened to that thing. How were Jake Hughes and
his mother? But did she really care? No. She cared
about Harry, where he was, how he was, and if he
would join them. From what Flo said, there was a war
starting out there. Would Harry survive it? Hell, he'd
survived their own personal war. Why she cared about
him so deeply, she didn't understand. It was a con-
flicted love. She couldn't stand him; they did nothing
but argue or annoy one another; their marriage had
worked at first but then dissolved into a codependency
that Dr. Phil would have had a field day with.

It shocked her, this feeling that perhaps she couldn't
live without him. It made no sense, it was laughable—
hell, she was a survivor too, wasn't she? She'd never
defined herself by her man the way she felt Aileene
did. But she had come to feel so secure in this relationship that had made her feel young again, made
her feel alive again, that she doubted she could ever
live without it.

She polished off another bottle of Cragganmore at
about five in the morning. That left only one more.
She would conserve this time, she promised herself,
vowed not to let it get the best of her. But just as she
was about to go back upstairs, she heard a girl's voice
calling for help. She hurried to Susan's door, about to
turn the handle when Aileene showed up as well. The
confrontation was silent this time, and Dolores backed
off as Aileene prepared another syringe.

Upstairs once again, directly above Susan's room,
she could hear the girl's painful cries slowly reduced
to a whimper. Maybe she should ask Aileene to give
her a shot of the stuff, Dolores thought. It was probably better than booze. Sure made Susan sleep. Dolores
tried to sleep too, but it just didn't happen. She wished
she could be downstairs holding Susan's hand, wiping

her forehead, aiding in some small way. She thought Aileene's Nurse Ratched routine was cold and without feeling; everyone needed love and attention when they were sick, no matter how long it lasted or how much pain you were in. The longing to be needed made her start thinking the worst about Harry, that he'd been attacked like Flo Brennan had, that he was lying in the snow somewhere, bleeding, that he'd been killed. Or, worse, that he'd decided not to come. That he had decided he didn't need her, didn't want to be with her, didn't want to see her again. She thought her life had become a cliché, the older woman with the younger man who had kept her young, who had now grown tired of her . . .

She finally drifted into an alcoholic sleep and dreamed that Bob was sitting on the bed next to her. She tried to turn over the other way, but bumped into him. He really *was* there. "You awake?" he asked.

"Yes."

"Rest well?"

"Are you nuts?"

"Aileene is still sleeping. She was up with Susan a lot of the night."

"I'm sure. Have you heard from anyone?"

He smiled. "That's why I woke you up. We've heard from Harry."

She shot up like he'd just doused her with ice water. "How? Cell phone?"

He shook his head. "We communicated through Cameron."

"How?" she demanded.

"Shortwave radio. Cameron reminded me that Michael had one when he was a teenager—a phase he went through."

"His truck-driver phase," she quipped.

He laughed. "Harry, maybe, but not Mike. Anyhow,

I found it and we got it to work. Cameron said that Harry got through to him on somebody's cell early this morning and he's on his way."

She closed her eyes and felt good again. "Oh, thank God."

He took her hand in his. And opened up. "The toughest thing about all this is worrying for my kids, Dee."

She saw he was revealing a deep fear. She kissed his cheek. "But Harry is on his way and Michael is safe—we know that for sure now."

"Doesn't mean Harry'll get here." He got up and walked to the window. "It's bad out there. I kept getting up and staring out the front window all night long. Flo's house seems to be overrun with people. Others keep going up the hill. I heard more gunshots, I swear." He showed her that he had a pistol in his pocket. "My boys are out there somewhere. And my daughter-in-law and first grandchild."

Dolores tried to get his spirits up. "Michael is fine. You said he's with friends and they are safe."

Bob nodded. "I suppose you're right. They're probably home with everyone playing cards or something."

"I'm frightened, though, from what happened to Flo. Frightened for Harry out on the streets."

"Hey," Bob cautioned. "I know my boy, and you do too. When Harry sets his mind to something, he accomplishes it. He'll make it."

She turned to lift her glass. It was empty. The bottle sat on the floor. She picked it up and took a slug from it, never moving her eyes from Bob's.

"Dee . . ."

"I've never done that in front of anyone but Harry. I feel like I'm playing Martha in *Who's Afraid of Virginia Woolf?*" She tried to laugh, but it didn't feel genuine. "I'm scared, Bob. It's the only thing that helps."

"Dee, I want you to know something."

She wanted to hear it. "Yes?"

"You have us. Always."

Tears welled up in her eyes. Bob came back to the bed and pulled her into his strong arms. She cried. "I needed to know that, I really did," she whispered. "Sometimes . . . sometimes it gets so lonely and I get so afraid . . . if only Harry could say that . . ."

"He feels it," Bob assured her, pulling his head back to look into her black eyes. "He can be a shit, we all know that, but he does have a heart and that heart loves you."

Suddenly they heard Herschel barking. Bob grabbed the pistol from his pocket, jumped up and hurried downstairs. Dee followed on his heels, but once they got to Susan's room they saw that it was not dangerous—the dog was indeed looking out the window, but at a coyote that seemed cold and disoriented in the middle of the pool patio.

"Auntie Dee," Susan said in her drugged state, using her favorite term of affection for her much older sister-in-law, "will you sit with me for a while?"

Dee looked thrilled to do so. "Yes, darling, of course I will."

Bob smiled at the scene. It was what they both needed right now. "If the coyote's gone, I'll take the dog out and feed him." When he walked out, he saw that Dee was glowing, the first time he'd seen her smile since she'd arrived.

Michael and Matthew walked into the building across the street from the Kings Carriage House, where they had spent the rest of the early-morning hours, and told the others what the fire department—no trucks could get there, only two inspectors had come in an SUV—had learned. The jolt of the accident did indeed rupture the propane tank line leading to the gas burners, causing the canister to explode. The building had been reduced to rubble; it was astonishing that only Parijata had been killed. Her loss was devastating, but it could have been much worse.

"There's a shelter they want us to go to," Matthew informed them. Everyone realized they could not stay forever in the crowded lobby of the small building where they'd taken refuge.

"Hollywood High," Michael added. "Over on Highland."

Tim turned to Matthew. "I could help the animals there. We all could be of use."

Wendy nodded wholeheartedly. "I need to be there too."

So it was agreed. They would go to Hollywood High School. They dressed as warmly as they could, thanked the people who had helped them and went outside again. As they gathered in front of the building on Kings Road for one last look at what had been their home, they saw two men carrying a black plastic body bag from what had been Parijata's apartment. Michael felt something give in his stomach, as if not quite believing it was real. Wendy held back tears. Everyone was silent. As the men passed what was left of the snowman, it collapsed into the snow.

Then, braving the wind and the icy cold—they pulled their scarves up over their mouths because you could get frostbite in ten minutes—they set out toward yet another home.

Harry Hanwell felt as though he'd been walking for months. He was tired, irritable, cold and hungry. He

spent an hour off his feet in a restaurant that had heat
but no food, camped there along with some homeless
people—the most susceptible to the storm's fury—and
a waitress who made him laugh, one of those big girls
with lacquered hair and a thousand jokes who seemed
to have been born in a coffee shop. Oddly enough,
no one questioned the fire hose slung over his shoulder. When he slept, he slept atop it, as he had the
night before in his father's office lobby.

Emerging onto the street again, Harry saw two surreal scenes that seemed as if they had come from opposite movies. In the center of what had been Wilshire
Boulevard and was now reminiscent of a ski slope,
five little kids, bundled so tightly that they looked like
little blow-up dolls, were playing in the snow, tossing
snowballs at one another while two mothers looked
on, shivering but enjoying the joy they could give their
children. Just halfway down the same block, Harry
saw feet sticking out from a pile of white that had
blown into a storefront, the protected area that led to
the front door. Someone had frozen to death while
trying to hide from the blizzard's fury, and was still
there under the drift.

He stopped in a church that was now doubling as a
shelter. He waited there only long enough to thaw out
yet again and get a couple of high-protein bars from
a girl who was handing them out. He drank some
water, took a bottle with him for the trek, used the
bathroom and even brushed his teeth with his fingers
and some Crest from a tube that someone had left
lying there.

When he set out again, the sugar and the rest had
ignited his energy, and he pushed through the drifts
faster than before. All along the way, he saw few people. Now and then he glimpsed a vehicle, usually rescue operations, moving down one street or another,

but the landscape was desolate. Everyone was smartly staying inside.

In pulling the fire hose back up when it started to slide down his shoulder, he felt a lump inside his coat. Reaching in, he was shocked to find the cell phone that the woman at his father's building had let him use. Not even thinking, he'd put it in his pocket after using it. He hadn't meant to steal it. He doubted it would work, but he tried anyway, and indeed, there was no signal. A block later, he gave it another shot, since there was still some battery time left. But it was useless. Three blocks later, he gave it one more try, and this time it was hopeful—he reached a recording after dialing Dee that told him the circuits were over-loaded. He kept trying every few blocks anyway, but it never rang through.

If the average citizen of Los Angeles felt helpless in the face of the crisis, prisoners locked up in cells felt completely vulnerable. One jail in particular was more conducive to the inmates' terror, the one in downtown L.A. where the cells were on the top floor, above a large municipal building. There, one hundred feet up, the wind and snow howled fiercely, incessantly, much worse than at ground level. It was here that Charles Manson had spent much time years before while he was being tried. It was also here that Jeffrey King had been held after being arrested on the rape charge.

Tensions were so high that the prisoners were confined to their cells for fear of a riot. There was no way to avoid the cold in the cellblock areas. Heating had always been inadequate. Clothing was at a premium. Food was diminishing. Freedom was always prominent in a prisoner's mind, but with the weather crisis and the sense of doom, the notion of getting out was replaced simply by a wish to stay alive. The prisoners felt they were locked in a concentration camp.

The problem was a difficult one. Inmates could be moved to other locations only in the best of weather, with the best protection. Half the police force in the city couldn't even be located. There was trouble enough on the streets; a jail break wasn't needed, and that might happen if the officials tried to move the men. The outlook was bleak.

Below, on the street, the occasional relative came by, hoping to give food to their loved ones, but the doors were shut tight. The place was understaffed and the risk of letting anyone else in too great. A woman stood under a small window at the Sybil Brand Institute, the Los Angeles detention center for women. Her sick and hungry drug-ridden daughter was in the building, and she had brought hot soup in a thermos. Not being able to get in, she just stood there in the terrible weather, chilled, crying, praying.

In a sense, her daughter had it easier. Whereas her mother had to deal with the realities of the storm, the girl had only to sit and wait. For redemption, or for doom.

On a wall in a shared cell, a woman had written DEATH TO PIGS. LET THEM FREEZE.

On a bathroom wall in the men's jail, another familiar message appeared: FOLLOW THE KING. HE WILL LEAD THE KINGS TO SAFETY.

Loretta Zane felt the gun pressing to her neck. The black kid was shaking, not only from cold but from his own terror. He needed a fix, or food, or sleep, something that would calm his bloodshot eyes. He'd shown up only minutes before, along with another band of people who were now homeless, people who had been living in the vicinity of the Hollywood Freeway and Silverlake Boulevard, where most everything had burned through the night. Fires were rampant. Even the LaBianca house had burned down, forcing Loretta and her band of misfits to take over Florence Brennan's house. The boy went directly to the kitchen when he arrived, only to find it stripped of anything to eat. Back in the living room, he pulled the gun on Loretta, who he'd been told was the leader.

"What are you doing?" she snapped at him. "Put the gun down. Jeffrey King is not your enemy."

"Who?" he asked with a blink of his eyes.

"Jeffrey King. Many of us are his followers. He'll help you."

"You talking Jeffrey My Man King the Lakers star?"

She smiled with pride. "Oh yes. *The* King."

"He gonna feed me? He gonna feed my mama?"

"When this is over, we'll have a new beginning, a utopia. We won't want for nourishment."

"I hungry now." He waved the gun in her face. "How come there be no food in this house?"

"We ate it. There are a lot of people here," she said to him, pretending he was not scaring her.

"My mama, she not be eating in two days."

"The other houses have food. Go take one." Loretta motioned to the front door. "Take the big house with the gates across the street. You'll find a feast."

He lowered the pistol. "I'm cold, you know?"

She touched his hand, motherly. "I know. We all are. But it'll change. We'll make it through. Jeffrey will keep us alive."

"The King be a great player, but I don't think he gonna give me some chicken tonight, you dig?"

"Jeffrey King is more than a former ballplayer."

"He crazy, Mama say."

She just grinned. "Stick with us and you'll see how

crazy he is." She looked into his young eyes. "You have a gun. That's good. Get some others together, take that house across the street," she urged. "Bring us some food back."

The boy set out, looking as if he was going to do just that.

Cameron was talking to Bob excitedly on the short-wave radio. "We got a call up here from Michael. From a soldier whose vehicle they were in."

"No way." Bob was thrilled but surprised. "Whose vehicle? Where? What happened? How are they?"

"On their way to Hollywood High, the shelter there. Their building burned down."

"My God!"

"But the family's okay. Wendy knew about the shelter—it's an automatic part of any disaster plan for the city. Christ, Bob, you should see it from up here—when you can see through the snow. Buildings are burning everywhere, heavy black smoke is swirling to the heavens, and there's no fire department left. Water mains are bursting."

"My pool drain valve froze up like an ice sculpture."

"South Central is bad. Murders, looting like crazy."

"Isn't the Guard on the streets?"

"Looters are simply trying to stay alive. Why stop them? Markets are cleared out, delivery trucks that got stuck in the snow have been emptied—one Albertson's driver was killed to get to the eggs and milk. Even ships out in Long Beach Harbor have been attacked."

"I didn't know it was that bad. We live a pretty rarefied life in these hills."

"There's a sense of doom and panic on the streets. Can't say I blame them."

"What's the president doing about it?" Bob asked.

"He's bringing the Marines up from Camp Pendleton by boat, to land on the beaches at Venice, Manhattan, Redondo, Santa Monica, Will Rogers. We're going to need strength, authority. Only men in uniform can provide that. It's partly psychological, and it's important as hell. How's Susan?"

"Bad."

"She hold out a few more days?"

"She'll have to."

Cameron heard the fear in Bob's voice. "Be straight with me, my friend. Can she make it a few more days?"

Bob was as honest as he could be. "I doubt it."

Cameron was silent for a moment. Then he said, "I'm working on something, Bob. I'm trying to get her out. I promise you, I'll do something for her. Just give me a little time."

"I believe you, Cameron. Thanks."

Bob went into the library and told Aileene, Dolores and Flo what he'd heard. Aileene was knitting, Flo was lost in a coffee table book on flowers, and Dolores was trying to read a magazine, but she kept looking out the window. Her Scotch was gone. But Bob still had brandy, whiskey and vodka. And she knew that was the last of it, so she was trying to pace herself, to hold out. If this thing lasted much longer, she thought, she'd be stealing holy wine from the good fathers next door. No, Harry was coming. She had to believe that. She had to remain in control. He would come and then she wouldn't drink again. Ever. She promised God, if he somehow got there, she would quit.

Bob was assessing the height of the drifts from the window near the piano when he saw a curious sight. A group of people—they looked young, dressed in gang chic, some blacks and Hispanics, he was sure, but not positive about all of them—were making their way up the driveway of the house just under them, on the other side of the brick wall. He feared for Robin and Rosie, the two women who had the kind of relationship that anyone, straight or gay, dreamed of having: they'd been together for thirty years. They'd both had big corporate jobs, then got out to reinvent themselves. Robin (who was a reader) now ran a used-book store, while Rosie (who had the wanderlust) had opened her own travel agency. Since the little bookstore on Vermont Avenue virtually ran itself, they found themselves traveling a lot. They were seldom home, for the discount Rosie got them on cruise ships provided the best place in the world for Robin to read books. In fact, both Bob and Aileene had thought they were in the Caribbean when the snow started. Until last night, when Aileene noticed lights were on in their house.

Bob had gone over by the back way, through the only opening in the brick wall, the connecting wooden gate off his driveway, forging through the snow, to make sure that they were all right. Indeed, they were, they said, "snug as bugs in rugs." They'd invited Bob in for tea, which he was delighted to drink, and regaled him with stories of unusual events over the years on this very street, for they'd lived here even longer than he and Aileene had. A dusting of snow—of all things—back in the early 1970s, which caused a big accident right out front of Bob's house. A gas-main leak that forced all the residents to evacuate overnight in the early 1980s. The time when some escapee from a mental institution was hiding in the center of the hill, right down in back of Bob's tennis court, and five helicopters with high-intensity searchlights suddenly turned midnight to noon and scared the hell out of everyone. And the LaBianca murders. "That was probably the worst," Rosie said.

"No." Robin disagreed. "The worst was when they re-created the whole gruesome thing by filming— twice—*Helter Skelter* on the street. It was ghastly."

Bob had left feeling sure they were safe, healthy, warm and happy. But now, watching what looked like a group of derelicts forging up their driveway, he was worried. Would they have invited them over? Bob didn't know much about their families or friends, but he and Aileene knew they had big hearts. Perhaps Bob was only being jumpy, Aileene cautioned. Perhaps this was none of his business. Flo said she didn't trust it at all. It was exactly what had happened to her.

Bob went downstairs, to a locked cabinet in the furnace room, just in case. From the cabinet he pulled out a shotgun and ammunition. He wasn't really sure why he was doing it. He already had a pistol. But Cameron's words about the looters, the lawlessness, had given him pause. And Flo's experience was proof of the inherent danger out there. He took the gun upstairs and hid it behind the door of the broom closet off the laundry room. He didn't want the women to be alarmed.

In the library, Aileene saw Dolores had no interest in the magazine she was holding. "You should do something to occupy the time."

"Like?" she snapped.

Aileene looked at a loss. She glanced at her cookbook collection on a shelf. "Bake."

Dolores almost laughed. "Bake?"

Flo laughed. "There goes my Atkins diet."

Aileene said, "The gas is still on. It'll go, just like

the electricity will go. It's out in most places, Cameron told Bob."

While the entire notion of baking was foreign to Dee, Flo smiled and looked enthusiastic. "Oh, heck with Atkins. It sounds like a good idea."

Aileene's voice got very perky suddenly, as if Flo's enthusiasm filled her with inspiration. "Come on, Dee. We'll bake up everything we can get our hands on while the oven still works."

Dolores looked at her as if she was speaking Chinese. "You must be kidding."

Aileene stood up. "It would be very constructive."

Then Dolores got it. "Oh, shit. Right. Get me off the bottle."

"That isn't it at all!" Aileene retorted.

"Don't patronize me."

"How dare you? I was just thinking of something to do to help."

Flo tried to say something, but Dolores turned away and muttered, "I want to help Susan, but you act like I'm carrying the plague. You watch me like I'm some kind of zoo animal. Like I'm deranged, or diseased, drinking in your precious house. *Let's bake cookies, Dee!*" Dolores almost spat. "Please."

Aileene lost it. "*Drunk*. Yes, that's what you are. And it isn't helping any of us. You ask for liquor as if it's plasma and you sit here on your big butt staring out the window in some lost hope, and what are you going to do if, for some reason, God forbid, he *doesn't* show up and the bottles are suddenly all empty?"

Flo stood with her mouth open, aghast, not knowing what to say.

Bob entered, stunned by what he was hearing. Dolores, at a loss for words, feeling slapped across the face, jumped to her feet and ran upstairs, tears breaking at the landing. Aileene sat down, slumped in the chair, and put her head in her hands. Flo wisely retreated from the room.

"Honey," Bob asked, "why did you do that? She didn't deserve that."

Aileene only muttered, "I am not sorry I said it."

He just stared at her, gave her time. In a minute she looked up at him, remorseful. "I was too harsh. I realize that." He sat on the arm of the chair and took her hand. "Oh, Bob, I'm just so afraid, on edge, and everything's getting to me. I can't stand it that the kids aren't here! I want Harry here more than Dee does, and I'm faulting her for worrying? What's the matter with me?"

"We're all pressed to the limit," Bob said, trying to comfort her. "But there's no sense in making it worse. Dee is very fragile, Aileene."

"Aren't we all right now?" Aileene closed her eyes. She needed time. Time to sit there and think about how to go up and apologize to her daughter-in-law.

When Bob crouched down to put another log on the fire there, he froze when he heard the gunshot. It sounded as if it had come from the driveway. He ran into the living room. Aileene followed him. Flo came down the steps. "They're doing it again!"

Bob waved the women back. "No! Stay there. Stay away!"

They obeyed as he fell to his knees and crept along the wall to the window.

But when he peeked out, he saw nothing but white snow falling.

The U.S. Army truck pulled up to the doors leading to the Hollywood High School gymnasium, and twenty-five cold but hopeful people got out, among them Wendy and Michael and Rachel, Tim and Matthew, Penelope, Jim and Kenny—all that was left of life in the Kings Carriage House. They walked inside, into the warm, humid air, where their faces fell. The place was in utter chaos, with hundreds upon hundreds of people on cots, on the floor, crammed into every available inch of space, children crying, dogs barking, hopeless faces, doctors and nurses, the smell of medicine and sweat and tears.

The group settled together in a corner, but within half an hour Tim had begun to help the paramedics, and Wendy was comforting other families who'd just come in from the cold. Even Michael sat with a group of youngsters who recognized him from television, telling them jokes and stories to get their mind off the situation. Matthew felt proud watching Tim move among the examining tables in a white doctor's coat. Finally they were doing something, not merely waiting it out. Matthew pitched in and rolled bandages and felt useful.

Hours later, Tim joined him on the single cot they were able to procure. It was not comfortable, but they slept in one another's arms. Michael caught a few winks as well, but Rachel was fussy and Wendy needed to hold her. Kenny listened to music. A girl he thought was pretty offered to let him use her iPod for a while. "I downloaded a lot of stuff," she said. "Legally." Jim Farrick sat riveted by a woman from Russia who told a group of people a harrowing story of one awful winter under communism. Penelope was wracked with memories of the fire and sat, awake, her head pounding.

Wendy too. The image of their building aflame and of Parijata's body being carried out in that black plastic bag would haunt her forever.

It was twilight when an exhausted Harry Hanwell reached the corner of Wilshire and Western, and turned left, feeling a momentary excitement because at the top of Western Avenue lay Los Feliz. But it was a long way still, and he felt he was going to die. He was hungry and wet and cold and ornery. But he'd make it. And to accomplish that, his body needed fuel.

Food. There was a restaurant across the street. The doors were wide open. He headed toward it. Once he was inside, the four people huddled there eyed him with suspicion, and a woman told him there was no food, it had been gone a long time ago. None of them so much as questioned the fire hose over his shoulder. When he turned to go, a voice came from what he assumed was the kitchen. "Found something, Stella!"

Stella, who'd been the one to tell Harry that coming there was for naught, jumped to her feet. "It's mine!" she growled, as if she had just found gold in the hills and was staking her claim. "It's ours!"

A man came from the kitchen carrying a huge vat of ice cream. Ice cream, of all things, in this weather. "Butter pecan," he said, "if you can believe that. Hey, Stella? My favorite flavor. Am I telling the truth?"

Stella found a soup spoon and dug into it. When Harry and another man moved closer, she grabbed a knife—albeit a bread knife—and faced them angrily. But the man pulled her hand down. "Stella, they're hungry too. There's plenty to go around." And for the next half hour, all of them feasted on the delicious ice cream, until it was all gone.

Suddenly, however, a huge Army vehicle pulled up on the street outside. Three other people rushed into the restaurant and told Harry and the others to be careful, that they were shooting looters. Indeed, uniformed men with guns were coming toward the building. The squatters ran through the kitchen to get out the back way.

In the kitchen, Harry saw a sack of sugar, one of
flour, a plastic bottle of vegetable oil larger than the
ones he'd always passed by in Costco. As he hurried
out the back door to the alley, he was surprised at
what he found. People were rushing from the rear
entrances to shops that lined the street, their arms
filled with stuff they were carrying away. A cop fired
a gun into the air. "Stop! We will shoot looters!"

"Like hell," a man called out. "I got four kids to
feed and my old father too. Nobody's gonna shoot me
for feeding my family."

No one shot anyone. Harry made his way up the
alley, wanting only to get back to the relative sanity
of the street. He pushed through drifts, colliding with
a woman who was hurrying out of a clothing store,
carrying sweaters under her arm. Harry reached out
to keep her from falling into the snow, but as he did
a bullet passed between them. "Shit!" He fell on top
of the woman as another shot hit the wall behind
where his head had just been. He swore that he'd felt
it singe his forehead as it passed by.

Suddenly several kids dashed out of the same clothing store, dragging coats and sweaters with them. Behind them emerged a man with a gun in his hand,
shooting aimlessly at them. A Guardsman jumped
from his perch atop a fence and shot into the snow in
front of the man, preventing him from killing one of
the looters, giving Harry a chance to grab the man's
leg and cause him to fall. The soldiers arrested him
and dragged him off.

One told Harry, "It was his store, and he's got a
right to protect it. But you don't kill kids for a goddamned coat."

The woman Harry had run into brushed snow off
her shoulders. "I think you saved my life, mister."

Harry's face suddenly felt hot, as if someone had sprayed him with coffee or poured boiling water on his head.

The woman's smile turned to horror. "My God, you're hit!"

When Harry reached up to touch his face, his hand was covered with blood. He almost fainted.

"I'm a nurse," the woman said. "Let me see." She studied the wound above his hairline. "That was close. I think your hair held the blood for a while—it's matted with it. But it didn't penetrate. It just grazed you."

"Jesus," Harry muttered.

The woman thought for a moment. "Come with me. My name's Janohn."

"Who?"

She grinned. "Janohn. Janohn Bunck."

"You make that up?" Harry asked.

"My mom did." She looked at his head. "I'll bandage you up," she said. "Least I can do." Then she pulled him toward the door of the clothing store.

"I'm headed up Western," Harry protested.

"Not tonight, you're not. You're coming down the street with me so you can have a good night's sleep and save that blood for tomorrow." She glanced up at the sky. " 'Cause you're gonna need it, buster."

At her house, which took them almost an hour to get to even though it was only three blocks away, she and her oldest son cleaned and bandaged the wound while Harry joked about the world crawling with strange "J" names—Janohn and Jinger. Blood had run down Harry's neck and soaked his sweatshirt; he took it off so she could wash it for him. The oldest kid, Augustine, a high school wrestler, gave him one of his that was even softer and warmer. "So, you rest a bit," Janohn finally said, "while I put together some dinner.

It's gonna be makeshift, but we have a good amount of stuff in the pantry."

Harry smiled. "Thank you. You're very kind."

Later, as he sat eating with the woman, her mother and her three kids, Harry kept glancing toward the little covered porch that they'd come through to get to the kitchen. That was where he'd left the fire hose. It worried him, but there was no way to get it inside, no way to hold on to it while he slept, or it would draw unnecessary attention to itself. After the warm food and delicious hot chocolate, Harry curled up on a battered sofa in the corner of the big kitchen, falling asleep immediately, even as the women did the dishes, banging pots and pans, the kids talking all around him.

Snow was exhausting.

They had waited for more gunshots, but they never came. Except for the blowing snow, everything outside the house seemed quiet. Lights at Robin and Rosie's continued to burn. Bob even thought he got a glimpse of one of them through their dining room window. Perhaps he was overreacting, or perhaps the shots had come from across the street where the squatters were still occupying Florence's house. When the lights in Robin and Rosie's started to flicker, Bob looked at one of his own living room lamps, waiting for them to do the same. They did.

Dolores had just come from the shower upstairs when everything went black. Just as she muttered, fishing around in the dark for the candle Aileene had put on the dresser, they came back on again. She lit the candle to be safe, and plugged in the hair dryer. And that did it. Blackness. The power was gone completely. With a wet head wrapped in a towel, Dolores brushed her teeth by candlelight.

They had known, of course, that this would happen. It had happened all over town, so they had candles ready, but it was another thing again to have to use them. The house took on an eerie glow, not nearly as romantic as it was when they dined by candlelight. Bob lit a rusty kerosene camping lantern he'd brought in from the garage and set it up in the kitchen. It looked ludicrous sitting in the middle of the polished-granite counter. But it worked.

The wind howled through the fir trees. It seemed to be getting even colder now that night was approaching. Dolores stretched out on the sofa in front of the fireplace, pulling her fur coat over her for more warmth. She'd accepted Aileene's apology half-heartedly, which did little to relieve the tension between them. Flo found a book of crossword puzzles and immersed herself in them. Aileene sat in one of the chairs facing the fireplace, knitting. Dolores tried to make conversation to take the edge off. "I hope Harry's somewhere safe for the night."

"Yes," Aileene responded.

"I'm sure the other kids are fine. There's resilience in youth." Dolores was truly trying to make Aileene not worry so much.

"Yes," was the cold response.

Dolores tried again. "Susan will make it through. It's got to change. It can't go on like this forever."

"I hope you're right," Aileene responded more warmly. The truth was Aileene was indeed worried about all her children, but she was worried about Dolores as well. Her dependency on alcohol was almost more than she could take. It seemed to have tripled since she'd shown up. She had finished off the Scotch and was down to the last of their liquor now. There was vodka, but what would she do when that was gone? Aileene looked at her sitting there all bundled up, loaded to the gills, watching the last of their ice cubes swirl around in her glass. *Maybe she's the lucky one,* Aileene thought. *She's lost in a fog, in her own world.* It was Dee's way of dealing with it. Why did it bother her so much? Aileene, whose fingers were nearly raw from knitting so tirelessly, so obsessively, wondered who was the fool here.

And yet why wasn't she rip-snorting drunk? Aileene just realized that. Dolores wasn't really plastered. She had teetered on the stairs on the way to the shower, prompting Aileene's fears that she might slip and fall in the shower stall. She slurred some words, but wisely didn't speak much. Booze usually made people more talkative; it seemed to have the opposite effect on Dolores, who was normally quite gregarious. The weather and the liquor and the lack of happiness in her life had depressed her. Aileene felt truly sorry for her and wished she could express it. And that she hadn't let her temper get the best of her.

Aileene set her knitting down and walked to the window overlooking the front yard. She strained to see into Robin and Rosie's dining room window, where candles were now burning. Yes, they'd been wrong about the gunshots. They hadn't come from there. And she was glad to see it, sure that the girls, who were gracious hosts, had simply opened their door to help shelter people with them. There was nothing to worry about, nothing amiss.

Walking back to her chair, Aileene stopped and un-wrapped Dolores' hand from her drink and set the glass on the coffee table. She'd fallen asleep balancing it on her chest. In the reflection of the dancing flames in the fire, Aileene stared at the woman. She had been so beautiful, movie star beautiful. She still was, in a way. Everyone blamed Harry for what had happened to her, for what she'd become. Everyone but Aileene—it wasn't just his fault. People had control over their lives and destinies, she believed firmly, and one person could not completely change another, rescue another, cause him or her to give up their spirit. Dolores had to have been willing to give up, in collusion with it, enabling the downward slide.

But on another level, Aileene felt sorry for anyone who would choose to be Harry's wife. She knew how formidable Harry could be, and she realized that no woman she'd ever met could match him for sheer drive. She surmised that Dolores was more fragile than most who attain great career heights. The stories about Streisand, J. Lo, or even old names like Barbara Stanwyck and Joan Crawford being bitches were probably true—but they had to be, didn't they, to make it in the first place? Aileene doubted that Dolores, for all her talent, had ever really had the guts to sustain a career in show business. If she had, she wouldn't have gotten lost so easily, wouldn't have given up. Harry, for all his greed and arrogance and lack of consideration, really did try to revive her career. He cared about her, at least at one time. What Aileene faulted Dolores for was the fact that she seemed to put it all on Harry's shoulders—hell, she was the performer, she was the star, she had an obligation to shine at what he arranged for her—and took no responsibility for her fading talent and aging charms. The booze didn't help either.

Then too, Harry had played his fair share, and no one knew it better—and it was no more painful to anyone—than his mom. He had a roving eye. He deserted Dee for weeks at a time, giving other clients more attention than he gave the client who was also his wife. Their arguments were brutal, legendary. How did any spouse deal with tabloid headlines about her husband and Madonna? Or all the others they'd linked Harry with, right or wrong.

Harry could suffer too, and had spent many a night back in Los Feliz since their marriage, running from Dolores' "drunken rages" and fits. And Harry wasn't the only one to leave; Dolores walked out on him countless times. Off to Mexico, Paris. One time she quite literally disappeared, and it took two months and a private detective to find her in the Caribbean. They made up, as always. But it didn't last long. The fights continued, the jealousies, the infidelities, the knock-down-drag-outs, and the days of wine and roses.

Aileene knew that Dee's real humiliation came because the names Harry was linked with were not only other women, but *younger* women. Not that Madonna was a spring chicken anymore, but certainly she was younger than Dolores. It was easier for a guy Harry's age to get young girls than it was for a woman Dee's age to find men Harry's age—May/December from either perspective—but the fact that it was always so public made Aileene feel a sense of shame. Harry was constantly being pictured not only with actresses he represented as one of CAA's top agents, but with waitresses, ski bunnies, flight attendants and unnamed "companions" as well. Aileene suspected that the constant media coverage of her seclusion and his dalliances cemented Dolores' relationship with the bottle. It was her way out. Perhaps too, because her drinking caused him such grief, it was her way of getting back at him for the way he hurt her with the affairs.

Over the years, Aileene had seen Dee falling-down drunk only a few times, and though it sickened her, she tolerated it. Harry always apologized for the discomfort. Aileene and Bob accepted it once they learned Dee had tried to dry out at clinics three

times—even Betty Ford—and failed, but Aileene had
never seen her drink what she'd put away just in this
one day. Her body and brain had to be saturated. Why
was she not comatose? Or was she? Aileene shook
her a little, and Dolores awakened slightly, rubbed her
nose, said, "Yes, fire . . ." And went back to sleep.
Feeling relief that she was still there, Aileene wondered if it was the fright, the fear, that was keeping
her so loosely tethered to sobriety? Was it the worry
about Harry and the panic over the weather that was
keeping her from passing out cold? Scotch. All that
Scotch. And . . . Aileene reached out and turned the
bottle around. And now vodka.

"Honey?" It was Bob's voice.

"Yes, I'm sorry." She looked up at him in the doorway, appearing a little startled.

"You okay?"

She nodded.

"I'm closing up the library. There are too many
windows, the air seems to be coming in from around
them."

"This is a well-constructed house," Flo said. "Built
when? Long before mine, I imagine."

"1929," Aileene answered. She knew the age of
every structure in the area.

Flo shook her head. "Mine felt like there were holes
in the wall."

Bob said, "The library is feeling that way to me
with the wind that's picked up."

The women helped Bob carry the plants that sat
near the library windows into the living room. If they
could save them, they would. Aileene wondered what
would be left alive outside after this stuff melted.
Could anything survive this brutal cold? Then she
looked at the shelves and pulled down four books she

had always planned to read. "This might be the pro-
verbial rainy day."

"And then some." Bob shut the heating vent, pulled
the shades, blew out the candle, closed the double
doors and locked them.

"Why did you do that?" Aileene asked.

He shrugged. "Dunno." But he did know. The gunshot earlier had worried him. When he looked out the
upstairs windows and could see past the swirling snow,
he saw bright orange spots on the horizon. Fires. A
great portion of the city was in flames. Where would
those people go, those who were burned out of their
apartments and houses? Here. They would come here.
Uphill. To the Hollywood hills, Beverly Hills, Los
Feliz. And that sent shivers through him. He had
made sure, without his wife knowing, that every window and door in the big house was secured. But still
it worried him.

The house next door, Robin and Rosie's house,
where he could see a candle burning on the dining
room table and several figures moving past it—that
was what worried him most.

Harry opened his eyes to see someone lying on the
battered futon across the room from him. It was Augustine. The house was quiet now, and only one candle burned atop the TV. "You been in dreamland,
man," the boy said.

"I was tired."

"I usually play video games at night."

"Not tonight, huh?"

The boy shrugged. "Sucks."

Harry sat up and rubbed the sleep from his eyes.
"What's your favorite? Video game."

"Practice Run."

"Cool."

"But I like *Grand Theft Auto* almost as much. Hey, your head okay? Mom told me to ask you."

Harry had almost forgotten he'd been shot. He looked at the wound in a small mirror on the wall. "Fine. Don't even feel it."

The boy got up. He was wearing baggy black basketball shorts and a thick sweatshirt. He found himself a box of Ritz Bits in a cabinet and offered Harry some. "Peanut butter."

"Thanks." Harry took a handful. "So, you wrestle, huh? What school?"

"First-year community college. Ma couldn't afford to send me to a big school, but that's okay."

"What are you studying?"

"Girls."

Harry laughed. "And?"

"Communications."

"What do you want to do?"

The boy started laughing. "Tell the truth, I want to be a weatherman."

"Shit," Harry said. "My brother is one. I suspect there's a mob out hunting him as we speak."

"Who is he?"

"Michael Hanwell."

The boy lit up. "He's awesome! Very cool. The stand-up weather guy."

"He's nuts, all right." Harry popped the rest of the Ritz into his mouth. "What do they call you?"

"Huh?"

"For short. Gus?"

"Augie." The boy brought his feet up under him. "Hey, what's in the hose?"

Harry's antennae went rigid. "None of your business."

"I'm curious by nature."

Harry suddenly wondered if the boy was being a

clever dude or was he playing him? "Papers. Important papers."

"Keeps 'em dry." The kid looked impressed. Like Harry was smart. "That's pretty ingenious. What do you do?"

"I'm an agent. Talent agent. Movies and stuff."

"You know Jon Stewart?"

"Sure."

The kid grinned. "Tell him hi." He pulled a blanket around his naked legs.

"You sleeping in here too?"

"This is where I always sleep. This is no palace, man."

Harry had never even considered that people might sleep in the room off the kitchen. When you had seven thousand square feet with two guest suites plus a separate pool house you didn't think about such things.

"You saving, like, contracts and stuff?"

"Pardon me?" Harry said.

"In the hose. To keep dry. Like Brad Pitt's latest movie deal?"

Harry grinned. "Something like that."

"I mean it," the boy said. "Tell them Augustine Bunck said hello."

"I'll have them send you autographed pictures."

Harry tossed and turned for nearly an hour, listening to the wind rattle the screens outside the windows. He made sure the boy was fast asleep before he even dared close his eyes, figuring he might want to actually see Brad's "contracts." Several times in the night, he thought about getting up and slipping out, but in the dark with the wind doing what it was doing, he knew he wouldn't get far. He needed to recharge his batteries, gain strength. Sleep would do that. The kid was harmless. Another weather nut like Mike. Go to sleep, Harry Hanwell. You got a hell of a trek in front of you tomorrow.

*   *   *

Cameron rubbed his eyes as he looked over reports coming in from designated shelters all over the city. "We're going to have to get people to open private homes as well," he said to General Van Hecke. "All the public buildings and movie theaters and churches and soundstages won't hold the people who have already lost their homes."

Van Hecke laughed. "We're supposed to expect that movie stars will open the mansion doors and welcome the masses? Try getting past the electric gates and the ferocious dogs of those compounds in Bel Air. Fat chance."

"Report in that says Jeffrey King's mansion went up in smoke."

"I heard it was a bomb."

Cameron groaned. "He won't be universally mourned."

"Who says he didn't survive it?"

Cameron nodded. "You know, I always wondered what 'bleak' meant. But I think I now know." Then he took a deep breath. "General, I want to request something personal. There's a family I'm very close to, and my goddaughter is sick. Very sick. I want them to be the first people out of here when we can do it . . ."

Bob sat with Aileene in the little sitting room off their master bedroom. Even though the furnace that provided heat for the upstairs was still working, they'd decided to let Dolores sleep it off in front of the fire in the living room. Flo took Dee's place in the guest room bed. Susan had been given another shot, and so she was good for the night, though Bob would look in on her now and then. Bob and Aileene's bedroom was very warm—thank God for old-fashioned gravity furnaces—and they decided to hole up there as if they were in a small cabin in the Canadian Rockies. Banff. Lake Louise. Someplace gorgeously romantic and remote.

"Listen to this," Bob said, reading from a book. *"The storm fostered a spirit of camaraderie in the city. Bars were jammed with customers who could not get home. At the Rail Bar, bartender Dick Lewis ordered ten patrons to leave as each group of ten entered; he feared the floor would cave in under the crowd's weight. His wife, Dee"*—Bob smiled—"Imagine that!" He continued. *"His wife, Dee, stood guard at the door with an iron fist."*

"What are you reading?"

"Snow stories. Paperback I found on the shelf. Probably one of Michael's. This is about the Big Freeze of 1977." Bob read on. *"At Salvatore's Italian Gardens Restaurant in upstate New York, free sandwiches for everyone replaced costly Chateaubriand."*

"God," Aileene said with a grin, "Harry would starve first."

"Fire departments set up soup and spaghetti lines. The Salvation Army served meals to twenty-five thousand people, clothed four thousand, and gave medical supplies to three thousand. Citizens offered their snowmobiles for emergency rescue missions."

"You think anyone in Los Feliz owns such a thing?"

"Residents without electricity or gas found others willing to take them into their homes." Bob stopped and took a deep breath. "I could be reading about L.A. Just change the location." He read on and his expression changed. Then again, aloud, *"Buffalo also discovered its dark side during the siege. There was widespread looting of abandoned vehicles—"*

"Dee's car, for sure," Aileene interjected.

"—and vacant jewelry stores and drugstores. On a sin-

gle night, sixty arrests were made by justifiably angry police. But, finally, Buffalo got help. President Carter—"

"Carter!" she gasped. It had been a long time ago.

"President Carter first declared a regional state of emergency so that federal funds could be used to remove snow and restore health and safety services. The Army, under the direction of Lieutenant Parker Van Hecke, flew three hundred men in from—" Bob paused. "He got a few more stripes since then."

"Money from Congress won't help us," Aileene said. "Buffalo may have been hit hard, but they're used to it. Everyone there keeps long johns in the closet and snow boots and big pots of winter stew on the stove. We don't. We don't know from this kind of thing. We've lost our lights and next will be our heat and our wits. No one can fly in to help us, because nothing can fly in this. No one is going to remove the snow, because no one knows how. Tell the general up on the hill behind us to go back to Siberia where he belongs. He can't do anything here." She held back a flood of emotion. "There's no hope."

"Honey," he said, reaching for her hand, but she pulled away, saying she was going down to check on Susan, and hurried out.

Susan struggled to get out of bed. She staggered at first but caught herself on the windowsill. Herschel, ever at her side, shook off sleep and wagged his tail. She looked outside, but could see nothing. But she could tell it was snowing harder than . . . than yesterday? She wasn't even sure what day this was. She opened her door. Herschel ran into the kitchen to eat while Susan crept into the living room. Auntie Dee was snoring on the sofa. She looked like a hibernating bear under her dark mink coat. Susan smiled.

She saw the library doors were closed and locked,

and she realized it must have been getting too cold. The house had a chill in it now. Demerol kept her temperature up, even made her sweat. But feeling clammy made it seem even colder. Back in her bedroom, she pushed the curtains aside and opened one of the French doors to the terrace. It took all her strength, but she did it. The narcotic was working and she felt almost like she was floating. There was no pain at all now. She reached out and grabbed a handful of snow. Just holding it made her feel wonderful. She tossed it back outside and rubbed her fingers over the flakes that were blowing against the glass. Oh, if only she could go outside for a while and play in it! She wished she could sit at her computer and write about it in her blog. She bet kids all over town were talking about it.

She cringed and fell forward a little. A sharp pain went through her stomach and radiated through her back as she arched backward. She reached up and tugged the door shut and eased herself down into bed again. She went as long as she could, biting on her thumb, holding her pillow tight with her fists, contorting her body into every conceivable position that might ease the sudden pain. Just as she felt she was going to scream, her mother entered the room.

Aileene held her and sat with her while she lay there pressing her fists into the small of her back, which gave her some relief. Aileene worried that it was too early for another hypo—it had only been two hours and she was supposed to wait four—but then said who the hell cares? They had plenty and her daughter didn't deserve this hell and she had to do something for her in this hideous snowbound situation. She prepared another syringe and gave her the shot and held her in her arms until the pain relinquished its intensity.

What disquieted her was that she knew it was getting worse. Much worse. Like the weather. They would not be going to any hospital soon, and no doctor was going to come to them. Susan needed an operation, and Aileene feared she needed it yesterday. She glanced at the window. What in the world were they going to do?

Susan read her mother's mind, but didn't voice her thoughts: that she wanted to be in a hospital now. She had always before wanted to stay home during the attacks, but this was different. She knew it was worse, she knew she needed care, she wanted that operation they had told her about, wanted for once in her young life to be well. She wanted that more than anything in the world.

Even more than the chance to play in the snow.

Dolores suddenly awoke and paced the living room with nervous energy and fears for hours. Her supply was running out. Soon it would be gone. Just knowing that meant she couldn't sleep. She stood at the window looking out over the lawn. She could see a house burning only a few blocks down the hill. Harry. Where was he this dark night? Would he come?

She looked everywhere for cigarettes. She'd given up smoking when she and Harry started dating, when he once told her he wouldn't kiss her with that taste in her mouth. She'd only had ten or twenty in all this time, not counting the ones in Jake's car. What she wouldn't give for one drag tonight. It might soothe her nerves. It might help her sleep. Hell, it used to help her stage fright, and in many an all-night recording session.

Recording session. She drifted over to the piano and sat down. Depressing the soft pedal, she played a chord. Not one in particular, just F major, a key she liked to sing in. She thought of her old friend Dusty Springfield. Dee had gone to her funeral in Oxfordshire, the Parish Church of St. Mary the Virgin, Henley-on-Thames. Cried her eyes out, standing with Cilla Black and Elton and Elvis Costello as the horse-driven glass carriage passed them. Dusty had been her favorite, her idol, her friend. Coming onto the music scene only about ten years after Dusty had, Dolores even recorded a song with her, but Dusty being Dusty, someone who was very particular and exacting about what she allowed to reach the public, it was never released. Dolores remembered Neil Tennant's eulogy—God, but she loved the Pet Shop Boys—that broke their hearts. Breast cancer. Dolores brought her hands to her own bosom. There but for the grace of God go I. Then she sang a few lines of "Wishin' and Hopin'" and felt teary-eyed. Boy, did she wish and did she hope now.

She changed keys several times, and lapsed into her favorite Sondheim song, "Send in the Clowns." She had enough miles on her, having been around the block more than a few times, to play Desiree now, so why didn't somebody cast her in a revival of the goddamned thing? Ah, a little night music indeed. If there were ever a night for madness, she thought, this was it. *A Midwinter Night's Dream.* Make that nightmare. ". . . making my entrance again with my usual flair."

Dolores took her hands from the keyboard and laughed out loud, remembering a party up at Burt Bacharach and Angie Dickinson's house in the old days, back when they were married, after a concert Dionne had given at the Greek Theater. All night long she and Dionne Warwick were giggly and silly. When Burt started tinkling the keys, he eventually played some Sondheim. Dolores sang the line she'd just sung,

". . . making my entrance again . . ." but as she warbled the words ". . . with my usual flair," she pulled out a Flair pen from her purse and held it in the air. Burt laughed so hard he said he almost peed in his pants on the piano bench.

Or was that at Carol Lawrence and Bob Goulet's a few years later when Jerry Herman was at the piano? Dee was feeling confused. No, Jerry would never play Sondheim, what was she thinking? Jerry, dear sweet Jerry. What she'd give to star in a revival of *Mame!* Christ, it could have been at Steve's place itself, his apartment in the Village. She'd spent many a wonderful night there. All her old friends. Bernadette Peters, Dorothy Collins, and the other Dorothy, Loudon. Even Lenny Bernstein a few times. Oh, the time she and Patti LuPone did a duet—what had they sung? Something from *The Fantasticks*. Or was it a Lloyd Webber? God knew, those were the days. Until Harry came along. Until Harry swept her off her feet, made her feel young again. Until Harry ruined her life.

She grabbed the bottle from the coffee table and refilled her glass. Then she sat again at the keyboard and tried it fresh. "Isn't it rich? Aren't we a pair?" And then she realized she wasn't alone. But no, it wasn't Aileene come downstairs to tell her to shut up. It was Susan. Smiling. Suddenly sitting next to her.

"Auntie Dee, I love your singing," she said softly.

Dee took her fingers from the keys. "Honey, you all right?" She put both hands on the girl's shoulders. "What are you doing up?"

"I didn't want to wake Mom and Dad. I got up to get an ice cube. For my lips."

Dolores inspected her lips. They were dry and cracked. Probably from the drugs dehydrating her. "There's no electricity, baby. No more cubes." But

Dolores had an idea. "Here, this will work better."
She stood up and turned the handle on the window
behind the piano.

"What are you doing?"

"Getting you some ice." She pulled it open just
enough to reach out and grab a handful of snow, com-
pressing it to the size of a tennis ball, and then handed
it to the girl. "This will work better. It's wet and cool
and soft."

Susan grinned through her discomfort. And Dolores
could see that she was in pain; her eyes were sunken
and her face could not mask it. She looked pale, and
frail, and weak. "Play some more, okay?"

Dee winked. "Okay." She played "Try to Remember." "This is from the first show I ever did onstage.
It's a pretty song. I think Patti LuPone and I once
sang it in a duet."

Susan listened and gently pressed her head against
Dolores' shoulder. "I said a prayer for Harry tonight.
I prayed he would get here all right."

"Thank you, dear," Dolores responded.

"Mom bought me a lot of old musicals I never
heard of. I saw one on TV last week. It was called
Show Boat."

Dolores stopped what she was playing and put her
hands together. "I love *Show Boat*. One of the great
old shows." She thought for a moment, then hit the
keyboard again. *"Fish got to swim, birds got to fly, I
got to love one man till I die. Can't help lovin' dat man
of mine."* Harry Hanwell. Dat man of mine.

"You sing it so nicely," Susan purred.

Dolores closed her eyes and continued softly. *"Tell
me he's lazy, tell me he's slow, tell me I'm crazy,
(maybe I know.) Can't help lovin' dat man of mine."*
She hummed a little, pressing her head against Susan's

on her shoulder. *"When he goes away, dat's a rainy day, and when he comes back, dat day is fine, de sun will shine!"*

"It's beautiful," Susan whispered. She played chords to accompany Dolores, a real duet on the piano.

"He kin come home as late as can be . . ." Dolores felt tears again. Harry, where are you? When are you coming home? *"Home without him ain't no home to me. Can't help lovin' dat man of mine."*

A voice from across the room cut the music like a cold sharp knife. "Susan, what are you doing?" Aileene came hurrying toward them in her robe. "Dee, what were you thinking?"

"Mom, I'm all right. Auntie Dee didn't do anything wrong. I came out to sing with her."

Aileene stopped in her tracks. Something astonished her. Susan was smiling, smiling for the first time in weeks. She bit her lip and drew in a breath. She felt foolish and embarrassed. "Well," she said, trying to soften the moment, "I heard it too and I felt like I wanted to sing along."

Dolores shot her a look. *My ass you did,* she thought.

Aileene walked to the piano and put one arm around her daughter and the other on her daughter-in-law's shoulder. "Remember the good old days, when we'd have a big noisy dinner party and then we'd sing for hours around the piano?"

"Michael would do imitations," Susan remembered.

"We'd try to do the entire score from the latest Broadway hit," Dolores said, realizing that Aileene really was trying to be less cold and demanding.

Aileene laughed. "I could never sing. I used to pretend, but I have no voice at all."

"Mine's shot too," Dolores quipped.

"No, it's not," Aileene surprised Dolores by saying. "It's still as lovely and fresh as it has ever been."

Dolores was moved. She sensed that Aileene wasn't just saying it to try to make up. She was being genuine. She meant it. "Thanks, Aileene."

Aileene turned to Susan. "You really should get back to bed, honey."

Susan nodded, and let her mom help her to her feet as Dee wondered what might be fitting to play for Aileene's exit? If only she knew "Ride of the Valkyries." No, that was being tacky. *Shame on me!* But as she played various chords and tinkled the keys, she felt choked up. Susan had done that to her. Even Aileene. Family, the good old days—it was such a distant but distinctly wonderful memory. Dolores wished for a moment she could be Susan's age again. She wished they could work up an act together, get a job in summer stock. They could be Judy and Liza at Carnegie Hall. Mother and daughter, kinda like sisters. The reversal in Dee and Susan's case, sisters-in-law who were like mother and daughter. Oh, the dreams. And how they die. Life was unfair. Proof of that statement was this little girl, in terrible pain, crawling back into her bed, perhaps only days from death.

Dee stopped suddenly, hating herself for even thinking that. She got up and slugged down the booze. Susan was not going to die—she couldn't dare think that. It was the hopelessness of her own life, her own marriage, her own situation, her own dead career that was making her project this depressing ending onto others. She had to stop. She had to do something to change her thinking. But the only thing she could think of was to drink more.

It was still dark when Bob and Aileene sat up with a start. Someone had knocked hard on the master bedroom door and then shouted their names. Flo stepped in, looking upset, sounding very concerned. "I'm sorry to wake you, I didn't want to alarm you . . ."

"Susan?" Bob asked, sure something had happened.

"No, Dolores."

Aileene breathed a sigh of relief, getting her wits about her. She'd been sound asleep and waking this way made her heart pound. Bob took her hand and looked up at their guest. "What about her?"

"She's gone."

"Gone?"

"Going. I mean, she's out there. She's outside."

Bob jumped from the bed. "What's she doing out there?"

"I woke up and went downstairs and found her putting her coat and my boots on." Flo tried to sound serious, even though the words, when Dolores had uttered them at the time, were comic. " 'I have made a catastrophic discovery,' she said to me. 'I have run out of liquor.' "

"Oh my," Aileene muttered.

Bob was already at the window. "It's too dark to see anything. You sure she went out?"

"Yes, the side door to the driveway. I yelled at her, begged her to come back, but she was heading down the hill."

"How long ago?" Bob asked, sliding into his pants even though he still had his flannel pajama bottoms on.

"Just a few minutes," Flo answered.

Bob forced the window open. A pile of snow, which had gathered on the outer windowsill, fell into the room. "Dee!" he called out into the dead of night. "Dee, come back!" But she didn't hear him, or if she did she ignored him. He slammed the window shut. "Goddamn it," he muttered, fastening his pants.

Flo said, "She was up all night. I heard the piano and couldn't sleep and went down to talk to her."

"Yes, we heard the concert as well," Aileene said.

"Four feet of snow and she's out walking in it," Bob said, pulling a sweatshirt over his head. "She's probably delirious, out looking for Harry."

"Or booze." Aileene saw Bob stuff his feet into his boots. "Bob, you're not going out there."

"Of course I'm going out there. I have to stop her." He headed for the stairs. Aileene and Flo followed. "Someone's got to talk sense into her."

"Bob, please don't get lost . . ."

Bob reached the main floor. "How am I going to get lost in my own front yard?" He pulled his ski jacket from the hall closet and put it on.

"She got a head start. You might have to chase her a long way."

"Aileene, come on. She can barely walk in the house, she's so tipsy. How far is she going to get in four feet of snow?"

Flo added, "The poor dear doesn't have the right shoes."

Bob turned the front yard lights on, opened the front door, kicked away the snow that had drifted there and disappeared.

Aileene ran back upstairs, to the master bedroom window, which gave her the only real vantage point to see the entire front yard and part of the street leading down the hill. By the lights from the lampposts on either side of the gates, she could now see Dolores, who had already reached the gates and was trying to open them by pulling the manual lever in the concealed control box in the frozen ivy. But the snow had stopped the slatted iron gates from moving more than a few inches, and Dolores was desperately trying to fit through. Just as she did, Bob caught up to her.

Aileene held her breath as she watched what looked like an argument.

In the snow, through the gate, with one hand grasping her coat sleeve, Bob cried out, "Dee, tell me where you're going!"

"I have to do this, Bob. Please don't try to stop me," she cried.

Bob felt her pulling away. He held on tighter. "Dee, wait a minute. This is madness. You can't do this."

"I need a drink, Bob." She looked desperate, starved. "You understand—I know you do."

"I do. I do. But—"

"No," she cried, and wrenched away from him, almost falling down. "I finished the last bottle. Harry isn't coming. I can't handle this. I'm no good at this. I can't get through this sober. I'll find a liquor store and I'll be back."

Bob thought she was losing her mind. "Closest liquor store is all the way over on Hyperion. But no store will have anything left on the shelves. I'll find you something in the house. We have wine, yes, for sure we have wine."

"I'll stop at neighbors' houses—someone will understand. Please, let me do this, Bob. Please." She started off down the street. She had no idea where the sidewalk stopped and the road began. "I'll knock on doors. Aileene will hate me for disgracing her to the neighbors, but I don't know what else . . ." Her voice drifted off in the wind.

Bob pushed the gates farther apart and slid through. "Dee! No! Don't do this."

She stopped and turned back toward him. "I know you're afraid I won't make it. Well, I *won't* make it without some Scotch." Her knees almost gave way. She had to reach out for Robin and Rosie's stone retaining wall to steady herself.

Bob called out, "It's not that at all. It's the danger. You know what they did to Flo. We have to stay in our homes. It's too risky."

Dolores closed her eyes and said softly, "I want Harry to come. I want this to stop. I want it all to stop. Oh, God, please make it stop . . ."

Bob tried to make a grab for her, but she pulled away and he took a spill, slipping on the ice under the snow, falling backward. When he pulled himself back to his feet, Dolores was gone. He saw her about five or six car lengths down the street and he gave it one more shot. "Dee! Dee!"

She turned back to him.

He tried another tack. "The Morinas' house. Go there. The second one up from the corner, on the left side."

Dolores turned to look down the hill.

"There," Bob said, "the one behind the trees. They're a wonderful couple. Their son Adam plays on our tennis court. Go to them." Then he pointed to the house next door to him, the one they were standing right down in front of. "Don't go to Robin and Rosie's."

"It's closer," she said.

"I don't know what's going on over there. Stay away, Dee."

She nodded. "The Morinas."

"Yes, Sally and Tony. They'll know you. They both work in television."

She reached out even though she was nowhere near close enough to touch him. "Bob, thank you. For understanding."

"Shit," he suddenly said, "to hell with this. I'll go with you. I can't let you do this alone."

"You don't have to do that," she cried, but he was already at her side, taking her arm.

But just as they started to descend the hill, Bob heard a faint voice cry out. He froze. It was Aileene. Dolores heard it too. They turned to see Aileene in the upstairs bedroom window, pushing the screen out of its frame, screaming at Bob, waving her hands frantically. They could not understand what she was saying. The wind was still fierce, and the snow acted as unwanted insulation.

"Go to her," Dolores said.

Bob waved back to his wife and saw her pull her hands inside the window. "I don't know what's wrong. Something must have happened." Aileene again beckoned him, waving him toward the house.

"Susan," Dolores said.

A shiver pierced Bob's heart. "Oh, my God." Without hesitation, he took off, turning up the hill, back to the gates, back toward the driveway.

"I'll be back very soon," Dee promised. She sounded suddenly encouraged and less desperate. "I'll say a prayer for Susan."

But he did not hear her. His mind was already in the house.

"Honey!" Bob called as he stomped snow from his boots just inside the door. "What happened? Is it Susan?"

Aileene was hurrying down the stairs. "No, it's Cameron. He called on the shortwave radio. I didn't know what to do. I don't know how to work it."

Bob was relieved that it wasn't an emergency with their daughter. And distressed that he might have missed something important. "What did he say?"

"He just kept saying, 'Bob, are you there? Can you hear me?' He said something had come up, he thought he could help."

"Help?"

Aileene nodded.

"Help what? How?"

She shrugged. "I don't know. That was when I called out to you. I didn't want to lose him."

Bob hurried to the radio in the kitchen, and fiddled with it, trying in vain to reach Cameron. It only crackled in response. "Listen, we can't let this happen again. Here's what you do if another call comes through . . ."

Aileene listened attentively and when he was through she sat down at the kitchen table. "Tell me about Dolores," she said. "Where did she go?"

Bob shook his head. "To find booze."

"I was right."

"I couldn't talk sense into her. I tried."

Aileene shook her head. "After her ordeal getting here that first night, I wouldn't think she'd ever want to walk in snow again."

"Addiction is a powerful motivation." Bob looked sad as he followed her into the kitchen. "I think she's in worse shape than we thought."

"There's not much we can do about it now. Clear your mind. Coffee?"

"Sure."

Aileene started to put beans into the grinder but immediately stopped herself. "What am I doing?"

"Do we have instant?"

She laughed. "When have we *ever* had instant coffee?" She opened a cabinet and took out a box of teas. "I didn't even realize they still made it."

"Tea is good," Bob said, watching her light the gas on the range with a match. "Just like my mom had to do with her Tappan back when I was a kid."

"I hope it doesn't go the way of the electricity." She turned up the flame under the kettle and held her hands near it to warm her cold fingers.

"Susan still asleep?"

Aileene nodded. "I peeked in. She and Herschel are both out cold."

"Flo?"

"I think she went back to bed," Aileene told him. She fixed a bowl of cereal, dopping on some plain yogurt that she had kept cold in the window, just the way he liked it. There was one banana left, so she sliced it over the bowl and kept a small piece for herself. But when she set it down in front of him, he didn't even notice. He was preoccupied, staring at the snow outside the kitchen window as the light of day threatened to arrive. "Bob?" she asked gently. "What's wrong?"

"Thinking about Mike and the family," he said softly. "Wondering where Harry might be. How long Susan can hold out. Dee. What Cameron meant. All of it."

Dolores pulled her fur coat tight around her. She remembered when she did that Christmas movie and had to stand singing in much the same getup as she had on now, in front of a fan that blasted her with snow, creating such a wind that it blew the hood of her coat off and then her wig as well. But this was no movie. She should be so lucky.

She made it only a few steps before she fell. She found she was at the foot of Robin and Rosie's driveway. What she saw seemed miraculous. Someone had shoveled the driveway's center, and it looked like feet had packed down the snow leading up it so it would be a lot easier to climb. And the house itself looked inviting. She could see candles burning in the windows. There were signs of life.

She glanced down the hill toward the house Bob had told her to go to, the Morinas' place. It looked forbidding. She seriously wondered if anyone was even there. She could not make out whether or not smoke was coming from the chimney because of the big eucalyptus trees blocking her view, and it was still dark outside. A glance up at the house she was in front of told her a fire was burning. She could see white smoke puffing from the chimney. But Bob had warned her not to go there. He could have been too cautious, overreacting. Christ, going to them would be so much easier—just climb the already shoveled hill, knock on the door, beg a little booze, and hightail it back to Bob's around the back of the house, through the wooden gate in the wall. Yes. It would be so much easier.

As she picked herself up, she heard a cracking sound coming from behind her. Standing on both feet now, shaking the snow from her mink, she feared a tree branch was breaking under the weight of the snow. But she was wrong. The heat told her she was wrong. On the other side of the street, directly across from Bob's house, the beautiful edifice that Florence Brennan had called home was now in flames. Dolores hurried up the shoveled driveway as fast as she could.

As she approached the front door, she heard voices. Robin and Rosie had always been fun, gracious hosts. She knew they entertained often and well; in fact, years before, Dee and Harry had joined them for a barbecue where, Dee recalled, the wine and beer flowed freely and they even turned her on to Ardbeg, an Islay single malt she'd never heard of. Surely they would have some today.

At the front door, Dolores looked down over the snowy front yard to see people pouring out of Flo Brennan's house. With the fire behind them, they were mere silhouettes, but it seemed to her that they looked like squatters—hobos, they used to call them in Dolores' day—homeless and desperate people. Or perhaps they were just regular people who had reached their limit. Disasters changed people. Never did Dolores imagine she would be doing anything so humiliating as knocking on strangers' doors to beg some liquor. Dense, heavy smoke shot through the snow on the roof of Flo's house. It looked like some kind of surrealistic landscape with steam exploding from deep geysers. All at once, the flames roared through the rooftop, and the snow turned to vapor as it fell into the structure, into the blaze that had engulfed the entire house.

Dolores heard voices down at the front end of the house she was now standing next to. She figured everyone inside had rushed to the windows in the dining room to see what was happening just across the street. She adjusted her turban, shook off more snow, and knocked. Someone heard it—the voices hushed. "Hello?" she called out. "It's Dee Hanwell from next door." She pounded with her knuckles. "Robin? Rosie?" She knocked on the tall window glass next to the door. "It's Dolores, Bob's daughter-in-law from next door? Can you let me in?"

There was no response. Which she thought strange. Maybe Bob was right. Maybe this was dangerous. She tried to peer in through the window she'd just rapped on, but the glass was frosted. She rang the bell, but of course without electricity it didn't work. She pounded again, called their names again, but still nothing. They weren't going to let her in.

She turned her head and looked down the hill. From the steps there she had a better view of the Morina house. It indeed looked devoid of life. *Good for them,* she thought. Maybe they had the good luck to be vacationing on Maui this week. She glanced at other buildings. The apartment building next door seemed forbidding, dark and difficult to get to. There were plenty of other houses, but could she make it through the snow to any of them? Getting up this driveway—and it had been shoveled—had been ghastly enough. Then she thought of the back door.

Perhaps it was open. If it was, she would just waltz on in and there really would be nothing they could do about it. If they didn't want more company, they could give her a bottle or two or three to get rid of her. Or perhaps she could just filch one. In her stupor, she'd forgotten about the gunshots, the danger. All that was important now was finding a bottle of liquor. They were probably all at the front windows watching the fire anyhow. Sure, this would be easy—slip into the rear of the house where nobody was. Probably the coldest part too, for the fireplace was at the opposite end. She got her hopes up. She should have thought of this first.

But getting to the door was harder than she'd thought it would be. Not that it was so far. It was that the snow back there had not been walked on like that in the driveway. It was thick and dense and deep. She didn't feel very cold—perhaps because she was insulated by the liquor still in her bloodstream—but maneuvering was hell. The drifts reached up to her knees in spots, and it took her forever just to get back toward the garage and then ascend the three or four stairsteps leading up from the driveway.

Making her way around the back corner of the house was treacherous because she felt herself slipping on the ice that was under the snow—oh God, she thought, she'd already forgotten the ice storm!—and she held on to the downspout of the rain pipe to steady herself. Under a window, she heard arguing. Aha. She hadn't been hearing things. They were there. She would just politely ask to borrow a bottle of Scotch. Or two, if they had it. They'd understand.

But long before she made it to the rear door to press the bell there, she stepped on something that felt like a big rock covered with snow. She slipped as she did so, almost falling. Reaching out to grab the wall of the house to steady herself, she saw what looked like another hand reaching up to hers. She blinked. She was seeing things. She looked down at her foot, which was pressing against the hard object in the snow, and this time she brushed some of the snow away. And found a head. A woman's head. Rosie's head.

Gasping for breath and shivering not from cold but from fright, she bent down and brushed the snow from the face. She had thought that somehow Rosie had gone outside and fallen, and couldn't get up, and had died of exposure without her partner inside realizing she was gone. But that theory was debunked when she saw that there was a bullet hole in the middle of her forehead.

She dropped the unimaginable object in her hands and started to scream, but the snow acted like insulation and she could barely even hear herself. That's when she looked back at the imaginary hand and realized that it was not her imagination; a hand was indeed reaching up from the drift up against the corner of the house by the door. She had seen this hand before. The ring on it was the one Robin had proudly showed her that Rosie had bought her for their twenty-fifth anniversary.

Fearing for her life, she knew she had to get back to Bob's house, just fifteen feet away. She would be safe there. She could warn them. She turned and assessed the difficulty of climbing the snowbank that blanketed the stairs leading up to Bob's driveway. She could do it, she had to do it. But at that moment, the back door of the house started to open and she saw the barrel of a shotgun poke out.

She had no choice but to head back the way she had come, down the driveway, terrified.

Just as the black sky started to lighten to gray.

The Sixth Day
Tuesday, January 20
High Temperature 19 Degrees, Low 9 Degrees

Harry had not slept well, waking every ten minutes to keep one eye on the boy sleeping across the floor from him and one on the fire hose on the little porch. But when the sun started pushing its way behind the clouds, he fell into a deep sleep, snoring loudly, almost comatose. When he did awaken, he jumped up with a start. Janohn and her mother were in the kitchen, cooking something over what appeared to be a can of Sterno, like you'd use out camping. The two youngest kids were playing with building blocks and dolls on the floor. Augustine was nowhere to be seen. Harry looked out on the porch. Sure enough, the fire hose was gone. "Where'd it go?" he shouted, jumping up.

The kids froze. The women turned to him.

"The hose. Where's my fire hose? Augustine took it, didn't he? Where is he?"

"Hush now," Janohn said. "No cause for alarm. How's your head this morning?"

Harry had completely forgotten he'd been shot. He

didn't care. The only thing important today was the paintings. "Where is he? Where'd he go with it?" Harry was beside himself. He'd hadn't come all this way to lose the priceless paintings to some kid who probably had never even heard of Vincent van Gogh.

Harry heard a smashing sound coming from the porch and turned. Augustine was out there, crashing a big hammer into what until that moment had been a chair. The boy was breaking up wooden objects so they could burn them to stay warm. Indeed, the spot where the hose had been hanging on the back of a chair on the porch was now a pile of broken and splintered remains of chairs, bookcases and nightstands. Harry tried to push open the door to the porch, but a big piece of wood blocked it. "Hey, you!" he shouted to the boy outside. "Get in here!"

Augustine looked up as if to say, "Are you talking to me?"

"What in hell are you all riled up about?" Janohn asked Harry.

"Stop the yelling," the old lady grumbled. "No cause for shouting."

"Yes, you!" Harry bellowed to Augustine, who was pointing toward himself questioningly. Augustine opened the porch door. "Where's the fire hose?" Harry immediately shouted.

"Calm down, calm down," the old lady again admonished.

"Man, what?" the boy asked, brushing snow from his shoulders.

"What did you do with it? If you burned it—"

Augustine rolled his eyes. "Come on, man, I wouldn't burn it. It's hanging right here." He pointed to the wall just outside the back door. "On the light fixture. I needed to bust up the chair it was hanging on."

"Let me out there," Harry ordered and the boy pulled away the piece of wood that was wedged against the kitchen door. Harry hurried onto the cold porch, stepped over the pile of soon-to-be-burned furniture pieces, and suddenly felt foolish. Sure enough, he could clearly see the edge of the hose hanging exactly where the boy said. It was frozen solid, of course, but he figured that would not harm the paintings; they must have been frozen as he carried them the day before. When he felt his socks getting wet from the snow that had fallen from the boy's jacket, he realized he wasn't even wearing his boots. He hurried back inside without an explanation.

"Sorry," he told the women. "Important papers and stuff, you know?" He rubbed his arms to warm up. "God, but it's cold out there."

Mother and daughter exchanged glances. They'd let this madman spend the night?

"Sorry," Harry said, reading their minds. "I'm a little edgy."

"Augustine's been getting chairs from the restaurant we met in," Janohn said. "We can't chop up all our furniture to burn."

"Why not?" the old woman snapped. "It's crap anyway."

"Ma," Janohn moaned.

"Taught my girl a lotta things," the woman said, wiping her hands with a dish towel, "but taste wasn't one of 'em."

"Ma, not today, okay?"

"Marrying that scuzzball Joaquin should have been the tip-off."

Ah, Harry thought. That's why the boy's skin was so dark.

"He was a nice guy when I married him, Ma. He became a scumbag later."

Harry snickered. "Is there coffee in that pot?" He was looking at the roaring flames in the fireplace, which had a makeshift grate—probably from a Weber grill, he thought—set in it on bricks.

"Sure enough," Janohn said, handing him a mug.

Harry poured himself some boiling coffee. "I should be on my way."

"You're crazy," the woman's mother said with a shake of her head. "Everyone has gone nuts."

"I have to get to my family's place," Harry explained. "My wife is there. I'm going to try to go straight up Western to Los Feliz Boulevard. If I can't do that, I'll head over to Vermont and take that up."

"Crazy, people are crazy," the old woman snorted again.

"Mother," Janohn admonished.

The old gal slammed both fists down on the worn Formica next to the sink. "This is God's curse. Revenge. It's our punishment for evil ways!"

"Mother!" Janohn rolled her eyes. "You sound like that Jeffrey King guy."

"He's right. It's the end of the world."

"Oh, here we go. Put in the earplugs."

"For killing the Kennedy boys," the old woman cried. "For that space shuttle accident. For electing Bush, both of them! For destroying the land, polluting the rivers. For terrorists using the name of God as a reason to murder."

"Mom, enough!"

"No," Harry said. "She's right. I agree. The world's ugly, intolerable. We need to each find our little niche—our desert island—and retreat there forever. Otherwise we're all just going to hell."

"Amen," the old lady said just as Augustine entered. "Get that wet coat off and warm yourself. You'll catch your death."

Augustine did that, as he related a story. "I talked to the soldier. He said people from the central core of the city are taking to the mountains, killing people if they resist letting them into their homes. Everybody's trying to reach the expensive houses where there are supplies and fireplaces."

Harry was thinking about his own beautiful home and who might be camped there right now. He smiled at the thought. Dolores would blow a gasket. He didn't care. He had decided to give it up forever at the moment he reached to cut the canvas of the first painting.

"Guy said the electricity is out everywhere. He even said he heard some people have committed suicide, thinking it's Armageddon."

The old lady blessed herself. "Told ya."

"He said every road leading out of the city is filled with abandoned vehicles, overturned buses, snow blowing over them. He said shortwave radio is the only way to communicate now. It's snowing all the way to Palm Springs. Over four feet here, the guy said."

"I have to get going," Harry said, hearing that. He stared out the porch windows. "It's let up a bit and that will help."

He got up, used the bathroom, dressed and said good-bye to the family who had sheltered him. Janohn slid a plastic-wrapped hunk of brownie into his pocket. "You'll need this later," she assured him.

"Thanks." Harry hugged her. "Thank you too, Mrs . . . ?" He realized he didn't even know her name.

"Calistoga," the woman said. She saw his reaction. "Yeah, yeah, we're an old California family, what can I tell you?"

Harry said, "Well, at least now I know why Jonohn got such a name."

"They call me Callie."

Harry felt a stirring, remembering Calla again.

"All you heard here was 'Ma' and 'Granny,' but I answer to Callie. Calistoga Caldwell." She looked at her daughter again. "Change yours back to Caldwell. How you can go through life with a last name like Bunck, I just don't know."

"You guys stay warm, and stay together," Harry told them. "Hey, Augie, you take care of them, you hear me?"

Augustine nodded.

"And God bless you," Harry added. He almost laughed that he said it, for he couldn't remember ever using that line in his entire life. He didn't even believe in God. Where had that come from? He knew. It was what they expected to hear. Just as he'd done with clients and possible employers of those clients. It was one of the reasons he was so successful. He could be a chameleon.

Callie was having none of it. "God? What's God got to do with this? That King guy is right. God turned his back on us long ago."

"Ma, hush up," the woman warned her.

"I heard King's compound out in the Valley blew itself off the face of the earth."

"So there is a God," the old lady snorted.

"I never understood King's appeal," Harry said. "I mean, twenty of his followers are doing time for torching car dealers that sold SUVs. He's an environmental terrorist, a cult leader, and he's still walking free."

Janohn said, "Lots of Enron guys are still living high on the hog."

Augie interjected, "I heard he might be dead."

"Good." Harry zipped up his ski jacket.

Janohn hugged him. "Harry Hanwell, you take care now. When this is over, you come back to see us."

"Yeah," Augustine said, "and bring Brad and Jon Stewart."

Harry swatted him on the back and headed out into the storm.

Again.

Augustine was right behind him as he lifted the fire hose off its hook. The kid watched him as he hoisted it on his shoulder, realizing it felt heaver than he'd remembered. "I'd drag it behind me," Augustine said.

"Huh?" Harry realized what he was saying. It was going to be difficult carrying it now that the snow was deeper. But dragging it could harm the paintings. "I don't want snow to get inside it."

"I have an idea," the boy said, opening the porch door again. He grabbed an industrial-sized, triple-gauge black plastic garbage bag and shook out the contents. About a hundred CDs from Best Buy that hadn't even been opened.

"I see you've been doing a little scavenging this morning yourself," Harry observed.

"Yeah, well, who knows if I'll ever get to play them. Take the bag. It'll fit it."

It did. The hose fit into it and there was enough slack for Harry to tie a good tight noose at the top. This way he could drag it over the snow behind him rather than attempting to keep it on his shoulder. "Good thinking, kid. Thanks."

"See ya," Augustine said.

"Yeah."

When Harry got back to Western Avenue he realized that things had changed. The winds that had howled all night had drifted snow as high as seven feet in some places. The street, a major Los Angeles thoroughfare, was unrecognizable, covered with snow, but the center had been packed down by National Guard vehicles and city trucks equipped with snow tires and chains. It looked to Harry like an ice festival carving of one of the elevated freeways in the city. Cars and buses were resting where they had haphazardly been abandoned by their drivers. The smoke from fires seemed to blanket the sky, creeping into his nostrils with every breath.

He pushed on, determined to get to his father's house by nightfall. If anyone could find a way out, it was his dad. He was connected, in the right places. Hell, Michael's godfather was the greatest weather brain the world had ever known. Cameron would take care of them all. Harry had visions of the whole family boarding a plane after an escorted ride to the airport in an Army truck. His father's dream was different: Bob envisioned a helicopter landing to get Susan to surgery. That was all that was important. But Harry had no idea. The family was scattered. Some of them were warm and safe on Waverly Drive. Michael and Wendy and the baby were in the gymnasium at Hollywood High. And Harry was crawling up Western Avenue, making his way north, uphill all the way. Would they ever come together? Hell, Harry didn't much care. Ultimately he wanted only to save himself and the future that lay in the bag he was pulling.

Every time he felt broken, defeated by the cold, Harry thought about the treasure he was dragging behind him, and his spirit translated into energy. He sweated as he plodded on, despite his weariness and weakness—he hadn't really eaten a meal in days. The piece of brownie the woman had given him increased his strength for a time, but as with all sugar rushes, the descent was awful. He wished she had put some dope in them. He wanted to curl up and just let himself freeze to death—*an easy way out,* he thought to himself. Then he pictured himself on that island some-

where, lying there in a hammock between two towering, swaying palms, a rum drink in his hand, his skin
tanned and buff, a naked native Calla at his side, lying
only feet from the villa that contained two of the most
beautiful pieces of art ever created.

And he forged on.

Michael and Wendy and the others had slept from
sheer exhaustion and sadness. The loss of Parijata and
their building, the aching in their bones from all they'd
done in the past days, the emotional strain—
everything was taking its toll. And this morning they
found they had more responsibility. Tim woke up to
the need to help the pets, mainly cats and dogs, that
people had brought to the shelter with them, many of
them suffering from frostbite. He did the best he could
without the proper medication and utensils. He
thought about statistics. He had so often read about
some eighty thousand people killed in a flood in some
country like China or a devastating earthquake in Iran
that wiped out a whole village. But who ever thought
of animals at a time like that? No one ever issued
statistics on them. They were living creatures, more
innocent than any human being. He knew there were
about seventy-five million pets living in Los Angeles.
What about them? They couldn't loot stores for food
and clothing. They were completely dependent. Someone had to help them. He would do what he could.

Wendy volunteered as the director of her section. A
council was formed—were they on a reality show?—to
keep the place running smoothly, and Wendy helped,
taking charge, calming them and assuring them they
were safe. Jim, Matthew, Kenny and Michael joined
other young men to make trips outside into the snow
on the football field, to retrieve dropped parcels of
food and water and medication, even magazines and

candy that choppers had brought in when the winds died down in the early morning. There was bickering over the parcels once they brought them inside, but, Michael told Wendy, "That's your problem to deal with." She gave him an exasperated look. People were out to save themselves and they all felt entitled. In an age of entitlement, sharing wasn't easy. Wendy tried to keep order and divide the supplies evenly and fairly.

Everyone shared their stories, each one worse than the last. Everyone thought they had had it hard until they heard what the person lying on the next cot had gone through. Stories of anguish, loss, perseverance. Frightening stories of being robbed, held up at gunpoint, left in the snow to die. One woman had crawled to the shelter with a broken leg after she and her husband had tried in vain to push their car out of the snow, and then gravity took hold and ran him over, killing him, then rolled over her leg. A little boy had walked for blocks alone to the shelter after his mother and sister, who had been right behind him fighting the angry wind and falling snow, simply, incredibly, disappeared. A rabbi who had been knocked unconscious on the street woke up to find his boots missing—and spent two days walking to the shelter in his socks. A doctor feared his toes might have to be amputated.

One woman came in with a tale that riveted everyone. "I heard from my brother, who is with the LAPD, that someone re-created the Sharon Tate murders."

Michael, Wendy and several of the others couldn't believe what they were hearing. "What do you mean, 're-created'?"

"They broke in and killed everyone in that house. Just like the Manson clan did."

"Who's Manson?" someone asked.

"You're too young," the woman answered.

Tim remembered a TV show on one of the anniversaries of the crime. "They knocked that house down. It doesn't exist anymore."

"New house, same exact place." The woman telling this story did not appear to be crazy. "The night the snow started, MSNBC did a report on that rally of Jeffrey King's followers. It was being held out where Spahn Ranch once was."

"Where Manson and the Family lived," Tim recalled.

"Yes. My brother said the cops paid little attention because the coming storm was priority. But he said that Manson slogans like DEATH TO PIGS and HELTER SKELTER had been written in the snow when it started falling that first night, out at the Getty Museum and other places around town. It was suddenly showing up. Someone wrote it on a door of a house in Brentwood that was broken into, and it was on the door of the house where the Tate place once stood."

"My parents live two doors from the LaBianca house," Michael said, feeling suddenly uneasy.

The woman nodded. "Probably happened there too. It's Manson's prediction, my brother said."

"What prediction?" Penelope asked, appalled, mesmerized.

"The race war. Black people would rise up and take over the white homes and kill them all. It seems to be happening because of the snow."

Wendy said, "Poor people are trying to save themselves, that's all. Black, Hispanic, Vietnamese, it doesn't matter. It's not a race war. It's human nature."

"Murder is human nature?" Penelope asked.

The woman who'd been relating the story just shook her head. "When hasn't it been, honey?"

Michael asked the woman whose brother was a cop, "Jeffrey King was telling his followers that they were the only people who were going to survive this?"

"My brother confirmed that his compound out in the Valley blew up. It was a bomb lab waiting to explode."

"So he won't emerge as the new Messiah when this is over?" Tim asked with a facetious grin on his face.

"No one knows if he was in the place at the time it happened."

"No matter whether he's still around or not," Michael retorted, his voice filled with determination, "we're all gonna be around when this is over. We're going to get through this just fine."

Bob felt Aileene shaking him and realized that he'd fallen asleep right there on the kitchen table, next to the shortwave radio. It was light now, or at least lighter than what he'd remembered when he closed his eyes. He rubbed those eyes and tried to focus.

Aileene greeted him with bad news. "The furnace gave out."

"Which one?"

"Upstairs. I went back to bed after you nodded off—I didn't want to disturb you, thought if Cameron called again you'd want to be there—and when I got up it was freezing up there."

He sat up and nodded. "How's Susan?"

"Not good. She didn't seem to need another shot, but she's getting dehydrated. It's tough for her to keep water down. I begged her to drink, but the pain is too great."

He looked gravely concerned. "She should be on an IV." He got up. "Stay here by the radio while I check the furnace room. Oh, how's Dee?"

Aileene looked puzzled. "Dee?"

His eyes flickered with worry. "She's not back?"

She shook her head. "Not yet."

Fear flashed across his face. He hurried to the dining room and looked out over the expansive yard. It was still snowing, but there was no sign of new footprints in the driveway. But then he thought he saw her—no, wait, it was someone else. A woman on the street. Another woman, two guys, people crossing the street, going up the driveway next door, up to Rosie and Robin's . . .

Aileene, watching next to him, was startled as well. "Where are those people going?"

"Where are they *coming* from?" he asked.

His answer came by way of a cry of anguish, a woman's voice coming from upstairs. Bob and Aileene turned, walked to the foot of the staircase in the foyer, and heard it again. It was Flo. She sounded the way she'd sounded when she told him how her dog had been killed. Bob ran up the stairs, with Aileene on his heels. "Flo?" he called out. "Flo, what is it?"

She was standing in the upstairs hall, staring out at the same scene they'd been looking at, but she had a better vantage point by being up higher. "My house," she whispered, trembling so that Aileene grabbed her, thinking she was going to collapse. "My beautiful, beautiful home. I woke up and looked out as I was about to go down the stairs—"

It was gone. Smoke was still rising from the collapsed structure, embers still burning, but you wouldn't guess it had once been a beautiful Mission-style bungalow. "My God," Bob exclaimed when he realized what had happened. He'd not been able to see it from the dining room window.

"Oh, no," Aileene said, pulling Flo into her arms. "Oh, honey, I'm so sorry."

Bob thought things through. "It had to have happened after I came back inside. I was right in front of it, out there with Dee, and everything was fine. I don't believe it."

"The people we saw going up Robin and Rosie's drive, they must have come from Flo's house," Aileene surmised.

Bob nodded. "So they have taken over next door as well." The words "we're next" were on his lips, but he didn't want to upset them more. "You're okay, Flo. It can be rebuilt. You can't."

She tried for humor. "Wish I could. Younger, thinner, blonder."

"You're safe. That's what counts," Aileene assured her.

Flo tried to hold her tears in, but she started sobbing. "I came all the way from Elgin, Illinois, to find a new life here when my husband passed away. This was where I was going to live for the rest of my days. That house was where I was going to die."

"You almost did," Aileene reminded her.

Bob took her hand and said, "Flo, be grateful you got out with your life."

Aileene, still looking out at the ugly steaming and smoking black mess across the pure white snow, suddenly gasped. "Bob, there's a body lying in the yard."

"Our yard?"

"No," Flo said, seeing it too. "Mine."

Bob saw it now. A person just a few feet from the collapsed structure, lying facedown in the snow. He took Flo's hand. She shivered.

Aileene thought it wasn't wise to continue looking at the devastation, so she led Flo downstairs to the kitchen. Bob went down the second flight of stairs, to the icy-cold family room, and opened the door to the furnace room. Yes, the furnace that serviced the upper level of the house was cold. The hot water heater and the main furnace were fine. He turned the gas valve leading to the upstairs furnace off, waited, then turned it on again. Without the spark of the automatic pilot, he lit a match, but the flame wouldn't catch. That was it for the upstairs heat. Thank God that the other furnace seemed fine. They'd bunk in the living room. Things could be worse. He just was glad he had defied everyone who'd told him to put in forced-air heat over the years. Gravity heat did not depend on electricity for power. Just like the new and efficient water heater.

When Bob came from the furnace room, something he'd missed in the family room grabbed his attention. There was a huge pile of used Kleenex on the sofa. An empty vodka bottle. A photo of Harry and Dolores at their wedding, which usually adorned the mantel along with several other family memories, lay on the couch too. Dee had been sitting there, crying, drinking, probably feeling her life ending. Bob closed his eyes. *Why did I let her go? Why in the hell didn't I drag her back?* He knew that if she was not found, he'd never forgive himself.

He walked to the windows that flanked the driveway. Snow was still falling, but not as hard as yesterday. Perhaps it was finally letting up. Good. That meant rescue efforts wouldn't be as difficult. Maybe someone would find Dolores walking—if she was still out there—and take her in. Better still, maybe she was safe and sound at the Morinas'. Yes, that was it, Bob told himself. She'd done what he'd told her and she was drunk as a skunk in a guest room while Sally and Tony planned a miniseries based on this incredible experience.

He opened the door to the driveway. He thought he could make out small indentations in the snow, which probably were his and Dee's footprints from early morning, leading downhill. He looked at the wall that separated his driveway from Rosie and Robin's and wished Dee would just walk through the wooden gate. He almost shivered when he got his wish.

But it wasn't Dee. It wasn't a woman. The gate swung open and a slightly crazed-looking young man wearing a heavy, tattered parka suddenly appeared. He held a baseball bat over his shoulder. His eyes looked vacant.

He froze as he saw Bob standing there in his doorway off the driveway. They eyeballed one another, sizing each other up. Bob glared as hard and as fiercely as he could, trembling inside but not about to show it. In a moment, the boy gave up, turned, slammed the gate shut so hard that snow fell from the top of it about six or eight feet down the driveway, and then Bob closed the door and locked it.

He decided, at that moment, to keep the gun on him at all times. And to have the shotgun at the ready. No one would do to them what they had done to Flo Brennan.

Across the country, the American people heard a special report by Peter Jennings on the phenomenon that had been called Ice Storm L.A., and was now being changed to the Great Los Angeles Blizzard. "The president, just out of a Cabinet meeting, issued a statement that everything will and is being done to help stricken Southern California. And what is the state of the snowbound city which at this time of the year should be having a little rain at most? Well, reports in say the reality of the situation staggers the imagination. Certainly the mounting damage reports that we have been hearing so far do. No American city has suffered so, ever. Only San Francisco perhaps could claim it went through worse hell with the great earthquake and fire, and there the residents were taken by surprise. What has happened and is happening in Los Angeles has been previewed by the increasingly bad weather for months now. The death toll is near fifteen thousand at this time, and how many more are injured or missing is anyone's guess.

"The city is totally crippled. The port was closed after two freighters collided, blocking the right-of-way. The airports have been closed for days; the railroads are not running. Nothing with wheels can move except for specially equipped military vehicles. The Army is trying to get snowmobiles, tractors, trucks with snow tires into the city as fast as they can, but most passages are blocked. The automobile, the symbol of Los Angeles, is nowhere. They're all buried in the snow.

"The commercial outlook is just as poor. Hollywood has shut down. Industry halted. There's little natural gas left and no way to get any supplies in. Electricity doesn't exist. Warehouses and mills are silent, empty. Out in the harbor in the Pacific, a pipeline that runs underwater to the shore from a point where super-tankers unload their Alaskan oil has begun to leak, but nothing can be done now to stop it. By the time something can be done the environmental damage may be worse than that from the Exxon *Valdez*. Ships with precious heating oil sit frozen in ice in Los Angeles Harbor."

Across the country, people sat in front of their television sets and computer screens with their mouths open, trying to comprehend such stories. It wasn't too difficult for those who lived in places where it did snow and where lousy weather was common. It wasn't difficult either for people who had visited California and knew that the possibility of such a thing as snow was unthinkable, with all those beautiful ocean breezes, those palm trees, the pools and the oranges ripe for picking. The people who had no real fixed image of California in their minds felt it was too bad, of course, but they really didn't understand how unique and far-reaching the disaster had become. And they wouldn't understand until it affected them—economically—in the months to come. What would happen when there was almost no fruit left in the stores? No vegetables? When none of their favorite TV shows returned? When no new movies were opening? Then they'd understand.

At the end of the broadcast, Peter Jennings added breaking news. "We have confirmation from the West Coast that Jeffrey King, the former Los Angeles Lakers star and controversial cult leader, is dead. His mansion in the San Fernando Valley blew up yesterday when bomb-making ingredients exploded and set off a chain reaction in the arsenal that was part of the compound. It was speculated, but not confirmed, that King was killed in that accident.

"The reality, it turns out, was very different. Mr. King's body was discovered almost two miles from the compound. He was found alone, along with a suitcase filled with money and painkillers that authorities believe he was addicted to, apparently attempting to flee. The man who set himself up as a kind of prophet—some say 'messiah'—who was going to lead his followers to glory after Armageddon, apparently froze to death trying to get out of the situation that he had assured his disciples they would be the only people to survive."

Michael heard the Peter Jennings broadcast because of an electrical generator that had been brought to the shelter. He was seriously beginning to wonder how long they could hold out. Supplies were gone, and people were pouring through the door by the hundreds. Fights were breaking out, people were dealing drugs, some overdosing, others demanding medical care when the doctors were trying to focus on those in the worst shape. Two babies had been born and a teenage boy had been stabbed. He wanted to get out of here. He wanted to try to get to his parents' house.

Wendy, tired and wan, flopped onto the cot they shared. "A bag of cookies."

Michael wasn't sure he'd heard her right. "Cookies?"

"A bag of cookies. Someone beat a little girl for a bag of cookies and left her to die out there."

He shook his head. It was worse than he thought.

Wendy laughed. "And then I talked to a woman who dragged a man, a diabetic who hadn't eaten, two whole blocks to get him some food. He was dead-weight, zapped because of an insulin reaction. She's about seventy, and small. It's amazing. The stories, amazing."

"You look wiped," he said.

She nodded. "I've been up since four."

"I didn't realize." He took her hand and bent forward and kissed her.

Her eyes looked playful. "Oh, what I'd give to be able to be in our own bed, making love right now."

He blinked. He hadn't expected her to say that.

"People think the funniest things at times like this," she said, trying to joke.

"I fed the baby," he told her, "but people are fighting over baby food. There isn't much."

She nodded. And thought for a moment. And finally said, "Let's do it. Let's go to your dad's."

"You serious?" He was shocked.

"Where people are civilized."

"This from the girl who was going to save the world?"

She closed her eyes. "Right now, if we save ourselves it will be a miracle."

Michael hugged her. "We will. I promise we will."

She snuggled into his arms. "Michael," she said very seriously, "why did this happen? Why did it snow?"

He thought for a long moment. "The freaky conditions were right for it, honey. Global warming is my best guess."

"Doesn't that mean the world is getting warmer?"

He smiled and kissed her forehead. "That's what everyone thinks. But what it really means is the air is full of carbon dioxide and particulate matter—grit, dust, carbons from industry and agriculture, car exhaust, even the butter flavoring on microwave popcorn."

"Crap?" she asked.

"Crap. And it screens out sunlight. The average temperature of the Northern Hemisphere has lessened by four degrees since 1970. The finest meteorological minds generally agree that a six-degree drop would produce a full-scale ice age."

"My God." She shivered. It was one thing to hear it on television, but quite another to be told it by her husband while nestled in his arms.

"It's not just here, though this is extreme. Russia's winter, the worst in memory, began in August."

"But they're used to it," Wendy asserted.

"Yup. No palm trees to worry about. Western Europe, after the most devastating drought in history, is living through a colder-than-usual winter, while oddly enough, parts of Scandinavia are bathed in sunshine. China is awash in hurricanes and endless rain."

"So you think it's ultimately humans' fault."

He just held her tight. Then he said, "Listen, the snowfall has lessened. The storm is weakening, as it had to. It's going to warm up."

"So that's good news," she said, sitting up to look at him.

"It's bad news. So bad that I think it's important to get out as fast as we can."

"But," she said, not understanding, "if it's weakening, then won't it be all right?"

"Think about it, Wendy," he said. He had a grave look on his face. "What's going to happen to all this snow when it warms up?"

She got it. "It's going to melt."

"And go where?"

She blinked. "Oh, my."

"Yeah. What's the worst scourge Southern California gets after fires? What am I always reporting on right after fire season?"

"Floods. There's no vegetation to hold the water when the rain comes."

"Los Feliz is at a higher elevation. If there's any place we want to be in the next few days, it's up high." He stood up. "You get Rachel ready and I'll see if the shortwave guy can get Cameron for me. He can relay a message to Dad that we're coming."

Without argument, Wendy nodded, sat up and started to dress the baby.

Michael hit on the soldier manning the shortwave radio. They'd become friendly in the time they'd been there, and the guy was one of Michael's fans. He was happy to arrange for Michael to speak to Cameron, but said he could possibly even do one better. He might be able to reach Michael's father directly.

Only minutes later Michael found himself talking to his dad. "It's me, Dad! Mike!"

"Oh my God," Bob said. "Aileene, it's our son—"

"Dad, you and Mom okay? Susan?"

"We're fine, Michael," Aileene cried out.

Bob continued. "But Susan's not good. It's real bad, Mike. We're praying that Cameron can find a way to get us out."

"How's Dee? Is Harry there?" Michael waited for an answer, but none came. "Dad, what's wrong?"

"Harry never made it. Dee went out looking for booze and hasn't returned."

Michael was stunned. "Oh no. But hey, she could be fine. Someone could have taken her in, she could have gone to a shelter like we're in, anything."

"I hope."

"Dad, is it safe up there?" Again the silence. "We hear stories that would make your skin crawl."

"Everything is quiet and safe here in the house, Mike. But the street, I'm not sure. Vagrants—probably driven from their apartments in Silverlake and Echo Park—took over the house across the street. Florence Brennan, our neighbor, she's here with us now. They burned it down this morning."

Michael nodded. "I've heard lots of stories like that."

"And I don't know what's going on next door, but I don't like it."

"We want to come there, Dad. But if you think it's too risky—"

"Mike, I just don't know. You have to be the judge. I want you here, we all want you here, but you've got a little baby to protect."

"I know."

"Thing is, Cameron has real power, real clout. If anyone can help us it's him."

"I got ya, Dad."

"Rachel, she's okay?" Bob asked.

Michael turned to see Wendy holding Rachel on her shoulder, all buttoned up in her hooded Baby Gap jacket. "She's fine. She's the lucky one—she has no idea what's going on." Michael locked eyes with Wendy. She nodded in answer to his unasked question. "Dad, we're coming."

"Okay, Michael," Bob said, relieved and yet worried, "but you be careful now. Your mother is standing here nodding, ready to jump for joy. We will be watching and waiting. When I see you out there, I'll come down to help. It's treacherous, but you already know that. Just keep an eye out on the streets, you never know what people might do when they're so desperate."

"We're leaving now, Dad. It's early. We hope to be there by nightfall."

"God bless, Michael."

Michael suddenly heard his mother. "Michael, we love you, and Wendy and Rachel, and please be careful . . ."

"Hey, Dad, Mom," Michael said, "I love you too."

Michael thanked the soldier and walked back to Wendy. "Ready?"

She smiled and nodded, pulling her jacket on. They said good-bye to Penelope, to Jim and to Kenny, and to Tim and Matthew, and others there that they had come to know. Then they gathered their few things and walked to the door. "Let's do it," Michael said, and they went out the door.

Harry dropped to his knees, feeling as though he was going to faint. The stubble on his face had frozen into a mask of ice. He felt it with his glove, then cracked it off, and his chin itched. He let himself fall backward into the snow, and he took a deep breath. It seemed, as he lay there looking up, that it was stopping. The wind was blowing it around, but he was quite sure it wasn't coming down as it had for the past two days. And that was good. It meant he might make it to his parents' house by night.

He figured he was at the halfway mark from where he had spent last night. He had lost considerable time dragging the unwieldy fire hose. But, seeing that it was what this whole trek was about, he wasn't complaining. He had pulled it most of the way, the plastic bag sliding fairly easily over the ice and snow, but when that had become difficult at times, he'd hoisted the ponderous baggage to either of his shoulders, and it took a toll. He ached from head to toe.

He assessed where he was. Between Sunset and Hollywood boulevards. Streets of dreams, he thought with a chuckle. But dreams were his only hope, his only motivation, so why was he laughing? He told himself to get his ass in gear and get moving again. He was in front of a tacky furniture store whose windows had been boarded up with plywood. What he wouldn't give to just crawl in there and curl up on one of those tacky fake-leather sofas for the rest of the day. But he couldn't. He had several more miles to go.

He trudged through the muck until he found himself standing in front of an adult bookstore, which amused him. Peeking inside for the hell of it, he saw a candle burning on the counter. Christ, were they open for business? No. There were two teenaged boys sitting on the floor, trying to stay warm with a blanket and the lift to their libidos that the pile of scattered magazines around them was no doubt providing. In front of them lay a half-empty box from Dunkin' Donuts. When they became aware of Harry's presence, one of the boys grabbed the box and pulled it to his chest. In the room full of expensive marital aids and sexual toys and DVDs and girlie magazines, the only thing of value was the food. "It's cool, guys," Harry said, nodding to them, letting them know he wasn't to be feared. "Just getting the chill off."

"Uh, yeah," one boy said, his voice heavy with distrust.

The other one said, "Dude, you don't mess with us, we don't mess with you, dig?"

Harry thought he'd best depart. As he turned, a porn magazine on a rack grabbed his attention. The naked girl on the cover looked a lot like Calla, the waitress at the Getty. Not Callie (thank God!), the old woman who had screamed about God's retribution for their sins. He snickered, grabbed it, rolled it up and slid it in his pocket. Hell, maybe it *was* her.

Next door was a massage parlor filled with homeless people. Next to that was a convenience store with a CLOSED sign in the window. Peering inside, because he too was hungry and thought there might be something left on the shelves, he saw an enormous black man sitting facing the window with a pistol in his lap. Harry jerked and moved away as fast as he could.

On the corner was a fried chicken place. A man opened the door and welcomed him, beckoning him inside. "Come on in, come in, we're all in this together," he said.

"Hey, I don't mind if I do," Harry said, thankfully.

The place was warm—they had one of the ovens going, the door open like a furnace—and there were bits of food left sitting on trays. Harry picked at some as a woman poured him a glass of tepid water. Everyone was tired and numb. No one but Harry seemed to be in any hurry to go anywhere. "My building, it done burn down last night," a woman dressed in red explained. "I got me my kids and here we are and here we gonna sit till this is over. Amen."

"Amen, sister," an old man in a preacher's collar said. "God have mercy."

A man about Harry's age said, "I hear they're putting people in the subway tunnels. I guess that's good shelter."

Harry blinked. "Never thought about that."

"That's where you'd go in a nuclear attack," another guy offered, "and this is worse, so it makes sense."

"Nobody be puttin' me in any sewer tunnel down there," the woman in red said. "Lordy, the thought of it makes my skin crawl."

The preacher said, "You do what you got to do to stay warm." To Harry, he said, "You are welcome to stay with us here, my friend, until help comes."

"I've seen Army vehicles on the streets," Harry offered.

"Plenty of them," one man added, "but they don't have food, they don't have clothes, they don't have electricity. What's the good of a big ol' motherfucking Hummer thing—pardon my language, ladies—if it's got nothing good to bring you?"

"Amen."

Harry rested a bit, putting his feet up. He knew someone would ask and it only took about five minutes. "So what's in the bag there?"

Harry smiled. "Everything I have left in the world."

"Amen."

And, Harry thought without saying, *my ticket out.*

"We're taking the fucking house next door," Andy screamed at Loretta. "I saw the guy earlier. He's a big guy. He's willing to fight. But all we need is a couple of more people."

"I'm in," called one from across the room. They were sitting in what had been Robin and Rosie's comfortable living room but now looked like a homeless camp under a freeway overpass. Since the house across the street had burned down, half of those squatters had come here, and the others had fled to other big homes on the street. But the people who had gathered here were mostly hard-core King followers. And Loretta was still controlling them.

But she was comfy in Robin and Rosie's digs. "We're fine here. We are okay."

"You lost your nerve?" Andy asked.

Loretta looked at him as if he had betrayed her. Another guy, with wild eyes and unruly hair, laughed at her. "Big lady with the big mouth, for years she's saying death to pigs and follow the King and we're going to be vanquished and now what?"

"You don't even know what the word 'vanquished' means," Loretta spit at him.

"I know that I don't like this joint. I know that we don't have no firewood left. I know the food is gone and I'm fucking hungry. I know that the place next door is loaded. And warm. And bigger than this. The King says we will stay alive. We can stay alive better over there."

A man at the front window called them over. "Look out, look," he said. "With the snow stopping, you can see it. L.A. on fire."

They moved to the windows, amazed. "Mass movement to the rich neighborhoods," one said. "It's the dream become reality," piped up another.

"I want the house next door," Andy said again. "I've never been in a house like that."

"That's not what it's about!" Loretta chided him. "The King said we were to take houses to stay alive until we were the only ones left, not to do it for fun or some feeling of power."

Andy turned on her. "You're a fucking control freak, Loretta. It has to be done our way or no way. Screw that. I'm taking the house next door."

"Do what you want," she snapped. She drifted back to the center of the room, near the fireplace where it was warmer. She looked right at Andy again. "Go," she said, almost spitting. "Go, kill them all, take everything they got, move in. But remember it's not over. The King has not been vindicated."

"Big word," the one with the unruly hair said through the gap made by a missing tooth. "Goes along with 'vanquished.' "

"Screw you."

Andy put on his coat. "I'm going over there. I'm gonna scope it out, see how many of them there are, what we need to do."

"But," Loretta said, "don't just walk in shooting. We've come this far, we can't risk any of us dying now. We have to plan this one. That place might have the food and warmth we need to make it through to the end." She walked to Andy and kissed him on the cheek. "Be careful, though."

"Why?"

"Because I think the guy next door will fight back."

The shortwave radio crackled. Aileene, who was at the sink in the kitchen, shouted to Bob, who was looking out the front window at the street, praying to see Dolores making her way up the hill with bottles in hand. Bob rushed to the radio, heard Cameron's voice, and this time they connected. "Cameron, you tried to reach me earlier—what's up?"

"Bob, I can't talk long. Van Hecke says it's a go. We'll get you out by helicopter. The storm is reversing, the end is coming."

Aileene rushed over and put her hands on her husband's shoulder. "When?"

"When?" Bob asked.

"Tomorrow, I hope. They say there are going to be high winds all day, so by tomorrow I think we're going to see rescue vehicles coming in here."

Bob said, "Mike should be here by then."

Cameron cleared his throat. "You should see it from up here, Bob. They're using flamethrowers to clear landing pads for the choppers. When it melts, the water flows down the side of the mountain and turns to ice. It's something. And it's a clue to what's coming."

"Melting snow." Bob grimaced. He had not even thought about where it would all go. "Oh man."

"Two things," Cameron said. "We have a Santa Ana condition brewing. High-pressure system over the Pacific Northwest and a low-pressure system settling off the southwest coast. The winds will blow from the northeast over the mountains, and as they drop through the passes near L.A., they will warm from compression."

"What's the second thing?"

"Rain. On top of the melting snow."

"Santa Anas are dry, hot winds," Bob argued. "They don't carry rain."

"We're being threatened on two fronts. There's a mild Santa Ana condition brewing, but the big danger is out in the ocean. There's a powerhouse of a tropical storm being held at bay by what's over us now."

"In other words," Bob reiterated, "it's time to leave."

"I'll be in touch. Be ready to get up here tomorrow. It's not going to be easy. Take Commonwealth Avenue and head up through Griffith Park, past the Greek Theatre. That road has been used by the teams stationed here, so it's navigable."

"I can't get a car out of my driveway. The streets are impassable."

"I mean hike up Commonwealth."

"Jesus."

"There's no other choice, Bob. I'll be in touch later. Hey, wait—any word from Harry?"

"Unfortunately, nothing."

"Sorry. I gotta go. Out."

As Harry Hanwell was making his way up the slope to Los Feliz, his wife was making her way down. Scared and thoroughly spooked by what she'd seen at the house next door to Bob's, and frightened for her own life when she saw the tip of the gun through the opening back door, Dolores had fled down the driveway, falling, sliding on her butt halfway, then at the street she turned toward Bob's property again, wanting to warn them, wanting to get back inside for safety, but people were coming up the road, torches burning in their hands like that mob scene she had never forgotten from the original *Frankenstein* movie, searching for higher ground. She hid in the bushes for what seemed the longest time. But not all of them were violent or angry. A man and woman spotted her and asked if they could do anything to help.

"Can you help me get the gates open over there?" She pointed to the gates protecting Bob's driveway.

The couple looked daunted. "I don't have much strength left," the man said.

The woman asked, "Is this the street that the Cardinal Manning Retreat House is on?"

"Yes, yes," Dolores said. "It used to be a convent. Right up there."

"We're Catholic and we thought they might be taking people in."

Dolores said, "Yes, I'm sure they are."

"Come with us, dear," the kind woman urged her.

"No. They won't have what I need."

Not understanding, they politely thanked her and continued on through the deep snow. She almost followed them, but she was fairly sure the good fathers had no liquor. But wait a minute—there were a lot of drunks in the priesthood. And they had holy wine for Mass. Why hadn't she gone there in the first place? Hell, they probably had a wine cellar that could keep her happy for days. Now it was too late. The couple had disappeared in the darkness up the street. She was afraid to go back up the hill. She needed something to drink.

She made her way to the place Bob had told her to go, Sally and Tony Morina's house, but she had been right. It looked like no one had been there for weeks. She thought about smashing the window and forcing her way inside, but stopped herself—was she as bad as the people who had done that to Robin and Rosie? The thought that she could be violent to get a drink shook her, and she hurried away from the edifice, determined not to harm anyone or anyone's property. At a house on the corner of Waverly Drive and Rowena, she talked to a woman who told her she was a Mormon and had never had a drop of liquor in her life, and proceeded to give Dee a lecture on how her life would be bettered if she would only give up "the drink." Dolores walked away in the middle of the sermon.

On the street again, just as the sun was coming up and the sky going from black to gray, she fell. But before she could get up, she heard the roar of an engine. It sounded like a speedboat. When she turned, she saw a cute young soldier sitting on some kind of snowmobile. He'd pulled up right next to her. "Hey, lady, you okay?"

Dolores sweet-talked him into giving her a ride. She told him she needed to get some medicine for her family at a market. He told her he thought most of the stores had been looted, but he would give her a lift down to the corner of Hyperion and Griffith Park Boulevard, where he thought there was a supermarket. "I live in Glendale," he explained, "so I don't know this area real well."

"Hey," she said, "I'm so grateful."

He helped her up and situated her behind him on the vehicle. "Glendale has fared the best," he said, " 'cause the Armenian community there really banded together to help everyone."

"I live in Beverly Hills," she offered. "They don't band together very well."

"Hold on to me."

She did. She closed her eyes for a moment, wishing he was Harry. "What is this thing?"

"Rescue vehicle they use at ski resorts," the boy explained to her. "Kinda fun, huh?"

"Yeah. Fun."

She was cold, hungover, desperate for a drink, her emotions completely numbed by what she'd witnessed at the neighbor's house. She told the boy about it as they drove. "A body, a woman's body in the snow . . . someone I knew . . . they're killing people to take over their houses . . ."

He gave no real response other than shrugging. "I know, I know," he said, as if he had been hearing it all day.

As they moved down the hill that was Griffith Park Boulevard, they passed groups of people heading up-hill, carrying sacks on their backs, dragging posses-sions, holding babies, looking desperate. *Poor devils,* Dolores thought. She searched the faces for Harry, but he wasn't among them. She wouldn't give up hope, though.

When she saw the shopping center on the corner of Hyperion Avenue, she asked him to stop. There was the Mayfair Market, Trader Joe's across the street, places where there might be just one bottle someone had missed. She thanked the officer, gave him a little kiss on the cheek. "You sure you're going to be all right?" he asked.

"Hey," she said, trying to add some humor, "I got this far, didn't I? So we had a little snow. Big deal." She pulled her turban down over her ears and set out toward the market as the snowmobile moved on.

She made her way into what had been the parking lot, which now looked like a meadow in Kansas. A sea of ice and snow. She leaned against the metal pipes that corraled the used shopping carts. The sign RETURN CARTS HERE was just visible atop the drift; she had no idea what was under it. Carts and cars, for all she knew. She needed a drink. Now. It had been way too long.

She made her way to the doors of the building, finding that all the windows had been shattered. Snow had blown into the big, empty space. Drifts had formed against the shelves. Inside, a big display of Tide containers looked like a snow mountain at a miniature golf course. As she moved toward the aisles, she saw toothpaste and mouthwash lying under icicles. Deodorants and shampoos. She pushed some frozen eyedrops aside and found a tube of ChapStick. It was cold and hard, but it soothed her lips.

She made her way to the sign that said LIQUOR. There was nothing left but a few broken bottles. She pushed the snow aside with her hands. Her leather gloves were soaked, her fingers hardly moving. There were no intact bottles to be found. The wind suddenly created a shrill, crying sound as it echoed through the vast empty space. She cupped her hands over her ears. "Stop!" she cried out, and fled back to the parking lot, then plowed through the snow to the street.

She tried the Trader Joe's. Inside, it was the same story. Everything that could be eaten or drunk was gone, including the booze. She saw the signs for "Two

Buck Chuck" Merlot and Chardonnay that she and Harry and nearly everybody in the country bought by the case. But only the signs were there; the cases had long disappeared. She scrounged around—she and several others looking for food—and discovered a plastic container of chocolate-covered almonds. Getting it open was not easy, and when she used her teeth to rip the safety band, they sprayed all over the snow. She laughed out loud. It looked like dog shit on the streets of New York back before owners were ordered to pick it up. She ate a few of them and felt energy returning.

Back outside, she noticed the bar. MJ's, the plaque said in front. It was sandwiched between two other businesses, almost nondescript, as if you had to know it was there. She pushed her way through the snow to the front door, which was unlocked. She stepped inside. It was dark, and damp, and cold, but not as cold as outside.

As her eyes got used to the darkness, she saw the bar, a pool table, a stack of local gay magazines. But all the liquor had been cleared out. She went behind the bar to be sure, opening cabinets, doors, looking in the dishwasher, but nothing. She saw a door leading to a back room, and went in there. On a hunch, she came across an unopened case that said SMIRNOFF on the side. Ripping it open, she discovered three bottles of Smirnoff vodka, three of Bombay Sapphire gin, a bottle of Absolut Peppar, and—pay dirt—three of J&B Scotch. She grabbed a J&B and opened it, pouring it down her throat. Tears filled her eyes. She cried out in a mixture of laughter and pain, looking at herself sadly with an objective and pathetic eye, yet able to laugh at the stereotypical ridiculousness of the moment. She was an addict who had just found her fix. She hated herself.

She spilled half of it down her neck, but she didn't care. There was enough to waste. She was in heaven, gleeful. "Harry!" she cried out as if the lord might hear and suddenly make him appear. "Oh, Harry," she then moaned, and the moan gave way to tears that wouldn't stop.

Michael shouted to Wendy, who was just behind him, "I feel like a refugee you see in the movies leaving the village burning behind him."

She too was blown away by what they were encountering. Buildings ransacked, gutted, burning. Others completely razed by explosions. Dead bodies in the snow. People, everywhere, going every which way in panic, trying to save themselves. Half the people in Los Angeles, Wendy guessed, were homeless now, just as they were. They all wanted food, someplace to warm up, wait it out. Until it was over. If it was ever going to end. Everyone seemed completely self-possessed. No one even spoke to anybody else. She'd never seen people so distrustful and guarded in her life.

Michael said hello to a woman who had dried blood at the corner of her mouth. She was huddled in the doorway of a store on Hollywood Boulevard. "Don't touch me!" she screamed at him, crawling into a ball. "Don't come near me." She clutched her purse to her chest. Michael moved on.

But for all the horror stories they'd heard at Hollywood High, Michael found people not to be the "animals" he was expecting. Everyone had one major purpose: survival. Everyone was out for the same thing. But not collectively. There were no marauding bands of looters on the streets, no gangs taking over, no mobs following a leader to storm the mansion, nothing like that. People were moving toward higher ground, yes, that was certain. But it all seemed so unorganized; every man for himself. And it made sense. The Los Angeles Basin was like a big pool. Fill it and the people standing deep inside will drown. You had to move to the top; you had to swim.

Rachel cried constantly, which worried Michael but not Wendy. She said she'd be worried if the baby *didn't* cry. They took turns carrying her, Michael more than Wendy, for his legs were longer and he had an easier time moving through the snow. The street, Hollywood Boulevard, was a major artery, and it had been traveled constantly since the snowstorm had begun. Cars were buried all along it, but the snow was so high now that paths went right over some cars, and around others, probably big trucks and SUVs. Subway entrances were almost clear of snow, trampled by the foot traffic to reach shelter in the depths of the tunnels. Michael suddenly wondered, when nearing the Red Line station, what would happen when it started to melt. Could the subway system absorb all that water?

Houses seemed to have sunk into the earth because the snow was so high. In some cases, drifts reached the rooftops or at least the windows. The wind had changed the landscape of the city completely. It was as if Michael, when he was a kid and had a train set, had dumped soap powder all over the miniature city and puffed his cheeks out to blow it around. The thing that looked the strangest was the snow clinging to the palm trees. It was so incongruous that it was hard to accept as real.

At Western Avenue, they stopped and assessed the situation. "I think we should head up to Los Feliz Boulevard and take that to the house."

Wendy disagreed. "If we kept going straight on Hollywood we wouldn't have to climb the hill."

"We would eventually," Michael pointed out, "no matter which street we take. I think our chances are better on Los Feliz because it's a bigger road and more heavily traveled."

Wendy nodded. It made sense. They turned north and climbed until they got to Franklin Avenue. There, Wendy felt like her legs were going to give out. "I have to rest," she gasped, handing him the baby. "I just need to catch my breath."

He put a hand on her shoulder as she sat down on what appeared to be the hood of a car. "You okay?"

She nodded, breathing deeply. "No sleep . . . this climb . . . it's worse than a day at the gym."

Michael suddenly saw something. A big Army vehicle was dropping people off just a few doors down from them. It looked like a family—the grandparents, little kids, a couple about Michael and Wendy's age. Curious, Michael waved to one of the soldiers, who approached him once the people were safely inside a house. "What's up?" the man asked.

"Hey, I'm Michael Hanwell. I'm the weatherman on KTLA."

"I wouldn't admit that publicly if I were you," the guy joked.

"You gave those people a ride?"

The soldier nodded. "They were out walking all night. Left their house to come up to a cousin's place here. I think they got burned out. We're helping any way we can."

"My wife and baby and I are trying to get to my parents' place. It's just south of Los Feliz Boulevard, over near Griffith Park Boulevard. Any chance you're going that way?"

The soldier nodded. "We're heading up to the observatory. There's a command post up there."

Michael said, "Yes, my godfather, Cameron Malcolm,

is up there. He's the meteorologist who's helping with the rescue efforts."

The soldier smiled. "I saw him earlier. Hey, sure. Here, let me carry the kid." Michael handed Rachel over to him. She immediately stopped fussing. "Hey, he likes me."

"She," Wendy corrected him. "Rachel's her name."

The soldier nuzzled Rachel with his cold nose. "Hey, little girl, come on, we're gonna give you a ride to your grandparents' place."

Dolores felt warm now, almost hot. She thought maybe the weather had changed suddenly, so she crawled to the back door—she had drunk so much so fast that she feared she could not walk—and saw the forbidding winds and swirling snow. Nothing had changed at all. But she was all right now. She was going to make it. She was going to warm up and re-gain her strength and then head on back to Bob's. It wasn't that far. She could make it by nightfall, even carrying a couple of bottles. Maybe Harry was there now. Maybe he'd made it too. She hoped so, because what had happened at the house next door could have just as well happened to them. Harry could protect them from the murderous intruders, he was strong. She laughed out loud. Strong? A shark. Nobody fucked with Harry Hanwell. That was part of the rea-son she was so attracted to him.

Dolores closed her eyes. She asked her brain to stop working. If only she could just go on without having to think. To remember. If only she could just forget everything. She opened the second bottle of J&B. It wasn't her favorite brand, but delirious beggars couldn't be choosers. "I'd prefer Dewar's," she said out loud, and broke into laughter. Her stomach hurt and pains shot up through her chest. She felt good and warm and almost serene, but she was in agony. It seemed difficult to breathe. She needed air.

She went out the way she'd entered, the front way, but there was a fight going on out there, a fight over some kind of vehicle it seemed, and so she closed the door and retreated. She'd have to go out the alley door and figure out how to double back to Rowena. In the rear storage room, she chose the third bottle of J&B and a bottle of gin and stuffed them into the deep pockets of her mink coat. They weighed her down, but she didn't mind. She opened the door and headed out.

The alley was more of a parking lot, and she easily maneuvered herself to the street. Once there, however, she realized she'd forgotten her gloves. No matter, she could keep her hands gripping to the bottles in her pockets, and Bob's wasn't so far—or was it?

She got to the corner of Hyperion and suddenly wasn't sure which way she was supposed to go. She chose straight ahead, along the side of the building where it seemed easier to walk, where she had something to lean against. *Oh, I'm tipsy, I'm really tipsy.* She grinned, thinking that's what she'd be saying to Harry if he were here. But he wasn't. She was alone. But she would make it. Aileene would be horrified that she returned with two bottles of hooch, but hey, she got them from a bar, she didn't beg them off the neighbors. To hell with Aileene.

She spied an alley leading up from Rowena, and she turned into it. She remembered going up it once when she'd walked Herschel with Susan—Christ, she did that to have a cigarette without Harry knowing, didn't she?—or did they? It was an alley, but was it this one? Yes, she was sure, it led to Waverly, right next to Flo Brennan's house, or what had been her house. Dolores looked up. She thought she could see the outline of Bob's castle in the distance. Yes, she was going the right way.

She realized soon, however, that choosing the alley was a mistake. No one had walked there in days, so the snow was loose and thick and she sank into it too easily. But there was no turning back. She would have to make it work. *Take your time, just focus, concentrate,* she told herself. She pulled herself along, grasping the top of a chain-link fence, the side of a truck parked behind a building. She heard voices and looked up, saw some faces peering out of a window, looking down at her, this mysteriously elegant figure in black mink and a turban from Saks Fifth Avenue, drunkenly making her way through the snowbound alley.

Black. She was all in black. As if she was in mourning. In fact, this was the turban she'd worn to Dusty's wake, the outfit she had said good-bye to so many friends in, seen so many contemporaries buried in. Who was she mourning now? Rosie and Robin? Harry? Los Angeles? Her innocence? Shit, she thought with a grin, that had died a long time ago.

She stopped walking, gasping for breath. Tears welled up in her eyes. Harry was dead, that was what she had been fighting, been denying. He would have been there, he would have come, he was strong. Strong! Harry would never be coming.

She slid down into a squatting position against a garage door, yanked out the full bottle of J&B and opened it. Cursing herself for leaving the other bottle in the bar, she put it to her mouth and chugged it down. She had to fight the paranoia, the melancholy. Wasn't this what always happened? Didn't she always start obsessing on the dead career and the lack of love and the terrible, terrifying loneliness? Not this time! She pulled herself up to her feet again. Not this time! This time she would not give in to it. She would enjoy this absurd winter wonderland. She would prove to them—to herself—that she could do it.

Damn him anyway, she thought as she charged through the snow. Damn him for leaving her, for abandoning her for his precious art opening, dumping her just like he dumped her car. Just to spite him, she would live, she'd make it. She would show them all she was just as strong as Harry. The house is just up the hill, at the end of the alley . . .

With the last bit of energy she had in her body, and a burst fueled by the spirits, she continued to climb up the incline of the alleyway.

She didn't notice the figures moving in the snow behind her.

Only two miles from the alley where Dolores was walking, a big open-air Jeep with massive snow tires and chains was churning its way down Los Feliz Boulevard. Michael sat up front with the driver, the soldier who'd agreed to give them a ride. Wendy was in back with the baby and the other soldier, and two other people they had picked up as they climbed the hill on Western Avenue. They were teenagers who had been trapped in a movie theater on Sunset Boulevard when the snow began and were desperately trying to get home. They lived only blocks from the Hanwell house.

"The worst is over," Michael was telling the driver. "It's warming already. Can you tell?"

The driver pulled his collar up. "I'm not sure. I'm not used to this."

"It is. And that means this is going to melt. That's my big fear. Where's this water going to go?"

The driver shivered. "They're gonna start evacuating people by chopper tomorrow, I heard. Probably special cases, ill people, important people."

"Yeah, movie stars and politicians first," Wendy quipped.

"My little sister is very sick," Michael said.

"I'm sorry," the driver said. They passed a group of people trudging along. "I wish I could pick them all up. You feel so damned helpless . . ."

Michael turned to look at them. There was a man helping his wife, two kids who seemed to be enjoying it, another older man who was struggling. A guy who was dragging a plastic garbage bag behind him. Another who was—"Stop!" Michael shouted, turning his head to look at the people again, craning his neck. "Wait! Stop!"

"Huh?" the driver said, hitting the brake. The vehicle slid.

"Stop, stop!" Michael peered back over his right shoulder. "Jesus, it's Harry! That's my brother." He had recognized the guy dragging the garbage bag. "Harry!" Michael shouted, jumping to his feet, holding on to the top of the windshield as the driver brought the vehicle to a stop. "Harry, over here!"

Harry Hanwell, his face red, his beard covered with ice, was sure he heard his name being called, but he knew he was hallucinating. But when he heard it again, he looked up. He didn't believe his eyes. He blinked three times before the realization set in and the adrenaline started surging. "Mike?" he whispered. He saw the figure shouting, waving, saw him jump from the vehicle and start toward him. "Michael?"

They collapsed in each other's arms, falling into the snow like little kids who were playing. They'd never been so happy to see one another in their lives. Harry grabbed his little brother, shook him, wrestled him, hugged him. "Mike, Mike, how? Where'd you come from? How did you . . . ?"

Michael looked into his eyes and kissed him. He

couldn't ever remember kissing another guy on the lips, but there was always a first time. Emotions were bursting. "You're okay, you're here, we're near the house . . ."

Harry was crying.

Michael felt his heart leap as he helped his brother up. "I don't believe we found you! Dad gave you up for lost. Dolores too. Nobody had heard from you."

"I'm too nasty to die," Harry joked.

Michael laughed, patted him on the back, brushing the snow off him, and said, "Come on. These guys are giving us a ride to Dad's."

"That's cool." Harry saw Wendy beckoning with her arms from the Jeep, and he waved back to her. "I'm glad you're all okay," he told his brother.

"Yeah, we're fine, fine." Michael looked to see that Harry was still pulling the bag behind him. "Hey, bro, none of my business, I know, but what the hell is in there?"

"Stuff."

Aileene put bread crumbs out for the birds. On top of the patio table just under the overhang of the back roof, where the snow had not piled so high. If this was an unbelievable horror for humans, she couldn't imagine what small creatures thought of it. She watched from Susan's window as what seemed like hundreds of them suddenly came from hiding and ate. Herschel licked the window, barking at them, but even the sight of him didn't scare them away; they were that famished.

Susan was famished as well, for she had not eaten in one week's time. But she was not hungry. The pain was excruciating, and it did not let up. She was weakening and her color was the color of the snow. Her pulse was slower, and her eyes, when open, focused

only in a drugged stare. Aileene and Bob looked at
one another just above her bed. She groaned in pain,
twisting on her side, trying to press her fist into the
place in her upper back where she felt it the most.
"Can we give her another shot?" Bob asked.

Aileene shook her head. "It's been less than two
hours."

He bit his lip. "They're not lasting long."

"No," she said gravely.

He looked out the window. "It's stopping."

She sounded hopeful. "I know. Bob, will Cameron—?"

Suddenly Flo's voice penetrated the house. "Bob!
Bob, come quick!"

Bob shared a concerned look with his wife, then
hurried out of Susan's room, closing the door. He
knew that Flo had been sitting on the piano bench in
the living room, watching the situation on the street,
hoping to see Dolores returning. But she was focused
on more immediate concerns; the sight of a man—no,
it was just a boy—coming up the driveway with a rifle
in his hand. He was followed by two others who
looked just like him.

"What is it, Flo?" Bob asked as he entered the
room.

"Look."

He did. He recognized him. "That's the same kid
who came through the gate from Robin and Rosie's
yesterday."

"He has a gun." She looked at Bob with frightened eyes.

"So do I." Bob hurried to the foyer closet where
the shotgun was waiting. He picked it up, cocked it
and waited. "Is he coming up the front steps?"

Flo tried to see, looking straight down. "No. I don't

think so. I think he's going to the door off the driveway."

Bob said, "Stay here, Flo. Keep an eye out." Then he hurried downstairs.

He heard the door handle rattle. He stood back, lifting the gun. He didn't want to hurt anyone, least of all a young man who was simply desperate for food and shelter, but he needed to protect his loved ones. He shouted, "Go away. I told you to go away."

"We're taking this house!" Andy shouted in a shrill voice. "You got no choice, man."

Bob again shouted, "Get out of here."

"Open the fucking door, man!"

Bob held his ground. His voice was firm. "Go away."

"We're Kings! We are followers of Jeffrey King and we're the only people who are going to survive this!"

"Jeffrey King is dead, you moron," Bob shouted. "His compound out in Chatsworth blew up yesterday."

"No way, man. No fucking way that—" The blast came before his words had even finished coming out of his mouth. It blew the handle off the door. Metal flew across the room—startling Bob so that he jumped back—and a gaping hole appeared where the hardware had been. Bob heard someone scream from upstairs. The intruder kicked at the door, hard. He would be inside in seconds.

"I'm warning you—" Bob lifted the gun. This confrontation wasn't going to be diffused. "Don't make me shoot you."

Another kick. The door swung open. The shotgun quickly caught Bob in its sights. Andy was about to blow him away.

But Bob shot first.

As the young man crumpled into the snow outside
the door, Bob felt his guts turn over. He'd just shot
someone younger than his second son, someone else's
son, a kid, a boy. He dropped the gun, rushing to the
figure whose blood was turning the snow pink. Quickly
turning him over, Bob felt his pulse, looked to see
where the bullet had hit, but knew there was no hope.
The front of the boy's jacket was soaked with blood
and gore. He gasped twice. And died.

Outside the window, the others who were following
him had fled.

Bob felt his emotions falling out of his control. He
reached out, pulling the young man into his arms,
holding him against him the way Bob knew his own
parents would do if they were here, wishing to hell he
could breathe life back into him, wishing to hell this
had never happened, wishing none of them had even
been here to get into this kind of situation. Feeling
the warmth of the boy's blood soaking into his clothes,
Bob pulled away and dragged him into the room. He
looked at this person he'd just killed. The first person
he'd killed in his life. Even in Vietnam, he'd not had
to kill anyone. He thought he could only be in his
early twenties at most. Bob knelt down and closed the
boy's eyes.

Aileene appeared at the bottom of the stairs. "Oh,
no, Bob . . ." She brought her hands up to her mouth
as she witnessed the sight.

"Aileene, get out of here."

She was beside herself. "He's dead? Oh my God!"
Bob walked over to her, tried to take her in his arms
and explain, but she saw the blood on his clothes.
"You're hurt! He shot you!"

"No, no, I'm fine. I shot him. It's his blood."

Aileene looked anguished, not quite understanding.
"You killed him?"

He was about to explain that he had had no choice, but he heard Flo shout again.

"Bob, they're coming up the drive!"

"Aileene, get upstairs, get Flo, go into Susan's room. And stay there."

"What are you—?"

"Take this." He handed her the pistol.

She trembled, her eyes darting from the gun to his face.

"Don't open the door for anyone."

"Bob . . ."

"Go!"

She knew he wasn't kidding, and she trusted his judgment. She hightailed it up the stairs just as they heard Flo screaming that more people were coming up toward the house.

Bob grabbed the shotgun and stepped outside. Brandishing the weapon like some gunslinger in an old Western cowboy movie, he stood his ground, in the center of his driveway just outside the downstairs door of the house, facing about five or six people— none of them looked like they were armed—who were climbing up the drive. "Don't come a step closer," he warned, cocking the gun.

They stopped.

"I shot and killed your scout. I'll shoot and kill anyone else who takes another step in this direction."

No one moved. No one said a word.

"We're all in this together. We're all in the same situation. We'll help anyone who needs shelter or clothing or whatever food we have left. But we will not be killed for it."

An awful moment that seemed like hours but in reality was only seconds froze the scene in time. Finally, a woman turned and started back down the hill. Two more figures did the same. Then another. And another. But one moved closer to Bob. "Please, sir," the man said, "I don't have a weapon, I'm not a violent man. My wife is pregnant. She's very sick, next door, with those crazy King followers."

Bob nodded. "One of them tried to shoot his way into my house."

The man shook his weary head. "They think King is going to save them."

"He's dead," Bob said.

"We heard that rumor."

"It's confirmed," Bob assured him.

"Thank God. But, no matter, they're all crazy. My wife needs some food. That's all I want."

"Take your hands out of your pockets," Bob ordered. The man did. There was no gun in either hand. "Come up here." The man walked toward Bob, struggling in the snow. Bob quickly patted his pockets, and then lowered his gun. "Come inside."

The man cringed when he saw the body lying on the floor of the family room. "I think his name was Andy. He was the worst of them. He killed the women who owned the house next door."

Bob was aghast. "Robin? Rosie? They're dead?"

The man nodded. "He threatened everyone. He was high on some kind of drugs as well as King rhetoric." He looked down at the boy with an expression of contempt. "He slapped my wife across the face." Bob thought he was going to spit on the body. "Throw him out in the snow. He doesn't deserve to be in your house."

Bob went to the storage pantry off the furnace room where they kept the bulk items they bought at Costco. He pulled a Trader Joe's bag from a pile on top of the spare refrigerator and handed it to the man, who held it open as Bob put in a box of cereal, several cans of soup, a large jar of olives, some crackers and cookies and a container of Waleed's pita chips, which Bob thought looked tempting. He hadn't even known that they were there.

The man looked up at Bob with grateful eyes. "Bless you," was all he said, and he slipped out, eager to get back to the house next door and to his wife.

"Go the back way," Bob said at the door, pointing to the gate in the fence. "Just push it open. Why did you all come up the driveway anyway?"

"We tried to get into a house across the street, next to the one that burned. But it was full of people as well. Then we saw your gate was ajar. We didn't know that Andy was up here already."

So his name was Andy. The boy Bob had killed. Younger than his own Michael.

"It's going to be over soon," Bob promised the man. "It's warming. Can't you feel it?"

The man looked up. No more snow was falling. He nodded. He lifted the little black knob and pushed on the piece of wall that was the gate and it opened. "Thank you," he called back to Bob, and disappeared through it.

Bob hurried back inside the house, closing the door, but it would not stay shut. The hardware was missing; it could not latch. He dragged one of the easy chairs from next to the fireplace over to the doorway and pushed it up against the wood. Then he rushed upstairs to tell the women what had happened, and that it was safe.

At least for now.

As the big Jeep's gargantuan wheels ground through the snow, Harry told Michael and Wendy what had happened to him since he got "trapped" at the Getty by the initial snowstorm. He made no mention of stealing two priceless paintings. "I went to my office,

the only place I could think of to spend the night—
Dee had already taken off for Dad's—and then set
out from there on foot.''

Michael and Wendy were amazed that he'd come
across the city on foot. "I always knew you were
strong, bro,'' Michael told him, "but this beats all.''

Wendy filled Harry in on what had happened to
them and to their building.

"Cameron thinks he can get Susan out,'' Michael
said.

"The rest of us?''

Wendy shot Harry a look. "This experience hasn't
changed you any, I see.''

Harry stood his ground. "I'm not being selfish,
Wendy. We all want to save ourselves.''

Michael interrupted. "What's important is Susan's
life. She comes first. We'll see what kind of evacuation
plans Cameron says they've come up with. Thing now
is to get to Dad's so we'll all be together.''

"Dee will be happy to see you, Harry,'' Wendy said.

Harry's response was anything but enthusiastic.
"Yeah.'' He seemed to think about it. "If she knows
who I am.''

"What do you mean?'' Michael asked.

"She's always three sheets to the wind in the best
of times. I can't imagine what this has done to her.''

The Jeep slowed. They were nearing the intersection at Vermont Avenue. Three or four Army trucks
were parked there, soldiers were milling about, there
was another Jeep with a big red cross painted on it,
and several people were lined up outside it. The soldier who was driving stopped and said, "Give me a
second,'' and hopped out, leaving the engine running.
The soldier riding in the back with Wendy went
with him.

The other two people who had been riding with

them decided to get out here and make the last of the trek on foot. "We can do the same," Michael suggested. "It's only a few blocks."

"No, it's not," Harry argued, and he was right. "We're only at Vermont. There's a couple of miles still. I know it seems closer, but we're always doing it by car."

Wendy nodded. "Amazing how much bigger L.A. is when you have to walk it."

The soldier who was driving returned to them. "My partner's needed here. In fact, they want us and this vehicle up at the observatory. They've cleared the drive all the way up there. But I promised you a ride home and I'm gonna keep my word."

"Hey, man, thanks," Harry said.

The soldier clarified his statement. "I'm doing it for the baby."

Wendy reached out and touched the back of his head. "She thanks you too."

The soldier put the Jeep in gear and it continued its journey east on Los Feliz Boulevard. "I don't know how close I can get you, but at least to the foot of Waverly Drive."

"You know the area," Michael said.

"Yeah," the young man said with a smile. "I went to Marshall High. Grew up on Avocado Street. This is my neighborhood." The radio crackled. The soldier answered, identifying himself. "Yeah, I read you," he said. "Taking some folks to their house, got a little baby here I don't want to see have to be carried through the snow."

"Is that the observatory?" Michael interjected. The soldier nodded. "Tell them your passenger is Michael Hanwell. That he knows Cameron Malcolm."

The soldier did just that, and in seconds Michael heard Cameron's voice. "Mike? Mike Hanwell?"

"Cameron!"

"Mike, I just talked to your dad. You at his house?"

"Almost."

"We're going to get you out. All of you."

Harry slapped Wendy five. Wendy hugged the baby. "It's going to be over soon," she promised her daughter. "This big adventure. Oh, the stories you're going to grow up telling."

"Or being told," Harry added.

Cameron told Michael to have Bob contact him when they were all at the house. "Hey, Cameron, is it over?"

"I think. But the worst is yet to come."

"Rain?"

"Yes. And Santa Anas. Man, don't you miss reading the daily NWB reports?"

"It's going to flood," Michael said. "The real danger is the water."

"You got it."

The radio crackled. "I'll have Dad call you when we're there."

"Over and out," Cameron said.

Just as he did, the Jeep turned right on Griffith Park Boulevard. It slid as it descended the hill there, scraping something under the snow that they assumed was another vehicle that had been buried by the blizzard. "God, I miss skiing," the driver said, grinning. "I know this sounds nuts, but I'm kinda enjoying this. I used to—"

His words were cut short by an attack so sudden and out of nowhere that they didn't realize what was happening until it occurred. Jumping onto the running board of the Jeep, a man holding a big knife stabbed the driver in the back of the neck so quickly and cleanly that only a small spurt of blood hit Michael on the shoulder. The vehicle twisted when the man jumped off, turning suddenly as the soldier's body fell to the right, against Michael and scraping against another car covered with snow.

It took a moment for the three occupants of the Jeep to realize what had happened, what was happening. Someone had killed the driver. The Jeep was out of control. Michael grabbed the soldier's body, holding him in place as Harry, who was right behind him, reached over and grabbed the wheel, trying to steady it, keeping them from crashing, heading into a snowdrift that would act as a brake. They hit with a thud. Wendy grasped the baby tightly, bracing both of them with one hand.

As soon as the vehicle stopped moving and Michael, breathless, holding the dead soldier in his lap, gasped, "Who did this?" they had their answer. The man brandishing the knife leaped over the back of the Jeep, grabbed Wendy from behind, putting one hand over her face and holding the blade at her throat with the other. Michael gaped at the crazed man at his wife's neck as the soldier's lifeless body bled down the legs of his jeans.

Harry thought fast. Grabbing Rachel out of Wendy's grasp, he handed her to Michael. He said to the man, "You hurt her and you're dead."

"I'm getting out," the guy sputtered. "I'm taking this. Nobody's gonna stop me."

"Go ahead," Michael said, protecting Rachel with his body. "Nobody wants to stop you. Don't hurt her. We aren't going to fight you."

"Get out," the shaking man ordered, pressing his fingers into Wendy's eye, her nose, her mouth. She moaned in fear.

"Don't hurt her, I said!" Michael shouted at him fiercely.

Observing the situation, Harry had no intention of getting out, of letting this bastard win. He was sud-

denly filled with fire, with a burst of energy. He
twisted around, reaching up to grab the hand holding
the knife, and pulled it away from Wendy's neck.
"Go," he yelled to her. She jumped out of the Jeep,
then grabbed Rachel from Michael. Harry was standing in the vehicle now, both of his hands grasping the
assailant's hands, the knife blade glinting up above
them. From the front seat, Michael slammed his fist
into the assailant's stomach, but as he doubled over,
he plunged the knife into Harry's chest.

When the big blade exited his flesh, Harry gasped in
white-hot pain. But adrenaline surged and he went ber-
serk. He pummeled the guy. They smashed each other
into the steering wheel, twisted in the bloodied seat, the
knife almost slashing Michael. Blood gushed from Harry's chest, making him even more crazed. He growled
and flipped the assailant over the side into the snow,
and Michael leaped down onto his chest. The man let
out a gasp of air as Michael's weight crushed his lungs.

But the assailant was like Rasputin, lifting the knife
in the air yet again, and Harry held his breath as he
saw the man was about to stab his brother in the back.
Stunned by his own pain and loss of blood, Harry
jumped down in rage and grabbed the knife just before it hit Michael's spine, throwing it far into the
snow, where it disappeared. Standing there, he kicked
the man again and again as Michael lifted himself up.
Harry didn't stop beating the man with his boot until
he looked like a bloodied corpse. Michael finally
pulled him away. "Harry, stop. Stop. You'll kill him."

Harry, out of breath, out of blood, gasped, looked
his brother in the eye, and collapsed.

Dolores stopped to catch her breath. Her hands,
without the protection of her gloves, were bleeding
now; her face was nearly completely frostbitten. Even

her teeth were chilled to the nerves. She plodded along through the alley as the winds kicked up the top layer of soft snow. Her body was wracked with pain. Snot ran from her nose into her mouth, and she had to use the sleeve of her mink to wipe it away. Every time she stopped, she took a drink. One of the bottles was already empty.

But Bob's house was just up the hill. At the end of the alley. She could see the roofline now that the snow had stopped falling. Only a little farther. Or was it? Was this some kind of mirage, like the one she had had to pretend to see in a cheap *Lawrence of Arabia* clone? Was any of this real?

She fell again, and this time she didn't even make an effort to move. She needed to rest, to warm herself. She yanked the last bottle from her pocket. Opened it. Drank from it. She shut her eyes and felt sunlight hitting her face. Christ, she really must be drunk. Sunshine? She opened her eyes and realized it almost was, up there trying to push through the clouds. *Oh God,* she thought, *it's almost over, the nightmare is finished.* She took another hit of the liquid gold. She felt it heating her up. She could go on. She got up.

But almost immediately she stumbled and fell again. This time she couldn't move. She was facedown in the snow.

The three figures that had been following her stopped as well, crouching. She looked as though she'd had it. But they weren't sure. "Wait a few minutes," the oldest of the three said. "We got time."

The female in the group nodded. "It's worth it," she said in anticipation.

"Oh my God," Flo Brennan cried, frightened to death again. "Someone is pushing the gate open farther. They're coming back!"

Bob, gun ready, hurried to the window. Sure enough, a man was pulling violently at the gates, at each side, trying to open them all the way. Bob thought that odd—why? There was plenty of room to walk between them, as the others had done earlier. Why would they want to open them the full width of the driveway? Bob looked beyond the gates. Some kind of vehicle that appeared to be an open-air Jeep was sitting in the middle of the street, aimed at the driveway. "Jesus," he said. "They're coming in Jeeps now."

He opened the window next to the piano and stood in it with the shotgun poised. "Hey, you! You down there!"

The figure looked up.

"Get out. I'm warning you, I'll shoot. Go away."

"Dad," the voice shouted. "Dad, it's me. It's Mike!"

Bob took his finger off the trigger, shaking. Looking through the scope, he saw the young man's face. The face of his son. *Michael!* "Oh God, dear God, it's them. Mike is here!"

"What?" Aileene called as she came from Susan's room.

"Mike!" Bob shouted, rushing past her, down the stairs to the lower level. "They're here, Aileene. Michael and Wendy are *here*."

When Bob got to the bottom of the driveway, Wendy was already steering the Jeep up the incline. "It won't make it," Bob warned as he neared the gates. "The snow's too deep."

"We have to, Dad," Michael yelled. "Harry's hurt. He can't walk."

Harry? Bob glimpsed the figure slumped over in the backseat. "Oh my God." He ran down to Michael,

put his arm over his shoulder, but there would be time
for hugs later.

Michael was beside himself. "I think he's dying,
Dad. He's lost a lot of blood. He got stabbed. Someone wanted to take the Jeep."

As they approached the Jeep, which was half in the
driveway and half in the street, Bob said, "Rachel?"
Then he saw his grandchild lying on the other seat,
next to her mother, crying violently.

"This thing is pretty powerful," Michael said. "It's
got chains too. You wouldn't believe what it plowed
through."

"Get on," Bob said. "The weight will help." He
jumped to the running board. "Wendy, let me. You
hold the baby." She switched seats without argument.
Bob slid behind the wheel. Michael got on too, sitting
in back, one hand on his brother's shoulder.

"Here we go," Bob said, gunning the machine in
the lowest gear, and slowly it churned and protested
and struggled, but it made it past the gates, cutting
through the snow with the powerful energy of the
motor, crawling slowly but steadily up the steep grade
of the driveway. They held their breath, but it made
it to the house. Bob stopped it right outside the lower-
level door, which was open since he'd yanked the protective chair away in his rush to get down to Michael.

They carried Harry inside, passing the frozen, dead
body lying there on the floor of the family room. Michael did a double take. Wendy gasped. Aileene
rushed to her, took her and the baby in her arms, then
kissed her son and said a prayer as Bob and Michael
carried Harry up the steps to the warmth of the living
room fire.

Wendy did her best to explain what had happened
as Aileene calmed the fussing baby and Flo Brennan

went upstairs to get them some warm, dry clothes. Bob and Michael ripped Harry's shirt from his body and looked at the wound. The knife had penetrated his chest but not his heart, nor had it punctured a lung or an artery. "I think he was very lucky," Bob said. "I think it's just loss of blood. I'll get some water— we've got the teakettle on—and some towels and antibiotic."

"And some Demerol," Michael suggested.

Bob nodded. "Absolutely."

Harry gasped and his eyes flickered. Michael held his head up, resting him on his knees, and said, "You're home, now, bro. You're gonna be all right."

"Yeah," Harry said weakly, trying to grin, "but did I get the bastard?"

"You did, Harry. You sure did," Michael said, as Bob rushed back in with the teakettle filled with hot water, towels, and one of Susan's hypos. "Does it hurt, Harry?"

"Feels," Harry gasped, "like somebody shoved jagged steel into my chest."

"Someone did."

Bob slid the needle into his shoulder. In fifteen minutes he wouldn't feel pain at all, would sleep, would rest. "Aileene, we have to keep him from getting dehydrated, give him something to build up his strength, something with iron."

"Not a good time to cook liver and onions," Harry joked.

"Dad," Michael said, remembering as Bob dabbed the ugly wound in Harry's heaving chest with a wet towel, "you're supposed to call Cameron. I talked to him in the Jeep. He said he thinks he can get us all out."

Harry twisted in pain as Bob pressed the towel

against his pectoral muscle. "I know I'm hurting you, but we need to clean you up."

"Dolores," Harry whispered. "Where's Dee? I thought she was here."

No one answered.

Dolores lay there in the snow clutching the bottle in her fist. She heard voices above her. She wanted to lift her head up, but she couldn't. She wanted to say something to them, but she couldn't. Was she frozen? Too drunk? Too exhausted? Was she dead? She made out a male voice asking, "You think she's dead?" No, she couldn't be dead, not if she was hearing someone asking if she was dead.

Then another voice. "Yeah, hell yes."

"You want it?"

The girl said, "It's why we followed her, stupid. Mom needs it."

"Yeah. And it's getting dark. No one's watching."

Dolores suddenly felt like she was getting a massage. Hands moved all over her, up and down each arm, her shoulders, her face covered with a cooling mud pack. It felt delightful. Was she in a spa? Wasn't that a kicker! From desperation in an alley to being pummeled by some woman with her hair in a bun in a lavish day spa. But now, suddenly, she felt cold. She was back in the alley. And her coat was missing. Gone. She lay in the snow in her turban, her slacks and sweater and her boots. No, someone was pulling them off as well. Maybe they would rub her feet too. That would feel so good.

It was Aileene! No, not Aileene, she'd never be that kind. It was Flo, no, maybe it was Bob helping get them off her. She'd made it home, made it up the hill, she'd done it. The bed was cold, but that was because

the heat was out and she hadn't slept in it. It would
warm up. If she just closed her eyes, she could sleep,
and she would eventually wake up fresh and warm
and . . .

She turned her head from side to side, trying to get
used to the lumpy pillow. There was no feeling left in
her body. Her hair was spilling out from under her
turban; she could feel it on her neck. Bob and Aileene
were gone now, and thank God, for she didn't want
anyone to see her looking like this. A fright. A mess.
In the morning she'd be better. She would pull herself
together, get herself looking like a million bucks, like
she had in the old days. Like on her album covers.
And then Harry would come. And she would promise
him, not another drink. Forever. And this time she
would mean it.

She closed her eyes focusing on that thought and
fell into a deep, deep sleep.

Within two hours she was gone.

Dolores Delanova-Hanwell had frozen to death less
than two blocks from the foot of Bob's driveway.

The Seventh Day
Wednesday, January 21
High Temperature 74 Degrees, Reached by Noon

They talked through most of the night, taking turns sleeping and keeping watch over both Harry and Susan, or standing guard in the window. Flo could not bring herself to hold a gun, so she tended to Harry expertly. She had been a nurse before she'd been married so she knew what she was doing. And she had a kind bedside manner. She even got him to drink some soup and made him swallow vitamin pills. When she found some iron tablets Aileene had in a cupboard, she encouraged him to get them down as well. She knew he would need strength in the morning.

For Bob had talked to Carter, who told them that a massive rescue effort would begin, weather willing, the next day. Helicopters were going to come into the city with supplies and medicine, and the neediest people would be flown out. The Hanwells qualified, Cameron assured them, not only because of Susan, but because of Harry. Plus, Bob himself was important to the city. Cameron told Bob that Mayor Zarian and other officials wanted him to help them in this most dire time of public relations—he had to somehow look to this being over and plan a campaign to win people back to Southern California. "It'll take more than that," he warned Cameron. "Maybe a miracle."

Susan's pain worsened. The Demerol was having little effect now. Harry refused a second shot when Aileene wanted to give him one around midnight, preferring to keep his mind alert and live with the pain. Flo had dressed his wound, put his arm in a sling, and cleaned up the blood that had soaked into his hair and skin; she gave him a bath as any nurse might give a bedridden patient, her face flushed at times when she realized she was touching the skin of a very handsome and well-built man just under thirty, especially as he flirted with her playfully.

Wendy guessed, rightly, that Harry was trying to deny what they all knew was the truth: Dee was not coming back. It had been too long, it was too cold out there, it was too dangerous. Harry said, "She's holed up in a bar somewhere, found herself a drinking buddy, she's singing her old hits, she's fine." But Wendy knew he didn't believe it. Something, some unspoken sense of things, some intuition, told them she wasn't ever coming back.

The living room sofa, facing the fireplace, had been turned into Harry's hospital bed. When Michael got up at three a.m. to do his time watching at the window, he saw his brother was awake. "I never said thanks."

"What for?" Harry asked.

"Saving Wendy. All of us."

"I've done worse to studio heads," Harry joked. "Those bastards would just as soon stick a knife in you as give you the deal you're asking for."

"People are monsters."

"Always have been, brother." Harry sucked down some water from a plastic bottle. "We all should have listened to you, Mike, and gotten out of town when we could have."

"I should have listened to myself," Michael added, smiling. "I just never really believed it was going to get this bad."

Harry looked at the fireplace. His jacket was on the floor drying near the glowing logs. "Hey, Mike."

"Yeah?"

"In my jacket. I got a hot porn magazine."

"Huh?"

Harry laughed. "From a store over on Western I stopped in. Like old times, huh?"

Michael remembered. "Oh, man, I'll never forget. I was only about twelve, I think, when you came home with all that filth."

"You were fourteen. Don't even remember the classmate who gave it to me. Said his parents were onto his collection, couldn't risk keeping it at home anymore."

"Jerry Anderson was his name."

"Hey, right. And we cut that hole in the material covering the box spring to hide it."

Michael reminded him, "*You* did that, to *my* box spring. That's why Mom found it."

"She found it 'cause you said you wanted a lock on your door. Talk about giving parents reason to snoop."

Michael laughed. "Remember how Dad tried to give us that lecture Mom told him to give, and how we knew he really wasn't mad, wasn't really serious?"

Harry rolled his eyes. "A couple of years later he told me that was pretty wild stuff we had."

"Mom said he burned it."

"Like hell he did. I'll bet it's still out in the garage somewhere in his workbench."

Michael laughed again and looked out the window. He looked alarmed. Somebody was walking up the hill with a burning patio torch in his hand. It worried Michael, and he rose to his feet, gun ready.

"What?" Harry asked.

Michael said nothing, peering outside. Because the fire lighted the room, it was difficult to see clearly, but thank God it wasn't snowing any longer. The flaming torch stopped at the front gates—it looked like someone was rattling them—but they gave up, and the patio flame, and the people it was guiding, continued up the hillside. "Good thing we padlocked it," Michael said. "It worked."

Michael had not only secured the gate before dark, he and his father had also boarded up and nailed shut the lower-level door. The house was their fortress and they would secure it the best they could. And protect it with their lives.

The baby fussed, but Wendy fed her and soon she was fast asleep again. They'd taken mattresses down to the main floor, giving them all places to sleep. The night dragged on. Harry slept soundly. Aileene hardly shut her eyes. Bob tossed and turned. Flo dreamed she was back home across the street. Michael, perhaps because of the talk of the porn collection and the thought of those naked girls turning him on so in his early teenage years, curled up next to his wife, felt sexually aroused, but told himself this was not the time or the place to fool around. But it did tell him that he was still alive, and that life was going to go on.

If they made it out.

*   *   *

"How you doing, sis?" Michael asked Susan as he sat down on the floor next to her bed.

"Michael," she whispered, opening her eyes, taking a moment to focus. "I heard your voice, but I thought I dreamed it."

"Mom told you we had come, but I don't think you were aware. We're all here—me, Wendy and Rachel. Harry too."

"Where were you?"

"Out there," he said, nodding toward the window. "The tundra." He brought his hand up to brush her hair from her cheek. He had never seen her look like this, so ill, so on the brink. He'd been in hospital after hospital with her, had been there through the worst of the attacks of pain, but she'd never looked like she was about to die. That's how she looked this morning. Her eyes were sunken deep into their sockets. It frightened him and made him forget his own aches and pains.

"You don't look so hot," she said to him.

"It's the beard," he said. He scratched it. "I think it's kinda cool myself."

"You look old."

"Distinguished?"

"Creepy."

"You should see Harry."

She giggled. But then she winced from pain. Michael helped her turn to her side. She was weak, feeble. How would they get her out? Harry might be able to walk with help, but Susan certainly couldn't, especially not out there.

"Michael?"

"Yeah, sis?"

"Can Auntie Dee come and sing to me?"

Michael bit his lip. "Sure, pumpkin, but later, okay?

You get some rest now. We're going to get out today. We're going to be leaving. To get you some help. So you get your strength. Promise?"

She tried to smile but she couldn't manage it.

Michael stepped out of her room and closed the door.

"Jesus, Mom, she's dying!" Michael shouted at his mother upstairs in the master bedroom, where Aileene was standing with her arms full of clothes.

"Don't say that!" she admonished him. "I won't hear that. It's bad enough with Dolores disappearing out there somewhere, Harry almost bleeding to death, not knowing if any of us are going to make it out of—"

He cut her off. "She's almost in a coma, Ma. I never expected it to be so bad."

She nodded and took his hands. "I know. I know."

Then he saw her vulnerability surfacing, the sensitive girl coming forth from hiding under the guise of the determined woman who would be their rock. "Mom, I'm sorry I yelled." He took her in his arms and held her gently.

When she felt tears coming, she pulled back. "If I start crying, Michael, I'm just not going to stop. Here." She thrust some clothes into his arms. "I found the warmest things I think will fit. Plus there's an old pair of your jeans you left here after you painted the new kitchen window. They're folded on top of the dryer." She pulled open a drawer in the dresser. "And some of your father's undershorts."

"You want me to wear Dad's underwear?" he asked in shock.

"This is no time to be funny."

"Funny? It's disgusting. Besides, Ma, I don't wear any."

"Information I don't need to hear," she said, handing him a pair of briefs. "They'll help keep you warm. We have to get up that hill."

"We have a Jeep. It'll take us."

She shook her head. "And what happened when you were last in that Jeep? Your brother almost died because of it. We might have to climb, Michael. Your father is getting those snowshoes we put away in the garage years ago. I only hope they're still there." She dug in the underwear drawer for a pair of long johns. "Your father could wear these. I think we should see if Cameron can get through to Dr. Shemonsky. Find out where she is. Where we can take Susan."

"Mom," Michael said, looking at her with respectful eyes, "I'm impressed. I know how much you're hurting, and yet you still take charge."

Aileene turned to him and deflated for half a second, looking suddenly lost and vulnerable again. "Michael," she said softly, "if I didn't, I would simply come apart."

Out of the frying pan and into the fire, the old cliché goes, and it was like that this morning in Los Angeles. People fled their flimsy buildings and packed themselves into larger flimsy buildings. On the west side of the city, several hundred people waited out the snow inside one of the Fox soundstages. Everyone was nervous, hungry, tired, but they shared a sense of relief from the hell of what they'd already been through. It was becoming bearable. But then . . .

It started with a sound. A moan, a ghoulish cry from the depths of some horror film, as if some giant were groaning before making his kill. The giant was the roof. The weight of the collected ice and snow was too much to bear. Like many a supermarket and warehouse roof before it, it simply came down. On hundreds of innocent faces staring up at the ceiling. A ceiling that was now upon them.

The same thing happened in the middle of town, at the Staples Center, where thousands of people were gathered today not to see a Lakers or Clippers game or to hear a rock concert or attend a Jeffrey King rally, but for shelter from the storm. The drifting snow, thousands and thousands of pounds of wet buildup, had pushed the roof, which had not been constructed to withstand weight like that, to its breaking point. When the ceiling started to fall in, they rushed for the doors, hundreds being trampled to death. But they were the lucky ones, the ones who died quickly. The rest would freeze to death in agony while caught under thousands and thousands of pounds of ice and snow and twisted metal.

No building with a flat roof was safe. They had not been built to withstand anything more than the weight of perhaps a few inches of water. Trouble was, most big buildings in the Los Angeles Basin had those exact same roofs.

The roof of the Hanwell house was peaked, and made from Spanish tile. It was solid and secure. When the snow started to melt, it would slide off to the ground. But the family hoped they would not be around to see that. "I don't know when we can go," Bob told them, keeping watch in the front window. "Cameron promised he'd call us with the word."

They sat and waited and waited. Harry seemed to be gaining strength. He ate, took Advil, kept drinking water. Aileene fixed everyone some food, a soup she'd made with cans of broth and vegetables and a chicken from the freezer that had defrosted. She was amazed the gas was still working. She served the hot soup with Ritz crackers and a box of See's candy for dessert. Flo moaned that if she died, Dr. Atkins wasn't going to let God admit her to heaven. When Susan screamed in pain from her room, Flo, rattled because of the uncertainty they were facing, started to cry. Wendy put her arms around the stranger, hoping to comfort her. "It's almost over," Wendy promised her. "This horror is almost finished."

Michael helped feed Harry his soup, because he could use only one arm. As he gobbled it down, Harry said, "Mike, the bag I was dragging. It still in the Jeep?"

Michael hadn't given it a thought. "Hell if I know."

Harry's eyes flared. "I gotta know, Mike. Go down and check."

"What can be so important?" Wendy asked.

Harry thought he'd use a line that had worked before. "Contracts, important client stuff. Life has to go on after this is over. I saved my most important files."

"Files?" Michael looked distrustful. "What's in there, the whole filing cabinet?"

"What do you mean?" Harry asked.

"That thing was heavy. You were using all your strength dragging it."

"I shoved them in a fire hose to keep them from getting wet," Harry explained.

"Pretty good idea." Bob had to admit that.

"Mike," Harry said, "placate me. Go down, see if it's still there."

Michael nodded. "Okay. You just tell Charlize Theron that she owes *me* when her next million-dollar check arrives." He left the room.

Bob said, "Do you represent her, Harry?" But before Harry could answer, he jumped to his feet. "It's Dolores!"

Everyone got up, rushed to the window. "What? Where?"

"At the gates. Look!" Bob said.

They saw a woman in a black fur coat trying to pry the gates open.

"It looks like her," Aileene said.

"Without the turban . . . Is that her hair?" Flo asked.

"Dee?" Harry said, straining to sit up, to see.

Bob shoved the window open. "Dee! Dolores!" he shouted.

"Bob, Michael should be just outside the garage," Aileene reminded him.

"Mike, can you hear me?" Bob yelled as loudly as he could.

"Yeah, Dad," came the faint reply. "I'm by the Jeep."

"Mike, go down the driveway. Dolores is at the gates!" Bob waved at the woman, but it looked like she was taking a step backward, like she was leaving. "Dee, no!"

They all saw Michael hurrying down the drive, sliding in the snow, calling out to the woman as they had, but she kept going.

"She's scared," Bob said.

"She's drunk," Aileene said.

"It's not her," Flo offered.

Indeed, it was not, Michael realized when he got down there. The woman who was walking away was wearing a black fur coat, she had the same shape and hair, but it wasn't his brother's wife. "Don't mean no harm," she said to him, afraid, hurrying away.

Michael got into the Jeep, started it and turned it around in the driveway in front of the garage doors so it was now facing downhill. As he was about to get out, he noticed the garbage bag on the floor where Harry had set it, right behind the backseat. There was snow on it, and blood, so he ripped it open to discover, indeed, just as Harry had said, a fire hose. Frozen solid. He lifted it and set it over his arm, just as he saw a figure move through the gate on the left side of the Jeep, a young man who jumped him and wrestled him to the ground.

Michael fought back, punching him. The guy got off a swing, hitting Michael in the jaw, but when the guy jumped up and rushed to the boarded-up downstairs door of the house, Michael grabbed him, twisted him around and kneed him in the balls. The guy bent over, cried out in pain, looked up and spit into Michael's face. Michael slammed him into the stucco and rapped his head against it, knocking him out. Then he dragged him back through the wooden gate and closed it, leaving him there as a warning to others that might think about coming through the gate.

He picked up the bag with the stupid fire hose and started up the back steps.

Inside the house, everyone stared at the figure who had just appeared in the living room. It was a slight woman in her late fifties who looked like she was not quite there, like she'd been shattered by all she'd experienced. "Please forgive the intrusion," she said. "I was next door. The situation there has become untenable. I didn't know what to do . . ."

"Are you all right?" Bob asked.

"What do you want here?" Aileene asked with distrust. "Why did you come here?"

"I didn't know where else to go. I was in the house across the street when it burned down. Then—"

"That was my house," Flo told her. "My home."

Loretta nodded. "I'm so sorry. The same thing happened to mine. Way down the hill. Days ago. I didn't know where else to go."

"Well, you can't stay here," Aileene said.

Bob walked toward her. "How did you get in? Didn't you see my son in the driveway?"

Loretta said, "He was going down the hill as I came through the gate at the back of the house. I was careful. I didn't want anyone to see where I was going, for fear they'd follow."

Michael walked in behind her. He was startled. Harry's eyes quickly focused on him. "Is it there?"

"Right inside the back door," Michael said. "Who is she?"

"An intruder," Aileene said clearly.

Bob asked the woman, "How many people are next door?"

"A hundred at least. They're hungry and angry and a few are inciting them."

"We have one of them down in the family room. He's dead."

"I know. Andy was the worst," Loretta said. "Frightened me terribly."

"He was a Jeffrey King follower," Flo offered.

Loretta nodded, looking disapproving. "They are all over the neighborhood. Very misguided."

"I'll say," Michael said.

"We can give you some food if you want," Aileene offered, warming to her slightly. "We don't mean to be selfish. We are just being protective."

"I understand," the woman said. "I am hungry. My name is Loretta Zane. I'm on the Los Angeles City Council." She looked at Bob with a puzzled expression. "I swear we have met before."

He nodded. "I've been to several council meetings. Bob Hanwell. I've done PR for the city many times."

"Ah, of course. Hanwell Public Relations."

"These are my sons, Harry and Michael, Michael's

wife, Wendy, my wife, Aileene, and Flo, our neighbor."

"Where was your house, Loretta?" Flo asked her.

"Echo Park."

Harry, who had been listening, said, "You traveled almost as far as I did. Why this street? How'd you end up here?"

"I didn't know where I was," the woman said, taking off her coat and gloves. "I am so grateful to you all for your hospitality." She walked around the sofa to Bob, who was still standing in the window by the piano. "Thank you, sir, thank you so much."

Bob offered his hand, but the woman, surprisingly, aimed to embrace him. He looked puzzled, glancing at Aileene over her shoulder as she pressed herself to him. Aileene shook her head. Harry looked even more distrustful. Michael just stared, trying to remember what he knew about this woman that unsettled him.

What none of them saw was that Loretta, as she hugged Bob, looked straight out the window and held her position for a moment, so the man who was peering up from the dining room window in Robin and Rosie's house knew she was in.

While Loretta ate in the living room, Bob called Michael into the kitchen to talk to Cameron on the shortwave. "Mike, I've been talking to Washington, San Francisco, the National Weather Bureau and some of the major universities that have been studying the situation, and they all agree—rain will come, with rapidly rising temperatures, bringing flooding of such magnitude that it might put the 2004 tsunami to shame."

Michael said, "How do you tell ten million people to move to high ground through seven feet of snow?"

"You'd be amazed at what people can do to survive," Cameron said.

Bob interjected, "Cameron, stop the airdrops, the hell with supplies. Use boats and choppers to get people out, for mass evacuation."

"We'd need every whirlybird in the world," Cameron said.

"So get them," Bob said, knowing it could be done.

"Dad," Michael warned, "we're talking about going from—what?—twenty degrees to seventy or eighty in a matter of a day. That's going to be like turning a hose on an ant colony."

"It's going to be like opening the Hoover Dam on them." Cameron cleared his throat. "So here's what I want you to do. The rains will be here by early morning. I want you to start up before dawn, get up here before the sun comes up. Before the winds come, which could ground all aircraft. You'll be in the first helicopter that takes off, I promise you."

Bob asked Michael a few moments later why he looked so worried.

"Rain," Mike said. "The worst is still to come."

When Loretta had finished eating, Aileene nicely but firmly urged her to leave. "Can we give you anything to take with you?"

"I'm afraid to go back there," the woman said, making no move to get up.

"Jeffrey King's followers?" Flo asked.

Michael's eyes flashed. Yes. He connected this woman to Jeffrey King. But how? Why? She had indicated his followers were demented. She sounded like she disapproved of them.

"You can't stay here," Bob said. But he couldn't give a good reason why. They had room, they had plenty of firewood, they had gas that cooked food.

And they were leaving before morning. Something about the woman worried him. It was just a feeling.

One that Harry shared. "We want to keep this just family," he said. "If we let you in, we will have to let others in."

"Perhaps you should," the woman answered brusquely. "I would share my good fortune if I had it."

Harry glared at her. "I'm a selfish kind of guy," he said, making no excuses. He turned to his father.

Bob said, "Loretta, I'm sorry. I mean, hell, I suddenly feel like we're on that show—what's it called?"

"Survivor?" Flo offered.

"Yes. Like we're sitting at the tribal council, voting someone out."

Loretta demurred. "I understand. I'm just really grateful for your hospitality." She stood up. "While it lasted."

Bitch, Aileene thought, having had enough. *Get out of my house.*

It came to Michael suddenly, in a flash. "You stood up for Jeffrey King!"

They all stared at him. Loretta said nothing.

"Yes, that's it. That rally, the one MSNBC carried. People were talking about it at the shelter. You told Contessa you were a supporter of his. That's why you've been next door. Andy was one of your henchmen."

Florence was aghast. "King's crazy followers killed Lady. Threw me out of my own home. Burned it down. You were with them!"

"You are not welcome in our home," Aileene said firmly. "I want you out."

"I'll walk you back to the street," Michael offered, wanting to be sure they were rid of her. "Let's go. Your leader is dead. If you want to stay alive you'd better leave now."

Loretta suddenly grabbed her chest and fainted. Dead away. Her knees sagged and gave out, and she crumpled to the carpet before Michael could break her fall. She hit her head on the coffee table. "Jesus!" Harry said.

"My God!" Flo gasped.

Aileene wanted to scream. She had instinctively distrusted this woman from the moment she'd waltzed into their home, and what Michael had realized about her had put her over the edge. "Throw her out into the snow," she said, "like she did to others."

"Mom," Michael said, "you don't mean that."

As Bob helped Michael put Loretta in a chair, Aileene fled the room, angry and upset.

Bob found his wife in the chilly master bedroom, sitting on the bed, her hands clasped together. "Mike went down to the garage to put the snowshoes and skis into the Jeep. They might come in handy."

She said nothing.

"We should each carry a backpack. Food, for energy, Susan's medicine, rope in case we need to tie ourselves together to climb."

She still said nothing.

"It's getting dark. But warmer."

Nothing.

"Aileene, say something."

"I want that woman out of my house."

He blinked. "I do too, honey, but I think she might have had a slight heart attack."

"I think she's pulling the wool over our eyes."

He shook his head. "We can't be sure." Then he looked out the window. "Oh Jesus."

"What?"

"The Morina house is burning. Look, even the trees are on fire."

She jumped up and joined him at the window. Sure enough, that beautiful English Tudor home was engulfed in flames. "Just like Flo's," she said softly. "It's what's going to happen next door. And here too."

"Don't say that."

"I don't think we'll ever get out."

"We will. Leaving Loretta Zane behind to pay for her sins."

"Even if we do get out, I don't think we'll see our beautiful home again."

"Aileene, honey." He took hold of her shoulders. "The reality is that the flooding might take the house before anyone has a chance to burn it down. The snow is starting to melt. Mike said it's drizzling a bit already. We need to get some sleep because we have to be up and out of here around four."

Aileene closed her eyes in anguish.

"Susan won't make it much beyond that. We have to get her on that helicopter, honey. We don't have a choice. We have to save our daughter."

"Bob," she whispered, letting him pull her closer. "Bob, I can't take much more. I just don't think I can hold it together much longer—"

"None of us can, honey," Bob said, holding her tight, trying to make her feel his strength, his love. But then, honestly baring his soul, he added, "Including me."

At ten in the evening, Michael came inside with two skis and a hammer in his hands. "I have an idea. In case we have to walk or climb some of the way." He started taking everything off the coffee table.

"What are you doing?" Harry asked.

"Building a sled. For you if you need it. And for Susan."

"I'm gonna walk, brother," Harry vowed.

"Michael," his mother said, objecting, "I bought that at Sloan's, when we first moved in. You can't."

But he did. He knocked the legs off it and nailed the skis where they'd been. It was primitive, but it would work.

Bob brought a box in from the garage and set it on the dryer. Inside was their camping equipment, several backpacks and rolled-up sleeping bags. "We'll all carry a pack except Wendy—you'll have the baby—and Harry."

Good, Harry thought. *I'll be carrying the fire hose. Somehow.*

"Wendy," Aileene said, "I think we still have that baby sling carrier thing that you left here last month."

"Great," Wendy said. "That'll make it so much easier."

Bob said, "We'll pack one of the backpacks with food, one with medicine and stuff, another with the rope for climbing, and one with important papers and things that you might want to take, Aileene."

She nodded.

Flo, keeping a close eye on Loretta, saw her eyes flicker and open. "Where are you planning on going?" Loretta asked weakly.

Bob answered for everyone. "Higher ground."

At two o'clock, when everyone was asleep, Loretta, having miraculously recovered from her "heart attack," drifted to the living room window. She reached into her pocket and pulled out a little flashlight, which she clicked on and off two times.

Looking down at the window in the house next door, she waited for the response. It took a moment, but it came. Two distinct flashes of light. Good. They'd seen it. They knew she was inside. Now where were they? What was keeping them? The family would be leaving soon, throwing her out. She could grab one of the shotguns and hold the family at bay while the Kings entered. It was time to show these people who this house really belonged to. It was time to prove to them that Jeffrey King could not possibly be dead!

Loretta saw Harry struggling to get up, so she went back to the chair, pretending once again to sleep.

Harry sat there, assessing his strength. There wasn't much. But he had made it here and he would make it out. And the fire hose would go with him. It wouldn't take up any room on the floor of the Jeep. But if they had to walk, hike, climb, that was another story. Being so weak, he knew he would never be able to carry the hose, and he seriously doubted that anyone else was going to offer to do it for him.

He stood up. It took him a moment to get his bearings. Loretta stared at him. He ignored her and walked to the kitchen, where he dug out the industrial-sized roll of plastic wrap that his mother always kept in a deep drawer. Putting it under his good arm, he grabbed a sharp bread knife from the block on the counter and carefully opened Susan's door.

She was sound asleep as a result of the drugs. Herschel ran up to him, wagging his tail as Harry rubbed his head. He set down the plastic wrap and then went to the back door, where Michael had said he put the fire hose. In his vision, it glowed. He picked it up reverently, all his enthusiasm and determination returning, and dragged it with one arm, feeling considerable pain, into his little sister's room.

She slept through it all as he cut the ends off the hose where the pieces of raincoat had been stuffed. Then, feeling where the paintings started and ended inside the hose, he sliced it in the middle. He pulled the precious treasures from the two pieces and quivered with delight at the sight of them. He unrolled them, stared at them for what seemed a lifetime, pleased that they had survived the journey so well. Hell, why wouldn't they? They'd survived centuries!

When Susan moaned, he quickly cut off enough plastic wrap to cover each one, to protect it from moisture, and set them atop one another. Then he returned to the laundry room just outside Susan's door, where Bob had placed the backpacks he'd found in the garage. The paintings would not fit into one of them, but there were two bedrolls there. That would be perfect. Harry could make the case that one could come in handy, and he would be the martyr to carry it. So he unfastened the buckles and took it to the privacy of Susan's room. On the floor, he unrolled it, put the paintings inside, and rolled it back up again. It absolutely did not appear the slightest bit suspicious; it simply looked like a sleeping bag. And it weighed a tenth of what the fire hose did; it would be easy for him to carry.

Harry thought it through. He had to have a better reason for taking it. What would he say? He would make the point that one sleeping bag would be a kind of insurance policy in case someone got hurt or injured. They could put the person in it and conceivably pull the bundle up the hill. Someone would dismiss the notion, saying the Jeep would take them the whole way, blah blah.

But Harry would win. He knew how to do that.

When he finished, he replaced the kitchen knife, put the plastic wrap back in the big drawer he'd found it in and carried the bedroll with him back into the living room. It was almost three in the morning.

Only an hour to go.

Harry flopped back on the sofa with pain in his shoulder, dropping the bedroll next to him, and fell asleep immediately.

Loretta really began to worry. It was three fifteen

in the morning and no one had shown up. Had they
lost their nerve? Were they too weary? Too hungry,
too tired, too scared? She began to burn. Cowards.
They were all cowards. They talked of being proud of
Squeaky and Tex, but they were as bad as the pigs
themselves. Jeffrey King was not dead. Impossible.
Unthinkable. It was a clever move to protect himself.
She lay there, pretending to sleep, praying for the
sound of people at the doors and windows.

Bob woke up. He slipped away from the others,
who were still fast asleep, and showered for what he
feared could be the last time in his own home, grateful
that the gas was still working, that the pilot light was
still lit, that the water was still hot even though the
master bedroom was frigid. He put on the long underwear Aileene had found for him and dressed in cordu-
roys, but he didn't don the silk undershirt he had often
worn skiing, worrying that it might be too warm today
if what Michael said came true, that it would feel like
summer again real fast. As he was tying his shoes,
Aileene walked into the bedroom. "You had the last
watch?" he asked her.

She nodded. "I took over for Michael. Bob, we're
not taking that awful woman with us."

"Loretta? Who suggested that?"

"She's deranged and pathetic. She must be realizing
her King isn't going to save her. That's why she's here
and not leading the band of thugs any longer. She's
going to want to come."

"She's not coming with us," he said firmly. "We're
being kind enough in leaving her here."

"Not in this house," she said loudly, firmly.

Bob nodded. "Let the ghost of her Jeffrey rescue
her."

Aileene looked sad. "If only we could take something with us, things we treasure."

Bob shook his head. "It's enough we have the chance to save our daughter, and our boys, and ourselves."

"And dear Flo. I'm just sorry it took this disaster to get to know her better."

"It takes something like this to bring people together," Bob said. "And isn't that a sad statement?"

In the living room, everyone had awakened. Harry asked Michael, "What time is it?"

"Three thirty. Ugh." He'd slept again for only twenty minutes.

Wendy stretched. She looked at Rachel, next to her, wrapped in a blanket on the mattress on the floor by the piano. "She slept all night."

"How do you feel, Harry?" Michael asked, rubbing his eyes, trying to wake up.

"Better. Stronger. When do we go?"

"Soon."

"I'm going to freshen up," Flo told them, and left the room.

Which left Loretta sitting there staring at all of them. "I feel better too. But I don't understand what's going on. This seems very organized. You're not only going to 'higher ground'—you have a plan. Somebody's waiting for you."

"Yes, well," Michael said, "don't concern yourself with it."

"I'm naturally curious," Loretta said.

"You're nuts," Harry corrected her. "So much for Armageddon, huh, baby?"

Michael ended the discussion once and for all. And he said it to her face. "Where we're going is none of your goddamned business."

Michael brushed his teeth and opened the back door. He could feel the difference. The air felt humid, the warmth noticeable. When he stepped out, the snow, instead of crunching under his feet as it had done for days, felt wet, packing down easily. He picked up some in his hand and clenched it in his fist. It made a ball and he threw it into the darkness of the deep, empty pool. He looked up at the sky and felt the light drizzle hit his face.

Earlier the night before, though the Hanwells hadn't heard him, Brian Williams had condensed it for the rest of the country. "There is an unearthly silence in the city," he had said, "punctuated only by explosions and the cries of the homeless, the hungry, the cold. No one knows the death toll. Thousands have frozen to death, some in their tracks as they searched for a way out. Officials say when the snow melts, the bodies will be more plentiful than the palm trees. In the past few days, we have reported murders for chocolate bars, killings for a winter coat. Now that seems to be changing. People are numb, losing energy, perhaps even the instinct, to survive. On top of that we have heard incredible tales of neighbors helping neighbors, even strangers, of people coming together to do the same thing, survive."

Peter Jennings summed it up a bit more dramatically. "Even with the fate of the city still unknown at this time, what is now and will forever be known as Ice Storm L.A. will go down in history as one of the most awesome and gruesome tragedies mankind has ever known."

Aileene packed a big purse full of things she couldn't live without. A pearl ring that Bob had given her on their twenty-fifth anniversary. A gold necklace she'd fallen in love with when they were in Rome. An antique brooch that had been her mother's. She also stuffed in things of sentimental value. Some of the children's report cards from school, family photographs, a few legal documents, things she felt they could not live without. The purse had a shoulder strap. Bob would tell her it was too heavy. But she would carry it. She could not leave it behind.

Wendy had already packed a backpack full of baby stuff, but then, because she didn't know where they were going or how long they'd be there, even for sure if they were going to get out, she gathered up the last of the baby bottles with formula, diapers and old baby clothes that Bob had found in the attic, things that the baby might need if they ran into trouble. Since the backpack was full, she wrapped them in a sleeping bag she found in the laundry room and went outside to stash it under the seat of the Jeep.

While she did that, Bob and Michael went downstairs and ripped open the boarded-up doorway. Then they dragged Andy's body out into the snow, around the corner near the garage, so Susan would not see it and become upset. Michael went down to the gates at the front of the driveway and unlocked the padlock and pulled the gates wide open. The street seemed silent, almost eerie.

When he got back to the house, he and Bob went upstairs, to find that Loretta Zane was gone. She had disappeared. "She must have gone out the door by the pool," Flo surmised.

They were glad. Aileene was particularly relieved. But no one really cared, because she was unimportant at this point. She could have the place if she wanted it.

Aileene dressed Susan in her ski jacket and Bob carried her down the stairs to the lower level. Aileene said, "Honey, it's going to be all right. We're going for a ride, a little adventure. At the end of it, we're going to get you to the doctor."

Flo came down and got into the rear seat of the

Jeep. The backpacks, sled, skis, snowshoes, ropes had all been put in or tied to the vehicle. Flo thought she would look very much like Granny on *The Beverly Hillbillies*, a television show she remembered from her youth, riding atop this cluttered vehicle to a new life. When Bob lifted Susan up and inside, Flo buckled her firmly into the seat next to her and let her body rest against hers. Herschel ran out of the house, dragging his leash and harness, hurried through the snow and leaped into the vehicle, hiding under the seat at Susan's feet. Bob turned and waited for the others in the darkness, holding the kerosene lamp so they could see.

Upstairs, Michael helped his brother to his feet. "You okay?"

Harry nodded, trying to gather his strength. Michael started to lead him away from the sofa. Harry resisted. "Mike, the bedroll."

"The what?"

"There, on the floor. I need it."

"What for?"

"Mike, don't ask questions."

"You'll fall over if I let you go."

Indeed, Harry was tottering. Moving the paintings had sapped all his strength, and he was going to need strength no matter how the day ended. "Mike, come back for it. Promise me."

"Yeah, yeah," Michael said, a shoulder under his arm, trying to lead him toward the stairs to go down.

In the family room, Aileene watched as Harry appeared, leaning on his little brother's shoulder. "I'm doing fine, fine," he said to his mother, anticipating her fears. "It's Mike we gotta be worried about. He doesn't feel too steady to me."

"Jesus, for a skinny guy, you're heavy." Michael groaned.

"Solid muscle," Harry boasted.

"No, it's the bullshit you're so full of," Michael shot back.

"That too," Harry admitted.

"Stop it, you two," Aileene said, laughing.

Harry pulled his arm from Michael's shoulder, wanting to do it himself. And he did. He walked to the door without help, although he did let his mother take his hand. Then he turned back to Michael and said, "Go back up and get the bedroll by the couch."

"Harry, come on," Michael said, sure they would not need it. "There's no room. It's stupid."

Harry looked at the bag slung over his mother's shoulder. "Mom has a bag full of silverware or something," Harry protested.

Aileene shot him a look. Then she looked back at Michael. "At least he doesn't want the fire hose."

"Who's gonna carry it?" Michael asked. "Everyone has backpacks except—"

"I know the assignments, Mike," Harry said testily, "but I'm carrying it. That's all there is to it."

"Enough already," Aileene cried out. "Stop this bickering." Michael and Harry both stiffened. They had seldom heard their mother's voice rise to such a high pitch. "Get it, Michael, if only to placate him. We don't have time to waste."

Harry bristled at her superior tone. But if it accomplished what he needed, he could easily overlook it.

"I'll lock the door at the top of the stairs here and go down the back way with it," Michael said. "I'll meet you outside."

Michael passed Wendy coming down with Rachel bouncing in front of her as he ran back up the steps. "I'll be right there. Get in the Jeep," he called out.

In the family room Wendy told Aileene they were

ready. "I put some extra Pampers and stuff for her in the Jeep earlier."

"Let's go, then," Aileene said.

Bob walked in. "What's taking so long?"

"It's okay, Dad," Harry said, reaching out for his shoulder. "Help me out."

Bob let Harry grab his shoulder, and he aided him walking out the door. Wendy followed with the baby. But Aileene didn't move. She stood still. She was leaving her home, a house she loved, the place where she had conceived and raised her children, the place where she'd thought she would live out the rest of her days. Well, hell yes, she would. "We'll be back," she said aloud. "We will be back." Then she turned and left, shutting the broken door behind her.

But when she stepped outside, when she saw that everyone but Michael was in the Jeep, she heard voices and they frightened her. Robin and Rosie's yard was filled with people. She heard Loretta's voice, trying to incite people, trying to egg them on. She heard someone say they had the guns, that Jeffrey King wasn't really dead. "Bob!" she shouted.

"Get in, get in," Bob said. He'd heard the voices too. And he knew what was coming. He jumped into the front seat of the Jeep, next to his wife and Harry, and started the engine just as Michael hurried down the stairway leading from the patio to the garage. Hershel barked and growled.

Michael had seen the torches in the yard next door from the higher level. "Dad, they're coming here!" he shouted.

"Mike, come on!" Bob yelled.

Michael tried to make it to the Jeep before the mob came through the fence. As he did, the bedroll fell to the snow.

"No!" Harry cried. "Mike, pick it up!"

Michael stopped, not realizing what had happened.

"To hell with it," Bob said.

Harry jumped up, trying to get out of the vehicle.

His mother grabbed him, holding him there. "Harry, have you lost your mind?"

"Mike," Harry shouted, "get it, grab it!"

Michael bent over to pick it up just as Wendy turned to see what they were talking about, but instead she saw the gunfire, the explosion that ripped through the darkness. She held her breath and bent over to protect her daughter.

Loretta appeared in the open gate in the wall with a mob of angry, desperate, hungry, dazed people behind her. Herschel tried to bolt from the vehicle, but Flo held tightly to his leash. And then there was another gunshot, aimed at Michael. Had he not bent down to grab the sleeping bag, the second shot would not have missed his head. The dog hid under the seat. "Dad, go, go!" he shouted, heaving the bedroll up into the back of the Jeep and grabbing hold of the vehicle just as the intruders arrived. They poured through the opening in the fence, like creatures from *Night of the Living Dead*, just as the Jeep started to move down the driveway, pulling Michael behind it.

"Shoot them!" Loretta ordered.

"Let them go!" another voice said.

"Take us with you!" another pleaded.

"Don't leave us, please . . ."

Suddenly Loretta threw herself toward the Jeep, grabbing Michael's leg as the Jeep descended the hill. He kicked as she was dragged along, trying to get her hands off his pants leg. "You'll kill yourself," he yelled. "Let go . . ."

"Please, please, take me with, take me with," Loretta pleaded. "He said we'd live, he promised to save us . . . he said we'd make it!"

As they heard her pathetic litany, Michael pulled himself up into the Jeep, but still Loretta was fastened to his leg. The dog, who had been cowering, scared by the gunshots, under the backseat, suddenly growled and snapped at her. "Herschel, yes," Michael said, thinking quickly. And the dog bit the woman's hand, causing her to let go. She fell and doubled over in the middle of the driveway. Another shot rang out, but it didn't hit the Jeep. In a moment, the Jeep moved through the gates.

"Harry," Bob warned his son, "keep your arms inside." Harry pulled his shoulder in just as the side of the Jeep scraped against the right gate. The snowshoes that Bob had tied there broke into pieces and fell off. But they were out in the street.

All the way down it, Aileene stared back at her beloved house. The fire was still burning in the living room, making the windows look warm and comforting. That was how she would remember it if she never got to see it again. Warm and inviting. A place of refuge from the storm. A place of love.

She put her arm around Harry and said, "Hold on, everyone. You know how your father drives."

It took them over an hour to go only a mile, but they encountered almost no problems and little interference. The mob had not followed them past their driveway. There was no one on the streets at this hour—which was precisely why they were traveling just before dawn. The warm clothes they'd dressed in became unbearable, and one by one, they started to shed layers. Flo helped Susan out of her ski jacket Aileene had dressed her in, but then worried that the girl might have a fever, for she was burning up. Harry handed her his bottle of drinking water, but Susan could not sip it. She was delirious.

They took Los Feliz Boulevard because it had been heavily traveled—it was the way the soldier had driven the Jeep to bring them to Los Feliz—planning to take Commonwealth Avenue up the steep incline toward Griffith Park. The snow was slippery now because it was starting to melt. The drizzle was getting stronger. By the time they made the turn onto Commonwealth, they were soaked. The headlights caught nothing but daunting melting drifts in their glare. Flo was sure they were not going to make it. She held her breath in fear, and gripped Susan's hand. Sensing her fears, Wendy reached around Susan, who was between them, and patted her shoulder. "It's going to be okay, Flo. Trust that."

Bob gunned the engine and as the night started to turn to day, the big Jeep crawled up the mountainside toward redemption.

Or disaster.

On the top of that mountain, Cameron Malcolm stood drenched. The rain was really coming down now, sooner than he'd anticipated and harder than he'd expected. Weather, he thought, laughing. Who the hell could predict it? He watched the rain hit the snow, watched the mounds of it lessen before his eyes, already seeing, in the early-morning haze, rivers starting to form as the water made its way down the hill.

Parker Van Hecke joined him out there, puffing on a cigar. "Sunrise," he said.

Cameron nodded. "The last day."

"They on their way?"

Cameron nodded again. "They'll be here."

The general groaned. "I gotta get the governor out.

He's been in his Malibu place all the time. We thought he was in Sacramento."

"We gotta get everybody out."

Van Hecke shook his head. "We're gonna give it a goddamned good try, Cameron." He choked a bit on the smoke, then coughed up some phlegm and spit into the snow. "And that's all anybody can expect us to do."

With the sunrise came the rain, drenching rain that made Bob wish the Jeep had a roof. The wet could not be good for Susan, and it was not good for driving. He did everything he could to keep the wheel steady, but despite the huge wheels covered with chains, they slipped and slid every few yards. Halfway up the hill, the Jeep hit something in the middle of the road. They jolted forward, but the seat belts saved them. Bob backed up as Michael jumped out and investigated what was in their path. He dug into the mound of melting snow in front of them and discovered an abandoned Mini Cooper. "Dad, you'll have to go around it."

Bob looked right and left and nodded. Backing up some more, he turned the wheel to the right, said, "Hold on, everybody," and jammed his foot on the accelerator. The Jeep seemed to leap into the air as it plowed through the mound of snow at the curb and sailed across the front yard of a mansion. Wendy caught a glimpse of people looking out the windows of the house, probably thinking they were imagining this. Bob stopped once he got the vehicle back into the street and Michael climbed on. "Go, Dad!" And Bob did.

When they reached the entrance to the park itself, Harry warned his father of something. "Dad, when-

ever I went running up here, there was a chain across
the road. If it's there now, you've got to bust through
it. Build up some steam."

"Got it," Bob said, again slamming his foot on the
accelerator. Indeed, under the snow, the heavy chain
snapped and broke and flew into the air.

"We did it," Harry said. "Too cool."

The Jeep strained and groaned as they moved
through the park, on a road that had had few vehicles
on it since the snow started. Several times they all
thought they were stuck for good. At one point,
Wendy gave Aileene the baby so she could take the
wheel while Bob and Michael got out to rock the Jeep
in the snow when they were stuck. When they reached
the entrance to the Greek Theatre, where the road
joined Vermont Avenue, they cheered. But the rain
was coming down so hard Bob could barely see, and
already arroyos of water and mud were cutting into
the hillside. The place was washing away.

They got another half mile up the hill, just past a
picnic area and the parking lot for the Greek, and
then the Jeep stopped. Just stopped. The engine
coughed and died. Bob tried to restart it, but it was
pointless.

"What are we going to do now?" Flo cried, shaking
with cold from the rain.

"Climb," Michael said. "Come on, everybody out.
We're going to continue up the road on foot."

Inside 3449 Waverly Drive, an uncontrollable Loretta, her bleeding hands wrapped in towels, barked
orders. But no one paid any attention. People dug
through drawers to find dry clothes, they raided the
pantry and kitchen to nourish themselves, they found
medicine and drugs and wine and water. Loretta
spouted her usual hyperbole about Charlie and how

he had finally been vindicated, but no one even bothered listening. The King was dead. They all knew it. So now how were they going to be saved? It looked like the family who had just left in the Jeep were the ones who were going to save themselves. People were exhausted. People were sick of this. To hell with Loretta's race war, her silly ravings. They just wanted to stay here until the rain stopped and the sun came out again.

When Loretta ordered two of the more militant of Jeffrey's followers to torch the place, one of the boys asked why. "Because these people were hateful. They were the epitome of what Jeffrey resents."

Someone just laughed.

"The people who owned this house reject the King! They sent Charlie and the others to prison for life!" she shouted. "These people—" She looked around and grasped a framed photo of the family that sat on the grand piano. "These people," she said again, brandishing the photo in front of them, "are your enemy. These people got away. We let them get away. They don't deserve to come back to this house. We must show them that we are—"

One of the boys pulled out a pistol and shot her through the chest. Then he turned and nonchalantly walked away. "Christ, she got on my nerves," he muttered.

"Yeah, dude, she be annoying as hell," the other boy said. "I want something to eat. They got any Oreos? I got me a taste for Oreos."

Loretta had been shot, but she wasn't dead. Slowly, she crawled over the scraps of coffee table legs that Michael had bashed to pieces, to the fireplace, where she reached in and pulled a burning stick from the fire. It singed her fingers, but she held it nonetheless. She would do what the cowards wouldn't do. She

would burn this place to the ground if she had to do
it herself. She would die in the fire, but she would die
knowing that what she had believed in all these years
was not for nothing. She would die proudly. And join
her beloved Jeffrey.

But before she could press the burning stick into
the flammable silk and brocade of the sofa, another
young man who had been watching simply stepped on
her hand. He smelled burning flesh as he ground his
big Dr. Martens boot onto the flame, putting it out,
crushing Loretta's hand as well. Then he stepped back
as he saw her looking up at him.

And then he watched her die.

It was after six in the morning and they were not
yet there. Cameron, standing outside the observatory
in his yellow hooded slicker, began to have his doubts
about the family making it up the hill. He saw that
the snow was nearly gone from the mountaintop and
little was left around the observatory building. Water
was rushing down from the hills above, water with a
force that could cut steel. Chunks of the parking lot
were already torn away. He could make out one major
stream—it looked like a stampeding river—beginning
to take trees with it as it dug a deep canyon into
the side of the hill, directly toward a group of Los
Feliz homes.

He imagined that the same situation existed in all
of L.A.'s canyons. A canyon would be the worst place
to be. Those homes would be the first to slide down
to their destiny, toward the middle of the city, where
the mass of humanity had chosen to leave. He remembered that La Cienega Boulevard had once been a
major runoff from the water in the mountains, years
and years before Los Angeles was even half the size

it was now. He could well imagine the asphalt of the long street ripped up by water by ten this morning.

He wondered suddenly about the subway tunnels. Had word gotten out—did the *people* get out? This water had come faster than expected. The temperature was about fifty degrees already and climbing. He looked down the road leading to the parking lots where the helicopters sat waiting. Would it stay intact? Would Bob and his family even make it up the road?

He recalled something he'd just read, a story about Colorado's Big Thompson River Canyon back in 1976. Communities had disappeared in minutes, streets and homes and stores wiped off the map with a splash of water. It happened because of a bad rainstorm up in the mountains. It was as simple as that. There had been no warnings of such a flood, only of thunderstorms up at the top of the canyon. Forty thousand cubic feet of water per second flowed through a section called the Narrows, which had been only twelve feet deep and was, by the time it was over, thirty feet deep. Cameron did some math in his head and realized that was three hundred and twenty gallons per second. Not that the same would happen here today, but the water was going to be amazingly plentiful, amazingly strong.

He looked over the city from the side of the observatory building and thought it wasn't wrong to assume the entire city could be, in the end, washed right out into the ocean. This arid place, where in past years droughts had done so much damage. It almost made him laugh. This was not some remote area in China before they built the Three Gorges Dam on the Yangtze. This was Tinseltown, Hollywood, L.A., the Big Orange, the Coast, SoCal. This was truly amazing.

He turned to go back inside, but something caught

his eye and he moved closer to study it. The water was digging deep ruts all around, trenches surrounding the base of the building. It was as though someone was scraping the earth away from it—and all it was perched on was earth. What would happen when that earth was no longer there? What he saw was a deep, wide crack in the foundation of the building. The Griffith Park Observatory, built in the 1920s, was cracking. Part of it could conceivably crumble and go rolling down the hill. Into someone's backyard.

Already, incredibly, the rains of the late night and early morning, combined with the rapidly rising temperatures, were taking their toll on Los Angeles. Dodger Stadium had cracked open and collapsed because it had been built on a land-filled base, which eroded faster than the rain seemed to fall. The Pacific Coast Highway from Santa Monica north to Point Dume above Malibu—what had been Malibu—was completely wiped out by massive mud slides. On that highway, the original J. Paul Getty Museum had crumbled into the Pacific. The Pacific Palisades had literally disappeared; Palisades Park was now one slope of mud and twisted underground telephone lines and chunks of what had been Ocean Avenue.

The same was true of the desirable canyons. Houses had oozed down the sides of the hills, stranding residents who climbed up trees or telephone poles or streetlight posts that hadn't fallen and killing many others. The entire hillside in Benedict Canyon, where many years ago Charles Manson's followers had slaughtered innocent people, disappeared under a rolling quake of mud. Downtown, the Disney Concert Hall stood proudly unscathed on its hill with the rain beading off its shiny and distinctive roof, almost as a defiant symbol of Los Angelenos' resilience. But across the street the foundation of the Dorothy Chandler Pavilion, filled with thousands of refugees from the storm, cracked in several places, threatening the collapse of the building.

The Hanwell party knew they needed luck.

Bob cupped his eyes with his hands and looked up the hill. They didn't have a choice. "We go straight up the side."

Michael gritted his teeth and nodded reluctantly. He put on the heaviest of the backpacks, the one with the food in it. Bob strapped on the one with Susan's medicine, Flo took the light one with the rope, and Aileene put her arms into the one she'd filled with important papers. She also put the strap of her heavy shoulder bag over her head, so she wouldn't lose it. Michael helped put the bedroll on Harry's back. Wendy saw that he was in obvious pain and offered to carry it. "I can do it," she assured him. "It'll balance the baby."

"I'm fine," Harry insisted.

Bob and Michael unleashed the sled that had been tied to the other side of the Jeep and fastened Susan to it. Herschel jumped on with her, and Aileene secured his leash and harness tightly so he would not fall off and be swept down the hill. And they started to move.

Bob and Michael led, followed by Aileene and Flo, who pulled Susan and the dog on the sled, which worked fine through snow but was difficult to drag through the muddy areas. The rain was depleting the entire area of snow more quickly than they would have thought. "It's warm rain," Michael explained. "When you dump ice cubes into your sink, what do you do to get rid of them fast?"

"Run hot water," Flo answered, understanding.

"That's what's happening here."

The odds were against them, and it was an immense struggle. They did fine for the first hour, but then they had a major setback. The road, the path of which they were climbing on foot, suddenly disappeared. A wide river of water had cut through it, ripping out the asphalt, taking the dirt beneath it. All they could see was a swirling, fierce river of brown water, roaring as if to beckon them. Michael and Bob, leading the group, took a step back. They could not cross it. What would they do?

Michael put his head up high, felt the wind. "The rain is going to stop. It's diminishing already. When it does, the northeasterly dry winds are going to blow in. The Santa Anas let the rains slip in first, and now they want their turn."

"Is that good?" Harry, leaning against his brother, asked.

"It's going to ravage the city," Michael answered.

"Not much left to ravage," Aileene added.

They left the roadway and moved into the trees. Harry and Wendy, carrying Rachel in a baby carrier attached to her neck, brought up the rear. When the winds came and the sun was out, the snow here would be gone in a flash; thankfully, at this hour, it was still pretty thick. They were soaked to the bone, and it was getting warmer and warmer, so they began to discard their heavy jackets and protective clothing. Michael felt weighted down by the backpack filled with water and candy bars for energy. He had to hang it from a tree branch while they stripped off their jackets, to keep from risking it going down the hill with the water.

"Who's got the rope?" Bob asked.

Flo said she did. She pulled her backpack off and handed it to him. He tied the rope around his waist,

then around Michael's, stringing them all together so
they were linked like hikers climbing Mount Everest.
They tossed the backpack away. Less weight made it
easier to climb.

"Harry," Aileene told her son, "we're not going to
need that either."

"We might," Harry protested. "Someone falls and
can't walk, we can pull them in the sleeping bag."
Even though he was in excruciating pain, he'd rather
lose his arm than the bedroll. He felt faint at times
and breathed heavily.

"It's really kind of you, Harry," Wendy said.

Kind of me? Harry wondered why she said that.

There were other problems. Flo could not move as
fast as the others. Thus, everyone's pace was slower
than it should have been. Even when Michael took
the baby from his wife and Wendy and Bob took over
pulling the sled, they could not move faster than Flo's
stride. The deadweight of the sled, of Susan's body,
was difficult. Sometimes three of them had to lift it to
get through the trees. Susan remained delirious, crying
out at times, looking as though she'd passed out at
others. They stopped constantly to make sure she was
breathing all right. Her head burned with fever, and
her parched lips were beginning to bleed, even though
a steady stream of water was hitting her face.

"We gotta stop again," Michael said suddenly.

"Why?" Bob asked. They'd just regained their pace.

"I have to take a leak."

Harry laughed.

Michael handed the baby back to Wendy and went
behind a tree while they waited.

Wendy was the only person who didn't have good
boots—none at the house had fit her. Her shoes were
wet, muddy, nearly falling apart. Her pants kept snag-
ging on branches and bushes that miraculously ap-

peared out of the snow. She'd cut her legs and
scratched her hands—they had long since discarded
their gloves because it was now so warm.

Rachel cried incessantly. Wendy asked them to stop
so she could feed her. They sheltered under a big tree,
and she put a bottle in the girl's mouth, which stopped
her tears for a few minutes, but a few minutes only.
Once they started moving again, the baby resumed
squealing. Wendy held in what she was feeling—*I can't
stand it!*—because she knew she would have to.

They were about one third of the way up when the
hill suddenly got steep. Looking up, they could not
even see the tip of the observatory building from their
vantage point. Bob tethered the lead rope around a
small tree, but Michael was leery. "Dad, I swear it
doesn't look strong enough."

Bob tested it. "It's okay, Mike." He pulled himself
up a few feet and looked back, then beckoned to the
others to do the same. They started to move, but suddenly they heard Bob shout. He fell backward, and
Michael caught him. The tree had simply come out of
the ground. Unlike other parts of the country where
the soil freezes deep, the freeze Los Angeles had experienced was on the surface only; the minute the
snow defrosted, so did the earth. Snow and ice seemed
to come down the hill with Bob. He hit another tree,
cracking his back, and Michael grabbed him just as
he was about to fall farther, taking all of them along
with him.

"Dad, you okay?"

Bob gasped for breath and nodded. "Sorry."

"It's all right. You didn't know. I'll lead for a
while."

"Yeah," Bob said gratefully. "I don't have much
strength left."

"Ditch the pack," Michael said, and Bob did. Then

Michael helped him up, braved the rain and slush and mud and led the party. Bob and Aileene pulled the sled, Wendy held Rachel, Flo let Harry lean on her—he even let her carry the bedroll for a while—but he was having the most difficulty now. His chest hurt and his legs felt numb, the way they had making the long trek from Beverly Hills to his father's house in the punishing blizzard. But what was on his back would make it all worth it. Hell, they could amputate his legs for all he cared, it would still be worth it. He was carrying the world on his back.

They shed even more clothing as they climbed. Everyone was down to sweaters, and even that seemed oppressive in the heat. Michael thought it had to be seventy already. Aileene could stand it no more. She asked everyone to stop while she took her sweater off and stood only in her blouse. Flo did the same, and the men stripped to undershirts. Wendy, who had been wearing a sweatshirt she couldn't breathe in, took it off and stood in her bra. "So who the hell's going to see me?" she quipped, and they all laughed for the first time in hours. Michael peeled off his shirt, wearing only his old painting jeans now, backpack against his skin.

Harry was still in his ski outfit. He was reluctant to set down the bedroll for fear that the water would push it down the hill. He would suffer. It was a good cause.

Cameron walked around the building again. As the hours passed, the situation became more critical. The building was cracking in many places. The back wall over the hillside was nearly suspended in air, the earth having washed out from under it. He went up to one of the large telescopes and searched his pocket for quarters. Surprisingly, it worked. He looked through it, focusing not on the sky but on the city below. The entire basin still seemed to be filled with snow, but he could once again see the red-tile rooftops and the flat asphalt roofs of large buildings and apartment houses. He happened to pan in on a house on stilts on a hillside in the Silverlake area. Then he saw it just fall down the hill.

He knew the same thing was happening all over the city. The earth was nothing but water mixed with soil. Six-plus feet of snow would turn to water. It would wash away even the biggest and strongest buildings in the downtown area. He pictured the Bonaventure Hotel, with its cylindrical glass walls that looked to him like a set of canisters, imploding into the lake in its lobby. He knew the sewers would overflow and the storm drains would reach capacity within hours and even city streets would become seaways, carrying houses and patio furniture and trees and cars and people out into the ocean. He already doubted that many of the beach cities were still standing. If only the rain would stop. Then they'd have the chance to get people out. He didn't want another Santa Barbara. There really was no Santa Barbara left. The rains, which had started there hours before they reached Los Angeles, had washed most of the city into the Pacific.

Cameron was right. At that very moment, all across America, newscasts were reporting the change in the weather in Southern California. The temperature in Los Angeles was seventy-two and rising, and it wasn't even noon. Mud slides reported by military command posts were the worst in the history of the state where there had been terrible mud slides since people started recording them.

No city was being spared. San Francisco had missed the snow, but now some six inches of rain had fallen in less than twenty-four hours. The entire San Joaquin

Valley was a lake; no city there had been spared flooding and some towns had been completely wiped out. There were virtually no crops left in the state of California, which would cause an economic shock that would affect the entire world. The total snowfall had been six feet seven inches in only five days' time. Now it was melting faster than it had piled up. It was easy to do the math.

In the industrial heart of the city, rail yards had ceased working, trains freezing where they'd stopped. Now the rains knocked the tracks from their holdings, washed out their underpinnings, and whole trains simply toppled over. The concrete aqueduct that was called—euphemistically—the Los Angeles River, where kids usually skateboarded, rode bikes or attempted the more rigorous extreme sports, filled with flash floods and overflowed its banks. It was built on a natural riverbed, however, and the overflowing water had begun to undermine the tall buildings throughout downtown.

At the Dorothy Chandler Pavilion, the split down the center of the building widened, sending crystal chandeliers smashing to the marble floors, causing windows to fall out, crushing those who were fleeing. At the Blue Line subway stop in Long Beach, a tidal wave of water hit the people who had sought refuge there, and melting snow flowed down stairs, escalators, through air shafts, drowning them instantly. Olivera Street, the birthplace of the pueblo and the Spanish mission that had become the city of Los Angeles, was gone. An explosion in the Hilton Hotel rocked the nearby area, and the building crashed down onto the abandoned, snow-covered Harbor Freeway and burned. The exhibit halls of the convention center nearby were now large swimming pools.

Power lines arced and snapped and electrocuted

people all over the city, literally frying them in the streets. One of the tall and expensive condominium towers on the Wilshire Corridor between Beverly Hills and Westwood caught fire and went up like a torch, the orange glow lighting the wet skies. Roofs continued to cave in everywhere in the city, and walls followed them. People who had managed to stay in their homes through the siege were forced out now, and they tried to take refuge in cars that had been buried in the snow. But the water took them like rubber ducks in a bathtub, tossing them around as they moved with the force of the newly created rivers. All the major streets leading down from the hills, streets like Vermont and Western avenues, Doheny Drive, Robertson Boulevard, streets that had been full of life, became pathways of destruction; they were now rushing rivers, wiping out everything in their path.

The Arboretum near Pasadena was desolate, devoid now of any living plant. Pickfair, the famous tourist attraction that had once been the home of Mary Pickford and Douglas Fairbanks, already seized by hungry, homeless victims, burned to the ground; the panic-stricken people inside had tossed priceless antiques into the fire to stay warm, and the flames had been too powerful and had spread in a matter of minutes. Homes that were the anchors of movie star maps, houses that had once belonged to the big names like Lucille Ball, Bette Davis, Danny Thomas, Jimmy Stewart, and mansions owned by current stars like Cher, Barbra Streisand, Sting and Larry King were all lost to the mud. Parts of the San Fernando Valley resembled the Pacific Ocean.

The Hanwells were now at the halfway point. Harry's arm was terribly swollen; Aileene feared an infection had set in. They stopped for a moment when she remembered she had tossed a bottle of antibiotics that they'd picked up on their last trip to Tijuana into the backpack with medicine. She found it for Harry and made him swallow six capsules just to play it safe.

Michael leaped a big stream of water that was cutting sideways down the hillside. Then he reached out to help the others across, but his backpack got in the way. "I can't move with this thing on me," he said.

"Let's eat the food and toss it," Flo suggested.

"Last chance for high-protein bars," Michael said, handing them out. "And one Snickers." He gave the dog a treat that he'd pocketed before they left.

Flo grabbed the Snickers and took a bite of the gooey bar. "Dr. Atkins, forgive me."

"I thought you said the rain was stopping," Harry reminded his brother as he chewed on a Power Bar. It seemed to be still coming down in buckets.

"Can we get rid of anything else?" Bob asked.

"No," Aileene said quickly. "The one I have has papers and Susan's medical records in it. We may need that wherever we end up. I'm fine with it. And I'm not giving up my purse."

"Give me the bedroll, Harry," Wendy said. "I want to change the baby."

Harry blinked. "What?"

"The bedroll, the sleeping bag you're carrying."

He didn't understand. "What are you talking about? What's that got to do with changing the baby?"

"There were diapers in the backpack with the medicine that Bob tossed. But I put diapers and powder and salve in the bedroll. Stuff for Rachel. Just in case."

Harry swallowed hard, feeling his heart flutter, his life draining away. "No. Mike brought this down from the living room. I slept next to it. There's no baby stuff in here."

"Yes, there is," Wendy corrected him. "I packed it and put it in the Jeep when Michael went down to open the gates. It was under the seat."

There were two of them? That's why she thanked me for carrying it. I grabbed the wrong one. Harry's mouth gaped open. No, she had to be mistaken—she had to be wrong.

"The one I packed is a North Face. The other was Columbia Sportswear, I think."

He recalled the Columbia insignia as he'd opened it. But he wasn't thinking—he wasn't hearing her. He was in another world, numb, stunned, praying she was wrong. He fell to his knees in the mud, ripping the bedroll from his shoulder, and tore it open in seconds. Indeed, baby powder fell out, a packet of moist wipes, a tube of creamy Vaseline, and Pampers. "Nooooooo!" Harry cried like a hyena shrieking into the night.

"Harry," Michael said. "Easy, man."

Aileene looked perplexed. "I don't understand—"

"The other one, where is it?"

Michael shrugged. "Probably in the Jeep. I wasn't paying attention to what you were doing. You grabbed the wrong one."

"Shit. Shit!" Harry went ballistic. "Why didn't you say there were two of them?" he shouted at Wendy. "Why didn't you tell me you packed all that baby shit? How was I supposed to know there were two of them in the Jeep, goddammit?"

Michael reached out for Harry. "Hey, brother, easy now."

"Fuck you, Mike. And fuck you too, Wendy." He was seething.

"Harry, stop it." Aileene was almost spitting. "I won't hear this from you."

Harry looked up at the building above them, then down the hill from where they'd come. He had no choice. There was little time. He had to do it. He dropped the bedroll into the muck and untied himself from the rope linking all of them.

"Where are you going?" Bob demanded.

"Harry, no!" Flo said, realizing he was about to split off from them.

The dog barked because they were all shouting.

Michael tried to grab his brother, but Harry leaped down the incline, shouting, "The Jeep. I've got to get back to the Jeep." He slid in the mud, flailing, obsessed. He fell, got up again, covered with muck and pine needles, and then he was gone. He disappeared in the wet snow, in the rain, in the trees.

Bob's instinct was to go after him, but he stopped himself. "I can't get him. I can't."

"Dad, I don't understand," Michael said. "He's going back for a sleeping bag?"

"There's something in it," Aileene said. "That's the only explanation."

"Sure," Wendy said, realizing. "Whatever he had in that fire hose. He must have moved it to the bedroll."

"It's worth risking his life over?" Flo asked.

Michael wiped mud from his face. "People's priorities are different." He gazed down the hill, wondering if he would ever see his brother again. "God, Harry, why?"

"What could have been in there?" Bob asked. "Certainly not contracts like he said."

"Money?" Wendy asked.

"Oh, Harry," Aileene cried, feeling deep emotional pain. "Why? Why now, when we're almost there?"

"You're right, Mom—we are almost there. Harry will make it. He's strong. He's probably back at the Jeep already and heading up our way." He said it, but of course he didn't believe it. "Come on. Let's give it our best shot."

Suddenly, sunlight poked through. Just a glimpse, but real sun. Southern California sun. Rain was still falling, but there was hope. The wind that blew the raindrops into their faces was dry, and hot. The winds were Santa Anas. Soon the pine needles would dry, the drops of precipitation on the leaves of the trees would evaporate, the sky would be clear and helicopters could fly. "Hell, maybe we'll get a tan on the way out," Michael joked. The laughter filled them with hope.

Harry tumbled down the last few feet to the road. Finally, he was on flat ground, lodged against a tree. He looked like he'd just come off one of the survival reality shows, covered with mud, bleeding, panting. But he saw the Jeep, sitting there untouched in the drizzle that still came down despite the sun that was trying hard to break through the clouds. He pulled himself to his feet and hurried over to the vehicle. And there it was. His precious sleeping bag, all rolled up and secure under the rear seat. He lifted it into his arms and hugged it to him. This was what he'd done this for, this was why he'd survived all this. He wasn't leaving without it.

He fastened it to his good arm and turned back the way he'd come. It was daunting just looking at that hillside again, much less with the mud cascading down it much worse than when they'd set out to climb it hours earlier. But he could do it. He would do it. That island was out there waiting for him, that good life that he'd dreamed about. Dolores was gone now. He didn't even have that problem to worry about anymore. It was just Harry Hanwell and Vincent van Gogh. A partnership that would see him through the rest of his days.

He gritted his teeth and started back up the hill.

*   *   *

Cameron thought he could see movement. Not water, not trees swaying in the increasing wind, but skin, a human being, some slim man without a shirt. He called to him from above, but the guy didn't hear him. So he eased himself down a bit, holding onto the trunk of a tree, and then found firm footing on a rock and started toward them. He could finally make out the figure. It was a young man, wearing only jeans and hiking boots. Michael Hanwell. "Michael! Mike!" Cameron shouted with glee. They'd made it.

Michael looked up to see Cameron waving at him with both arms. "Cameron!" he yelled. He turned to the rest of them, who were about ten feet behind him. "I see him! I see Cameron! We made it!"

Not quite. There was still a ways to go, and it was the most difficult of all, because the water was taking everything in its path. Aileene remarked that it was like trying to climb up Niagara Falls. Mud and rocks and bits of pavement from the parking lot came rushing at them as though someone were tossing them, trying to hit them. There was no snow left under their feet at all, so it was nearly impossible to pull the sled. The dog added weight but they knew he would never be able to keep his paws rooted in the muck. Susan moaned and turned her head back and forth deliriously.

When Bob saw Cameron, his heart rate quickened. This was it, the end of the line, and they *would* make it. He felt a new surge of energy. It was going to be over in a matter of minutes. He grabbed Aileene's hand and squeezed it tightly. His feelings rushed through her body without the need for words.

"Thank God," Flo gasped. "Oh thank you, God."

Cameron reached out, and Michael's outstretched hand touched his. Their fingers clasped together and

Cameron helped lift him up onto the big rock. "We have to move fast," Cameron told him. "I fear the whole building is going to come down." Cameron patted his godson on the back. "I knew you'd do it."

Michael had no voice left. Shouting all the way up the hill had taken its toll on his vocal cords. He sat down and pulled on the rope with Cameron, yanking the sled up to the rock, where Bob untied Susan and lifted her from it. Aileene and Flo handed the dog up to the men on the rock, then took turns getting themselves up as Michael reached for the baby, handed Rachel to his father, and then helped Wendy get up to the safety of the rocky promontory. "Where's Harry?" Cameron asked. "I thought he was with you."

"Not anymore," Michael said, but his attention was drawn to the earth-shattering sound coming from above them. The observatory was beginning to collapse. What they heard was a wall coming down. They watched through bloodshot eyes as massive pieces of cement and steel and stucco rolled down the hill only thirty feet from them. One of the upper pillars on the southern wall fell out and crashed to the muddy earth. Three enormous pine trees collapsed under the weight.

"Oh my God," Wendy gasped.

"Come on," Cameron said. "We don't have time to play spectator." He helped them up off the rock, to the ground that the observatory sat on, where they saw a massive helicopter sitting on its side in the parking lot there, blades resting sideways on the ground. "It came apart as the parking lot split open," Cameron explained.

"How are we going to get out?" Bob said, his hopes dying.

"There," Cameron said, pointing above them, up

the hillside. "The landing pad above is still secure. We're going to take the tractor . . ."

As they headed toward it, Michael gave one last glance down the hillside, hoping that his brother would miraculously appear. But, of course, he didn't.

Nearby was a massive machine that looked like it could move heaven and earth. It was outfitted with an enormous plow in front of it, but the rear was huge and could hold all of them easier than the Jeep had. "Come on," Cameron urged, "as fast as you can." He grabbed Susan, carrying her in both arms toward the vehicle. The rest of them sloshed through the mud behind him. And they climbed onto the vehicle. Aileene sat down, put the heavy purse down, which she'd managed to hold on to throughout the treacherous climb, and then let Cameron set Susan into her arms. The dog leaped up of his own volition, followed by Michael, who turned to help Flo. But she had a terrible time. "I can't get my fat ass up there!" she shouted.

"Here," Cameron said, putting his arms under that particular piece of anatomy, heaving her up as Michael almost pulled his back out, but she was soon safely in the vehicle.

"Dear God," Flo promised, "you get us into that sky and I'm doing Atkins forever. I make a solemn vow. Never another hamburger bun as long as I live."

Cameron got inside and gave the soldier sitting in the cab of the vehicle the sign. It began to move, the gears grinding. "We were almost stopped by Jeffrey King's followers in our driveway," Bob told Cameron. "It was iffy."

"But God—the real God—was on our side," Aileene added as the vehicle moved toward the mountainside. Behind them they saw another pillar topple from the observatory, and what seemed like twenty or thirty soldiers rush from the building. The whole building was tilting now. It seemed to be hanging on the edge of the cliff by only a thread.

The tractor headed up the mushy road, closer to the landing pad, closer to the chopper, closer to freedom.

Harry pressed on, fighting the stream of water coming down at him. He would make it. There was no other choice. He'd win, he'd succeed in this the way he'd succeeded in everything in his life. He was a winner, not a loser. He had a grin on his face, a shit-eating grin, the grin of survival. And survive he would. He could feel the gentle breezes blowing over him as he sat in that hammock outside his villa on the shore. He could see the beautiful paintings hanging on the walls inside. He could think of nothing else. It was his motivation. The only thing that would save him.

He grabbed hold of a low tree branch and swung his knees up over the river of water that suddenly appeared from nowhere, almost chinning himself. He was using both hands now. There was no pain. The instinct to live overcame everything.

The huge vehicle came to a halt as close to a little makeshift building as it could. An officer rushed out, followed by General Van Hecke. "I've called in every damn thing that will fly," he shouted. "It's the best we can do now." He pointed toward two helicopters. The blades on the first one were already turning. "You people go ahead. I'll be on the next one. You get going."

Cameron led the group toward the enormous Army helicopter. They climbed aboard with the help of the military crew. But just as they were lifting Susan aboard, the ground suddenly rattled. At first they thought it was an earthquake, and they all turned in the direction the mind-boggling sound was coming from. What they saw was the most astonishing sight yet.

The Griffith Park Observatory crumbled before their eyes. It vanished. It collapsed and slid down the hill it had proudly sat on for an eternity. A mighty roar was its last hurrah. And all that was left was mud.

Harry Hanwell heard the sound and felt it in his feet, in his whole body. He had time only to look up once, to see the wall of concrete coming down upon him, like an avalanche hitting unprepared skiers in a disaster movie. He tried to cry out. His mouth opened but couldn't make a sound. The sky seemed to be raining pieces of the building. Trees fell with the walls of the observatory. The telescope, which had stood in the dome of the building and had been the whole purpose of the structure, sailed past Harry's nose. He toppled backward onto the bedroll as a chunk of plaster and tile and twisted steel bracing flattened him and ended his life with incredible power and force.

Water rushed down all around Harry's body, carrying pieces of the building into the canyons below. In the midst of it all, barely noticeable, pieces of brightly colored canvas, little chips of old oil paint, floated through the rushing water, all the way down to the road below, down the hillside and into the sewers.

When Cameron got into the helicopter, a soldier shut and locked the door. The pilot was ready to take off. The engines revved up. Wendy could feel the warmth of her baby against her breasts as Michael put his arm around her and rested his head on her shoulder. Bob and Aileene held hands. Susan opened her eyes and looked around. Herschel licked her nose and she smiled. Flo let the tears come down her cheeks, not even trying to stop them as they felt a jolt and all at once were in the sky.

They looked out over the mountains as they rose above the city, over the nightmare they'd just lived through, and soon they could see the vastness of the Los Angeles Basin and the blue water of the ocean. No one said a word. The roar of the blades above them filled the compartment. The only feeling in their hearts at that moment was relief. Relief that they had made it and that it was finally, for them, over.

As the chopper moved inland, away from the melting snow and rushing waters and death and destruction, a swarm of rescue helicopters suddenly appeared from over the surrounding mountaintops, filling the skies, bringing the one thing everyone in stricken Southern California had lost by this time. The sight of thousands of evacuation aircraft brought *hope*.

And, for the first time in over a month, there wasn't a cloud in the sky.

In fact, the sun was shining brightly.

RAIN FALL
by Barry Eisler
0-451-20915-X

John Rain kills people. For a living. His specialty: making it seem like they died of natural causes. But he won't kill just anyone. The target must be a principal player. And never a woman. John Rain may not be a good man, but he's good at what he does. Until he falls for the daughter of his last kill.

RAIN FALL was hailed as
ONE OF THE BEST BOOKS OF THE YEAR by
Publishers Weekly
San Jose Mercury News
New Press

And don't miss
HARD RAIN
0-451-21246-0

New York Times bestselling author

Sara Paretsky

"One of the best suspense stories this year."
—*The Buffalo News*

BLACKLIST

0-451-20969-9

As a favor to a client, V.I. Warshawski agrees to check up on an old mansion. But instead of a mysterious intruder, she discovers a dead man. V.I. is hired by the dead man's family to investigate—only to uncover buried secrets and betrayals spanning four generations.

"A thoughtful, high-tension mystery."
—*Washington Post Book World*

"A genuinely exciting and disturbing thriller."
—*Chicago Tribune*